TEZCATLIPOCA

Kiwamu Sato

YEN ON

NEW YORK

TEZCATLIPOCA

Kiwamu Sato

Translation by Stephen Paul
Cover art by Jun Kawana

TEZCATLIPOCA
© Kiwamu Sato 2021
First published in Japan in 2021 by KADOKAWA CORPORATION, Tokyo.
English translation rights arranged with KADOKAWA CORPORATION, Tokyo, through TUTTLE-MORI AGENCY, INC., Tokyo.

English translation © 2023 by Yen Press, LLC

Yen On
150 West 30th Street, 19th Floor
New York, NY 10001

Visit us at yenpress.com • facebook.com/yenpress • twitter.com/yenpress
yenpress.tumblr.com • instagram.com/yenpress

First Yen On Edition: February 2023
Edited by Yen On Editorial: Jordan Blanco
Designed by Yen Press Design: Wendy Chan

Yen On is an imprint of Yen Press, LLC.
The Yen On name and logo are trademarks of Yen Press, LLC.

Library of Congress Cataloging-in-Publication Data
Names: Sato, Kiwamu, 1977- author. Paul, Stephen (Translator), translator.
Title: Tezcatlipoca / Kiwamu Sato ; translation by Stephen Paul.
Other titles: Tezcatlipoca. English
Description: First Yen On edition. New York, NY : Yen On, 2023.
Identifiers: LCCN 2022048785 ISBN 9781975352127 (hardcover)
Subjects: LCGFT: Thrillers (Fiction) Light novels.
Classification: LCC PZ7.1.S26494 Te 2023 DDC [Fic]—dc23
LC record available at https://lccn.loc.gov/2022048785

ISBNs: 978-1-9753-5212-7 (hardcover)
978-1-9753-5213-4 (ebook)

10 9 8 7 6 5 4 3 2 1

LSC-C

Printed in the United States of America

CONTENTS

I
In Ixtli In Yollotl (Face and Heart)

II
Narco y Médico (Drug Dealer and Doctor)

III
El Patíbulo (The Gallows)

IV
Yohualli Ehecatl (Night and Wind)

Days Beyond the Calendar

I

In Ixtli In Yollotl
(Face and Heart)

Only the gods are real.

—Neil Gaiman, *American Gods*

01

cë

North of the United Mexican States, across the national border, lies El Dorado, the land of gold. This is a tale that some choose to believe, while others have no choice *but* to believe.

They walk through dust storms into the red sunrise, tracing a route without a road. They willingly traverse the perilous desert of rocks and cacti, making the sign of the cross and dragging their exhausted feet onward.

The Border Patrol of the United States of America awaits them, but there are only so many eyes that can watch. The border is simply too vast. Mexico and America share a boundary that runs nearly two thousand miles long—the world's largest smuggling zone. Hundreds of thousands of people cross the border illegally every year, using every means imaginable.

Not all of them survive the trip. Border Patrol helicopters drive migrants around like flocks of sheep, a tactic called *dusting* that human rights organizations decry as inhumane. A low-flying helicopter can threaten and scatter a group of travelers on foot, pushing them back toward Mexico. Escaping the helicopter often means separating from your companions, leaving them behind to brave the withering desert conditions alone. The fate of any lost in the arid wastes is indisputable.

Still, people continue to attempt to cross the border, desperate to escape a cycle of poverty without an exit. There's no choice but to make the journey to the empire of capitalism that shines like the sun: America.

* * *

Lucía was born in a city in northwest Mexico near the Pacific, and she would have done it, too. She wanted to try crossing into America. It was another life she could have led in some fantasy parallel world. But she didn't. She left the country, but not to the north.

In 1996, Lucía Sepúlveda was seventeen years old, a *mestizo*—part *indio*, part Spanish—with shiny black hair and even darker eyes, large and black like obsidian.

Her hometown of Culiacán, capital city of the state of Sinaloa, probably looked like an utterly ordinary place to tourists who didn't know better, not that they ever came to Culiacán. In truth, however, the city was ruled by forces outside the law: violence and fear. Streets weren't littered with dead bodies, but the city was a war zone all the same. The conflict was the sort that no UN peacekeeping force would solve: the drug war.

The cartel ruled the city, and its members, the narcos, were everywhere. Always watching. They weren't street-level pushers dealing drugs in furtive back alleys; they drove around in Lamborghinis and Ferraris. They carried assault rifles and resorted to terrorist acts if necessary.

The Mexican cartels had networks that extended beyond national borders. It was an international business. Their main export was *polvo de oro*, golden dust—cocaine. The biggest market was across the border in America, with Canada, the EU, and Australia serving to bolster their astronomical profits. No one ever worried about paying taxes on this kind of product.

Asia—Japan, the Philippines, and especially Indonesia—was seen as a growth market. There, cocaine took a back seat to sales of crystal meth. The cartels called it *hielo*, or ice.

The cartels owned coca farms in places like Colombia and Peru, where they oversaw cultivation, cocaine production, transport, and distribution all by themselves. They bought off politicians, officials, prosecutors, and police officers, absorbing them into the drug business. New ways to launder money were constantly being churned out. Methodical kidnapping, torture, and murder were part of the cartel's business, and an army of narcos supported the vast criminal enterprise. There was no headquarters office building with half-mirror windows reflecting the sky, nor were there CEOs in boardroom meetings, yet the cartels still possessed enough capital to influence world finance. No one crossed them. Freedom of speech was meaningless. Openly attacking the cartels was to invite the grim reaper into your home, where you and your family lived.

When she was a young girl in Culiacán, Lucía dreamed of going to a private school in Mexico City, but her parents, who ran a tiny market, couldn't possibly pay the monthly tuition of two thousand pesos. Lucía knew that she probably wasn't going to any local schools, either. Her parents had no connection to the drug business. They were poor and had debts. Lucía abandoned her dream of high school without speaking a word about it, deciding to help at the store.

On an afternoon in July, during the rainy season, two men came to the shop while she was working the register. One had a video camera running. They weren't locals. Perhaps they were tourists from Texas, although Culiacán wasn't a tourist destination at this point in time.

They weren't sightseers, but they *were* American. The one with the camera smiled at Lucía and said, "*Soy periodista.*" The other one didn't say anything. He just dropped a bag of almonds, a tube of sunscreen, and two Dos Equis Ambers onto the counter and paid silently.

Learning that they were journalists worried Lucía. There was only one topic people would come to this place to cover.

Her fears were well founded. The next day, the men came back to her shop with three narcos they'd made contact with somehow. They bought more Dos Equis Ambers and offered the chilled beers to the narcos, who wore baseball caps and bandannas to cover their faces. They started drinking, and then the interview began, right in the middle of the general store.

Lucía cursed the Americans' lack of sense and prayed to God that this wouldn't bring any trouble. She didn't want to hear what they were saying, but their murmurs were quite audible. There was no one else in the store. No one would dare come enter with them around.

The trio of men with pistols tucked into their belts seemed to enjoy having the camera on them.

"Do you believe you're the toughest guys in the world?" asked the American.

"Believe, like, in a religious way?" replied one of the narcos.

"No, in the real sense."

"I bet you *gringos'* military is tougher. The Marines."

"You think so?"

"We've had shootouts with the SEMAR. That's the Navy here. Special forces," said another narco. "I hear your Marines are better than them. So they probably got us beat."

The one who hadn't spoken yet chuckled. "But if they're *los más fuertes*, then we're the *silbato de la muerte*."

"What does that mean?" asked the American.

"It means if we blow the whistle, death comes for you."

They left their empty bottles at the register, and the man with the camera followed them.

Silbato de la muerte. The whistle of death. The sound of the words haunted Lucía, refusing to leave her ears.

The two Americans continued their coverage until the weekend. Lucía had started believing they had good luck and God's protection until Sunday morning, when they showed up dead in an empty lot on the outskirts of the neighborhood.

It was a mystery why the narcos had blown the whistle on them. Maybe they thought the men weren't journalists at all but undercover DEA agents. No matter how careful one tries to be, death comes swiftly and for the most trivial reasons. Both were shot in the forehead, the brain matter from their ruptured skulls coating the inside of their baseball caps like paste. Their video camera and recorder were gone, as were their wallets and identification. The only thing in the pocket of the cameraman's cargo pants was the tube of sunscreen purchased at Lucía's store.

When she saw the brief newspaper article about their deaths, she closed her eyes and sighed.

This is the town I live in.

Lucía had a brother named Julio. He was two years older than her, tall, skinny, and bony, with very wide shoulders. They were notable enough that his friends nicknamed him El Hombro.

Like so many others, Julio wanted to go to America and earn some money to send back to their poor parents.

To work as long and lucratively as possible, he needed to cross the border illegally.

The secret routes into America were controlled by the coyotes, immigrant smugglers with ties to the narcos. In other words, they were essentially a part of the cartels.

Julio tried desperately to find a smuggler who wasn't a coyote. His friends laughed at him and said it would be easier to get rich digging for emeralds, but Julio was undeterred.

Borrowing the help of a coyote created a connection to the narcos, one that lasted for life. They would force you to smuggle cocaine or sell on the street. You'd spend the rest of your days with nerves taut as wire.

At last, Julio found a man who claimed he wasn't a coyote. He alleged himself to be a former UN staffer, so Julio put his fate in the man's hands and paid him twenty thousand pesos that had taken ages to gather. It was a desperate gamble.

Two days later, a stranger approached Julio. "If you want to cross the border, it's another twenty thousand," he said. "If you can't pay, you'll have to smuggle cocaine across."

The man Julio had found was connected to the narcos, just like everybody else. It was as simple as that.

Julio refused those options. If he ferried drugs, he'd be trapped for the rest of his life. He wanted the twenty thousand pesos back, but there was nothing he could do about it. Ordinarily, that would've been the end of it:

You got tricked and lost your money to a bad bet. But not in Culiacán. Things only came to a conclusion when the narcos said they did.

Julio's remains turned up the next day. His eyes had been gouged out, and his tongue was removed. He was left naked in the street with each of his long, gangly limbs severed at the joint and placed nearby. They punished Julio for seeking a smuggler who wasn't a coyote, and they made an example out of him.

That was the end of Lucía's brother and his nineteen years of life.

The police came to dispose of the body, wearing black ski masks to conceal their faces. They put up yellow warning tape, took pictures, and quickly finished their examination. It was less than twenty minutes before the tape came down and the van drove off, taking Julio's body to Identification.

Blood stained the asphalt. The wind whipped up a sand devil. A scrawny dog came over, head drooping and ribs visible, drawn by the scent of the blood.

The narcos' scenes of slaughter were normal, like natural phenomena— nearly impossible to avoid. Like everyone else, Lucía understood one basic truth: No one was going to save you.

While her parents wept, Lucía arranged for a funeral. She sold all of Julio's possessions worth any money and did her best to remove every last physical memory of her brother.

Lucía realized this was the last chance to make up her mind. The fear would forever keep her trapped in this place if she didn't act now.

She didn't so much as leave a letter behind for her parents. Evidence would only lead to confusion and possibly the attention of the narcos. She had to vanish, leaving no trace. Without a word to anyone, she kissed the crucifix on the bedroom wall, then said good-bye to Culiacán, Sinaloa.

Unlike her brother, she didn't look for help from non-coyote smugglers. She didn't seek aid from anyone.

If crossing the northern border into America meant paying money to the narcos, then she wouldn't go to America at all.

Lucía headed south.

It was the solitary journey of a seventeen-year-old Mexican girl.

She did whatever she could to continue traveling south, sneaking into the trailer of a truck hauling a shipment of beef, wrapping herself in a blanket and sleeping beneath a tree, and riding on unfamiliar buses in unfamiliar states. She even hailed down a farm tractor driven by a shriveled old man and demanded a ride, despite it moving slower than an oxcart.

And no matter how friendly the smiles were, she never trusted anyone.

Home had taught her that lesson. If she sensed danger from another in any measure, she was ready to pull out the miniature machete hidden under her dress and kill. Even if it was an old grandmother.

Nayarit, Jalisco, Michoacán—after several days and nights, the seventeen-year-old girl arrived at Acapulco, the capital of the state of Guerrero, along the Pacific Ocean.

I'm still alive.

Lucía stared at the sky in a daze while the sea breeze blew against her face. She hadn't been raped and left behind with her throat slit, and she wasn't floating facedown in a mud-colored river. Hard as it was to believe, she'd come all this way on her own.

She made the sign of the cross and offered a prayer to Our Lady of Guadalupe. Despite her achievement, she took little joy in the moment. Lucía felt as though she'd aged decades, and her only feeling was a relief that felt close to resignation.

Acapulco in the '90s was a dazzling place packed with tourists. It felt like heaven compared to Culiacán.

In time, Acapulco, too, would become a drug war battleground. Tourists would vanish from the resorts, and killings would happen nightly, but that was in the years to come.

Lucía found work at a restaurant, where she wore the uniform and apron they provided, and brought drinks and food out to the tables. With her rich black hair, brown skin, and big obsidian eyes, she was quite popular with international guests, even though she only spoke Spanish. Some people visited the restaurant multiple times during their stay. Men asked her out on dates, and she got more tips than the other servers.

She always put on a cheery face in the restaurant, but it was only a facade. The horrors she'd experienced had bored a hole in her heart through which everything passed. On her shift, she stifled her natural wariness and masked her cold gaze; all smiles for the guests.

"*Buenas noches,*" she would say.

One hot May afternoon, a young white man in nice clothes came to the restaurant alone. The man drank a michelada and cut into his *carne a la tampiqueña* in silence. Eventually, he set down his knife and fork and began arranging matches on the corner of the table. He placed three vertically; their heads were white, and the center matchstick was broken in the middle.

Lucía's face twitched when she saw the matches. Pretending to have noticed nothing, she filled the young man's water glass and retreated to the kitchen. She pulled aside Alejandra, the coworker she felt closest to, and whispered, "Watch out for the guy at that table."

"Why?"

"Don't let him talk to you or learn your name."

"Did he say something to you?" asked Alejandra, who was Peruvian.

Lucía pursed her lips and said nothing.

A while later, the white man finished his meal, quietly dabbed at his lips with the napkin, left money for the bill and tip, and exited the restaurant. Lucía, who wasn't ready to relax yet, watched as Alejandra strode over to the table, cast a look at her, and collected the cash.

She returned with a grin. "Were you worried about the matches?"

Now it was Lucía's turn to look puzzled. Did Alejandra know what those matches meant?

"Are you trying to trick me into being scared?" Alejandra asked, laughing. "That sign means a narco's here, right? People like doing that for fun these days."

Before Lucía could find her voice, Alejandra grabbed the other girl's apron and jammed a bill into the pocket. "Here's your tip."

After their shift, Alejandra and Lucía went out for dinner, where the former told the latter about a TV drama called *Mandamiento*, or "Commandment."

It was a popular show that featured a famous Hollywood actor in the cast. The story was set in Acapulco, and the main character was a young narco trying to advance in the cartel's ranks. According to Alejandra, the practice of placing matches on the table showed up in several memorable scenes. So, either as a prank or because he thought it was cool, the young white man had merely been copying what he'd seen.

As she ate, Lucía felt ashamed of her terror. However, she couldn't laugh it off, either. Lucía had seen an actual match signal back home, as well as the gunfight that broke out afterward, which claimed her friend's life. She mentioned none of that to Alejandra, though.

Lucía thought of her brother, and then her parents. She'd abandoned her elderly father and mother, breaking God's commandment, and left home. *But who was the first to disobey God?* she thought. Who mutilated and murdered her brother and lived to tell the tale? Who was buying cocaine from them? The TV show? Tourists pretending they were narcos? The world was one big sick joke.

Lucía spent a year working in Acapulco. In the locker room after a shift, Alejandra told Lucía that she was quitting. Lucía's only friend undid her long hair, which she kept tied up for work, and shook it out. "I'm going back home to Peru for a bit, and then I'll be working in Japón."

That was a surprise. *Japón.* Lucía knew the name, of course, but she'd be hard pressed to find it on a map. Japanese tourists came to the restaurant, but she couldn't tell them apart from the Chinese ones.

"I'll get in on a short-term visa and do everything I can to make yen," Alejandra explained. "Japanese money is strong. You guys have America right next door, but Peruvians have to travel to Japan to get good work. Tokyo, Kawasaki, Nagoya, Osaka…"

The idea was a revelation to Lucía. And Alejandra was right. When Mexicans thought about a place of better opportunity, America was the only thing that came to mind. That was why they risked their lives to cross the border.

"If I can marry a Japanese man while I'm there, I'll be set for life," Alejandra said. She'd taken off her uniform and reached into a locker for the orange T-shirt on the hanger inside. "I'll be able to work as much as I want."

"Where is Japan?" Lucía was still in her waitress uniform. She hadn't even undone her sleeve buttons.

Alejandra wriggled around inside the T-shirt until her head popped out of the collar.

"Al borde del Pacífico." The edge of the Pacific.

02

öme

Lucía continued working at the restaurant after Alejandra left. She carried drinks and food, smiled for the tourists, and agreed to be in their pictures. On breaks, she smoked cigarettes out back. As she exhaled, Alejandra's voice echoed in her mind.

Al borde del Pacífico. The phrase sounded beautiful, poetic, and unforgettable. Guatemala, Costa Rica, Panama, Colombia, Peru, Brazil—no other country left a greater impression on her heart.

I want to go there.

Lucía stopped herself from thinking about it any further. It would never happen. She didn't know anyone there and didn't speak the language. Tracking down Alejandra would be impossible. Friendship among foreign laborers was like that of tourists: It began and ended in the same place. Even if Lucía found some Peruvian community in Japan, there'd be no place for a Mexican among them.

Despite so many factors, Lucía's longing for the far side of the sea continued to grow.

Why? she asked herself. *What do I imagine I'm going to do there?*

Were there an answer, it probably had nothing to do with hope for a better life or the pursuit of happiness. It was for a nearly empty heart.

Growing up in her hometown had left Lucía's chest empty, as though the center had been gouged out. Filling it was impossible, and Lucía didn't aspire to try. *Instead, I want to be even emptier.*

Her wish was to live as insubstantially as the wind. Perhaps that meant existing as a perpetual wanderer. Her journey out of Culiacán was still ongoing. She would travel to an unfamiliar land and become no one. Maybe she could finally forget everything about herself if she left Mexico, Peru, Argentina, and the Americas entirely. If she lived on an island in the Far East. Across a sea vaster than any desert.

Lucía considered joining one of those groups that traveled to Japan to work, the sort Alejandra had talked about, but there were no such opportunities in a tourist destination like Acapulco.

She'd brought her identification papers when leaving Culiacán, so she had a passport made at the office in Acapulco and looked into short-term visas to Japan. However, she learned that, unlike Peruvians or Colombians, Mexicans didn't need visas to travel to Japan. Without a visa, the maximum length of stay was six months. But if it was over ninety days, you would have to visit Japan's Ministry of Justice before the end of the stay to update your papers.

Lucía didn't want to get involved with officials in *any* country. They might deport her. But as long as she played her cards right, she could remain in Japan for half a year.

At Acapulco International Airport, Lucía boarded a plane for the first time in her life, marveling that she would cross the border without meeting an end like her brother. Yet for all the surrealness of that moment, the blue of the sea when viewed from above was even more unbelievable. Lucía trembled at the sight of the Pacific, which seemed an utter abyss. The next thing she knew, there was only white beyond the window, and it took the girl some time before understanding that the plane was flying through clouds. Above, far beyond the distant sky, was an eternal darkness, the likes of which Lucía had never seen.

Lucía reached *al borde del Pacífico* on Friday, July 3, 1998. She took a bus from Narita Airport into Tokyo and searched for jobs at restaurants, but she couldn't speak a word of Japanese, so they all turned her away. On top of that, no proper manager was going to hire someone who'd entered the country for tourism reasons.

She stayed at a business hotel. Every breath you took in this city cost money. The price of goods was shocking, but fortunately, Lucía finally managed to get a job. A man from the Kansai area of western Japan who managed a hotel in Roppongi agreed to hire her to tidy rooms without asking for an ID. After a quick tutorial from the Vietnamese cleaners who already worked there, Lucía scrubbed bathtubs, removed mattress sheets, and replaced the trash cans full of used condoms. The Japanese called this place a "love hotel," and it was a place expressly for having sex. Male and female prostitutes, students, normal adults: Everyone came here.

On Lucía's seventeenth day of work, the owner called her into his office. *He's going to fire me*, she thought. Perhaps he'd already called the police.

Dreading the worst, she opened the door to see the hotel owner sitting at the desk with a map open. As he had during her hiring interview, the manager spoke simply and slowly in Japanese, mixing in a smattering of English words. Lucía could only understand the English. She listened and asked a few questions when appropriate until she understood what the man was saying to her. It was fortunate she'd picked up a bit of English in Acapulco.

"South side, Kansai, Osaka. Mega city. You get it?" he said, pointing at the map. "In Nanba City, my friend business. Mahjong, Chinese game. They want woman worker. Good-looking, Chinese dress, you get it? *Gaijin* okay, no ID okay. You serve drinks, clean ashtray, pretty smile…"

The boss finished with a phrase in English, the most important part of all.

Three times the salary.

With an opportunity for a new job in her pocket, Lucía bought a Spanish-language map in Roppongi and rode the bullet train to Osaka, an all-new experience for her.

It was past one o'clock at night when she found the mixed-use building in a small back alley of Nanba. She mentioned the love hotel owner's name at the entrance and was told to wait outside. Eventually, a man came down the stairs, and he ushered her back up with him.

As the hotel owner had explained, there was a roomful of people playing the Chinese tile game mahjong on the second floor. Next, the man led her to the fourth floor, where no one was playing mahjong. Instead, there were men and women standing around tables lined with green felt and piled high with chips. The games here were roulette, poker, and blackjack. Not all of the players were Japanese.

The man tapped Lucía's shoulder and said in English, "This is yours." He handed her a large shopping bag. She took it and looked inside. It didn't contain a Chinese dress as advertised but a bunny-girl costume.

Lucía required no explanation to understand that this place was clearly a casino. However, she hadn't known until now that gambling was illegal in Japan. It was legal in Mexico.

Lucía stared into the bag and considered her options. She didn't have anywhere else to go, she could work here without an ID, and the pay was three times what she got for cleaning the hotel rooms.

Her new job began the following night. Lucía tied up her hair and wore the long bunny-ear headband, fishnet tights, and high-heeled pumps. She served drinks and light food to the gamblers at the illegal casino and learned bits of Japanese at the same time. The quoted salary turned out to be accurate, so she began accumulating some actual yen savings.

When her initial period of ninety days neared its end, she talked to the casino manager about it, and he gave her a certificate of enrollment at a Japanese language school—counterfeit, of course. She went to a local immigration office, told a made-up sob story about her struggle to continue her language studies, and successfully received an extension to her stay.

Lucía didn't make any friends like Alejandra back in Acapulco, so she was always alone. However, the good money she was earning allowed her time to learn about clothing and cosmetics. She went shopping to blow off steam, then visited the bar to drink. Brushing off the men who flocked to her was annoying, and she wished there was someplace she might drink in peace. One day, she asked the manager of the casino about it.

"You want to drink alone? Then drink at home. And if you don't want to do that, smoke cigars. You want a cigar lounge."

He told her about a place on Shinsaibashi-suji. All the customers at the cigar lounge were men, and there seemed to be an unspoken rule that women weren't allowed. The bartender tried to brush her off, but she gave him a large tip, and then he smiled as if nothing was wrong and gave her a bourbon on the house.

Lucía sipped her drink and savored the aroma of a Cuban cigar.

Once she was a regular, she started ordering mezcal that had been imported from Jalisco, Mexico. Lucía had always been curious about it since first spotting it on the shelf. Mezcal was a distilled liquor made from *maguey* and agave, and they put a worm inside the bottle. When she drank mezcal, Lucía got a certain look in her eyes that frightened the other regulars and the bartender. There was something cold and empty about it. Eventually, they began to assume that Lucía was some kind of high-priced Latin American call girl, the exclusive property of one of the local yakuza. After that, no one tried to hit on her anymore, and she was never asked how much for a night.

That winter, Lucía caught a cold from one of the casino regulars and requested to take the night off. The manager refused, however, telling her to show up, even if she was late. So Lucía took some medicine, put on her makeup, and wore a long coat and muffler. The fever made her reflection in the mirror hazy. She grabbed an Hermès bag a customer gave her, put on her boots, and left her apartment on unsteady legs.

Lucía was a full hour late to the casino, which opened at one in the morning, and when she got there, she stopped in her tracks at the sight of the mixed-use building bathed in red light. It looked like it was burning, but the red was not from fire. It was *la policía*.

Eleven cars from the Osaka Prefectural Police were there, lights flashing, and several vans, too. Lucía thought it strange that there were so many spectators nearby. The Japanese in Nanba walked right up to the yellow police tape to watch. In Culiacán, no one ever did that; you observed from around the corner or through the window like a sensible person. It kept you out of the line of fire if a gunfight broke out.

The crowd watched as the casino workers and guests were filed into the vans and taken away to the station. Lucía returned to her apartment at once. Although she worked under a false name, it was dangerous to remain in Nanba now. Anxious and trembling from chills, she gathered her belongings and considered her next step. She had nowhere to go. Anyone she could ask for help was connected to the casino in some way.

Should I try the cigar lounge in Shinsaibashi? No way. The men who visit there are the kind who will tell the police anything they want to know.

Lucía's fever was rising, the shivers were getting worse, and she was feeling sick to her stomach. Her six-month residency period was ending soon, too. She had to think of a solution to that problem. Lucía was exhausted, but she summoned enough strength to haul out her heavy suitcase and hail a taxi in the middle of the night, keeping careful watch for any officers on patrol.

"To Shin-Osaka Station," she told the driver. He said that the last train for the night was long gone, but she assured him that was all right. She was going to find a twenty-four-hour restaurant near the station and wait for the trains to start.

As the door shut and the taxi drove away, Lucía suddenly recalled a man's face—someone she'd met at the cigar lounge. He was one of the few who'd spoken to her there, but only once.

"What do you do?" he asked.

You were allowed to chat with friends at the cigar lounge, but for the most part, you didn't bother anyone else.

Lucía was there on her day off because she didn't want men hitting on her. This man was breaking the house rule. She exhaled smoke and ignored the man, glancing at the bartender instead. He returned the look with a wide grin.

This was something that Lucía hadn't understood at all when she first came to Japan, but she recognized it now. The bartender's smile was the sort she occasionally saw from the underground casino manager. It signaled an exception—a sign that the man here had a special relationship with the business.

"I work at a mahjong parlor," she said in halting Japanese to the man sitting two seats down. That was the answer the manager had instructed her to give.

"Mahjong? Did you say a mahjong parlor?" the man asked, staring keenly at the side of Lucía's face. "Where's this parlor?"

"Nanba."

"Do you stack tiles, Miss?"

"You mean, do I play mahjong?"

"Yes."

"No," Lucía replied. The Spanish *no*.

"Didn't think so." The man chuckled, shoulders bouncing slightly. He was still staring at her.

He ordered Lucía the most expensive bourbon at the bar, then smoked his cigar in silence. He opened his mouth just enough to allow a puff like vaporized dry ice to escape, floating, spiraling, toward the faded lights on the ceiling. Unlike the men at the casino who tried to grab her ass, he didn't tell dirty jokes or make aggressive moves. His hair was slicked back, and he wore rimless glasses. His suit fit him perfectly and was undoubtedly made to order. His necktie was held with a golden pin, and each of his cuff links contained a lustrous black stone.

"As it happens, I have my own place," he remarked. "A club. If you want to work for me, I'd be glad to talk. We hire foreigners and would be delighted to have someone like you. It's not in Osaka, though. What do you think? Care to chat business?"

Lucía shook her head. He'd asked her name, and she had given him the alias Alejandra, just in case.

The man stood from his seat, and the bartender recognized this as the signal to retrieve his coat. After sliding his arms through the sleeves, the man approached Lucía, placed an elbow on the counter, and looked into her eyes. "It's hard to survive, isn't it? Life throws so much at you. It's enough to leave even a pretty girl hollow. Just like your eyes."

While the taxi rolled along its route, Lucía rustled through her bag, searching for business cards. She didn't have a single one from casino patrons, but she kept some she'd received elsewhere.

She found it tucked into her pocketbook: the card from the man who ran a club that hired foreigners.

Club Sardis
Saiwai, Kawasaki, Kanagawa
Kozo Hijikata

Lucía turned the card over. There was a handwritten phone number, and the same information as on the front, only written in Japanese instead.

There was no house or street number anywhere, in either English or Japanese. Was there really a club? Was this just another casino? Lucía didn't know, but she also didn't have much choice.

After a long, dark night of waiting for the first train, Lucía finally closed her eyes in a seat on a bullet train to the Kanto region. She thought of Kozo Hijikata. Their conversation had lasted only ten minutes at most, but she could tell that he had the same air about him as the men who ran the casino. He was not a traditional businessman.

Lucía changed trains at Shinagawa Station and stopped again at Kawa-saki, where she used a pay phone to call the number on the card. She assumed nothing would come of it and kept her expectations low, but Kozo Hijikata himself answered the phone.

He came to get her and took her right to the club. It wasn't open in the middle of the day, but it was indeed real, as was the job offer. The establishment wasn't an underground casino, either. It seemed as though all of Lucía's concerns were unfounded. However, her intuition was correct about Kozo Hijikata. The man was a mobster. He ran a luxury club in Saiwai, and a warehouse in the harbor area.

Lucía wasn't alarmed to learn of the man's background. She knew this was going to happen. All that mattered was escaping the Osaka police and dealing with her residency period deadline. She started working as a hostess at the club in Kawasaki, and soon she was living with Kozo Hijikata.

The young woman told herself:

No matter how bad he is, he can't be as bad as the narcos in Mexico.

03

ëyi

Koshimo Hijikata was born in a hospital in Kawasaki on Wednesday, March 20, 2002. His recorded time of birth was 4:08 AM, and he weighed a hefty 4.3 kilograms.

His father, Kozo Hijikata, was a Japanese yakuza, and his mother, Lucía, was a Mexican who worked at his father's club. Because they were legally married, Lucía received resident status, and their son entered the world with Japanese citizenship.

The father couldn't stand the baby's crying and largely stayed away from the house, leaving twenty-three-year-old Lucía to raise her son alone. She had no relatives and no friends.

Kawasaki had many foreign workers, but very few were Mexican. There was no community for Lucía, and the marriage left her even more alone— materially satisfied but emotionally bereft.

That emptiness was something she desired.

Yet even things you desire can hurt you.

After her son's birth, she began to reflect on the home she'd abandoned. Now she had another tiny person with her who was just as alone in the world.

What am I supposed to tell him? Where are his roots? All I see are my brother's dead body and my screaming parents. All I have is emptiness and hatred. I have nothing but guilty memories.

Held captive by her past, Lucía did not bother to teach her Japanese-born son the local language, choosing to read from a Spanish Bible she managed to find at a used bookstore in the city instead. She also felt compelled to regale him with the legend of Our Lady of Guadalupe, which was not an official part of the Bible, but just as important to Mexicans. She repeated the story over and over.

Lucía also told him about her memories of the one time she visited Mexico City to experience the glory of the eve of Independence Day. At eleven o'clock on the night of September 15, before a packed crowd in El Zócalo, the president stood on the balcony of the National Palace and rang the Bell of Dolores, crying, "Long live Mexico!" The crowd repeated it back to him.

"¡Viva México! ¡Viva México!"

Fireworks stained the night sky in flashes of green, white, and red, the colors of the flag. Paratroopers performed a demonstration. Lucía walked with her brother down Paseo de la Reforma, which was built to resemble Champs-Élysées in Paris, her senses overwhelmed by the barrage of fireworks and the thundering roar of the crowd...

As Lucía regaled her son with the details of the story, her eyes gradually lost focus, and her grasp on the difference between memory and reality grew fuzzy. Young Koshimo couldn't understand what any of it meant. All he could do was stare at his mother's entranced face.

Koshimo didn't go to preschool or kindergarten. He stayed with his mother, only meeting his father occasionally. He learned Japanese from watching TV. When he was a bit older, he listened to the radio at low volume. He could understand the words but was totally unable to read or write. He entered an ordinary elementary school for Japanese children in the neighborhood, but he couldn't keep up with the classes. The other children laughed at him.

In 2011, an anti-yakuza measure—officially, an "organized crime exclusion ordinance"—was enacted in Kanagawa Prefecture, and Kozo

Hijikata suddenly found his life far more difficult. Conditions were already tough because of the worldwide recession that began three years earlier, and now the syndicate's bank accounts were being frozen left and right. Under the ordinance, he had to relinquish the high-end club. He focused instead on the harbor warehouse he still held, searching for chances to stem the losses. Unfortunately, the new law created a power vacuum that a rival Chinese group from Yokohama moved in to pounce on.

Kozo Hijikata had to sell off his cars, and he turned to drinking. He went back to scrapping on the street to blow off stress, an activity he hadn't done since becoming a yakuza lieutenant. He would get into fights with wannabe tough guys and young bikers, beat the crap out of them, and force them to strip naked and apologize.

After spending the night in the drunk tank, he'd come home in a foul mood and beat Lucía with no provocation. Koshimo watched his terrifying father abuse his mother. As this pattern wore on, Lucía talked less and less, showing fewer emotions. Eventually, she stopped cooking meals.

Koshimo, now nine years old, cooked on his own. He tried boiled spinach. He used the frying pan to cook eggs sunny side up, but the yolk burst because he couldn't crack the eggs right. He found some chicken in the freezer, boiled it in a pot, and added some salt. That, he decided, tasted the best of all. From then on, whenever he found chicken in the freezer, he always ate it.

Koshimo's mother, who was now a neglectful parent, did actually go out shopping now and then. She came home with a small amount of food and home supplies and was always curiously energetic. It was more abnormal than any natural activity; a state of agitation. She sang and laughed and even danced around the house.

Ironically, Lucía's liveliness came from a product of the narcos she so despised. It came to Kawasaki from across the ocean, but it wasn't *polvo de oro*, the narcos' most prized commodity. "As long as it's not cocaine," Lucía told herself, refusing to admit her betrayal.

"This is different," she told Koshimo, who was too young to understand, while she clutched a needle. "You don't snort it. It's just a little poke."

Koshimo was always hungry, and he hated going to school. He had no friends there, and couldn't keep up with the lessons. His family hadn't paid for the lunch program, and the teacher scolded him for it every day.

The spring he started fourth grade, Koshimo walked from his house to the Tama River, swung his backpack around with the textbooks inside, and hurled it into the flowing water. He stopped attending school from that day forward, and no one said a word to him about it.

His smiling mother lived in a haze of confusion and hallucinations. She would sit around with a vacant look in her eyes, then start dancing the next moment.

Koshimo took money from her wallet and went to the butcher, where he bought some cheap chicken breast. He boiled it in the pot, added salt, and devoured it. He crunched the bones, and drank every last drop of the liquid left in the pot.

Despite his crude, unbalanced diet, Koshimo grew taller by the day. Each time he looked into the bathroom mirror, cracked from where his mother had smashed a bottle against it, he was unnerved by what he saw. His shoulders were very wide, and his limbs were as long and thin as sticks. His cheeks were sunken, and when he took off his shirt, he could see his ribs.

By the time he was eleven, Koshimo was already over one hundred and seventy centimeters.

He listened to his mother mutter Spanish in her nightmares until dawn, and at six o'clock, he got up and made another meal of chicken. He washed the plate and used an empty can as a thermos. Like every other day, he took the can of water and a knife he stole from his father's room and went to a nearby children's park.

At the park, he would pick up dead sticks that had fallen from the trees, then sit on the bench and strip off the bark with the knife. Once the branch was nice and smooth, he carved delicate patterns into it. The arrangements were varied, from geometric shapes like circles and triangles, to images of dogs and birds.

Koshimo was not the only regular visitor to the children's park. Every single morning, an old man in a wheelchair showed up. He wore a tattered beanie and a dark blue work jacket. He pushed the wheelchair along by himself. His left hand had no pinky or ring finger.

The old man's daily activity was to smoke cigarettes beside the bench and read the bicycle race odds. He would mutter to himself and mark the players' names with a red pencil.

When Koshimo got thirsty, he drank the water from his can. There was a faucet at the park, but he found he could concentrate on his carving better when the water was close at hand. The boy carved symbols on his branches, and the old man in the wheelchair studied the odds. Neither one interfered with the other; they might as well have been invisible. For a long, long time, they never shared a single word.

One Saturday morning, six high schoolers who used the park as a late-night hangout spot came searching for something they'd lost. They'd never come by so early before and stopped when they spied an unfamiliar face.

They'd seen the old man in the wheelchair many times, but they didn't know the guy on the bench. His skin was on the darker side, and his black irises were bigger and deeper than a Japanese person's. He seemed foreign.

The boy who led the group of six wore a brand-new Puma coach jacket and a Grand Seiko watch that looked fresh out of the box. He'd bought both of them with money he made by scamming elderly people over the phone.

"Hey," called the boy in the fancy jacket in a friendly tone of voice. "You live around here?"

Koshimo kept his head down and continued to carve the branch in his hands.

"Did you see any earphones on the ground near this bench? They were my favorites."

Koshimo said nothing.

The boy in the coach jacket crouched down so he could look Koshimo in the face. "You from Peru?" he asked while lighting a joint. The high schoolers had been smoking weed in the park last night but never did so when it was bright out.

"Listen," the boy said. "There's a word, *shikato*. You might not know it because you're not from here, but it means 'to ignore someone.' There's a card game called *hanafuda*, and they have fancy pictures on them. The card for October has a deer turning its back on the moon. That's deer, *shika*, and ten, *to*. *Shikato*. Why is it a deer? Well, the guy at the casino taught me that it means 'disrespect.' It's not a tiger or a wolf but a wimpy little deer that's showing its ass to you. That's why they say never let anyone *shikato* you. Now, wasn't that nice of me? I taught you a lesson."

While the boy in the jacket gave his speech, one of his larger friends snuck around the back of the bench and quickly wrapped his arm around Koshimo's neck. It was a rear naked choke, or at least a crude approximation of one. His forearm compressed Koshimo's windpipe, and the younger boy lashed out.

"Holy shit, he's strong!" the large boy shouted. "C'mon, help me."

The others rushed over, and it took four high schoolers to hold down the eleven-year-old boy. The branch and knife fell from Koshimo's fingers.

The boy in the coach jacket picked up the knife and pointed it at Koshimo's pained, reddened face. "Don't fuckin' ignore me. When I ask you a question, you answer. If you don't understand Japanese, say *hello* or *buenos*-whatever."

The boy brought the knife's edge even closer to Koshimo's face until it pressed against his forehead. Blood trickled from the vertical line in the flesh. Excited, the boy added a horizontal cut. A trail of red oozed down Koshimo's face.

The old man in the wheelchair next to the bench continued to read the bicycle odds, ignoring the scuffle. No one perceived him anymore, like a rock on the side of the road.

"Tomorrow, you're gonna bring us tribute money," the boy said. He kicked the water can off the bench.

"Knock it off," the man in the wheelchair said abruptly. Koshimo had never heard him speak before.

With the attention of the teenagers on him, the old man looked up from the bicycle odds.

"That's Hijikata-san's son."

The boys holding Koshimo down panicked and let go of him at once. The arm blocking his windpipe let up, and Koshimo coughed painfully. There were tears in his eyes.

"Listen, old man," said the boy in the jacket, approaching the man in the wheelchair, "you better not be bullshitting."

"If you don't believe me, by all means, continue. I don't give a shit."

"You got proof?"

"Fuck proof," said the old man. "Take the boy to the office and ask for yourselves. Want me to go with you?"

He cackled and held up his hand. When the boy saw the missing fingers, he went pale and clammed up. If the old man was telling the truth, they would get worse than a beating. They wouldn't be going back home.

While Koshimo coughed and hacked, the six boys huddled up like soccer players before a match and whispered the name of the yakuza syndicate.

Koshimo could hear them, but the group's name and his father's affairs were none of his business. Once his breathing was steady, he got to his feet and walked over to the large boy who'd choked him. The boy was a teenager, but Koshimo was taller. He grabbed the boy's hair in his right hand and, despite fierce resistance, dragged him down to the ground, practically slamming him into the dirt.

The other five were stunned at the power in the skinny boy's frame. Loose hairs tangled in Koshimo's fingers.

The boy's head struck the ground, and he went still. The one in the coach jacket panicked and threw a rock at Koshimo. It struck his cheek with a dull smack. His right cheek was split and bleeding, as was the inside of his mouth. Driven to fury by the pain, Koshimo moved on the coach jacket high schooler with a terrifying look in his eyes.

The boy in the fancy windbreaker had grown up in Kawasaki, like Koshimo, and he'd seen a variety of messed-up adults. There was a class of people called "prison boys" who were despised even among yakuza. They were the lowest of the low rung in the system, the ones who couldn't control their own violent impulses. Because of this, they were constantly in and out of prison. One prison boy merely bumped shoulders with another tough guy at a hostess club, and he ended up hitting the other man dozens of times, covered his mouth with tape, and drove him to the Tama River. He tied up his hapless foe, dropped him alone into a little fishing boat, and sent him down the water. The boat was spotted at the mouth of the river, and the man was rescued before being swept out to Tokyo Bay. When the prison boy was arrested, he said without a hint of guilt, "What? If I was gonna kill him, I wouldn't have put him in the boat. What did I do wrong?"

The boy in the coach jacket also knew some "ultras." That was what they called the ultra-junkies; the people so strung out, they'd basically lost their minds. One ultra jumped barefoot out of a third-floor apartment onto asphalt. She dragged her right leg behind with the bone sticking out and made her way into a café across the street, then stuck her hand into the fish tank next to the automatic door and grabbed at the goldfish inside it. She laughed as she ate every last fish in the tank.

Clearly, this kid was in the same category as those people. He couldn't be dealt with using ordinary means. Koshimo's eyes flashed red with the blood that pulsed through them, and his gnashing teeth were stained the same color. He resembled a wild animal coated with the blood of his victims.

The boy had picked up Koshimo's knife and also had his own butterfly one, but there was fear deep in his bones. His opponent was no different from a prison boy or an ultra.

Shit, he thought. *My dad's a problem, but this guy's even worse. If I fight him, I'll get fucked up. He'll try to kill me. He's crazy.*

"*Te mato,*" Koshimo threatened.

"W-wait, wait," said the boy, overwhelmed by the murderous hostility. It took all of his willpower not to turn and run for his life. "I'm sorry."

The terrified boy gritted his teeth and took out a bunch of cash, then jammed it into the stomach pocket of Koshimo's cheap hoodie. That was the signal of retreat. The high schoolers tried to flee, abandoning their collapsed friend, but the old man in the wheelchair yelled at them. Two remained and tried to lift up the unconscious kid, but they had great difficulty. The boy Koshimo slammed to the ground was over eighty kilograms. After thirty seconds, he came to, staring at his two friends vacantly. He didn't seem to remember what had happened. The two who stayed behind offered him their shoulders, and the trio stumbled out of the children's park.

Koshimo picked up the broken stick, the whittling knife, and the empty can, and set them down on the bench. Then he walked to the park's faucet and turned the valve, washing the wounds on his forehead and cheek as he considered the old man in the wheelchair.

When he came back to the bench, the old man spoke first. "That was rough," he remarked. "But you've got a feel for scrapping. That's from your old man."

"You know me?"

"I do. Your mother's Mexican, ain't she?"

"Ouch," Koshimo murmured, touching his forehead, and then his cheek. *"Me duele aquí."*

"Go home and put ice on it."

"Okay. Bye."

"Hang on," the old man called. "Kid, how much did he stick in your bowl there?"

"Bowl..."

"That's the pocket over your stomach. Your bowl," the old man explained, pointing at his own gut.

Koshimo brushed stray hairs off his fingers and reached into the pocket. There were three crumpled-up ten-thousand-yen bills inside. Like a doctor tending to a patient, the old man casually reached over and took the bills from Koshimo, straightening them out. Then he pocketed two and returned one.

"That's a good bit of spending money you just earned," he said, grinning. Almost all his front teeth were gone. "You wanna go to the races next week?"

04

nähui

With the cool fall breeze blowing on his healing forehead and cheek, Koshimo sat on the bench in the park like always, enthusiastically carving a branch.

The wheelchair was parked next to the bench. But the old man wasn't reading the bicycle odds in the paper. He'd bought a portable TV with the money he won in the race the previous week, and listened to it with a set of earphones.

Koshimo whittled away with the knife in bliss until a shadow passed over him, and he looked up. The wheelchair had moved to rest right in front of him.

"Very fine work," said the old man, staring at the branch in Koshimo's hands. "Are those sparrows on it?"

"*Cuervos,*" Koshimo corrected him, then switched to Japanese. "Crows."

"Oh. Pardon me," said the old man. "But isn't it back-breaking to carve those little things in that flimsy stick? Why not get a thicker one?"

"Break my back? No. Why my back break?"

Koshimo returned to his task. He enjoyed carving the thinnest stick possible. When he was in the zone, he didn't have to feel hungry.

The man turned the right wheel of his chair to rotate, then had an idea and spun himself ninety degrees so he could speak to Koshimo, who'd turned away. "In Kawasaki, the only games to play are bicycles and horses. But there's also the game about putting the ball in the bucket. You ever seen this, kid?"

Before Koshimo could answer, the man in the wheelchair unplugged his earphones and showed him the brand-new portable TV. Large men were jockeying for a dark orange ball on the tiny screen. One of them tossed it against the ground. The ball bounced back up into his hand, and he repeated that action as he ran. Then he launched into a majestic jump, avoiding an opponent's outstretched arm, and tossed the ball into a net overhead.

"Nice." The old man grinned. He took a swig of whiskey from a pocket flask to fight off the autumn chill. "If only I could get some action on this."

Koshimo leaned forward to get a better look at the screen. He remembered a game during elementary school that resembled this, but he couldn't recall its name.

Is it the same? Maybe not.

He tried to envision his reflection in the mirror running around on the court like those tall men. However, the players fighting over the dark orange ball were bigger, faster, and stronger than him. They moved back and forth rapidly, scoring points and dashing from one end to the other, and time melted away. Koshimo's eyes darted back and forth across the screen. Two players collided; one fell onto the floor, and the other stood over him and looked down at his opponent. A whistle sounded. After a short pause, the game started up again. It was a wonder that the two men didn't get into a fight. A faded ginkgo leaf landed on Koshimo's head as he concentrated on the screen.

"Good stuff, huh?" said the old man.

"These people," said Koshimo. "What people are they?"

He was trying to ask what the name of the sport was, but the old man in the wheelchair said the name of an electronics company. The Kawasaki-based enterprise was the sponsor and namesake of the team the old man was rooting for. Mistaking that for the name of the sport, Koshimo repeated it over and over like a prayer from the Bible as he watched the second half of the game.

The old man in the wheelchair left, and Koshimo was alone in the children's park. When the sun began to set, he finally put the whittling knife away, picked up the four sticks he'd carved with patterns over the course of the day, and headed for the lot of the former machine parts factory. Shadows fell long across his path. The plant had gone out of business during the global financial crisis, and though the machines and parts had been removed, the empty building was never demolished. There was a sign prohibiting trespassers, and barbed wire. Getting in wasn't easy. According to the old man, drug dealers and buyers slipped in through a gap in the barbed wire to do business at night.

Koshimo knew that his mother did drugs; she had told him as much herself. She shot a drug that wasn't cocaine into her arm. *Does* Madre *come here to buy drugs?*

The cinder-block wall on the west side of the lot had collapsed, making it possible to get a bit nearer to the building. Koshimo hurled his sticks onto the stained sheet-iron roof.

The pile of branches on top of the rusted metal resembled a bird's nest. All of them were Koshimo's handiwork. The newer branches on the top were lighter in color, but the ones at the bottom were faded and dull. Every stick that he carved got thrown onto the roof of the abandoned factory: that was Koshimo's rule.

After stepping away from the crumbled wall, Koshimo stuck his hands into his hoodie pocket and pulled out the ten-thousand-yen bill from the teenager who'd looked ready to cry. He stared at the piece of paper.

Maybe he could use this money to buy the ball from the game the old man showed him. The sport where you ran around with the ball and threw it into the net.

After some consideration, Koshimo thought he remembered where to find a sporting goods store and walked west on Shinkawa Street, then crossed the pedestrian bridge into the neighborhood of Sakai and went down the road on the other side.

When he got to the dingy old sporting goods store run by an elderly couple, Koshimo sniffed back his snot and asked for the name of the electronics maker. The old couple told him where to find a nearby electronics shop. When he got there, he repeated his question. They showed him to a row of different light bulbs, leaving him utterly dumbfounded. How had this happened?

Dejected, Koshimo headed home with no ball. As he was crossing the pedestrian bridge out of Sakai, he passed some elementary school kids.

"I love Kawasaki, city of love." They were singing the garbage truck song. Koshimo was familiar with it, too. "I Love Kawasaki, City of Love" was the actual title of the song, but because garbage trucks always played the tune, children called it the garbage truck song. The kids ended their song abruptly, rushing over to the bridge railing and peering down. They'd noticed one of their classmates below, riding a bike. Together, they shouted:

"Where are you going?!"

The boy on the bicycle stopped, startled, and looked up at the bridge. As the children laughed and giggled, Koshimo descended the steps alone and continued on his way home.

Koshimo's mother was watching TV in the apartment. His father had to give up the high-end club, but she'd found work at a different one.

She must be going to work, Koshimo thought. *She's usually not awake at this time.*

Her hair was tied up, and she'd done her makeup. She wore fine clothes, smelled sweet, and sported clean nails. The woman was even thinner than her son, but she was a true beauty when not on drugs.

Ordinarily, Koshimo snuck money out of her wallet, but since she was sober, he asked for it instead. She refused, but he kept asking.

"Qué pesado," she scolded him, but Koshimo was satisfied. It wasn't the money he wanted.

Tezcatlipoca

05

mäcuïlli

As he grew taller, Koshimo learned to steal a variety of things: bicycles left on the side of the road, clothes, shoes, and carving knives from the hardware store. He didn't usually take food. He could buy chicken with the money he filched from his mother's wallet.

When he was twelve, Koshimo found himself living in a new home. The new yakuza ordinances reduced his father's income even further, so they had to leave the big apartment behind. They moved to a building in Kawasaki's Takatsu Ward, where an old school friend of his father's ran a hardware store on the first floor and rented out the upstairs for extra income.

They got to move in without paying a security deposit or any extra one-time fees, but just like the old place, Kozo Hijikata almost never stayed there. It was as though he didn't consider it his home. On the few occasions he did show up, he never gave Koshimo's mother any money for bills.

Instead, she paid the rent with money she made working at the club, and anything leftover went to drugs. Her coworkers at the club were selling to her.

Trash piled up in their new, smaller home. Koshimo's mother left her clothes all over the place. When trucks drove down the major road next to the building, the vibration rattled the windows.

It was sad that when he woke up on the second floor of the hardware store, he couldn't go to the familiar children's park and see the old man in the wheelchair. However, Koshimo was used to being lonely. He soon found another diversion to pursue.

He'd ride a stolen bicycle to Todoroki Ryokuchi, a park in Nakahara Ward, where the Todoroki Arena was. Then he'd buy a ticket at the window and watch a game. He could get in at the children's price if he brought his mother's insurance card. It wasn't until they moved to the Takatsu Ward that Koshimo figured out—on his own—that the sport's name was *basketball*, and what the old man had taught him was merely the name of the electronics-company-owned team based in Kawasaki.

At age twelve, Koshimo was already one hundred and eighty centimeters. When he walked through the lobby of the arena, the people he passed assumed that Koshimo was a local basketball player, but he'd never touched a basketball, and his grasp of the rules was loose at best. Still, he loved to watch the games.

The stands had many empty spots. Most of the people who showed up for an amateur company league match were associated with the companies, and there were few independent fans of the teams. Koshimo kept his hood low and always sat alone in the darker parts of the upper deck. The players looked huge to him. *I wonder if I'll be like them someday.*

Koshimo's favorite player was a Black man built like a tree. Kerry Ducasse played center, stood two hundred and ten centimeters, and weighed one hundred and twenty kilograms. On this particular day, he played a major role in the second half, helping the electronics company's team come from behind to win. After leaving the arena, Koshimo pedaled to a large sporting goods store in the Nakahara Ward. He'd already scoped the place out two days earlier. While the employees were busy inspecting a new shipment of inventory, Koshimo reached for a size-seven synthetic basketball. It was the first time he even touched a competition basketball, but Koshimo's long fingers were able to grasp and lift it one-handed, just like the adults did. He walked right out of the store, tossed his loot into the bicycle basket, and rode off into the wind, a bit faster than usual.

The following morning, he woke up early and returned to the neighborhood where he used to live. Koshimo had never traveled by train or bus on his own, so he always used a bike.

He went to the children's park, hoping to show the ball to the old man in the wheelchair, but the only things he found were a few wandering pigeons. He sat down on the bench and waited. By midday, the old man still wasn't there. Koshimo hadn't brought his stick-whittling knife, either. Since he was getting bored, he tried his hand at dribbling, and threw the ball against the trunk of a ginkgo tree in an imitation of shooting. He waited until the sun went down, but the old man never showed, so Koshimo gave up, returned the ball to his bike basket, and pedaled back to the apartment in Takatsu.

The old man in the wheelchair was dead. He'd been in an accident only six days before Koshimo returned to the children's park. Drunk from the whiskey in his flask, he'd fallen onto National Route 15, where a ten-ton truck laden with gravel ran over him and the wheelchair, instantly crushing the metal frame that supported his body. Screws and bolts flew across the road into the oncoming lanes, glinting in the sun as they bounced on the asphalt.

The Kanagawa Prefectural Police's First Mobile Traffic Unit and Mobile Patrol Unit cordoned off the site of the accident, and the Traffic Investigation Division examined the scene amid the exhaust fumes from trucks passing in open lanes. They took pictures of the brake marks, shards of headlights, remains of the whiskey flask, and scraps of flesh, diligently collecting them all up.

A member of the Traffic Investigation Division found something odd among the scattered pieces of the wheelchair on the opposite side of the road. It was a stick carved with fine images of birds and geometric symbols. Perhaps it was some private article belonging to the old man. If so, it would need to be given to his family.

Assuming any family shows up, the investigator mused.

He took a photo of the stick, then placed it inside a plastic bag for storage.

With a regulation size-seven basketball in his possession, Koshimo created a new daily schedule for himself. When he woke up above the hardware store, he took his knife, basketball, a can of brined mackerel, and a plastic bottle full of tap water, and walked to the bank of the Tama River. He didn't play with the basketball right away. First, he found a stick and carved patterns until midday. Without a watch, he was left to measure the passage of time by hunger. If he wasn't finished with a stick, he'd hide it in the grass and return for it the following day.

After eating the canned mackerel and drinking tap water from the bottle, Koshimo always took a nap on the riverbank. When the sun began to set, he took the basketball to Mizonokuchi Park. He stayed out until the evening for the same reason as he always did—there was nothing to do at home.

Middle and high school students on their way home whispered, wondering who *that* was: the person dribbling a basketball in the park without understanding the basics of how it worked. Koshimo tried to mimic Kerry Ducasse's dunk style, jumping up to grab a thick cherry tree branch overhead. It startled a crow, which took off squawking. Koshimo hung from the branch for a while, letting his feet dangle in the air.

The elementary school children passing through the park on their way to after-school tutoring saw the tall, lanky figure playing with his basketball in the dark, and nicknamed him Golem.

"Did you see Golem today?"

"Yeah, I did."

"What does he do, all alone like that?"

"He plays basketball."

"You call that basketball? He's just throwing it against a tree. He talks to birds, too. I think he's crazy."

06

chicuacë

Mizonokuchi Park was full of buzzing cicadas. People heading to the library just beyond the park hurried past Koshimo. It was still light out, but the library was closing soon.

Thirteen-year-old Koshimo watched these people from time to time as he continued practicing his unique dribbling style. He'd never gone inside the library. It reminded him of school, which he hated, and he couldn't read the kanji in the books anyway. The picture books seemed interesting, but he didn't want to sit with the little kids to read them.

Before long, the library doors were closed, and the western sky had reddened. It was as though a silent bomb had gone off in the city, and everything was on fire. The color that spanned the sky developed dark yellow and orange hints. Even a bit of green. Clouds resembled scars left by some gigantic monster's claws.

When the sun sunk lower, the red light turned the color of dark blood, and the clouds seemed like torn entrails. The gruesome portrait floated neatly onward to the west, and when Koshimo could no longer make out his shadow or the basketball's, he decided it was time to go home. He pulled up the bottom of his T-shirt to wipe the sweat from his forehead, then walked through the park, occasionally bouncing the ball. The cicadas in the trees around him filled the air with a constant droning, and a crow crossed the dark sky overhead.

During his trip home, Koshimo thought of his mother, who would be back at the apartment above the hardware store, muttering in Spanish under her breath. These days, he sometimes found her naked and passed out in the entryway or pissing herself in the kitchen. Occasionally, she screamed out of nowhere.

When he got to the main route with heavy traffic, Koshimo stopped dribbling. He wasn't so confident in his skill to trust the basketball wouldn't roll into the street. And that ball was a treasured friend. He palmed it, alternating between right and left, as he continued along.

The lights were still on in the hardware store. The owner and landlord sharpened knives for a fee, and when it got late, the people who worked in the kitchens of nearby bars brought their knives to him.

Koshimo had only been in the hardware store once, just after his family moved in. The owner, his father's friend, said "Hey" to Koshimo while smoking a cigarette. Koshimo dipped his head a little, then scanned the shelves to see if there were any knives suited to whittling. Had he found one, he would've stolen it, but the many pieces of cutlery were all for the kitchen. There was also a cheap golden kettle and a commercial stockpot, but that was it.

Koshimo climbed the stairs on the outside of the building, holding the basketball to his chest. The door to the upstairs apartment was unlocked; he heard screaming inside. Koshimo opened the door and saw his father, who hadn't been home in a month, kicking his fallen mother. She was clutching something to protect it. Her head was pointed downward to the tatami mat, her arms were folded under her stomach, and her long black hair hung to the ground. His father hunched down and grabbed her arm.

"That hurts!" she shouted in Japanese. "Stop it!"

"Pain in my ass," he snapped. "Do I have to cut your whole arm off?"

Koshimo stood in the doorway, staring with his shoes still on. He recalled the dark marks on his mother's arm, the ones she tried so hard to conceal. *Is he angry about the injections?* he wondered. *But those have been there for years. It makes no sense to be mad now.*

Koshimo watched them long enough to understand what his father was doing. He wasn't angry about the needle marks; he was trying to steal her ring. She wore a ring with gemstones on her left ring finger.

Kozo Hijikata wanted to sell Lucía's ring before she could.

"But it's the ring you gave me," she wailed.

Kozo knew that was a lie. She didn't have her wedding ring. She'd sold that one long ago.

The shiny item on her ring finger was a gift from a guest at the club on Nakamise-dori Street where Lucía worked. Five 0.08 carat Zambian emeralds studded the band. The man who'd given it to Lucía had an obsession with Latinas, and she hadn't bothered telling him that she was Kozo Hijikata's wife.

Surprised by Lucía's resistance and feeling exhausted, Kozo started smoking a cigarette. He didn't bother to use an ashtray, tapping the butt right over the tatami floor and staining the straw fiber.

An abrupt, high-pitched whistle caught Koshimo by surprise, and Kozo as well. A stainless-steel coffeepot was on the gas stove in the kitchen. It was squealing and issuing hot white steam.

Kozo Hijikata finally noticed Koshimo standing in the entryway with a basketball in his hands. He glowered at his son and said, "Turn off the stove."

Koshimo removed his shoes and walked in, then turned the knob.

"Come here," his father commanded. "Hold this woman's arms down."

Koshimo pretended not to hear, instead going for the sink with his head down. But his father's thick fingers seized his shoulder. Kozo pulled Koshimo around and forced him to lift his head until his eyes met his father's.

"Look at you," Kozo said, staring aghast up at his son. "You're even fuckin' bigger now. What the hell do you eat? Dog food?"

He's so small, Koshimo thought as he stared down at his father. Were the man lined up next to Kerry Ducasse, he'd seem like a child.

Once, Koshimo's father had been so frightening that the boy couldn't look at him, but each time they met, a little of that menace wore off. At one hundred and seventy-six centimeters, Kozo was not small; his arms, legs and neck were thick, and his chest was broad and powerful. But Koshimo had long outgrown his father. Kozo hadn't changed at all over the years—Koshimo had. Without realizing it, the boy started to smile.

The look of contempt on his son's face drove Kozo into a fury. He roared and slapped Koshimo on the cheek. It was a full-on strike, and Kozo's last bit of self-control was the only thing that kept it from being a closed-fist punch. A blow like that might have killed Koshimo.

Yet despite the hit, Koshimo stood his ground. He didn't even drop the basketball. And he was still smiling. What little rationality Kozo retained flew out the window, and he started to beat his son as if it were a street brawl in the red-light district.

Koshimo withstood the punishment, however, never losing his footing. Not only that, he shoved his long arms outward, still holding the basketball, and pushed his father away.

Kozo fell right onto his back, speechless. All he could do was gape with astonishment until the air returned to his lungs, at which point he haltingly lifted his head. He stared up at his swollen-cheeked son with utter disbelief. It was beyond him to process what had occurred. He'd never been knocked off his feet in a fight before. At least, not to his recollection.

His strength is off the charts, Kozo thought. *Is that my blood or his junkie mother's?* Once his coughing subsided, he leaped to his feet and yanked open the pantry. He was looking for a kitchen knife but couldn't find any. In fact, there weren't any in the apartment. Koshimo had gotten rid of them all because his mother would swing them around when she was in one of her states. The dagger and whittling knife Koshimo used to carve branches were hidden in the back of the closet.

The long knife Kozo had carried on his person for many years was no longer in his possession. These days, the police could easily haul him in for possession of a paper knife, to say nothing of a proper weapon. Instead of blades, mobsters carried tear gas for self-defense. But the idea of a yakuza using something like that instead of a true weapon seemed a joke to Kozo.

Koshimo's father kicked the pantry door in a fury and turned to leave the apartment. Koshimo heard him quickly descending the stairs outside and looked at his basketball. *He'll come back.*

Just as he expected, his father returned with a dangerous look on his face and a knife taken from the hardware store downstairs. It was a twenty-centimeter *gyuto* chef's knife that a local bar had left there for sharpening. The freshly honed edge shone faintly, like rain clouds before an evening shower.

Kozo, eyes bloodshot, thrust the knife, but Koshimo calmly backed away to avoid it. This movement was easier to predict than the wild, careening way that Lucía swung blades around.

The man had totally lost all rationality. He was trying to stab his own son.

When the knife came charging for his stomach, Koshimo stopped it with the basketball in his hands. The knife sank deep into the synthetic leather, and the ball popped loudly. It lost its resilience and fell to the floor, dead.

Anger surged in Koshimo. Kozo pulled the knife from the slain ball and attacked again. Father and son grappled. Kozo slashed at Koshimo's neck. The cut was shallow but spilled blood that painted patterns on the tatami. Koshimo grabbed his father's throat with one hand and squeezed on the carotid artery with incredible strength, lifting him off the ground with that arm alone. Kozo's eyes widened with shock and agony. His feet dangled. Koshimo showed no mercy. Just like his father.

"Why did you kill my friend?" Koshimo said.

His father's head struck the ceiling, breaking the light bulb overhead. Glass shattered, and the light went out. From deep in Kozo's thick neck came the sound of breaking bone.

In the sudden darkness, Lucía vacantly watched as her son's silhouette lifted her husband off the ground with his left arm. Kozo's toes hung weakly in the air and didn't seem to move.

The impossible present mingled with Lucía's regular drug-addled daze, assaulting her senses. Perspiration ran from her skin like a waterfall, and she delved into a reality of her mind's own making. She didn't see her husband and child. **Julio.** Her brother, with his broad shoulders, tall stature, and the nickname El Hombro, stood before her. He was strangling one of those loathsome narcos. A delighted Lucía became a seventeen-year-old girl again.

All around her was the scent of maguey stalks and alcohol—tequila and mezcal.

Julio's gotten his revenge, so we have to have a big party. Lucía was about to begin the preparations when a shadow fell over her eyes, and her brother disappeared.

She brushed sweat-slicked hair out of her eyes and stared into the darkness. Now it was her brother who was dead. She was plunged back into terrible despair. He'd been murdered after all. Lucía looked at the ring on her finger. *That's right,* she thought. *I was being chased. They were trying to steal my ring. But they can't have it. I'll sell it and use the money to get out of this town. I have to hurry. Have to hurry.*

Lucía peered up, ready to run, and saw the back of a terrifyingly tall man. He seemed to be gazing at her brother's corpse. He turned.

Sensing danger, Lucía noticed a small machete resting atop some nearby dried straw. It was the one she'd taken with her when leaving Culiacán. She lunged for the weapon, hair whipping violently, and lashed out at the narco who had tortured her nineteen-year-old brother.

Taken aback by the sight of his mother picking up the *gyuto* from the tatami and attacking, Koshimo reacted by hitting her. Awash with adrenaline from the fight with his father, he did not hold back. She slammed into the wall, fell onto her bottom, and collapsed like a puppet.

Koshimo spoke.

"Madre."

The owner of the hardware store, who was missing his freshly sharpened knife, wondered if he should contact the police or not. He smoked several cigarettes nervously as he listened to the noises from upstairs. Among the footsteps, he heard something popping. *That better not be a gun*, he thought. Once things got quiet, a disturbing image formed in his head.

Footsteps descended the stairs, and the door to the store opened. But instead of Kozo Hijikata coated with the blood of the family he'd murdered, the hardware owner saw his tall, mixed-race son. The boy was empty-handed. There was a large bloodstain on his T-shirt.

"Did you get slashed?" the man asked.

"Solo un poco," Koshimo replied, pointing to the wound on his neck.

"Where's your old man?"

"Llame a la policía, por favor."

"What?"

Koshimo was in such a feverish state that he didn't realize he was speaking Spanish. He repeated himself over and over, wondering why the message wasn't sinking in. *Please call the police.*

Many overlapping sirens raced down Fuchu-kaido Avenue, their flashing lights coloring the entrance of the hardware store the color of bright blood. When the officers opened the door to the upstairs apartment, they saw a thirteen-year-old boy sitting against the wall, tossing a wilted basketball up into the air. His parents' bodies lay nearby on the floor of the darkened room.

"Do you understand Japanese?" called an officer, the cold, strong beam of his flashlight shining on the boy.

07

chicöme

The inaccurate story that spread through the neighborhood after the incident claimed that a foreigner had invaded the home of a Japanese family and murdered them.

When the Criminal Affairs car returned to the Takatsu-Minami Police Station from the homicide scene, the media's cameras flashed at the tinted windows. They captured nothing but images of black windows, and even if they'd caught sight of the suspect, he was a minor and couldn't legally be displayed. Still, there was a certain news value to the image of a car carrying a murderer.

Koshimo was marched through the station in cuffs and a leash around his waist. Once they had tended to the light cut on his neck, they made him drink water and collected a urine sample to test for drugs. Then he was hauled to a room for questioning. The uniformed officer tied Koshimo's leash to the leg of the table and undid his handcuffs at last.

A man and woman entered, sitting across from Koshimo. The man was Assistant Inspector Nobuhiko Terashima from Criminal Affairs, and the woman was Patrol Officer Noriko Kasai from Community Safety. Officer Kasai was in charge of juvenile crimes.

"Just to confirm, is this you?" asked Assistant Inspector Terashima as he showed Koshimo a document.

"I don't think so," Koshimo replied, shaking his head. He didn't recognize the kanji on it.

"But this is your name," Kasai said gently. "It's your legal name. Do you understand what that means?"

Koshimo looked at what was printed on the form again.

土方小霜

Kasai said, "We're going to need you to sign a few forms, and I'd like for you to sign them like this. Using these kanji."

Koshimo could understand the first two, *Hijikata*, and he could write them, too. But he didn't know the following pair. He stared at them closely.

You read those last two as "Koshimo"?

He learned that his name had its own kanji while in a police questioning room.

Koshimo had thrown his backpack into the Tama River in elementary school and hadn't been to school since. The more information Kasai gleaned from questioning, the sooner she realized that the boy was mistaken about his own age.

"Koshimo," she said, "you weren't born in 2000, you were born in 2002. Your age isn't fifteen; you're thirteen."

"Thirteen," Koshimo repeated, nodding. *"Trece."*

"Can you tell me your father's name?"

"Kozo."

"Do you know what he does?"

"Yakuza. Mobster in Kawasaki."

"And your mother?"

"Madre." Koshimo scratched his nose.

The boy's parents were dead. According to the initial examination, his father perished from broken cervical vertebrae and a spinal cord separation, and his mother died from an external head wound. They'd have to wait for the coroner for more details, but both deaths seemed nearly instant, based on the state of the crime scene.

Tezcatlipoca

"*Madre* is Lucía," said Koshimo. " Lucía Sepúlveda, *Koshimo y Lucía.*"

"What does that mean?"

"It means Koshimo and Lucía."

He showed her how to write it out.

Koshimo y Lucía

"Do you know where your mother came from?" she asked.

"Mexico. Sinaloa, Culiacán. In Japanese, say *Mekishiko.*"

"Yes, Mexico." Kasai nodded. Internally, she groaned. "Were you at home all night?"

"I went home when it got dark."

"Around what time?" questioned Assistant Inspector Terashima.

The two wanted a record of events leading up to the murder of Koshimo's parents, but they found that his statements were useless when it came to time. He never checked the time. He couldn't even read an analog clock.

The questioners decided to talk about Koshimo's parents instead. He didn't know much about his father, so they asked about his mother instead.

"*Madre* loved *hielo.*"

They weren't sure what he meant by that and wondered if they'd misheard him.

"Did you say 'yellow'? She loved Asian men?" asked Kasai.

"No. Ice."

"Ice?"

"Yes. It's ice. But not ice."

"This kind of ice?" Terashima mimed a needle going into his arm. "Is that what your mother was doing?"

"*Sí,*" Koshimo replied.

After asking around the station, they confirmed that the Latin American term for crystal methamphetamine was *hielo*, or ice.

"Koshimo," said Kasai, "you don't do *hielo*, do you?"

The boys shook his head. "No."

There was a knock on the door to the questioning room. It was Inspector Taketoki Yoshimura from the Organized Crime Department of the Kanagawa Prefectural Police.

Inspector Yoshimura had rushed to Takatsu-Minami Station upon hearing from headquarters that Kozo Hijikata, lieutenant of the Ishizaki Shindokai organization, had been murdered. He spoke to Assistant Inspector Terashima, a former classmate at the academy, and they went out into the hallway.

Koshimo leaned back against the pipe-frame chair, staring idly at the ceiling. Officer Kasai, now alone with him in the room, tried to imagine the boy's future. Yakuza father, strung-out mother, mixed-race, neglected home life, no education. It was a combination of challenging circumstances for a child in Kawasaki, and while he needed to atone for the crime of killing his parents, he couldn't be wholly blamed for it. *He was born unlucky*, she concluded.

Yoshimura and Terashima returned to the questioning room. Yoshimura looked down at Koshimo and said, "Show me your arm." His voice was deep.

"Which one?" Koshimo asked.

"The arm you grabbed your dad's neck with."

They're looking for needle marks, Koshimo thought. *But I don't do that. Why don't they believe me?*

He dropped his long arm onto the table; he'd changed T-shirts at the station. Koshimo put his palm up, so the police could see the inside of his elbow.

Inspector Yoshimura was not looking for injection marks, though. After a long career in the Organized Crime department, his interest was in the boy's arm itself. "Flex your muscle a bit," he instructed.

Koshimo looked at the man blankly, not sure what he was after. Still, he obeyed, curling his fingers into a fist. It brought about a transformation in the boy's long, slender arm. Both his biceps and his forearm bulged, bringing thick veins to the surface.

The three police officers blinked. It was *just an arm*. No tattoos, no needle marks, no self-harm. Just a boy's limb. And yet it had just as much power as any handgun or blade they'd confiscate in Kawasaki. It was like a python had appeared atop the table, aggressive and capable of violence. The trio of adults understood that merely speaking with the boy was not going to give them a picture of his true nature.

Inspector Yoshimura had arrested many mobsters who were proud of their fighting ability. Out of all of them, only four or five were truly powerful, and they could be classified in a number of categories. However, the impression this boy gave off was unlike any other. It didn't even resemble his father's.

During middle school, Kozo Hijikata practiced sumo in Yokohama's Tsurumi Ward. When he went to high school in Kawasaki, he joined the American football team. He played running back and was good enough to be known all over the Kanto region for his skill.

He was also known for his skill in a brawl. He took a page out of the football book by wearing a mouthguard, and, knowing that others weren't so wise, broke his opponents' teeth. When he couldn't find someone to fight, he pretended to be drunk on the street and stumbled into people, apologizing. If they got angry with him, he would happily flip the switch and throw a punch.

Yoshimura went to a school in Yokohama, and he often heard about Hijikata, who was a year younger than him. Yoshimura was a heavyweight judo athlete talented enough to reach the national finals. The team was absolutely forbidden from getting involved in any violence, a rule that Yoshimura followed diligently. He enjoyed hearing stories about the foolish things delinquents did, though, and laughed them off with his teammates. Hanging out in the judo team locker room was a great way to hear nasty tales from all over the Kanagawa Prefecture. Those about the undefeated Kozo Hijikata painted the portrait of a true wild man. It was impossible to believe they were the exploits of a sixteen-year-old.

By one account, Hijikata barged drunkenly into a sports gym where he was not a member, ignored the staff's insistent commands, and benched one hundred and fifty kilograms without assistance. He broke a blood vessel and got a wicked nosebleed, then passed out and started snoring. The police showed up, slapped him awake, and kicked him out of the gym, bloody shirt and all.

When Yoshimura heard this story, he and his teammates discussed if it was actually possible to bench-press one hundred and fifty kilograms without assistance while drunk. They concluded that, like the tale about the fish that got away, this legend had grown a bit in the telling. But even lifting two hundred pounds demanded incredible strength while hammered.

There was another particularly telling story about Hijikata as well.

One July night, after a harsh round of football practice, he went out into the Horinouchi red-light district and got into a fight with a Nigerian barker. The Nigerian was a former boxer, standing at about two meters. Not only did Hijikata break the other man's front teeth, he grabbed his fist, broke his fingers, and tried to tear them off. When the police and paramedics arrived, the Nigerian was staring at his dangling, dislocated middle and ring fingers and screaming his head off.

Hijikata had a college scholarship lined up to play football, but in the summer of his last year of high school, he was arrested for possession of marijuana and lost the scholarship. He voluntarily dropped out of high school, and after that, his behavior worsened.

By the time Yoshimura had graduated college and taken a job with the Kanagawa Prefectural Police, Hijikata was already a member of a designated organized crime group and was often seen coming and going from the group's office.

The two never met in high school, and now that they were adults, they were on opposing sides of the police-yakuza dichotomy. Hijikata had never even heard Yoshimura's name, but when they finally came face-to-face, Yoshimura couldn't hold back his adrenaline.

The rumors about Hijikata were true. The two got into a shoving match in the yakuza office, but the mobster eventually gave up and let Yoshimura cuff him. That brief tussle was enough for Yoshimura to understand how powerful Hijikata was. There was no one else like that, even in judo. And

Hijikata hadn't taken the fight seriously. He was horsing around, smiling, and radiating confidence. Beneath the tattooed skin, his rippling muscles slumbered, waiting to strike. He wasn't the kind of person you wanted to face without backup. A firearm would be the only option.

Hijikata's strength and ferocity were famous, even among his fellow yakuza. If you disregarded his joking with police officers, he'd never lost a true fight.

And now he was dead. Just like that.

According to the coroner, Hijikata was one hundred and seventy-six centimeters and weighed one hundred and two kilograms. Yet he'd been lifted off the ground with one hand, smacked against the ceiling, and had his neck snapped. Inspector Yoshimura still actively visited the judo dojo at police headquarters for exercise, and he couldn't believe this state of events. No one was that powerful. How much grip, arm, and back strength would it take to accomplish such a thing? Not to mention instantaneous force. Against a man like Kozo Hijikata, no less.

If this thirteen-year-old boy killed him, then he was nothing short of a monster. The police had known that Hijikata had a son, but he had no prior criminal history, and they hadn't been paying attention to him.

To think he was raising a kid like this, Yoshimura thought. "That's enough. Relax."

Koshimo stopped flexing.

"Stand up," Yoshimura commanded.

"Let's put the cuffs back on, just in case," said Assistant Inspector Terashima.

"No, it's fine." Yoshimura gazed into Koshimo's eyes. "Behave yourself. Got that? Now stand."

Koshimo sullenly slid the pipe-frame chair backward, eliciting an unpleasant squeal, and he rose slowly to his feet. The rope was still tied around the table leg. He was six-foot-two. His head approached the ceiling, and when he looked at the door, his gaze traveled right over Inspector Yoshimura's head. Yoshimura looked up at the boy.

"Will I be put to death?" Koshimo asked.

Yoshimura didn't answer right away. He stared into Koshimo's eyes, then said, "After an examination at the hospital, you'll be tried. Depending on the results, you might go to juvy."

Because he's only thirteen, he'll likely go to a Type-One detention center, Yoshimura thought. He'd receive a corrective education and be back out within a few years. But, if possible, it would be better if the boy never got out at all.

"Oh, yeah," Koshimo said. "Will I be able to play basketball?"

Yoshimura fixed him with a glare. "Think about what you've done before you speak."

"It was *Padre*'s fault," Koshimo said. "He killed the basketball. It was my friend."

The room was silent. The three police agents stared at the thirteen-year-old and thought about the long, long days ahead of him.

"I haven't seen that guy around."
"Yeah, I wonder where he went."

After Koshimo was sent to Sagamihara Juvenile Detention Center in August of 2015, the boys who passed through Mizonokuchi Park at dusk noticed that Golem was gone.

They were disappointed that one of their favorite urban legends had suddenly vanished. Most likely, Golem lived in the sewers and climbed up to the surface from manholes. He threw the basketball against the trees to stun the bugs and birds so he could eat them.

Even after vanishing, Golem remained a topic of discussion among the children for a while. Some of them even kicked soccer balls against a tree trunk to mimic him.

But eventually, all mention of him died out. Once a new story arose about a four-eyed crocodile living in the Tama River, they'd forgotten him entirely.

08

chicuëyi

Executions, assassinations, corpses...

Men and women hung from the bridge without their heads, priest and procession were sprayed with submachine guns as they conducted a solemn funeral in the graveyard—**reality**.

Murders, retribution, sacrifice...

A burning school bus, screaming parents, circling helicopters, **reality**, armored police cars accelerating down the road to school.

Nightmares, atrocities, bodies...

Bombed buildings, limbs scattered across the floor, spilled viscera, **reality**, a pickup truck loaded with cocaine driving against a background of black smoke.

In the *guerra contra las drogas*, the accursed **reality** the country was facing, the battle in Nuevo Laredo, Tamaulipas, in northeastern Mexico, was the worst. Despair covered the land, and the cruel winds of death blew down every street. Open warfare between two cartels had turned the city into a hellscape.

Across the border in America, the *San Antonio Journal* had this to say in the morning edition of its September 11, 2015, paper:

> The latest drug war is reaching its final stage after two years
> of fighting. Just like Culiacán, Sinaloa in the northwest of

Mexico, the new lawless area is Nuevo Laredo, Tamaulipas, in the northeast. The citizens lead their lives, dogs walk the streets, cars drive by, and the traffic lights function, but the danger lurking throughout the city is immeasurable.

Right across the border with Texas, Nuevo Laredo is connected to the route of gold, Interstate 35. This vast stretch of highway traveling all the way to Minnesota carries forty percent of all the drugs smuggled into America from Mexico. That brings an astronomical amount of money into the pockets of drug dealers. Even if the current drug war in northeast Mexico resolves itself, the amount of cocaine won't change, only the web of connections supplying it, and the name of the cartel.

The forces that took control over the northwest are biding their time, watching the war in the northeast. The cartel based out of Sinaloa manages half of the drugs smuggled here from Mexico, and they are more than happy to watch their rivals duke it out. The more strength the others lose, the more their own territory stands to grow.

The old tyrants of the northeast, Los Casasolas, are in decline, fated to go the way of the Tyrannosaurus Rex. Soon, the Dogo Cartel's era will arrive.

The amount of cocaine that crosses the border won't change. And neither will the United States' status as the biggest marketplace.

San Antonio Journal

Born in Veracruz, the Casasola brothers pushed into northeast Mexico and grew Los Casasolas into a massive operation over two decades, but their territory was being devoured by the new Dogo Cartel, leading to gang warfare in 2013.

Any who'd defied Los Casasolas in the past died out. This new drug war drew the attention of the Mexican authorities, as well as the DEA and CIA over the border as well.

The leader of the Dogo Cartel was not a Mexican. He was Argentinean-born, and he named his cartel after the proud Dogo Argentino, a breed of fighting dog that could kill a puma.

Their choice of the world's greatest fighting dog as a symbol was appropriate. The Dogo Cartel possessed an aggressive nature; once they sank their teeth into Los Casasolas, they refused to let go, regardless of any retribution.

Hardly a day went by that the two cartels didn't get into a gunfight on the streets of Nuevo Laredo, spilling blood and empty cartridges onto the asphalt, and spreading death as they went.

Wherever they found their enemies, they started shooting, civilians be damned.

Over fifty narcos engaged in an urban battle, leaving every building within a radius of fifty yards riddled with bullet holes. Eighteen passengers died inside a *pesero*, a minibus caught in the cross fire, its windows and body unable to stop bullets. Some shots hit a van carrying some promising young baseball players, killing two. Their team held a solemn memorial game, but no one spoke an ill word about the cartels. No one dared mention their names.

The war only worsened to the point that local newspapers wouldn't speak of it anymore. They lamented the dead on their cover pages, but not a single article spoke the truth about the cartels responsible.

Los Casasolas y Cartel del Dogo.

Words that should have adorned the front page every single day but were never printed out of fear of retribution.

Ayoze Rubiales, 55, newspaper writer.

Tomás Tellechéa, 41, newspaper writer.

Perpétua Lucientes, 33, journalist.

Viviano Frías, 27, writer/blogger.

Angel Garza, 38, TV station producer.

There was no end to the list of people who bravely criticized the cartel war and were summarily threatened and executed for it. Their voices were buried under cold earth, and the blood running in the streets over them heralded the death of high-minded things like law, order, and journalism.

The media's self-imposed censorship on cartel topics began after the death of bestselling author Casimiro San Martín, who had his own information network and humanistic views. He staunchly criticized the corrupt relationship between Los Casasolas and the local police.

The cartel easily killed Casimiro's eleven round-the-clock bodyguards and abducted him. He wasn't seen again until five days later, in a chili-processing plant. The state of the body was so wretched that even the investigators who were used to the narcos' cruelty had difficulty examining it.

Right arm, left arm, right leg, left leg: none of them were recognizable. The forensics team concluded that they had frozen the seventy-three-year-old author's limbs while he was still alive, then smashed them with something hard, like a hammer. The official cause of death was shock from blood loss, but surely the terror and agony had stopped the elderly man's heart before that. That would forever be an educated guess, because they couldn't find the heart for confirmation. It was carved out of his body, leaving an empty cavity in his chest.

Los Casasolas' narcos launched a grenade through the bulletproof glass of a Dogo Cartel Jeep.

Unable to avoid the toppled, burning automobile, the vehicles behind it quickly piled up. The Casasola men promptly showered their enemies with bullets, tossing in the occasional hand grenade. Once they were out of ordnance, they approached the cars, looked for anyone still breathing, and dragged them out into the open, where they ripped off their clothes and slashed their carotid arteries. Recording executions and putting them on the internet was a regular activity at this point; the Dogo Cartel did the same thing. But there was no time to stand around filming during a battle as fierce as this one. They had to focus on killing as quickly as possible, before enemy reinforcements could arrive. They killed living human beings with the efficiency and impunity of slaughtering cattle or squashing bugs. It was the extreme limit of violence, of boundless terror, a hell with no end. Blood coated the street.

When the police special forces arrived, Los Casasolas exchanged fire with them gamely but largely withdrew. They'd spent an extravagant amount of ammunition on their rivals, but doing the same to the police would be a waste of expenses. That was the particular flavor of pragmatism the cartels favored. Ultimately, it was all a business.

Fighting the police with their helmets and armored vests would mean expending thousands, even tens of thousands of bullets. But if you attacked individual officers on their way to or from work, you could take them out with just a handful. That's what the cartels sent their *sicarios* to do.

Isolate and eliminate each commanding officer, one at a time, and kill their families, too. By placing a target in their sights 365 days a year, the cartels were able to keep cops frightened and pacified. Hostile prosecutors and judges could be similarly pressured. They would keep up the heat until their targets quit and fled to the land of *gringos*. Or else it would be just another body to add to the count.

Four brothers led Los Casasolas.

"El Pirámide," Bernardo Casasola.
"El Jaguar," Giovani Casasola.
"El Polvo," Valmiro Casasola.
"El Dedo," Duilio Casasola.

Their enemies, the Dogo Cartel, constructed a communication interception system rivaling that of the American DEA and were able to pin down the coordinates of Los Casasolas' hideout, a mansion on the outskirts of the city, and attacked in a way the four brothers never expected.

At four AM on September 9, 2015, they conducted a drone bombing of the sort the Americans did all the time in the Middle East.

The drone was huge, its wingspan a whole eight meters, and it buzzed through the darkness. It dropped a five-hundred-pound military bomb on the mansion, blasting it to pieces. Bernardo and Giovani, the first and second brothers, did not survive the initial explosion. All that remained of them were burning scraps of flesh—nothing that could be given a proper burial.

The third brother, Valmiro Casasola, escaped the attack by coincidence. He couldn't sleep, went out to smoke a cigarette, and wound up talking with the sentry at the gate. As he spun around to see the mansion exploding, his initial thought was that they'd been hit by an air-to-surface missile. So he was already looking at the sky when his subordinate came running across the grounds, pointing into the air and shouting.

Based on the size of the drone silhouette outlined against the moon and stars, Valmiro believed the attack might have come from SEMAR, the Mexican Navy. However, the Navy wouldn't forgo any attempt to capture targets and choose to bomb them.

Must be the Dogo Cartel, thought Valmiro.

His wife and children were hiding in the mansion's basement. Their escape tunnel was caved in, blocked by concrete, so by decision of the fourth brother, Duilio Casasola, the family was sent back up to ground level.

Valmiro could see the blood streaming from his brother's head. Duilio was carrying an AR-18, an American assault rifle. His favorite thing to do was feed his living enemies' fingers to pigs. It was why they called him El Dedo, "The Finger."

"¡Pinche cabrón!" Duilio swore, loading all of the brothers' families into armored cars. There was a Grand Cherokee and three Range Rovers. *"¡Vamos! ¡Vamos!"*

"No, alto," Valmiro warned, but a second bomb struck, shaking the ground and knocking over trees. A fireball erupted, blotting out Duilio's visage.

The car carrying Valmiro's wife and children had just taken off safely. A second huge drone chased after it. Its pursuit was precise; one of the Casasola men in the Cherokee leaned out the window and took aim with a Russian-made antitank launcher, but the drone had already dropped its payload at the calculated coordinates. All four cars flew into the air. The blast tore into the ground and took the lives of everyone in its vicinity.

Valmiro's radio buzzed with a warning that Dogo Cartel vehicles were on their way, but it was too late. The line of headlights was already visible.

He grabbed an armful of guns and grenades, tossed them into a Ram 1500 pickup, and sped down the forest road under the predawn sky, gunshots ringing out behind him. He kept his foot on the gas and considered the high-resolution camera the large drone was bound to be equipped with.

Will it be able to identify my face? Probably. So it'll follow.

Valmiro fled from the mansion hideout to an empty lot about thirty-one kilometers away and hid the pickup truck inside a shed that had been abandoned by the previous occupant. Leaving the car out where its roof was visible would make it an easy target. He didn't even have a moment to mourn his family. Valmiro promptly got down on his stomach in the tall grass and, checking carefully around him, radioed his subordinate, Andrés Mejía.

When Andrés showed up, he was carrying binoculars and a backpack stuffed with C-4. He pointed the binoculars toward the brightening sky, observing the graceful drone.

"That's a military drone," Andrés said, "but it's not air force. It looks a lot like a Boeing X-45 to me."

Andrés had been in the Mexican Army before he was a narco, and he knew quite a lot about weaponry. He handed the binoculars to Valmiro, who peered through the lenses. The eerie craft was almost eight meters long, with a gray, windowless body. It circled the sky over Nuevo Laredo. It was clear what the Dogo Cartel was looking for.

They've seen the footage of me escaping.

El Polvo: The Dust. It was a nickname known among narcos, law enforcement, and the world at large. He was the most vicious of the four brothers who led Los Casasolas. The Dogo Cartel had killed three of the siblings, but they hadn't finished the job yet.

Valmiro and Andrés waited out the large drone's search, then moved toward the center of the city. It wouldn't follow them there. Back in the Ram 1500, it was less than five minutes until Dogo vehicles spotted them, and a fierce gunfight broke out. The pickup's reinforced glass windshield cracked and went white, as if fogged from morning dew, before shattering. Tires burst, and the pickup skidded.

The two men jumped out of the car and returned fire. Andrés shot his gun and tossed a grenade but quickly took a bullet to his right shoulder; the blood splashed on Valmiro's cheek. Andrés collapsed to the ground and crawled away. Enemy bullets pinged off the asphalt and twanged against road signs.

Valmiro knew he couldn't save Andrés. He grabbed the backpack full of C-4 and ran in the opposite direction, toward the highway. Eventually, he spotted a Toyota truck stopped on the shoulder. The young farmer who owned it had just finished tying a sheet over the pile of chilis in the bed. Valmiro shot him through the head and let his body fall to the ground, then took the sombrero off and used it to hide his face as best he could.

Inside the truck, the farmer's wife was sitting in the passenger seat. Valmiro shot her in the face, opened the door, and kicked her body out. He quickly got back out of the truck and lifted the sheet over the bed to check the contents. He was worried the couple might have had a son back there, but it was just a mountain of chiles. Valmiro returned to the driver's seat.

He drove to a self-service gas station.

Valmiro stopped the truck at the corner of the lot and bought himself a pack of gum from a vending machine. Then he opened the backpack to check the C-4 detonator's phone number. It was wired up to a smart-phone, and calling it triggered the bomb. C-4 didn't explode from contact with bullets or being lit on fire. The detonator was necessary to set it off. Once he'd committed the number to memory, Valmiro inserted the deto-nator into one of the individually wrapped plastic explosive blocks, buried it under the mound of chilis, and left the gas station behind.

He drove east. When he found the folk-art stand he was looking for, he pulled off the road, lifted the farmer's sombrero for a slightly better peripheral view, then called Andrés on his wireless transceiver.

"Come to the folk-art stand," he said. "Where the cactus sign is."

Andrés was most likely either shot and killed or tortured and killed. Valmiro's message was not meant for him, but for the Dogo Cartel, who had picked up his radio.

At one o'clock in the afternoon, under the cloudy sky of the monsoon season, and with the folk-art stand with the cactus-shaped sign directly in view, Valmiro Casasola examined his face in the rearview mirror of the Toyota. He chewed a piece of the gum from the vending machine, spat it out, and stuck it to his forehead to keep the blood from trickling down into his eyes.

He took a deep breath and exhaled. He was forty-six, but his stam-ina still held, and his willpower was fierce. You couldn't survive as a narco without those qualities. His brothers, his men, his wife, his son, and his daughter were dead, but he wouldn't plead to heaven and ask, "Why, God?" nor would he sit in church and weep. That was for ordi-nary people.

The moment my family was killed was the moment my long quest for revenge began. My god doesn't forgive sin, Valmiro thought. His was the battle god that transcended hell itself. Yohualli Ehecatl, Night and Wind; Titlacauan, We Are His Slaves; Tezcatlipoca, the Smoking Mirror.

He checked the remaining bullets in the two guns on his lap. Four shots in the Austrian-made Glock 19, and three in the Swiss TP9 submachine gun. Both used the same ammunition: 9×19 mm Parabellum rounds.

Valmiro removed the bullets from the TP9 and moved them to the Glock 19. The SMG had higher initial velocity and range, but considering what he was about to do, it was better to put all of the ammo into the pistol, which was easier to fire.

He squeezed the pistol and lay down on the seat, slowing his breathing. No sound came through his left ear—the shock wave from the bombing had ruptured the eardrum. Valmiro felt dizzy. Perhaps his inner ear and semicircular ducts were damaged, ruining his sense of balance. He hadn't felt this bad since that night in Colombia.

Seven years ago, he'd ridden in a small submarine arranged by a Colombian cartel. The vessel was built in the jungle, and it could carry six passengers and their cocaine underwater. Its interior was as cramped as a prison cell, and the oxygen was thin. During the voyage along the bottom of the Gulf of Mexico, one of the Colombians threw up and fell unconscious. A putrid stink of vomit filled the craft, but it couldn't surface due to the watchful eyes of SEMAR, and there was no ventilation. Eventually, the man who vomited came to his senses, but his fellow Colombians were so furious with him that they shot the man as soon as they were back on land.

That steel coffin was awful, but at least we were traveling through the water, Valmiro thought. *It's worse now.*

El barco se hundió.

The *barco*, his ship, was the cartel. And when it sank, it took everything with it. Everything.

Valmiro sank into the driver's seat of the truck and gazed at the cactus sign, waiting. Once, foreign tourists had flocked to this folk-art store to buy items related to Día de los Muertos: skeleton dolls, altars, sugar skulls. Even when November was months away, colorful skills sold like candy. There were no tourists anymore. The building's sizable floor was empty and forlorn. Now the only patrons were locals. They bought the buckets and hoses and brooms that the manager acquired for cleaning the place.

A car pulled into the parking lot of the folk-art store. When it stopped, an old man and woman got out, along with their young grandson. He was about seven years old, and cradled a Batmobile in his arms as gently as if it were a puppy. Batman's supercar looked much too large to be a child's toy, and to Valmiro, the thick tires seemed as big around as orange slices. Perhaps it was an RC car.

The old man glanced around, then ushered his wife and grandson through the door under the big cactus sign. A minute later, five cars full of Dogo Cartel narcos showed up, as though to mock the visitors' fate. Armed men looking for El Polvo charged into the store, leaving three guards outside.

Valmiro started the pickup's engine, pointed it at the store, and pressed the gas pedal. When the guards started shooting at him, he ducked down, curled up, then jumped out of the open door.

He had plenty of experience jumping out of a moving car when he was young. One of the tried-and-true methods of smuggling in Mexico was to drive a pickup laden with cocaine off a cliff into the ocean, where the business partners were waiting with motorboats to collect the product as it floated on the waves. Valmiro and others would keep their hands on the wheel and bet money to see who could stay in the car the longest. It was a game of chicken. They would mark the spot where you jumped out with chalk.

After rolling onto the parking lot of the folk-art store, Valmiro got up on a knee and pulled the Glock's trigger, counting down the bullets.

Siete, seis, cinco…

He shot one of the guards who tried to dodge out of the way of the unmanned truck, shot the head of another who blasted at him with an MP5, and hit the third man in the gut with his sixth shot. The last one tried to get back up, but rather than finish him off, Valmiro hit the call button on his smartphone.

The truck plunged into the building right at the moment the C-4 buried under the mountain of chili peppers exploded. The windows shattered outward, and the asphalt shook. Black smoke erupted, and the cactus sign crumbled as it burned. A rat bolted out of the devastated building, coated in flame. It raced across the parking lot toward Valmiro and spun in a circle, burning horribly. Valmiro realized it wasn't a rat but a tire from a toy Batmobile.

09

chiucnähui

He hadn't gone out on his own with only a single bullet in his gun since he was a boy; it felt like a bad joke. Valmiro took bus after bus, placing calls to cities in Texas. He wasn't having conversations, just logging phone calls. Los Casasolas had a number of bases around the state. There was Laredo, just on the other side of the Río Bravo (which the *gringos* called Rio Grande) from Nuevo Laredo, and then Del Rio, Austin, and Dallas.

Where would a man go from Nuevo Laredo after his hideout was destroyed, his brothers were killed, and he was on the run from drone bombers? Valmiro was certain the Dogos believed he'd run north. They thought that El Polvo would flee to America in defeat.

Nuevo Laredo sat right next to the border, after all. Texas was much closer than the Casasola brothers' home of Veracruz. At the very least, if Valmiro was in America, he wouldn't need to worry about huge drones hunting him in an urban environment. Knowing they had his communications tapped, he sent the Dogo Cartel sniffing around the border between Texas and Tamaulipas, then tossed his smartphone away down an alley.

Sixteen-year-old Teodoro Forqué, better known as Lolo, worked at a little *carnecería* in Nuevo Laredo. He worshipped Los Casasolas, and even worked as a street dealer. While he wasn't seen as a cartel member, he was at least known a little within the criminal element of the area. Lolo had to support his family but was so poor, he couldn't even buy himself a gun.

Still, he dreamed of being a narco for Los Casasolas and making a bunch of money one day.

Lolo's father was a trainer at the racetrack who fell into drug trouble. A man from the Dogo Cartel named Sancho killed him. Lolo hoped to get revenge, but Sancho died soon after.

An older dealer told Lolo that it was El Polvo who'd killed him. "That means Sancho went through the usual torture. Your old man's been avenged." Valmiro, "El Polvo," had indeed murdered Sancho, but it had nothing to do with the death of Lolo's father. Still, it brought light to Lolo's heart. *One of the brothers who runs Los Casasolas, the most powerful cartel in all of Mexico, avenged my father!*

When El Polvo, that mysterious, distant figure, appeared without warning, Lolo barely batted an eyelash. He had no idea what Valmiro actually looked like.

"Whose bike is that?" Valmiro asked. A Bajaj CT 100, an Indian motorcycle, sat out front.

"Mine," said Lolo.

Valmiro took out a paper bill. When he saw the amount, Lolo quietly rejoiced. It almost felt unreal. Now he'd be able to buy a gun. Not a loaner but his own. It was the first step to being a real narco.

"Buy yourself a new one," Valmiro said, handing him the money. "You got a full helmet that covers the face? I'll buy that off you, too. And I want some water."

After quenching his thirst with the cup of water Lolo brought him, Valmiro slicked back his hair and washed his face until the cut on his forehead stopped bleeding. Then he took the key, sat on the bike he'd just bought, and checked the gasoline level.

Lolo quietly asked, "Is there anything else you need, *Señor*? Any *coca*?"

Valmiro shook his head, put the full-face helmet over his head, and turned on the engine. *"Hasta luego,"* he bid.

* * *

Valmiro headed south on Federal Highway 2 along the flow of the Río Bravo. He took in the passing scenery through the helmet's windshield, envisioning his escape route and thinking of the many hard days ahead of him. He would flee as far as necessary, and once he'd built up power again, he would exact his revenge on the Dogo Cartel for killing his family. He would even murder those who begged for their lives. *It'll take years to put the cartel back together and reclaim our plaza. But I'll do it all.*

The word *despair* meant nothing to Valmiro. He accepted the cruelty of the world, offered his blood to his god, and strode proudly through hell like a warrior. He was used to pain. He was used to praying to his Aztec god and walking side by side with agony.

Two hundred and sixty-seven kilometers later, Valmiro arrived in Reynosa and stopped at a *mercado*. He left the bike at the entrance to the crowded market, removed his helmet, and left it hanging conspicuously on the handlebars. The key was still in the engine. He walked a short way into the *mercado* and turned around in time to see a young man in a ragged T-shirt hurrying off with the bike.

Just take it as far away as you can, Valmiro urged him silently.

He told a cactus-seller that he'd lost his cell phone and paid the man to borrow an old BlackBerry. Valmiro placed a call to Miguel Trueba, a police detective. Miguel was a cartel informant working within the Reynosa Police.

Valmiro told him where they'd meet up, erased the call from the phone's history, then handed the BlackBerry back to the man.

He walked through the bustling marketplace and bought a premade torta from a stand. Instead of change, he asked for a set of plastic cooking gloves and savored the taste of beef and avocado as he strolled through the crowd.

He bought a shirt and slacks, then a kitchen knife at another store, and a cheap Chinese flashlight at yet another.

As he made his way west, the crowds dwindled, until finally dying out near a church. Valmiro strolled into the chapel, entered the confessional, removed the floor panel, and descended a set of stairs that led underground.

The channel heading east underneath Reynosa was known as Cuetz-palin among the senior Casasolas members. That meant *lizard* in Nahuatl, the language of the Aztec Empire. There were places within Mexico where it was still spoken today. Valmiro's *abuela* was from one such region.

Los Casasolas had a tunnel running between Tamaulipas and Texas, but before engaging in that massive project, they did a test dig in Reynosa. That was Cuetzpalin, a seventy-meter underground passage.

Valmiro turned on the flashlight, lowered his head, and proceeded. It was freezing inside the one-hundred-and-fifty-centimeter-high tunnel. He'd bought the clothes specifically for this; by the time he got out, he'd be covered in mud.

A rope ladder waited at the end of the passage, and Valmiro climbed it to the surface. He was now inside a hat warehouse. The space was full of cardboard boxes packed with all the different colored hats they sold at the *mercado*.

When he saw Miguel Trueba waiting for him, Valmiro clapped his hands and brushed the dirt off his clothes.

Trueba had pulled up in a Ford Explorer SUV with clean plates, the sort reserved for emergencies like this one. He was smoking a cigarette, having supposedly quit years ago.

"How's your daughter?" Valmiro asked.

"Fine," Trueba replied with a smile that even he had to know looked fake.

Los Casasolas had no future. A new age was coming, and Trueba was worried. *Should I kill El Polvo, Valmiro Casasola, right here and now? If I'm going to do it, this is the time. If he's the last survivor of Los Casasolas, that will be the end of it. But there's no way to know for sure. If any of his men are still lurking around, they'll come after me. They'll send* sicarios *to her boarding school in Mexico City and inflict hell on her.*

Trueba was a chief patrol agent and, in exchange for assisting Los Casasolas, received enough money to buy a new car, raise his five daughters, and pay for his elderly mother's care. His eldest attended the private school in Mexico City on the cartel's dime.

He could have shot Valmiro in the warehouse at any time, but he didn't even pull his gun. He gave Valmiro the key to the escape vehicle and a fake ID, as well as the name and departure time of the reefer ship he'd arranged in Veracruz to the south.

"I'm so tired." Valmiro sighed, dropping the key into his pocket. "I need to wipe off this sweat. Do you have a towel?"

"A handkerchief."

Valmiro took it and cleaned his face. *"Gracias por todo,"* he said, walking over to Trueba, and putting his arm around the other man's back. It was a Mexican-style side hug. Trueba returned the gesture, circling his arm around Valmiro's back.

Like a magician performing sleight of hand, Valmiro flipped open the handkerchief and placed it on Trueba's head. Now he wouldn't get any splashback. With his right hand, Valmiro drew his pistol and pressed it to Trueba's temple, pulling the trigger. It was all one smooth motion. The gunshot echoed throughout the warehouse. The dirty cop collapsed to the concrete floor, handkerchief stained with blood and brain matter.

The Dogo Cartel would've killed him eventually. They'd have sniffed him out, kidnapped him, and tortured him into giving up El Polvo's destination. Whether Trueba knew it or not, there was only death for him. As Valmiro looked down on the body, he thought, *You were a good man. You worked hard and faithfully.*

He tossed the Glock 19 aside, having fired its last bullet, and took the pistol from the dirty cop's holster. Then he tore the dead man's shirt off. He put on the plastic food-preparation gloves from the market and stuck the knife he bought into the cadaver's chest, working it vertically and putting his strength into it, until he severed the sternum. The sound of sawing and cracking filled the warehouse, and the dead man's head lolled left and right. Once the sturdy breastbone opened top to bottom, Valmiro cut out the intrusive ribs, then stuck his arm into the cavity he'd created. It was still warm. The heart was beating. He squeezed it with his left hand, and with the knife in his right, severed the thick aortic valve. Blood poured out of it, but with practiced ease, Valmiro lifted the heart and laid it on top of the corpse's face. Then he offered a prayer in Nahuatl.

In ixtli in yollotl. A face and a heart.

The face and heart of the confused fool were thus bound together, and Miguel Trueba was sacrificed to Valmiro's god.

Valmiro didn't believe in Jesus Christ or Santa Muerte, the saint of death who was the object of devotion for all narcos. Instead, he placed faith in a power from before the Spaniards wiped out the Aztec Empire, long before Christianity came to this land.

10

mahtlactli

He intended to travel south from Tamaulipas; not into America. Instead of following the smuggling route of the cartel's primary product, cocaine, he would hide by moving with its secondary product: *hielo*.

Whether on the motorcycle or hunched underground in the Cuetzpalin, Valmiro's mind was constantly working on his escape plan.

Almost all of the cartel's cocaine went north to America, the biggest marketplace, but some of their other drugs went south instead. The biggest one of those was *hielo*.

Ice, methamphetamine, a potent stimulant. Unlike cocaine, which was derived naturally from coca leaves, *hielo* was manufactured via an artificial process, and was first synthesized from ephedrin in 1893 by Nagai Nagayoshi, a Japanese chemist and professor. In the 1930s, its ability to stimulate the nervous system was discovered, after which it was sold in Germany as Pervitin, and in Japan as Hiropon. Despite the eventual recognition that the substance harmed the brain and its subsequent banning, it became a major product for black markets around the world.

The *hielo* manufactured in Los Casasolas' lab in Tamaulipas largely moved along two routes, both of which involved naval shipping.

The first smuggling route went through the Gulf of Mexico, down the Caribbean Sea, made land in Venezuela, and then traveled into Brazil.

The second trail moved south over the Caribbean, then through the Panama Canal and into the Pacific. After stopping in Chile, it was brought by land to Argentina. In the capital city of Buenos Aires, it would be loaded onto a ship again to cross the South Pacific to Australia. And the trip didn't end there. Drug capitalism and the properties of the free market intertwined like Ouroboros, spreading products ever outward, so that drugs produced in Mexico found their way to destinations like Indonesia and Japan.

Valmiro's plan to escape the Dogo Cartel involved the use of that second route. He drove Miguel Trueba's Ford Explorer south out of Reynosa toward the port of Veracruz, where the reefer ship was waiting for him.

The city of Veracruz in the state of the same name was where the Casasola brothers grew up. It represented Valmiro's roots, and it was also, in a sense, the origin of modern Mexico. This was where Mexico's history began, and where the Aztecs' history came crashing down.

In 1519, in what is currently known as the Gulf of Mexico, a Spaniard led armed troops to make landfall. He was a conquistador with a pale, grayish face and faint whiskers.

Hernán Cortés was thirty-four at the time. He created a settlement along the water and named it Villa Rica de la Vera Cruz, the rich village of the true cross. This was the basis for what later became Veracruz.

With a base established, Cortés's forces marched west across the new continent they called Tierra Firme. The various tribes they met and fought along the way all succumbed to the Spaniards' modern weapons, but they offered strident warnings: Do not go to the kingdom to the west. You will all die.

Cortés's ambitions exceeded those of even Diego Velázquez de Cuéllar, governor of Cuba. He wanted to conquer the Aztec Kingdom, the most fearsome in all of Tierra Firme. And he intended to take all of the gold in the possession of the *indio* king.

"The first people to call themselves *Mexica* were the Aztecs," Valmiro's *abuela* told him when he was young. "The Spanish killed the Aztec king and destroyed the *teocalli*, the great temple. They ruined the city and built their palace and the Zócalo on top of it. Where do you suppose that is? Yes, Mexico City. Before then, it was a city called Tenochtitlan, a beautiful place like you've only seen in your dreams. They took everything, yet the Aztecs didn't allow the conquistadors to own them. The Spanish angered the Aztec gods. They only pretended to be absorbed into the white man's civilization. In truth, the Aztec gods are eating their entrails from within, cutting off their heads. This drug war, it never ends, does it? It's a curse. It was the Eastern men who brought the *opio*, but only because the Aztec gods called them here. Understand? The disaster wrought by the divine crosses the oceans and spreads across the entire world."

It was September in Veracruz, and the temperature was in the nineties. Four months had passed since the rainy season began. There was no precipitation that morning, and the waves of the Gulf of Mexico sparkled. As he stepped onto the refrigerator ship heading for the Panama Canal, Valmiro undid two buttons on his shirt and wiped the sweat from his brow. He squinted against the sun and breathed in the scent of the sea and the fishy stink that had permanently settled into the boat.

The flies buzzing around the deck followed out to sea. They alit upon Valmiro's shirt, then buzzed around some more before stopping again. He gazed at the water with their humming in his ear—only the right, because his left was still deaf. It was time for him to rest. Valmiro let his eyes close slowly. In his dream, jaguars raced across the landscape, eagles took flight, and snakes slithered through the desert dust, then lifted themselves up to strike.

The *abuela* who loved Valmiro and his brothers dearly and took care of them like a mother was named Libertad. It was a Spanish name given to her by her family—probably when she was three or four—because in this day and age, it was easier to have one of those.

Before she was given the name Libertad, her family and the other villagers called her Quiahuitl, the Nahuatl word for *rain*. Sometimes they called her Ome Quiahuitl, "Two Rain," based on the date of her birth in the Aztec calendar. But both of these were nicknames. Her true name was Tezcaquiahuitl, "Mirror Rain."

Libertad was an *indígena* born in Catemaco, Veracruz, a place located on a lake where the descendants of the Olmecs, Mayans, and Aztecs still lived. These people were initially known as *indios*, but as the times changed, the term was replaced by *indígena*, which was not considered to be an insult in the same way. But Libertad and many of the villagers told the whites and *mestizos* that they were *indios* anyway.

Some of the old Aztec rituals survived in her village. The *brujos*, keepers of the occult ways, spoke in a mixture of Spanish and Nahuatl, telling stories of Aztec mythology at night, lighting fires, burning copal incense, and performing rituals minor enough not to get shut down by the Mexican authorities. If they did *real* Aztec rituals, the entire village would be rounded up and arrested.

No matter how faint the fire or wisp of smoke, if it contained the *brujos'* holy power, it was a grand sight in young Libertad's eyes. She could see the massive blaze at the lost *teocalli*, and the vortex of smoke shrouding the statues of the gods around the altar. When combined with the *brujos'* whispers, Libertad found the Aztec universe opening before her, welcoming and nurturing her soul.

Having felt true holy power for herself, Libertad despised the rituals held in every village as shows to entice the tourists. They were flashy, but empty, and didn't open the door to the mysterious dreamworld in any way. Libertad stomped up to the home of one of these sideshow *brujos*, stood in the doorway, and accused him of being a liar and charlatan. *"Mentiroso!"* she spat, and for good measure, included the Nahuatl *"Iztlacatqui!"* as well. "Let the gods of the Mexicas devour you."

The *brujo* stuck his head out the window and threw ritual cacao beans and dried grass roots at his righteous little accuser to drive her off.

Libertad's family was extremely poor. One year, their livestock all died of a plague, leaving the family without any means to support itself. Libertad left the village at age sixteen.

She caught the eye of a white man visiting the lake at Catemaco on vacation, and he asked to marry her. He was Carlos Casasola from Veracruz, a *criollo*—a Mexican-born of pure Spanish descent. Carlos had inherited his grandfather's trading business, named after the family, and owned several boats at the port of Veracruz. Libertad chose to marry him in exchange for financial support for her family. Interracial mixing was happening all over Mexico at the time, but Carlos's lineage had not taken in a drop of *indígena* blood yet, a tacit admission of its racist views. Carlos was the first man in the family to take an indigenous woman for his wife.

Libertad had nothing like a dowry to offer and hardly any possessions to take with her to the mansion in Veracruz. She left Catemaco with some change, an adobe brick to remember her home by, an old whistle in a little burlap bag, and an obsidian knife a *brujo* had given her. Initially, she'd intended to bring the maguey thorn she used for prayer, but when informed they were sold at the market in Veracruz and could be acquired at any time, she reluctantly left hers behind.

If you traced the Casasola family line back far enough, you arrived at the conquistadors who destroyed the Aztec Empire in 1521. Carlos told Libertad as much ahead of time. But that didn't change her intention to help her family back in the village once she was married. There were *tons* of conquistador descendants in Mexico. *No matter what the president says about how equal we all are, this is* their *country.*

Libertad had to get used to an all-new way of life. Her husband, Carlos, allowed her to venture out into the port city and learn new things once a week. She heard all different kinds of talk: Spanish, English, other languages she'd never heard before. Economic opportunities, nonsensical schemes, sailors from various countries who showed up and left, traders, stevedores, and the massive *mercado*. Just a brief walk was enough to make her dizzy with all the information.

It hurt to see other *indio* girls like her selling themselves for a living. They came from other places, not Catemaco, and found opportunity in the big port. Soon there were rumors about Libertad—that she lived with a wealthy white man—and they envied her, and threw things at her when she passed.

However, some of the girls were more sociable, and Libertad got to be on good terms with a few. They sat together in the café, drinking hot *atole*, a beverage made of ground corn, and talked about their hometowns, smoked cigarettes, and shed the occasional tear. When they said good-bye, Libertad performed an Aztec-style prayer for the sex-worker girls.

The prayer involved the plucked thorns of a maguey leaf bought from the market. She would take a thorn and pierce her own earlobe, then sprinkle the bit of blood over smoke to cleanse bad luck and pray. In a modern twist, the smoke came from a cigarette on an ashtray, not proper copal incense. Still, Libertad's heart was one with the people of her long-lost kingdom. The maguey was the symbol of the Aztecs, the source ingredient for *pulque*, and held a sacred power. If she felt that the girl she was praying for had terrible misfortune in store and needed more power, Libertad would not hesitate to puncture her own fingertips or wrists to ensure there was sufficient blood to offer to the smoke.

When she returned to the mansion and Carlos asked about the bandages around her fingers, Libertad would say, "I got hurt when preparing some fish."

"Again?" he replied. "You're so clumsy."

As a port city, Veracruz had plenty of fish from all over the Gulf of Mexico available at the market. Carlos's favorite seafood was marlin soup.

Until she married a white man, Libertad had never eaten sweet, solid chocolate. The chocolate from her home village was a drink, the same way it had been in the Aztec days—a thick, sticky liquid of cacao, cornmeal, and chili peppers. When she was out on the town with her husband and ate solid chocolate from a sweets shop for the first time, the dirt-clump hardness and unnatural sweetness were so startling to her that she promptly spit it out.

Libertad experienced many things that were difficult to believe, but she didn't find life in the city to be enjoyable. The misery of urban impoverished people ran deeper than those back in the village, and the world seemed more chaotic and confused than it was at home.

When an earthquake struck, the people of Veracruz went outside and talked to their neighbors in hushed, worried tones about "magnitude" and "Richter," but Libertad found it strange that no one spoke of *ollin*. *Ollin* was a Nahuatl word meaning *movement* that symbolized earthquakes. It was the seventeenth of twenty symbols used in the Aztec calendar.

Whether the earth shook or not, earthquakes had been a part of the Aztec calendar from the beginning. That was the calendar, and the calendar was time itself. *This country truly has forgotten the Aztecs,* she thought.

The sun that shone upon the earth trampled by the Christian conquistadors, the moon that mournfully illuminated feasts ringing with Spanish songs, the temples smashed and buried underground—everywhere and in everything, the gods' boundless rage pulsed and seethed. Blood needed to be offered to the sun and moon. And with no one doing so, the gods grew angrier by the day. Nothing could quell the disaster now. It would only spread.

In this country, once home to the lakeside Aztec capital of Tenochtitlan, before the lake was erased to create the new capital of Mexico City, nearly every person was baptized into the Catholic faith.

Libertad's husband was a devout Catholic, and although he didn't control his wife to the extent that most men his age did, he didn't permit her to exhibit heretical Aztec leanings around other people. He wanted the beautiful young wife he'd found to play the part of a modest Christian woman.

She was baptized at the church, where the priest strictly instructed her, "You must discard the name Tezcaquiahuitl, which brings disaster. You must believe in Christ and be reborn in Him. Remove the names of the Aztec gods from your memory forever, for they are the Devil in another form."

Huitzilopochtli, Tlaloc, Xipe Totec, Mictlantecuhtli, Tlaltecuhtli, Xolotl, Coatlicue, Quetzalcoatl—and these were only a few. Libertad never forgot the names of the Aztec gods, no matter how much the Catholics insinuated they were the ravings of pagan savages.

Aztec mythology was as complex as a labyrinth; one god would transform into another and play multiple roles. The white men had difficulty understanding this world. The things that happened in the stories could not be explained as a simple clash between good and evil, with clear-cut lineages and godly family trees. Layers of dreams, glimpses of unfathomably deep logic beyond human means within a plane of chaos, mysterious power that trapped humanity in its clutches: these things were all *ollin*. They had the same power as the earthquake, and the myths brought destruction and rebirth to humanity.

Every person passes through day and night, waking and sleeping, sleeping and waking. Within this cycle, they contact the world of dreams, but far bigger than any individual's dream is the godly plane, and that can only be touched through the calendar.

The Aztecs used two calendars: the *tonalpohualli*, which had two hundred and sixty days, and the *xiuhpohualli*, which had three hundred and sixty-five.

In the *tonalpohualli*, a month was twenty days, and there were thirteen months in a year.

$$20 \times 13 = 260$$

This calendar was further broken up into *trecenas*, twenty periods of thirteen days each, in which each period was overseen by a different symbol. This was very important for divining fortunes.

The *xiuhpohualli*, meanwhile, was used to count months and years. Each month was twenty days, and a year was comprised of eighteen months.

$$20 \times 18 = 360$$

By adding five more unlucky days called *nemontemi* (days beyond the calendar) to the total, a year then became three hundred and sixty-five days. Every twenty days was another celebration of the gods, so such ritual festivities occurred year-round. Only the last five days were observed in silence, almost like a period of mourning.

It took a very long time for the two-hundred-and-sixty-day *tonalpohualli* and three-hundred-and-sixty-five-day *xiuhpohualli* to complete an entire cycle and align at the same position again. The lowest common multiple of those two numbers was eighteen thousand nine hundred and eighty.

$$18,980 \div 365 = 52$$

Fifty-two years.

To the Aztecs, the longest calendar cycle's final day was a portent of potential doom, much like the feared Judgment Day of Christianity but possibly with an even more destructive abyss lurking beneath it.

It was the day that time reached its end. The world would undergo death, and no one could say if a new calendar would follow, bringing its own fifty-two-year cycle, or not. Even the gods were ignorant to the world's ultimate fate.

On the day that a fifty-two-year calendar reached its end, the people would discard all their household tools and cleanse their homes. The priests in Tenochtitlan cast the old statues of the gods into Lake Texcoco. When the sun went down, all fires in the Aztec lands were extinguished. It was crucial that all flames of the past be snuffed.

Then came a night of absolute terror, when time ran out. It was not just darkness; time itself had burned out. Only the yawning mouth of nothingness awaited. Women and children wore evil-warding masks and hid in the granaries, praying that demons would not take them away.

The men stood watch, protecting their families, while the *tlamacazque*, the priests, observed the stars from the *teocalli* built atop the hill of Iztapalapa to the east. They were watching for Pleiades. When it passed the zenith, and the priests had observed that the next fifty-two-year cycle was beginning, they would carve out the heart of a human sacrifice and light a fire within that person's chest. The universe persevered in its work-ings because of the sacrifice. If the fire in the sacrifice's chest burned bright and beautiful, the sun would return. But if it went out, then time's flow perished, and destruction beyond human reckoning blotted out the heav-ens, calling demons and accursed monsters to the earth to slaughter all of humanity.

Once the fire was burning in the sacrifice's chest, the *tlamacazque* trans-ferred that flame to the altar, then they cast the removed heart into the light and heat. The fire was shared among many torches that were taken to all the temples, illuminating the shadows over the kingdom one at a time. Most of the people, however, trembled in the dark and held their breath through it all.

When at last the sun rose in the east, the people knew that another cycle had begun, and the two hundred thousand residents of the great city of Tenochtitlan rejoiced. They wept with joy, thanked the gods, and pulled out celebratory clothing they had hidden from the eyes of demons—the only things they kept when throwing all household items into the water. They decorated their heads with jade and quetzal feathers and donned clothing adorned with turquoise as beautiful as the surface of the lake seen from shore. The children wore stone earrings and deer pelts, holding sticks to mimic the priests. There was no distinction between the rich and poor. Elites and slaves alike stood side by side, singing and dancing.

The drums sounded, and the warriors of Huitzilopochtli, the "Left Side of the Hummingbird," donned their battle gear fashioned after Cuauhtli, brandished shields covered in feathers, and marched through the city of Tenochtitlan. Cuauhtli was one of the *trecena* symbols, a soaring eagle.

The people ate *tlaxcalli* made of cornmeal—later called tortillas by the conquistadors—drank pulque, burned copal, and pierced their earlobes with maguey thorns and sprinkled the blood over the smoke, praising the gods for allowing a new calendar cycle to begin.

At the top of the stepped pyramid temples called *teocalli*, rituals were held constantly starting from daybreak. Sacrifices were made to the gods and lasted through midday with no sign of stopping. Lives were given without end; to offer up one's blood and heart as food for the cosmos was a laudable act. If enemy soldiers taken prisoner were not sacrificed, they would go to hell instead. So the captives bathed to cleanse their bodies and were marched to the temple.

After removing the heart for the god to devour, the priests dumped the body below. The remains toppled down the long stone staircase, where a waiting attendant would cut off the head. This, too, was an offering. The people surrounded the headless body and severed the arms and legs. The god would eat the heart, but only the limbs were acceptable for the people. Following the strict precepts of the Aztec religion, the people seared the arms and legs and consumed them. Next to the human meat was cooked armadillo.

The finer arms among those sacrificed were offered to the *tlamacazqui*, whose face was painted in yellow and black. The god the priest served loved arms most, after hearts.

After receiving the limbs, the priest brought over a hundred slaves up the long stone steps of the *teocalli*. His followers blew death whistles. These sacrifices relinquished their hearts and arms to a terrifying being who could not be seen or touched.

The people celebrating the new fifty-two-year cycle noticed the *tlamacazqui* and slaves, and began to intone the names of the sacrificial god. Titlacauan ("We Are His Slaves"), Yohualli Ehecatl ("Night and Wind"), Necoc Yaotl ("Enemy of Both Sides")—all were the name of the same god. Possessor of eternal youth, reflector of all darkness: **Tezcatlipoca, the Smoking Mirror.**

11

mahtlactli-huan-cē

The scale of Libertad's rituals was nothing compared to the glory of the Aztec days, but she had to continue offering her prayers to the gods, even if she had nothing bigger than a little bundle of chiles to offer.

Unbeknownst to her husband, Libertad counted the days and weeks of the Aztec *tonalpohualli* and thought about the gods. She used the *xiuhpohualli* to mark the months and years. She was supposed to hold a celebration every twenty-day month, but of course, that wasn't possible.

In the same way that people looked forward to September for the Day of Independence and December for Christmas, the month of May, the hottest of the year, was very special to Libertad. When the dry season finally concluded, the Aztec sun blazed even hotter, as though consuming itself for strength. The sky was a fearsome shade of blue, sucking the water out of the soil. Punishing heat and a dryness that brought death to crops reached their peaks in May, when Tezcatlipoca reigned. Careful preparations were made throughout the year for Tezcatlipoca's festival, called Toxcatl, the same name as the fifth month.

When Libertad was growing up in Catemaco, the village elder summoned her one day. She was only six.

They walked along the shore of the lake, the elder slowly lagging farther behind until he stopped and spoke. "In the Aztec days, your ancestor was a *tlamacazqui* who served Tezcatlipoca. And he was also a military leader who stood at the head of the jaguar warriors. To be both priest and warrior was a great honor, as much as being a ruler, a *tlatoani*."

"Tezcatlipoca," Libertad repeated. The *brujos* had taught her about many gods, but that was a new name. It seemed similar to her own, she thought.

"As you know, the Aztecs created mirrors by polishing obsidian," the elder said. "They called mirrors *tezcatl*. The word *black* was *tliltic*. And to smoke was—"

"*Popoca.*"

"Smart girl. The name Tezcatlipoca is made of these three words. Many years ago, a *gringo* archaeologist came to the village. I heard him call Tezcatlipoca 'the Smoking Mirror.' They always want to name everything in their own language. So, Libertad, the 'Tezca' part of your name, Tezcaquiahuitl, is the sign of your ancestors' blood. Those who do not have that blood are not meant to put Tezca in their name. Yes, your family is poor. Your father and mother suffer to support you. But you are a special family. Don't ever forget that."

When she returned home, Libertad went to her father, who was sweating over the livestock, and relayed what she'd heard from the village elder. The moment he heard his six-year-old daughter say "Tezcatlipoca," he blanched, dropped the basket of feed, and looked around to confirm that no one else was present. Then he took Libertad into the back of the barn and stared into her young eyes.

"Don't ever speak that name aloud," he whispered, furious. The girl didn't understand why she was being scolded. They ought to be proud of their great ancestor. There was no reason to hide the truth of their god.

Libertad's father continued staring into his daughter's eyes. It was the way of children to do what they were told not to do. So he said, "When you must speak of him, use the name 'Yohualli Ehecatl,' and do it quietly. It is the same god. Do you understand? Don't speak his true name. Keep it secret within your heart, and lock it tight."

Much later, when she was grown, Libertad came to understand her father's feelings. He wasn't angry so much as frightened. He was afraid that if his daughter said the name **Tezcatlipoca**, it would bring back that dreadful god, once laid to rest by the conquistadors, from the depths of the earth, brimming with power once again. If that deity reawakened, then so would the great festival of Toxcatl at the end of the dry season, and his daughter's heart would be taken from her chest. If the god spoke through the *brujos* and demanded her heart, there could be no refusal. It was in the name *Titlacauan*: **We Are His Slaves.**

The village elder hadn't simply spoken of the past out of nostalgic longing. He was sending a message to Libertad's father through the girl. "If you worship Tezcatlipoca, you will receive strength that will pull your family out of poverty."

However, Libertad's father didn't want that kind of strength. To him, a little poverty was better than waking a cruel Aztec god from the ancient era.

In May, Libertad put on a hat, walked out into the Veracruz market and bought a live rooster. The merchant gave it to her in a cheap, bent wire cage. Next, she purchased an earthenware jar. It was about ten centimeters wide, and the sides were carved with Aztec-style skulls. It was a replica, a souvenir for tourists. They called them *réplicas de piezas arqueológicas*.

She took the squawking rooster around the back of the mansion, its flightless wings beating helplessly. Grabbing the burlap sack she brought from Catemaco when she was married, Libertad retrieved the obsidian knife from inside. The blade was a crude, Stone Age–type tool, but it was certainly up to the task of severing the rooster's head. Libertad hung the bird upside down to drain the blood into a tin bucket and plucked its feathers. Then she pressed the obsidian knife against its breast, dug deep, and removed the rooster's heart, an object only slightly larger than a quail's egg.

The young woman lit the copal incense resting in the jar, and when fragrant smoke began to rise, she placed the sacrificial heart over it. She sprinkled the blood in the bucket over the heart and smoke and spoke the god's name. In addition to Yohualli Ehecatl, he had the names Necoc Yaotl, and Titlacauan. These names indicated the greatness of the god to the Aztec people. They were not what the god called himself, merely titles that humanity ascribed to him. In other words, he did not even need to give his name. The humans simply praised him, celebrated him, and demonstrated their submission to him.

Before the copal had entirely burned away, Libertad placed the obsidian knife before the jar and whispered the god's true name in prayer.

> *O Great Tezcatlipoca.*
> *Grant us the end of the season of all-consuming drought,*
> *and allow the rain god Tlaloc to walk across the sky once more.*
> *Give the descendants of the Aztecs the gift of life.*
> *Allow us the chance to meet an honorable death.*
> *You are the great Yohualli Ehecatl.*
> *Titlacauan.*
> *Tezcatlipoca.*

With a quick burst of the *silbato de la muerte*, the whistle from her bag, she concluded the ritual and buried the entire jar, with the heart resting atop it, so that Carlos wouldn't discover the evidence of her heresy. If he caught sight of it, he would brand her a witch in his fury, then call for an exorcist, and she would never be allowed to walk to the market again.

Burying her offerings wasn't a waste in the slightest. Mictlantecuhtli dwelled beneath the soil. He was the god who ruled the underworld where all the wandering souls fell, though he wasn't as powerful as Tezcatlipoca.

Libertad placed the roast chicken on the supper table, and Carlos ate it with a fork and knife, none the wiser. Libertad didn't partake, only drinking soup, but she continued to cut portions for her husband. The rest of the meat was shared among the housemaids.

Libertad continued attending church, pretended to make the sign of the cross, and before long, she was blessed with a child. Her first was a boy. Two years later, she gave birth to a girl, and another girl the following year.

Isidoro, the eldest, was the apple of his father's eye. He was also spoiled by the maids, who sought their employer's approval. The boy grew up relying on others to do everything for him. After her childhood in the village, this was an unthinkable attitude for her son. It seemed impossible that he would grow capable of leading a commercial business, and she fretted constantly over the difficulty that was sure to come in his future.

Isidoro was lazy, but also keenly observant, sporting an acerbic, cynical wit similar to Carlos's. He realized that his mother worshipped Aztec gods and muttered loud enough for others to hear, "Oh, no, I'm going to hell. My mother's doing black magic."

Worried about her husband's mood and her social reputation, Libertad never spoke a word to her children about Aztec mythology.

One day, she took her daughters to the *mercado*, and one of them stopped in front of an *indígena* man in an alley.

The man was making fine carvings in a board about forty centimeters to a side. Tourists and foreign sailors watched, entranced by the artwork. Even though it wasn't finished, a few people were negotiating a price.

"That's amazing. What is it?" Libertad's daughters asked.

She gave them a troubled look and replied, "Oh, I don't know."

But in her heart, she knew. *That man is carving an image of Tlaltecuhtli, a fearsome monster of the earth. It is bigger than any of the ships that visit the port of Veracruz. Bigger than any whale. It is a violent and uncontrollable thing and does not understand words. Ultimately, Tezcatlipoca took his warrior form and fought the creature at sea, tearing it to pieces, but even then, it did not die. It was so strong, it devoured one of Tezcatlipoca's legs. Though I call it a monster, it, too, is an Aztec god...*

The man's depiction of the deity was adroit. Libertad was seized with a desire to talk to him about it, but this was the last time she ever saw the artist selling replicas of the decoration that sat on the throne of Moctezuma II.

Carlos Casasola made a healthy, steady profit through his business and never worried about the future. He had no illnesses, and hadn't been sick in years.

The premonition of death came to him without warning. He saw off a Casasola ship laden with silver and turquoise at the port, and on the way home, a stray dog came rushing up to him on the street and bit his hand.

The bite was shallow, and Carlos was able to tend to it himself, but when a sailor caught the dog with a net borrowed from a fisherman, he suggested that Carlos take the animal to a vet for examination. The sailor suspected the dog had a disease, and he knew the danger such infections posed.

They took the stray to the pound, and eventually someone from the Veracruz public health office contacted the Casasola company. "The dog was suffering from an acute form of rabies," the worker explained.

Carlos went to the hospital and had the bite wound disinfected again. The virus was in the dog's saliva. Despite the advances of medical science, the rabies virus was still ferociously deadly.

After a month of incubation, which he spent praying to God, Carlos developed symptoms of rabies. He had a flu-like fever, complained of pain around the bite, then collapsed and had to be taken to the hospital. When he awoke, he screamed and writhed, afflicted by hallucinations caused by the virus's effects on the brain.

Libertad watched as nurses in protective gear dragged off her husband, who drooled and wailed as though possessed by a demon. *He was cursed by the Aztec gods*, she thought.

A look at the calendar made it clear. The day Carlos was bitten by the rabid dog in the port was *Miquiztli*, first day of the *trecena* governed by the symbol of the skull. Death personified had come for him.

Those afflicted by rabies struggled to swallow because of extreme throat contractions. Ingesting liquid involved so much agony that a victim could fly into a panic from the mere sight of a glass of water. For this reason, the disease also went by the name hydrophobia. Understandably, the sight of an exorcist priest carrying a container full of holy water would also elicit this reaction. When Carlos saw the priest, who ignored the doctor's warnings not to enter the hospital room, the mere glimpse of the crucifix on the clergyman's chest made him think of holy water. Fear twisted his features, and he struggled to turn away. "Stay back! Don't come any closer," he pleaded hoarsely, cursing the priest.

Hallucinations, confusion, unending thirst, suffering. In the end, Carlos died without being able to say a proper good-bye to his family. The calendar caused Libertad's hair to stand on end. The curse of the gods, the rage of the ancestors. The day her husband died was the sixth day of the *trecena* started by Coatl, the Snake. This day was Chicuace Itzcuintli, the day of Six-Dog, ruled by the god of death, Mictlantecuhtli. Death sent the dog to drag Carlos's soul down to Mictlan, the underworld. This was the lowest level of the underground realm, where the souls of those who died naturally eventually came to rest. Lost souls eventually dissipated there, but most likely, Mictlantecuhtli intended to drive Carlos into an endless labyrinth without an exit. He would be trapped in another world, a plane of eternal suffering.

There were more ominous elements. Coatl, the Snake, was the symbol marking the entire *trecena* on the week of Carlos's death. Back in her little village in Catemaco, Libertad had asked the elder and a few *brujos* the name of her ancestor who had served Tezcatlipoca.

His glorious title—granted by none other than the highest of *tlatoani*, King Moctezuma II himself—was Tezcacoatl. Mirror Snake.

Isidoro grew up to be a fickle and lazy man, just as his mother had feared. He inherited the Casasola trading company, in accordance with the will stored in his father's safe. Despite Carlos's subordinates' lack of trust in Isidoro's business acumen, the new owner showed up at the office brimming with enthusiasm, did a passable amount of work, and then spent his nights drinking and wandering.

One day, he traveled out of state, claiming it was for business reasons, although he had none. While enjoying the nightlife of Oaxaca, he met Estrella, a *mestizo* girl born to a rich local family. Half a year later, they were married and went on to have five children.

Every one of them was a boy.

Blessed with grandchildren at a young age, Libertad showered the five with love, and they loved her in return.

Bernardo.

Giovani.

Valmiro.

Duilio.

Hugo.

After her husband's death, Libertad needed to play the part of a good Catholic on far fewer occasions, but as with her own children, she did not tell her grandsons about Aztec mythology. Her son and daughter-in-law wouldn't like it. To avoid antagonizing them, she did her best not to use any Nahuatl words when spending time with her grandsons.

On Catholic holidays, the boys surrounded Libertad excitedly, pulling her hand and saying, *"¡Vamos a la fiesta, abuelita!"*

"Pasarla bien," she would reply with a smile and a shake of her head, sending her grandsons off to enjoy themselves.

It's better to keep the stories of the gods to myself, Libertad reasoned.

The thing that finally changed her mind was when Hugo, the youngest of her grandsons, contracted rabies from a dog bite and died, just like her husband.

As the youngest, Hugo had not yet seen his maternal grandparents. So Estrella took him to Oaxaca in July, when the Guelaguetza festival was in full swing.

The Guelaguetza was a major celebration bringing together *indígenas* from various regions. Libertad knew about it but wasn't particularly interested. To her it was a tourist attraction, a form of entertainment for Christianized Mexico. It was not a ritual to bring back the old gods.

Entranced by the women dancing in their colorful traditional dresses, Hugo's mother failed to notice the dog that ran up or the cries of her son. She heard only the singing and drums that filled the street. Only when other tourists were bitten and people started to raise a fuss did she finally notice that something was wrong with her youngest child.

Poor Hugo was bitten on Ce Itzcuintli, the day of One-Dog; once again, the dog of death reared its head in the calendar.

After the incubation period, Hugo fell ill, much like his grandfather. He was covered in sweat, eyes bulged from pain and terror, unable to drink any water or speak, and his mouth was frozen in a rictus of silent screaming. He passed on the forty-fourth night after his fateful bite.

It was the fifth day of the *trecena* of Atl, or "Water." The god in control of that week was Chalchiuhtotolin, the "Jade Turkey"—one of the forms of Tezcatlipoca. And the day that Hugo died was Mahcuilli Acatl, "Five-Reed." The god who ruled over that day was none other than Tezcatlipoca himself.

Libertad was unable to sleep in the wake of the gods' merciless anger, plain as day on the calendar. She regretted not telling her grandsons about the Aztec gods and myths and wept as she pled for forgiveness.

I've betrayed the Aztecs worse than anyone, she thought. *And the gods delivered punishment upon my grandson. I should have realized that my husband's death was a warning. I should have known that Tezcatlipoca ordered Mictlantecuhtli to send that dog from the underworld.*

Hugo's parents, Isidoro and Estrella, argued so bitterly in their grief over their son's death that the police came to the house on a noise complaint. Libertad, however, had no more tears to shed.

Her eyes beheld the bonfire atop the *teocalli* in Tenochtitlan, capital of the Aztec Empire. The pain of her anguish was so great that it turned into a kind of intoxication, where the meaning of her husband's and grandson's deaths as told by the calendar rushed through her veins as the pure voice and will of the living gods.

The dog came from the underworld to tell me. Sweet Hugo, you died an exalted death; a sacrifice to Tezcatlipoca. Because of you, I have finally realized what he wants. From my five beloved grandsons, only you were taken, leaving four behind. I know what that means now. All of it was fate at work.

12

mahtlactli-huan-öme

Libertad stood before the cross-shaped gravestone that stood in the soil above Hugo's little casket but did not sign the cross. A month had passed since the boy's death, and the Catholic mourning period had just finished.

Her four living grandsons were with her at the plot, and she looked each of them in the eyes. "Bernardo, Giovani, Valmiro, Duilio, you mustn't cry anymore. From now on, the four of you are one. Four Casasola brothers as one. Understand? Listen closely."

When she spoke in hushed Spanish like this, Libertad's voice had a strangely compelling nature. It was the voice of the *brujos*.

Libertad called over Bernardo, the eldest. "Bernardo, the black Tezcatlipoca from the north will protect you. You are at the end of the cosmos, and there is no one beyond. You must watch over your younger brothers."

Next, she summoned Giovani, the second. "Giovani, the white Tezcatlipoca from the west will protect you. West is the direction that the Templo Mayor in Mexico City faces, so you mustn't forget your prayers to the Aztec gods."

Valmiro was next. "Valmiro, as the third, you are cautious and early to rise. That is a good thing. So the red Tezcatlipoca who protects the east will stay with you. You must wake up earlier than the others, stand in the darkness of the dawn before anyone else, and help your brothers."

Then she called Duilio. "You're the last, Duilio. As the fourth son, you'll have the protection of the blue Tezcatlipoca to the south, along with the god of war, Huitzilopochtli. You might be short, but you'll be much stronger soon."

It was an October afternoon. A row of cross-shaped Catholic graves shone in the sun. The day's portion of seasonal rain had yet to arrive. The four boys felt that their *abuelita* had told them something important and that they'd been given a role to play, but they didn't understand what it meant.

A cloud's shadow fell over the graveyard. Valmiro looked up at Libertad, squinting into the brightness of the sky, and asked, *"¿Qué es Tezcatlipoca?"*

The next day, Libertad left the mansion in her hat, and visited the market with her grandsons in tow. The Casasola family had cars, and a hired driver, but Libertad chose to ride in a *pesero*, a minibus. If she didn't teach the boys how people in the real world lived, they would turn into idle hedonists like Isidoro.

At the market, she bought a live rooster. The boys were delighted, and each of them wanted a chance to hold the cage. They ate tacos from a stand and took the *pesero* back home. Libertad held the chicken cage openly, not caring what anyone else thought. The driver certainly said nothing, because he knew she would give him a tip.

When they got back to the mansion, they let the rooster loose in the back. The boys had great fun chasing the bird, and when the lunch hour approached, Libertad decided it was time to put an end to that.

She caught the struggling rooster and cleanly chopped its head off with the obsidian knife. The headless bird flapped its wings, sending bloodied feathers flying. The boys went wide-eyed with shock at the sudden carnage. Duilio, who was now the youngest without Hugo around, began to cry. Between the rooster head rolling on the grass, the gouts of blood gushing into the tin bucket, and the dark, shining weapon in his *abuelita*'s hands, it all appeared like something out of a nightmare. The other three looked like they were holding back tears, too.

"It was the dual gods Ometeotl who created the world," Libertad said as she filled the bucket with rooster blood. "They was the first gods, born from nothing. They created themselves. And they were the only ones who could do such a thing."

"Is this in the Bible?" asked Bernardo, the oldest. His face was pale.

Libertad did not answer. She was careful to not say either *sí* or *no*. The boys' parents lived in the mansion, too, and they were Catholic. If she said a word against Christianity, it would lead to familial strife.

Instead, she just stared at the cut on the rooster's neck, then dangled it upside down again to drain the remaining blood. She would have preferred to leave the head on and remove the heart while it was still moving, but the blood needed to be drained if she was going to cook it later. "Then Ometeotl created something other than themselves out of nothing. First, Ometeotl created the basin of the world, with the four cardinal directions, and placed four gods on them. These were the Tezcatlipoca of north, south, east, and west. The four Tezcatlipocas were one god together, the night and the wind, and they rule the world."

The boys tried to remember the things she said to them at Hugo's grave. Black, white, red, blue, the four brothers were one—Duilio was too young to pronounce Tezcatlipoca properly, and when it came to the god of war Huitzilopochtli, who was his ally, he could only remember that it was *something*-pochtli.

Once the blood had stopped dripping from the bird's neck, Libertad started plucking its feathers. "After creating the world and the gods that live in it, Ometeotl went into hiding. Nobody knows where they went. It might be outside the bounds of the time that flows through the universe entirely. Because the first gods were gone, Tezcatlipoca became the oldest. As Tloque Nahuaque, god of gods, Tezcatlipoca is special among all deities. We are going to offer him a sacrificial heart now."

She cut open the chest of the headless rooster and removed the heart. The boys gazed at the heart resting on their *abuelita*'s palm. They recognized the little inverse triangle shape. It was very similar to the turquoise that their mother owned.

Copal burned in an earthenware vase, and the rooster's heart was placed among the sickly sweet smoke. She poured out the blood pooled in the tin bucket, too, bit by bit.

While Libertad chanted prayer words the boys didn't understand, they followed church custom, closing their eyes and drooping their heads forward.

When the prayer was over, they opened their eyes. The obsidian knife, slick with blood, shone in the sun. It was a frightening sight, like black ice.

Libertad could sense what they were thinking and scooped up the knife. "This was once the land of the Aztecs. There were other countries around them, but those were barely important. The Aztecs were the biggest. And the Aztecs took this obsidian, which is created in volcanoes, carved knives and arrowheads from it, and made mirrors. They called mirrors *tezcatl*. They were sacred things, only for kings and high priests. The mirror contains the power of Tezcatlipoca, who rules the darkness. There is nothing in the world darker than obsidian, and it reflects the fate of humanity. Obsidian has many faces, in the same way that Tezcatlipoca can change his form at will. Sometimes it cuts off the head of an enemy general, sometimes it carves out the heart of a sacrifice, and sometimes it becomes a mirror."

War, sacrifice, fate, gods…

Black shone with a light that contained both the brittleness of humanity and the endless darkness of the cosmos past the stars. These things were beyond the boys' understanding, but to their eyes, the rock was like something from another world that had come into their *abuelita*'s possession.

After a dinner of roasted chicken, Libertad summoned her grandsons to her room, and she sat them down at a table lit by flickering candlelight. In the gloom, she smoked tobacco, lit copal, and spread paper upon the table. It was *amatl*, a form of paper made from tree bark during the Aztec days. The boys had never seen it before.

Libertad poured the leftover rooster blood from the bucket into an ashtray, then dipped a quill into the blood. The boys' eyes danced at the beauty of the scarlet macaw feather that shimmered in the candlelight. It was the national bird of Honduras and widely beloved across Latin America.

"All around is a lake," Libertad said, drawing the outline of Lake Texcoco on the *amatl*, then the massive city that had loomed over it until the sixteenth century. Her hands moved with surprising dexterity. The rooster's blood formed lines on its own, floating up to the paper's surface from nothingness.

"Tenochtitlan," she said. "It means 'among the rocks and prickly pears.' This was the Aztecs' metropolis. They had a number of *teocalli* upon the lake, and all kinds of people lived there: gods, kings, priests, nobles, warriors, traders, prisoners, and slaves. There were no farmers living in Tenochtitlan. Do you know why that was? It was the same as the big cities of today. There were hundreds of thousands of people there, and those from other tribes would come to do business, so everyone in the city was able to make a living doing things other than farming. That was how rich and grand the Aztec nation was."

An illustration of the fallen kingdom began to fill in the blanks on the *amatl*. The canals of the city built atop the lake, its embankments, bridges, and the *chinampa*—floating gardens built atop rafts of reeds. Above it all stood the true form of the Templo Mayor that had been so unceremoniously destroyed by the Spaniards—a grand, stepped pyramid that worshipped two gods at its top.

On the right side of the west-facing *teocalli* was the shrine to Huitzilopochtli, god of war, the "left-handed hummingbird." Its wall was decorated with a *tzompantli*, a rack stuffed with human skulls. On the left side of the temple was the shrine to Tlaloc, the rain god, and at its entrance Libertad drew a human statue that archaeologists called a *chacmool*. It rested on its back, bearing a vessel for holding the blood and hearts of sacrifices.

"Can we see it if we go to Mexico City?" asked Giovani.

"Only the ruins and museums," Libertad replied. "The beautiful lake is no more. Cortés—the captain of the conquistadors—led such devastating irrigation projects that all of the water dried up. Listen closely. Your *abuelita* was born in Veracruz, but further back, your ancestor lived here, in Tenochtitlan. And he was a very important man. His blood flows in your veins now. Place your hands on this *amatl*. Close your eyes. I will show you what the Aztec city was like."

The four boys put their hands on the rooster-blood drawing and closed their eyes. The *amatl* was cool, and the smell of copal spicy-sweet. As Libertad spoke, her low voice brought forth the imagery of the Aztec Empire, as true as anything they could see in reality.

"We're going to take our canoes north from Tenochtitlan. Is everyone ready? What you can see ahead is a place called Tlatelolco. Do you see the vast market there? In Nahuatl, we call it a *tianquiztli*. It is far bigger than the market in Veracruz, and you can buy anything there. The first Spaniards to arrive thought they were dreaming; they couldn't believe their eyes. It was much, much larger than any market they'd seen in Rome or Constantinople. Twenty thousand people visited every day. Sixty thousand during the special market held once every five days. Now stick close to me, we're going to walk through it. You see all the women selling fruit? The men strutting about in their fancy clothes are the big merchants, called *pochteca*. Notice the men selling incense tubes packed with copal, and the women selling medicines of mixed honey and maguey. There are stands and sellers from here all the way to the lake shore. Corn, chiles, turkeys, ducks, puppies, roosters, hens, rattlesnakes, beans, cacao, torches, pine resin, and salvia blooms brought from the south. That man asking for *chalchihuitl* is looking for jade, and the woman speaking of *xihuitl* wants turquoise. The market continues. There is gold, there is silver, and there is greenstone. Earrings, tapestries, waistcloths, vanilla pods, cactus fruit, and *huauhtli*, which was a very important food to the Aztecs. Today, we call it amaranth. They sold feathers of the quetzal bird, which only nobility could wear, and macaw feathers, too. This quill I have is made from the feather of a macaw. You boys know what *pulque* is, but have you ever seen an otter pelt? There are badger pelts, too, and deer. Axes, earthenware, pots, the *amatl* you're resting your hands on now, so many dyes you couldn't count them all, male and female slaves. The nobles gave their slaves a good life.

Some people willingly offered themselves up to be slaves, in fact. It was the conquistadors who worked their slaves like common beasts. Now, do you see that crowd of people over there? There are skilled artisans demonstrating their abilities to onlookers. There's a man carving patterns into a *tecpatl* flint knife, and another man polishing an obsidian one. Only the nobles are wealthy enough to buy those, however. What do you think of Tlatelolco? The *tianquiztli* seems to go on forever, doesn't it? You couldn't possibly see it all in a single day. But that's not all there is here. Like Tenochtitlan, they have their own Templo Mayor. Focus your ears and listen closely."

Libertad began to beat the table as the boys held their eyes shut. It was quiet at first, but it grew steadily louder. **The sound of the drums from the *teocalli*.**

"Can you see it? A ritual has begun atop the *teocalli*, which stands as tall as a mountain. A sacrifice will be made to Tezcatlipoca. Can you see them being put on the stone altar? There are four *tlamacazque* there, each one holding a limb down."

Libertad beat the table harder.

"One more *tlamacazqui* is holding up an obsidian knife. You mustn't look away."

Libertad hit the table. The rhythm got faster. The *teocalli*'s drums.

"Look, a shining red jewel has been taken from the chest of the sacrifice. Do you know what it is?"

"Corazón," said Valmiro. The other three nodded, their eyes closed.

"You're very smart." Libertad beamed. "That's right. The Aztecs called it *yollotl*. Remember that word. When you take out the *yollotl*, you hold it up to the sky. Do you see? It's not an execution. You are offering food to the god."

"Like tacos?" asked Giovani.

"Yes. Human hearts are the gods' tortillas. Now the priests are tossing the body off the steps. Like water flowing over falls, it tumbles down and down. What's this? Are you crying, Duilio? There's nothing to be afraid of. The sacrifice is helping to support the world of the living. His soul has gone back to the heavens, and the body left behind is only an empty shell. Now, open your eyes."

When the boys did so, they felt as though their own hearts had been removed. Each touched his chest in the dark, to make sure there was no hole.

13

mahtlactli-huan-ëyi

Isidoro Casasola noticed that Libertad no longer bothered concealing her heretical interests from his sons. His wife, Estrella, told him with undisguised concern, "I wish she wouldn't do that around the boys."

Estrella was from Oaxaca, where many *indígenas* lived, and she liked to think she had a generous attitude toward the old cultures, but like almost everyone, she was raised in a strictly Catholic setting. In her mind, whether Mayan, Olmec, or Aztec, the memories of the fallen civilizations should be preserved as pleasurable things like decorative art and dances. They should not be brought into the present day as active religions.

"It's because *Madre* isn't Catholic," Isidoro told her, then went into his study and shut the door. He lit a cigar, poured himself a shot of tequila, and exhaled heavily.

He'd always found it difficult to understand his mother's way of thinking, but her fixation on the Aztecs was a constant. He'd seen his father get furious and slap her for it many times, but she never gave it up. Eventually, his father contracted rabies, suffered, and died. She probably saw his end as the anger of the Aztec gods come to life. Being in her presence made that clear. And when Hugo lost his life to rabies the same way, it must have had a profound effect on her.

Isidoro took another shot of tequila. *It's all well and good to be devout,* he thought. *But Mexico is a Catholic country. These Aztec kings like Moctezuma and Cuauhtemoc, they're historical figures whose names belong in textbooks, on street signs, and on liquor bottles. Templo Mayor is just a ruin for tourists. If you take these things seriously, people will think you're crazy. I understand why Estrella is worried. But what am I supposed to do?*

His mother wasn't just unfathomable to him; she was frightening and unapproachable. She'd never lectured him or beaten him. So why was he afraid of her?

There was one answer: Isidoro feared the strange and baffling sorcery that his mother revered, and he didn't want to admit that. Curses and magic weren't real. If they were, the Aztecs would have driven back the conquistadors…

Yet once Isidoro's inner child seized on an emotion, no amount of logic would drive it away. Isidoro's scorn for his rural Catemaco-born mother was a reflection of his terror. Even as an adult, he'd never once looked the woman in the eyes and spoken his mind to her.

Isidoro took another shot of tequila and wiped his mouth. As Estrella said, it might have some negative influence on their sons, but on the other hand, what knowledge didn't? Chemical experiments, if used for evil, could teach you how to kill. In other words, it was important to be tolerant. For now, the boys weren't denouncing María or Our Lady of Guadalupe. They respected Father Hidalgo, the Father of the Nation, as far as Isidoro knew. They went to Mass. If they started claiming they didn't want to go to Mass, that would mean that Libertad's teachings had crept beyond the boundaries of tolerance. That was where the line stood. He'd feel bad about it, but if it came to that, he'd have to remove her from the mansion. He'd set her up with a cheap little place in the country and make her live there alone.

Once his plan was set, Isidoro placed the shot glass on the desk and left the study. He called for the family driver, who waited in the mansion on standby. Isidoro didn't want to be home right now. He was in the mood to blow off steam at a casino, but he didn't have the money to gamble with at present. "Take me to the office at the port," he said to the driver.

Coddled by his father and raised soft and decadent, Isidoro believed himself to be an excellent businessman. It upset him that the senior members of his father's company didn't value his contributions and leadership.

In accordance with the will, Isidoro took over the Casasola enterprise at age twenty-seven and racked his brain for new profit streams that would match the current era.

His idea, adding to the silver and turquoise exports that the company had managed since his great-grandfather's generation, was to use those materials to fashion decorative items that the company would sell wholesale. Necklaces made of jade and feathers, silver rings and bracelets with embedded turquoise. The concept for the designs came from Libertad's love of Aztec art. This was how he advertised the line to buyers:

"Beautiful charms made the way the ancient Aztecs did, fashioned by Nahuatl-speaking indigenous artisans at our workshop located in Oaxaca."

In reality, the factory was in Veracruz, and there were zero pureblood *indígenas*. Nearly everyone at the workshop was *mestizo*, along with two Blacks from Bolivia and one Chinese immigrant who came from Chile. None of them knew a thing about Aztec mythology or spoke a word of Nahuatl. They merely labored in a factory to provide for their families.

When the hippie counterculture took over in the late 1960s in America, Aztec ornaments made by indigenous peoples sold like gangbusters. The Casasola company ships made regular trips out of Veracruz, laden with decorations and ornaments, and traveled up the Gulf of Mexico to America.

Isidoro also started selling jaguar and puma pelts to wealthy white buyers at exorbitant prices. And when he got them stuffed and mounted, he always made sure to save them for auctions, to jack up the prices even higher.

He felt that he had demonstrated his business acumen, but in fact, the sales of ornaments and furs were only a small percent of the company's overall income. The bedrock of the business remained exports of silver and turquoise.

The lifeline of the Casasola company was its tight connections to the mine owners of Mexico, which had been nurtured during Isidoro's great-grandfather's, grandfather's, and father's generations. Without them, there was nothing to load on the ships.

The senior employees who had worked with his father, Carlos, were concerned about Isidoro's heavy-handed negotiations with the mine owners. They warned him many times to improve his tactics, but Isidoro solidly ignored them.

Once an owner of a silver mine in the state of Guanajuato finally cut ties with Casasola, others quickly followed. Rival companies reaped the benefit of all those sources of silver and turquoise, and Casasola profits dried up. Several ships had to be sold, employees left, and bankruptcy loomed.

On September 15, the eve of Independence Day, when he would normally have been in Mexico City with friends, getting drunk in El Zócalo and shouting *"¡Viva México!"* with the crowd, Isidoro was instead sitting alone in the Casasola office, gazing at the port of Veracruz out the window.

Ships with their lights gleaming silently crossed dark sea, occasionally breaking the quiet with the blast of a steam whistle.

Isidoro smoked a cigarette, drank mezcal, and fiddled with the handgun on top of his desk. It was an old Colt revolver, a memento of his father. When he was young, Isidoro thought it was a relic from his conquistador ancestors. Once he was an adult, he learned that it was made much, much later than the sixteenth century, which was when the conquistadors toppled the Aztec kingdom.

He put the gun back on the desk, then looked up at the portrait of his great-grandfather that hung in the office. The man inside the frame scowled at his failure of a descendant, as though he knew how much debt the family company labored under.

I don't have to blow my brains out, Isidoro thought. *I can just get drunk and jump into the water. That will do the job.*

The phone rang.

It was a complaint from a partner in New York, wondering where his shipment was. Isidoro apologized, hung up, and promptly received another call. This one was from Barcelona, seeking a debt payment. The next came from Piraeus in Greece, then San Francisco, then a different company from New York, all looking to collect on debts.

With a tumbler full of mezcal in one hand, Isidoro rubbed his sleepy eyes and took yet another call. This one was from his wife.

"I've had it," Estrella said. "The boys were playing with fire in the backyard. Do you know what they were doing? Poking their own earlobes with cactus spikes. They were sprinkling their blood into the smoke. It's crazy. Anyone could see that it's black magic. This has completely ruined Independence Day. And it's all because you didn't keep your mother in line, because you're too weak. Well, I can't take it anymore. Get Libertad out of here, or I'm going to take the kids back to Oaxaca."

"They're not cactus spikes," Isidoro said.

"What?"

"They're not from cacti. They're maguey thorns. You know what that is, right? What they use to make *pulque*."

"What on earth are you talking about?"

"I'm getting work calls. I've got to hang up."

Isidoro put the receiver down, and Estrella's fury grew distant. He let the silence settle on his shoulders. Isidoro finished the mezcal in his cup, then pulled the bottle closer and poured more.

The phone rang.

"*Bueno,*" said Isidoro.

"You sound like shit," answered the man on the other end. "I want to talk to Isidoro Casasola."

"Speaking."

That phone call changed Isidoro's life. The man on the other end didn't want to complain or demand money. He was hoping to start a new business relationship.

The Casasola trading company had been operating for four generations, owned ships and warehouses in the port of Veracruz, and was on the verge of going out of business.

The narcos were aware of this, of course, and had been waiting for the right moment to contact Isidoro.

The first job was smuggling hash to New York.

By successfully shipping the bricks of hashish up north for two months, Isidoro gained the cartel's trust. Next they asked him to smuggle cocaine for them. Under the guidance of narcos who'd been dispatched for "instructional" purposes, he learned how to hide cocaine among piles of lumber. As the man in charge, Isidoro rode the ships himself and saw the product safely to Barcelona.

There were many places you could hide cocaine aside from lumber: inside frozen fish, in taxidermy eyeballs, behind framed paintings. Isidoro had managed to hold on to one last ship, and he kept it running at a constant clip, ferrying product from port to port. Soon the company's fortune had, in Isidoro's own words, "Come back from the dead like Lazarus."

The stacks of bills fell from the sky and bubbled up out of the ground.

Why didn't I get into this line of work from the start? Isidoro wondered, looking back at what had brought him here. Nothing from the past seemed real; it was all merely a nightmare. Thank God he was back in reality.

In exchange for moving their wares over the ocean, the cartel paid Casasola their respects and much more. They treated the coca farmers and street-level dealers like vermin, but they spared no expense on expanding and maintaining their shipping routes. It was more than worth the investment.

Major sums of money came flooding in, new faces filled the office, the debt vanished, Isidoro hired an accountant recommended by the cartel, then bought a yacht for his own pleasure and enjoyed it in the company of women.

There was no need to bow and scrape to those old mine owners; they were stuck behind the times. He bought silver and turquoise from new mines and resumed exporting them, but only at a third the previous output. Despite that, rumors soon spread that the Casasola company had come back from its troubles.

When he was younger, Isidoro had enjoyed the use of hash and cocaine in a party setting, but he never thought about selling it himself. That was seedy business, shameful stuff you did in back alleys. And it was so small, too. Not like scouting out vast excavation sites, making deals with mine owners, and exporting huge amounts of silver and turquoise. Or so he thought.

Now that belief had been completely overturned. Drugs were **big business**. Isidoro was shocked into a new way of thinking.

Transport's the most important aspect of the drug trade. The sea is covered with lanes of gold. I never would've believed there was this much money moving around until I got involved. This transcends the simple concept of making money. There's so much cash moving this way that it's more like tax income than business profits. Yes, call it a tax. There's an invisible country of drugs that crosses the seas, and people in every nation of the world are paying the drug tax…

When human beings faced danger, they possessed the ability to change their ways to survive, demonstrating an alacrity and dynamism that suggested they'd evolved and grown. And once the danger passed, they went right back to their old ways.

Having stabilized the Casasola company again, Isidoro basked in the flattery of those looking for a slice of his fortune, and he began to spend exorbitantly, as he'd done in the past. Isidoro had rescued the company from the brink of disaster, after all, and rebuilt its fleet of ships back to the number from the glory days. What harm was there in flaunting his success?

Intoxicated by wealth, he bought diamond rings, emerald-studded watches, and dozens of custom-made suits, and he spent his nights drowning in liquor and women.

He had no desire to go back to the mansion and get between his Aztec-obsessed mother and Catholic bitch wife. Instead, he traveled between the homes of five different mistresses, ignored his sons, worked, caroused, slept, awoke, and worked again.

As long as his ships full of cleverly hidden cocaine kept leaving port from Veracruz, he would continue to make ungodly sums.

Isidoro's lack of fear for the cartel and shows of extravagance were gathering attention. Despite never having killed a man, Isidoro fancied himself like all the other narcos—powerful and dangerous.

Eventually, he began demanding a higher cut from the cartel. Even worse, a poor personal judgment led to a major business failure.

A ship scheduled to unload in a West African port had to turn away before it could dock. The trouble arose because Isidoro had skimped out on the bribe to pay off the local coast guard. Isidoro claimed this was "just business," but it was a serious mistake on his part. If other narcos waiting on land hadn't noticed something was wrong and contacted the ship ahead of time, the vessel would have sailed right into port and quite possibly lost a few hundred kilos of cocaine. That kind of loss was the sort measured in hundreds of millions of pesos.

Suddenly, the tides shifted. It was time for Isidoro to serve a purpose: to send a warning about who was really in charge. The cartel's warning was not for him but those close to the man. The meaning would be lost on Isidoro, but everyone else would understand. And there would be no second chances if they failed to learn the first time.

The Mexican cartel got in touch with their business partners in a Colombian cartel and said, "We're going to kill the president of Casasola, but his ships will continue to sail." Then they unleashed their *sicarios*.

Isidoro's wealthy friends heard of his fate through whispers, yet not a single one of them thought, *The poor bastard*. Instead, they all cursed him. *The lucky bastard.*

He got to act as he pleased *and* survive for a few years in the drug world before it caught up to him.

Libertad offered a rooster to the gods in the mansion's backyard, ran her fingers through the blood in the bucket, then drizzled a little onto four small plates, one at a time. She told her grandsons, "Now drip that onto the ground before the gate."

It was six in the morning. The four took the plates, walked through the garden with its rich scent of dahlia flowers, and carefully made their way to the front gate, careful not to spill any of the blood.

There was a dead body waiting for them.

It looked like someone had placed a big doll there as a prank—a naked one. The head, arms, and legs were separated from the torso, resting separately. The sites of the cuts were dark and discolored, and the skin was bruised purple here and there.

A woman passing by the gate screamed, and when her voice died out, an eerie silence moved in. The four boys stood silently.

A maid who heard the scream came out to see, and slowly, carefully pulled open the gate. She walked out into the street and promptly fainted the moment she identified the corpse. Even then, the four boys were utterly still and did not spill the rooster blood. Eventually, Valmiro set his plate down at his feet, then ran into the backyard and found Libertad washing her hands at the well.

After hearing his report, she fixed him with a stare and asked, "Is that true?"

Valmiro nodded.

"You're absolutely certain?" Libertad asked again.

"Es verdad," replied Valmiro. *"Es mi padre."*

Libertad sighed heavily, but she did not fall to pieces. She went to the gate with Valmiro and saw the body, her other three grandsons, and the unconscious maid, in that order. A crowd was already gathering.

She ordered her grandsons to carry the parts of Isidoro's body into the backyard.

Bernardo and Giovani lifted the torso like a stretcher, while Duilio carried the two arms, crying. Libertad told Valmiro, "You carry the head." Once the boys had all gone into the yard, Libertad picked up the legs, dragging them behind her, then shut the gate and closed the bolt.

The boys put the separated parts of their father in their proper places and tried to stick the severed ends together, but it didn't work. The head, arms and legs refused to stay put, rolling at odd angles. The sight of their mutilated father eventually brought the other three boys to tears, too.

He barely spent any time at home with them, but they only remembered those occasions he was there; his smile and his voice. The sadness rose in them, then the hurt and anger, and lastly, the deep hatred.

Hugo and *Padre* were gone.

"Who did this?" Bernardo shouted.

"The narcos," said Libertad.

They looked up at her puffy eyes.

Libertad cheered up and encouraged the poor *indígena* whores working around the port, and she told their fortunes for free if they asked. In return, they'd told her all about the kinds of people that Isidoro had gotten involved with.

"It's a bad way to die," Libertad remarked. "Very bad."

"Why?" asked Valmiro through his sobs. "Didn't he die as a sacrifice, like Hugo?"

"He did," said Bernardo. "*Padre* got chopped up fighting with bad guys. He's an Aztec warrior. He became a tortilla for the gods, and he helped keep the world from being destroyed."

"Your father did not die fighting," said Libertad. "He didn't listen to others, he made a bad mistake, and he was killed. And Isidoro knows nothing of the Aztec gods."

"Then, is he going down to Mictlan?" Bernardo asked, frightened.

"Mictlan is the underworld, but it is not like Catholic hell. It's a land of darkness where the souls that weren't offered to the gods travel and learn. At the end of the journey, the souls disappear. I wish that he were going there, but he's not. Isidoro is going somewhere very different, to suffer a horrible fate."

"You have to help him, Libertad," cried Duilio.

"There is one way," Libertad said quietly, after a long pause, "one way to do it. We must *kill him again*."

The four boys held down their father's torso as instructed, and Libertad plunged the obsidian knife into his chest. She cut through the flesh, opened a hole, cut the bones, and removed the heart that had long ago lost its *ollin*.

"Point his face straight up," she stated.

Valmiro, who'd brought the head into the backyard, felt that this was probably his job. He grabbed Isidoro's head, which had rolled onto its side, put his hands on the cheeks, and pointed it upward. His dull, open eyes reflected the blue sky above.

Libertad placed the heart on top of Isidoro's face. The four were alarmed. What was *abuelita* doing?

"Just keep it propped up," Libertad ordered, then she reached into her burlap sack and retrieved something that looked like an Italian ocarina. Valmiro, who'd never seen an ocarina, thought it was shaped like an avocado, but upon spying its faded white color and contours in the sunlight, realized that the instrument looked exactly like a skull. It was a little skull, about the size of a baby's head.

Libertad breathed into the whistle, producing a sound like a woman sobbing. The noise got louder, bit by bit, until it was the wind howling outside the window, then the shrieks of a person being burned alive, and lastly, the screams of the damned from hell.

Frightened by the ghastly, ragged sound, all the boys except Valmiro clamped their hands over their ears. He would have done so, too, if he weren't holding up his father's head. He very nearly peed himself. But if he let go, the head would roll, and the heart would fall off his face. Valmiro worked very hard to conquer his fear.

Ehecachichtli, the wind whistled.

The Aztec whistles terrified the conquistadors in the sixteenth century, and it was hard to imagine any other instrument in the world producing such a chilling sound. The Spanish friars on the conquest labeled these *silbatos de la muerte*, whistles of death. When blown, the whistles summoned wind, lured the dead up from the depths to peer out upon the living, and lastly, brought about the ruler of all darkness, Yohualli Ehecatl, the "Night and Wind."

Libertad took her lips off the whistle and spoke.

"In ixtli in yollotl."

"Your father has died again." She took the heart in her right hand and raised it, looking at the four boys. "Now his soul will not go to some frightening, unknown place, but will rise into the cosmos where the gods are. Your father had to die twice because he made a mistake. That is why his first death was so terrible. You must know about the mistake that he made. So listen closely. Your father was *ahuicpa tic huica*."

The boys just stared at her.

"'He carries without carrying,'" Libertad explained. "It means he was only idly transporting the sacred heart that resides in his chest. He did not know what he was doing or the meaning of his life. He was a fool who lived only for his own pleasure."

"*Padre* was a fool?" Bernardo asked.

"That's right. Bernardo, Giovani, Valmiro, Duilio, none of you must be an *ahuicpa tic huica*."

"How can we make sure not to be that?" asked Giovani.

"Put a hand to your chest. Can you feel it beating? That's the key. Your *corazón*. Your *yollotl*. You haven't found it yet; you're too young to be connected to the gods. You feel the world with your *ixtli*, your face. Because your eyes lie within your face. But your face doesn't know the meaning of life. Children, like you, and foolish men, like your father, don't have their face and heart connected. They're all separate. You don't have a real face."

You don't have a real face. The boys put their hands to their cheeks just to check.

"A warrior fights and dies for his gods, and a human sacrifice gives up his body. When you have made a sacrifice for the gods, your face will behold this world properly for the first time. Then you will find your sacred heart. Your father didn't understand that. But you four are Aztec warriors. You must find your true *in ixtli in yollotl* and be there to help each other live."

Estrella helped up the maid who'd fainted out front and returned to the mansion. With trembling hands, she picked up the phone and placed a call to the police. Others in the neighborhood had already reported the incident, and cars were headed to the Casasola residence.

When the authorities arrived, they examined the bloodstains outside the gate and asked Estrella, "Where did the body go?"

Before she could answer, the officer who'd gone around the back of the mansion called the others.

Next to the quartered and beheaded body of Isidoro Casasola, with his heart extracted, stood an *indígena* woman and four children. She was holding a stone knife. The officers pointed their guns at her to make her drop the weapon, then handcuffed her behind her back.

Libertad was utterly stoic as they put her into the car and did not so much as peep in objection.

Her husband, torn to pieces by the narcos after a life of profligate excess; her Indigenous mother-in-law, who calmly cut him open and pulled out his heart in front of her grandsons; the boys, whose souls had been stolen by the Devil; an unending pagan ritual.

Estrella could not stand to be in the Casasola house in Veracruz for a moment longer. She began to go mad, wailing, throwing objects, and knocking over chairs. Soon after, she departed, alone, for her home in Oaxaca, taking none of her family assets with her.

Had Libertad committed blasphemy on Isidoro *after* his burial, she would have served a maximum five-year sentence. However, she'd carved open his chest with the obsidian knife before his burial. Given Isidoro's condition, it was clear he'd been killed by a cartel. In accordance with federal law, Libertad was fined and held for four days before she was released.

Back at the house, the living room was in a terrible state. Used plates were still on the table.

"*Abuelita*," called Valmiro, rushing down the stairs when he noticed she was home. "*Madre* left. Mila's not here, either."

Mila was a maid who'd worked for the Casasolas for four decades.

"You didn't go with your mother?"

"No."

"Where are Bernardo, Giovani, and Duilio?"

"They're here," Valmiro replied. "We're like you. We're Aztec warriors."

Libertad sold the family's possession and started charging for the fortune-telling she'd done previously done for free. By doing so, she was able to support the boys.

The Casasola company office remained at the port, but the cartel had completely taken over the business, and Libertad didn't see a single peso from it.

I want revenge against the ones who killed Padre.

Libertad understood the silent desire burning in the boys' hearts, and she respected it. Every human being was an *ahuicpa tic huica*, carrying without carrying. Only firm, unyielding will would awaken and guide them to the path to the gods: *in ixtli in yollotl*.

The brothers listened to Libertad's stories of the lost kingdom every night, never growing bored of them.

They learned many things through fear, and by knowing fear, they gained the wisdom to face reality. The stories were so interesting that they didn't need to pay money to go to the movie theater for entertainment. In fact, all the horror movies from America seemed to be rip-offs of Libertad's accounts.

In the summer of 1975, the eldest, Bernardo, went to the theater with his friends from school and saw *The Texas Chain Saw Massacre,* which was infamous for being scary. His friends covered their faces with their hands or ran out of the theater before the movie was done, but Bernardo wasn't frightened in the least. In fact, he was curious why people would pay money to see such a thing. What Leatherface did was the same as Xipe Totec, and much cruder. Xipe was the flayed god and regularly stripped the skin from slaves and pulled out their eyeballs, then wore them for himself. When the *xiuhpohualli* stated that it was Xipe Totec's festival day, the Aztecs who worshiped him would flay slaves accordingly, wear their skins for twenty days, dance, and chase others around.

After *The Texas Chain Saw Massacre,* Bernardo lost all interest in horror movies. He didn't even see *Friday the 13th* when it came out. He told his brothers it would be a waste of money. When *Friday the 13th Part 2* came to theaters a year later, people talked about the mask-wearing, machete-wielding killer, but he just seemed like a cheap imitation of real Aztec warriors.

While Libertad's stories were magical in effect, she was frankly realistic when it came to death. Within her tales of dreams and illusions, there was always an absolute marker of death. People died. They didn't come back to life. Dying in a good way returned the soul to the heavens, but that was no longer your present self. There was no afterlife. The soul was reincarnated. But before that, it was turned into a bird, so it never recalled its old existence. How could someone who didn't recall the past possibly be reborn as the same person?

The horrifying sound of the *ehecachichtli.* Tezcatlipoca sitting atop the *teocalli* and devouring the arms of sacrifices, watching Tenochtitlan sink into night. The sound of drums bound with snakeskin. A *tlamacazqui* priest worshiping the war god Huitzilopochtli giving a sacrifice's heart to a *cuauhtli,* an eagle. The *cuauhtli* grabbing the heart and flying off, upward through the thirteen layers of the heavens, dropping it into the indentation of the sacred stone. Quetzalcoatl carrying the stone to the sun. The *cuauhtli*, its job finished, descending and transforming into a *cozcacuauhtli*, a vulture, and proceeding farther down into the nine layers of the subterranean realm. The souls of those humans not sacrificed to the gods plunging headlong beside it, traveling through the nine dark layers, only reaching the deepest depths of Mictlan after four years. There, they met the terrifying skull-faced god of death, Mictlantecuhtli, evaporating at last and knowing release from the restless journey through utter blackness.

"As I've said many times, the important thing is how you die," Libertad said through the copal smoke. "It's how you use up your lives. That is crucial."

Through the blood and mythos of the fallen kingdom, the four boys came into contact with the order of the cosmos and the cruel nature of reality, thought hard about light and darkness, understood the importance of firm willpower, and forged stronger brotherly bonds.

As they gathered information on the cartel that executed their father and stole the family company their great-great-grandfather built, they began to believe the Mexican federal justice system incapable of punishing the men responsible. The narcos existed outside the law. In other words, working to become policemen or prosecutors was a waste of time and effort for the boys.

The most direct path to vengeance was to become the *enemy's enemy*. They would join an organization that rivaled the cartel that stole their father's life.

They grew in size and personality, intertwining with Aztec memories, reaching toward the plane of revenge—a future in which they became narcos.

Within this other cartel, home to the most ferocious men from all across Veracruz, the Casasola brothers' cruelty stood out above the others'. Stories of their exploits spread.

* * *

"They're fanatics who captured an enemy lieutenant, cut out his heart, and offered it to their Aztec god."

They stood at the front of every firefight. If a companion was in danger of being abducted, they charged at the enemy, swinging hatchets they used to sever arms. Dozens of narcos who should've been dragged off, mutilated, and slaughtered were saved by the Casasola brothers' astonishing courage. Although it was more like a fearless insanity than braphery.

Even the *sicarios* from their own organization feared them. The younger guys admired the Casasola brothers so much that they got tattoos of Aztec symbols like the Templo Mayor or eagle warriors, even the Nahuatl words *mitl chimalli*, or an arrow and shield, a metaphor for war. A few stopped going to Mass and started worshiping Aztec gods instead.

They never went out carousing in the pleasure district, and thus they never fell prey to the intricate intelligence network that enemy cartels had established using high-priced sex workers.

When they at last identified the *sicario* who did in their father, the brothers started a gun battle in broad daylight and took the man alive. Unfortunately, Valmiro's and Duilio's bullets punctured the man's stomach, exposing his entrails. He was liable to die soon. With the stink of the gunpowder on his hands stinging his nostrils, Valmiro called Libertad and asked, "Should we bring him to you?"

"No, you handle it," she replied. "But when you're done, bring his heart and left arm here."

They killed the wailing hitman, removed his heart, and cut off his left arm, then took them back to the mansion. Libertad was waiting for them. She carefully washed the heart and arm with water from the well out back, wiped them off, then shut them in the freezer.

The following May, the *sicario*'s heart and left arm were finally removed. The *xiuhpohualli* had reached Toxcatl, the festival day for Tezcatlipoca, so

Libertad opened up the freezer to retrieve the sacrifice for the temple. The heart would thaw at room temperature, but in order to make the left arm "easier for Tezcatlipoca to eat," she hit it with a hammer and broke it into fine pieces.

The sight of his *abuelita* carrying out this process with a smile gave Valmiro an idea for a form of torture that would surely terrify his enemies.

In the future, this idea would become his epithet, a nickname that defined him. El Polvo was a common term in the drug business, most often as *polvo de oro*, or "golden dust," the finest kind of cocaine. But the *dust* associated with Valmiro was a different thing altogether.

He froze the limbs of his kidnapped victims with liquid nitrogen, while they were still alive, then broke them with a steel hammer. His victims were forced to watch their own limbs shatter into powder.

After they'd enacted their revenge on the *sicario* who killed their father, the Casasola brothers continued killing narcos from the rival cartel. They offered the lieutenants' hearts to their god, and with each sacrifice, the brothers felt the sacred power they harbored growing stronger.

They killed, sold cocaine, bought weapons, killed again, and every now and then, gave money to the poor *indígena* prostitutes down at the port. The girls would prick their own ears with maguey thorns, cast the blood over incense smoke, and pray to demonstrate their gratitude to Libertad's grandsons, the Casasola brothers.

When Libertad fell ill with pneumonia, the brothers immediately bought out an entire five-bed hospital room just for her. They did their best to decorate her bedside with green quetzal feathers and jaguar pelts while she lay there, gaunt and tiny. They brought in gold and emeralds, and kept armed guards posted at the entrance to her room and around the floor twenty-four hours a day.

Out of the many presents from her grandsons, Libertad was most delighted with an obsidian mirror Valmiro bought from a man who'd dug it up illegally. It was a *tezcatl*, an Aztec-era mirror buried among ruins—an incarnation of Tezcatlipoca.

Libertad developed a high fever and looked even more haggard, and on Mahcuilli Calli (Five-House), fifth day of the *trecena* associated with Quiahuitl, the rain, she died.

Her grandsons took her remains, placed her in a special-made coffin, and sent her off with an assortment of feathers, pelts, ornaments, and the obsidian mirror.

As the sun descended in the west, they buried Libertad on a hill outside Veracruz, which they'd purchased for this purpose. It was a grave for Libertad alone, with no cross stuck in the ground above it.

They didn't need to take out her heart. She was not *ahuicpa tic huica*, but had been *in ixtli in yollotl* all along. They'd learned everything from her.

Beside Libertad's coffin was another. Inside it were the remains of her doctor, whom Valmiro had shot dead. He hadn't taken the doctor's life as punishment for failing to save their *abuelita*, though. It was to ensure Libertad's lonely soul would have company. She needed an attendant until her journey to the heavens was complete.

When high-born Aztecs died, their servants were buried along with them as an offering to the gods. They also buried eagles, monkeys, and even dogs with turquoise ear decorations. The beasts would serve the dead in the next stage, but the most valued followers were humans. Valmiro chose the doctor to be Libertad's attendant.

By the time the coffins were hidden under the soil, the entire hillside was dyed scarlet by the bloodlike sunset. They stood on the hill until the stars emerged. A gust of wind blew through the darkness, and they closed their eyes.

To dispel their grief over Libertad's passing, the Casasola brothers waged nonstop war.

The violence grew more heated. They destroyed the occupied Casasola company office building, then the cargo ships in the harbor, driving the rival cartel into ruin. They didn't just fight with their enemies; they ruthlessly turned their guns on the few narcos within their own organization who dared to compete with them.

The days of battle dragged on, spilling copious blood that the brothers offered to the gods as they counted off the days of the Aztec calendar.

They conquered Veracruz and the state of Tamaulipas to the north as well, announcing the birth of a new cartel: Los Casasolas.

Under constant scrutiny from the Mexican authorities, the DEA, and the CIA, the cartel's primary members were listed in the Americans' investigation materials as such:

Most Wanted Fugitives

Bernardo Carlos Casasola Valdés
a.k.a. "El Pirámide"

Jesus Giovani Casasola Valdés
a.k.a. "El Jaguar"

Valmiro Marcos Casasola Valdés
a.k.a. "El Polvo"

Juan Duilio Casasola Valdés
a.k.a. "El Dedo"

In 2015, a reefer ship left the port of Veracruz on a sunny September day and headed from the Gulf of Mexico to the Caribbean, then it passed through the Panama Canal into the Pacific Ocean and down to Santiago, capital of Chile, to pick up a shipment of salmon.

Valmiro disembarked and walked to a used auto dealership close to the dock. He checked the tires on a few of them first; there wouldn't be time to replace them after he made a purchase. He paid in cash for a Mitsubishi

Pajero that was covered in mud but with wheels in fairly good condition. Then he gave one of the window-washing kids hanging out on the curb a decent tip to scrub the dirt from the body.

Valmiro drove the Pajero to the border, then presented a fake passport to get into Argentina. The next leg of his trip was by air. He left the Pajero behind, got into an old propeller plane, and flew from the west end of Argentina to the east. The journey to Aeroparque Jorge Newbery in Buenos Aires was a tiresome one because the plane shook violently the whole way.

Entering the home country of the Dogo Cartel's leader was a big risk; his family and partners still lived there, after all. Valmiro could have simply boarded a boat in Chile heading across the Pacific, and left the Americas behind that much sooner.

However, he chose not to do that because this would confuse his enemy more.

Valmiro went to the port in Buenos Aires and made contact with a sailor on a container ship Los Casasolas had used many times to smuggle *hielo*. The man didn't recognize Valmiro, who gave an alias anyway.

After some negotiation, Valmiro was permitted to sneak onto the ship for thirty thousand dollars. Had the sailor known who he was dealing with, he would have demanded three times as much.

Valmiro requested a smartphone from the sailor and told him he would pay using a digital cryptocurrency. It was called Batista, a variant on an existing system that a Uruguayan programmer had modified, which was a favorite of the Colombian cartels.

The encryption, hidden in a string of letters and numbers, was split into three parts and tied to GPS data. When the ship Valmiro was on left the port, the first key was sent, at which point the sailor could use the key to receive 10 percent—in this case, three thousand dollars—in cryptocurrency. When the ship reached port, the sailor would receive 40 percent with the next key—twelve thousand dollars. In order for him to get the third key with the remaining half of the money, Valmiro's GPS would need to reach the encrypted coordinates of his destination, and the sailor required a password that Valmiro set ahead of time. Valmiro had to send the password himself once he'd arrived at his goal. Naturally, this meant he had to be *alive*. However, if Valmiro did nothing, then a public key would be sent automatically twenty-four hours after leaving the ship. This allowed the sailor to collect 30 percent of the remaining fifteen thousand dollars, or four thousand five hundred.

The Batista system was meant to reduce the risk of either a pay-first or pay-after method of conducting illegal business, disincentivizing betrayal before arrival and murder after arrival. It was an invention ideal for the drug business, ensuring drugs and weapons could pass to the other party securely.

With his trip secured, Valmiro went to eat dinner at a steakhouse in Buenos Aires as he waited for the night to pass. An elderly white couple at the table next to him asked him where the opera house was. Valmiro smiled as he answered, then watched them keenly after that. They had to be in their eighties, and they assumed he was a local. Either that or they were Dogo Cartel conspirators who were merely putting on an act.

"We came here from Switzerland," the wife said in Spanish. "We'll be leaving for Venezuela tomorrow."

He nodded and beamed. "You're quite the travelers, at your age."

Venezuela, Valmiro thought. *It's known for being a place where wanted narcos hide. But only if they're on the run from the American DEA. If you're running from cartels with connections all over Latin America, it's not safe.*

He rose from his seat and grinned at the elderly couple once more. *"Adiós,"* he said. "Enjoy your evening."

After midnight, Valmiro snuck onboard a shipping vessel registered to Panama with the sailor's help. The vessel was packed with steel containers in two sizes, twenty feet and forty. For a premium, clients could put their containers "under deck," while all others would be stacked "on deck."

Valmiro hoped to conceal himself in an under-deck container, but due to the suddenness of his request, there was no time to prepare a better option, and he had to go in an on-deck container.

The ship was bound for Monrovia, the capital of Liberia in West Africa. For the roughly twenty days the ship spent crossing the Atlantic, the on-deck containers weathered wind, rain, and seawater. And everyone knew what happened when the metal boxes were exposed to sunlight for a while. Valmiro was sealed in without a window, rocked by the waves, clutching his gun, with no chair or bed for comfort. It was the start of a long, harsh journey to smuggle the most precious cargo of all: himself.

Twice a day, the sailor came to deliver water and food to Valmiro's container. He drank the water and ate the can of fish. He drank no tequila or coffee and smoked no tobacco or marijuana. There were canisters of agricultural chemicals stored in the container, which he turned on their side and laid on top of. Before the dawn, it was as cold as a desert night on the sea, so Valmiro wrapped himself in a blanket for warmth. When he woke, he defecated into a plastic container and shut the lid.

Valmiro spent the days doing nothing but breathing in total darkness. There was no light to tell the time, but he could feel the sun. The fierce light, unobstructed at sea, turned the inside of the container into a searing hell. On top of that, the ship itself was nearing the equator as it drew closer to the African continent.

Conditions were perfect for death via heatstroke, but Valmiro persevered. It was agonizing, yet he wasn't afraid. *If I die here, I will offer my own heart to Tezcatlipoca. And if I don't die here, then I will simply offer him a heart acquired at my destination. The red Tezcatlipoca is with me. And so is Xipe Totec, the flayed god*, he thought.

He counted the days by three calendars, based on the number of meals the sailor brought him: the Aztec *tonalpohualli* and *xiuhpohualli*, and the Christian Gregorian calendar.

Any water he drank, lukewarm and unpleasant, dripped right out of him as sweat. He chewed antibiotic pills and found himself tormented by memories of the past in his heat-induced delirium. It was a chaotic vortex that intermixed with reality.

Dead roosters in the backyard, a Peruvian farm during a business excursion, coca trees, level-3 armored vehicles, men at the coca farm, cocaine manufacturers, someone screaming, *"Vamos, vamos,"* calculators displaying totals of cocaine in tons, ringing phones, *abuelita*'s voice, "The important thing is how you die," GPS coordinates, the streets of Berlin, fourteen kilos of liquid cocaine sold to an investor for three-point-two million euros, a bloody bathtub, his subordinates' betrayal, screams, women, torture videos on the internet, prosecutors begging for their lives, a writer dying with his arms and legs frozen, subordinates hung from a bridge, a Texas hotel, a pound of meth crystals sold for nine thousand dollars, liquid nitrogen tanks, a steel hammer, cocaine hidden in the stomach of a frozen fish, his sons, daughters, wife, and brothers blown sky-high by a drone, the wafting smoke of copal incense, walking through Tenochtitlan, riding a canoe, getting off at Tlatelolco, blood-stained *teocalli* steps, staircase pyramids, Tezcatlipoca, Yohualli Ehecatl, Titlacauan, he drowned this world in a flood, Nahui-Atl, his *abuelita*'s voice again, "Aztec warriors cut off the ears of every captive they took and offered them to the king of Culhuacán," we are Aztec warriors, we came from the legendary homeland of Aztlán, our blood was mixed with the Spanish, everything was stolen from us, but we have not vanished yet, we will march with the heads of captives in our hands, our power, shotguns, *silbato de la muerte*, obsidian knife, sacrificial arms offered to god, devouring the tender palm, just as we eat the chicken, we eat the chicken, we eat.

At the end of its voyage across the Atlantic Ocean, the container ship arrived in West Africa. At the port of Monrovia, Valmiro's on-deck container was lifted off and set down by a crane, and he exited at last with the sailor's help. He snuck into the warehouse, wobbling feverishly, scooped up water from a bucket with trembling hands and washed his face and body. Then he donned a cheap T-shirt and a pair of jeans. Valmiro's weight had dropped significantly from the twenty-two-day voyage, and he had to tighten his belt to keep the jeans from falling off his waist.

As the sun sank over the Equator, Valmiro moved among the dock-workers leaving for the day and made his way into the city.

He converted his money to Liberian dollars, bought an open-collared shirt, slacks, and leather shoes to freshen up his look. That done, Valmiro checked in at a hotel. After entering his room, he left by the emergency stairs, looking over his shoulder all the while, and slipped down an alley to a cheap motel instead. Once there, he sent voice data to certify the cryptocurrency transaction, concluding his business with the sailor. Now the man on the Panamanian ship had the remaining fifteen thousand dollars, and all of the encrypted location data was wiped clean.

Valmiro slept like a rock on the hard motel mattress and woke up in the morning. He walked to a busy road, hailed a cab, and said in English, "Take me to Madero International."

Madero International was a trading company based in Monrovia. Until the early nineteenth century, it had been known as Adele & Madero and made its money selling slaves and weapons.

Six years ago, the enterprise began assisting Los Casasolas with money laundering, and Valmiro had twice visited their headquarters. The capital of Liberia was not completely unfamiliar to him.

Los Casasolas rented a safe in the Madero International basement under the alias of "Francisco Martínez."

Valmiro took the key and opened the safe, pulling out the cash inside and a pair of crutches.

The crutches looked like the typical sort made of aluminum and rubber, but they weighed twice as much. They were made of a synthetic resin, a combination of glass fiber and liquid cocaine. It was the same method used to create false suitcases for smuggling, and once you separated the cocaine mixed throughout the entire set of crutches, you would have five million dollars' worth of coke.

Valmiro tucked the crutches under his arms and hailed a taxi. The driver offered to put the suitcase into the car for him, but never said a thing about the crutches. They were magic walking sticks Valmiro was confident would never leave his side.

A long stay in Monrovia was never the plan. Valmiro had a particular map of the world in his head that only a narco would understand, and he moved boldly.

First, he rode on a research vessel owned by an "environmental protection group," which traveled south across the Gulf of Guinea, down to Cape Town in South Africa. The organization that owned the ship was well known to African poachers. If you paid them enough money, they would let you transport animals whose commercial trade was prohibited by the Washington Convention. The ship also carried drugs and refugees.

Valmiro quickly left Cape Town and embarked on another grueling container journey. A second voyage of baking heat and darkness inside the container, taking antibiotic pills and withstanding sheer agony.

The shipping boat crossed the Indian Ocean and docked at Perth, Australia. When Valmiro walked through the coastal city with the crutches, people helpfully got out of his way.

He'd already traveled more than halfway around the globe from Veracruz, but Valmiro didn't stop here. Living in the narcos' world meant creating a maze with your tracks, because every manner of danger lurked out there and sought to follow you. Fail to hide your steps, and you wound up getting bombed, like in Nuevo Laredo.

Being situated on the west coast of Australia, Perth was closer to Southeast Asia than the capital city Canberra to the east, and there were many Asians living here. Valmiro spent money in the Asian community, followed leads, gained trustworthy collaborators, and arranged for yet another stow-away journey.

After losing their prey in Nuevo Laredo, the Dogo Cartel continued to search around the border between America and Mexico.

At this point, Valmiro had already left Australia and melted into the crowded chaos of Southeast Asia.

II

Narco y Médico
(Drug Dealer and Doctor)

And deeper in history, at the turn of the nineteenth century a booming market for shrunken heads in Europe sparked tribal wars in South America.

—Scott Carney, *The Red Market: On the Trail of the World's Organ Brokers, Bone Thieves, Blood Farmers, and Child Traffickers*

Capital, Deleuze and Guattari says, is a "motley painting of everything that ever was"; a strange hybrid of the ultra-modern and the archaic.

—Mark Fisher, *Capitalist Realism: Is There No Alternative?*

14

mahtlactli-huan-nähui

The keen instincts and skills of observation that Valmiro had honed in Mexico needed to be resized to match the city of Jakarta.

The language was a big hurdle, of course, but even without understanding the locals, there was a plethora of things to take in. There was much to be gleaned by taking his time to walk the streets and analyze what he saw. Where did the junkies gather? Who was selling on the street? Where did the women of the night eat before work? Where did the most robberies and murders occur? And which bridges did the dirty cops park their cars under?

Jakarta, the city on Java's northwest coast, was a port metropolis of over ten million people, far outclassing anything in the Los Casasolas base of Tamaulipas. A transforming mass of humanity that evolved by the day, it was an endless cauldron of heat and activity, owing to the waves of capitalism that crashed upon its shore.

The entire country was an indispensable market for the drug trade. As an archipelagic country, the Republic of Indonesia was spread across thousands of islands that covered as much distance east to west as the continental United States. It had the greatest land area of any country in Southeast Asia, and a population of two hundred and sixty million—the fourth highest in the world. This made the multiethnic nation the rising sun of new capitalism in Asia. And a new sun created new shadows for darkness to take shape.

Capitalism was the modern-day magic sigil here. Under its arcane system, all forms of desire slumbering in the depths of hell were brought into the daylight of reality—including things that were never meant to be.

Of all the different forms that capitalism's magic took, the most potent of all was surely drug enterprise. And having spent a lifetime standing at the center of it, Valmiro found that his new hideout of Jakarta had a darkness to it that was very familiar and easy to understand.

One of the city's features was its incredibly snarled traffic.

Lines of cars squatted and honked, belching exhaust fumes and going nowhere. Motorbike taxis wove their way through the lines, passengers in *bajaj* tricycles complained to their drivers, and buses trundled along special busways separated by concrete block walls. If you were traveling aboveground, the busway was ideal, Valmiro decided.

In places where the traffic was worst, they used a "three-in-one" system, in which a car was required to have at least three passengers in order to pass along certain routes. It was a clever attempt to ease traffic, but it only gave way for a new form of business. People would walk the streets near one of the checkpoints and knock on the window of any car that didn't have the required three passengers, offering to help them pass through the zone. Once past the traffic zone, the impromptu passenger, known as a "car jockey," received twenty thousand rupiahs from the driver for their help.

Twenty thousand rupiahs was only two American dollars, but that was valuable income for a jockey. Some of them were women with babies who took advantage of the fact that infants counted under the three-in-one rules. The baby didn't get any money of its own, but it did mean that one adult could do the work of two, increasing their desirability to the passing drivers. Some women even borrowed infants for the job.

Humans needed to make their livings, and their ingenuity at finding them kept the traffic problem going.

Valmiro went to one of the restricted roads to watch the jockeys in action. He was searching for a man who could help with his work.

Valmiro visited a high-end shopping mall in Jakarta that handled all manner of brand items, seeking to buy cologne. He didn't need it when lurking in a cheap motel, but if he needed to stay at a three-star hotel for whatever reason, expensive cologne was an excellent tool to help him manage the impression he gave off. As Mark Twain's famous novel demonstrated, there was a knack to playing the part in both high and low society, and the world of the narcos had taught Valmiro how to manage both.

The mall's clientele was apparent from the cars in the parking garage: Mercedes Benzes, BMWs, Porsches, and Ferraris. The entryway faced a huge plate glass window like something from a modern art museum, and there was a body and bag check to get inside.

Valmiro wasn't walking with the crutches infused with liquid cocaine. They could remain in his hotel room. He lifted his hands, submitting to the metal detector test from the security guard, gazed at the luxury cars in the parking garage under the blazing tropical sun, and recalled when he was just a low-rung cartel member.

They used to subject me to a metal detector test every time the boss called me to his home.

Storefronts for Chanel, Gucci, and Yves Saint Laurent passed by as Valmiro wove through the high-end watches and jewelry, making his way to the perfume area. Sporting a finely crafted appearance, Valmiro fit right in. He asked questions in English, and the young sales associate answered in kind.

After purchasing cologne, Valmiro went to a special cell-phone-only mall called ITC Roxy Mas. All the vendors inside sold phones and phone accessories.

The ratio of phones to the overall population of Indonesia was over 130 percent. Smartphones were considered a more indispensable part of daily life here than elsewhere. You could buy SIM cards at streetside vendors. And when buying them, you didn't need to show any proof of identity. All it took was some money to get a number.

This was perfect for Valmiro. At ITC Roxy Mas, he bought three smartphones—a Galaxy, an Oppo, and a BlackBerry. From sellers along Hayam Wuruk Street, he picked up three SIM cards from major mobile carriers in Indonesia: Indosat, Telkomsel, and XL.

With the help of a jockey who understood English, Valmiro was able to find a Spanish-speaking dealer in Jakarta. He bought some hash from the dealer, chatted a bit, gained information about the area, and spent some of his time learning Indonesian. The language was considered one of the simplest to learn. Compared to memorizing and deciphering the complex code words that narcos used for business, Valmiro found it no trouble at all to pick up vocabulary sufficient for basic communication.

Once Valmiro exchanged some of the dollars he'd cashed out in Australia for rupiahs, he asked the street dealer to put him in touch with someone who could arrange counterfeit documents. He then hired the document forger as an interpreter, reached out to the overseer of one of Jakarta's open-air markets, and after some careful negotiation, purchased a *kaki lima* wheeled cart and began his own business.

Valmiro placed the *kaki lima* on the east side of Mangga Besar Road, which ran east to west through one of Jakarta's pleasure districts.

He offered nothing more than cobra satay, Bintang beer, and two kinds of tea. The tea was for the Muslims who didn't imbibe alcohol. There were more Muslims in Indonesia than anywhere else on earth.

However, hardly any local Muslims patronized Valmiro's cart. Instead, he primarily saw foreign tourists interested in cobra satay.

Valmiro passed himself off as Peruvian, and had two different aliases, but he forced the two former jockeys he hired to work the cart to call him El Cocinero: "The Cook." Despite the title, Valmiro hardly ever prepared the live cobras for the cart; he let the two youngsters do it.

"Selamat malam!"

When curious tourists stopped at the cart, the two employees greeted them in the local language.

Just weeks earlier, the young men had been scraping together a living by riding in strangers' cars through the three-in-one zones for chump change. Now they killed and prepared cobras for cooking as though they'd been doing this job for years. One of them was a Javanese local, while the other was a Sundanese man from Sulawesi.

Cobra satay was hardly fine dining, but it was a regional delicacy in Jakarta. You couldn't buy cobra to eat just anywhere.

After an order was made, the cook removed a live cobra from the cage, gripped its neck tightly, and intentionally hit it on the head. The angered cobra bared its fangs in a sign of intimidation. The thrill of this little road-side show was part of the price. You had to be careful, however; many people were sent to the hospital with snakebites from the very thing they were selling.

Once the customers had their fill of cobra ferocity, the cook lopped off the animal's head. Any ordinary kitchen knife would do, but at Valmiro's stand, the employees used a traditional Javanese knife called a *keris*. The props were important. The exotic blade, with ripples along its length as though it were a snake itself, easily separated the cobra's head from its body. The creature continued to wriggle for several moments after the severing. Customers often grimaced with disgust at the carnage but also flushed with excitement. Their eyes locked onto the cobra's mouth, which opened and closed spitefully. After a long gaze at the gleaming, venomous fangs, patrons occasionally requested to take a picture.

"Go ahead," the cook would say. "But be careful. It can still bite, even as just a head. People have died that way before. Also, watch out if it shoots its saliva."

The cook turned the writhing, headless cobra upside down and poured the spurting blood into a shot glass. Its fresh blood was another crucial product, a beverage of unparalleled intensity. Some people couldn't take a single drop of its pungent warmth, while others were eager to down the whole shot.

Once drained of blood, the cobra was hung on a steel hook, skinned, and then chopped into hunks on a cutting board. The meat was skewered one chunk at a time, placed on a mesh grill, and cooked over a fire, then put on a plate and served.

The *kaki lima* of El Cocinero, the silent Peruvian, did not engage in aggressive advertisement or short-change customers. The business merely peddled cobra satay on the street. It was always the Javanese and Sundanese young men working at the cart—very few knew the owner was a Latin American man. Even if they did, the information had no value. There were as many food carts in Jakarta as stars in the sky, and while overseeing the market could be decent money, the daily income from a single *kaki lima* was going to be paltry no matter what.

It was a well-known fact that carts didn't turn a great profit, but Valmiro wasn't hoping to get rich selling cobra satay. He operated another business in the shadow of the first. He didn't expect to get wealthy with that, either, but it was a means to work himself deeper into the city's darkness. His eyes were sharp, and his ears pointed.

15

caxtölli

Valmiro met the Japanese man during his first *musim kemarau,* or dry season, in Jakarta.

It was Monday, June 6, 2016—the first day of Ramadan. Instead of being packed with the unmanageable traffic jams that were an inescapable part of life in Jakarta, the streets looked like a ghost town. The bike taxis and *bajajs* moved as smoothly as the busways, and those from religious minorities like the local Chinese and Australian businessmen, who normally couldn't speed around the city, raced by in their sports cars. Valmiro, who watched them go, was another outsider not taking part in the Islamic fast.

The effects of Ramadan extended to Mangga Besar Road. Most of the usual carts were absent, and Valmiro's Javanese and Sundanese employees were also away because of religious observance.

Valmiro made no attempt to pretend he was diligently minding the food cart, but lazily tending to it was a nice way to observe a much quieter Jakarta. Valmiro wore a baseball cap with the logo of a major Indonesian IT company on it, sat on an uneven round chair, drank some Bintang, and idly watched the cart while smoking Indonesian cigarettes from a red pack labeled DJARUM SUPER 16.

A stray dog trotted down the path, and Valmiro gazed up at the sky, which had a different shade of blue from Mexico's. The butts slowly multiplied around his feet as the time dragged on.

A group of white tourists approached the cart: two women and one man. They stared at the tangle of cobras in the cage with undisguised fear.

"Do they really skewer and grill these?" wondered a woman.

"Try for yourself," Valmiro replied in English. "They're very nutritious."

"Are they all king cobras?"

"Javan cobras," he answered. "All freshly caught and lively. Where are you from?"

"Canada."

"You should try one before you go. You'll never taste it anywhere else."

"Well, in that case…," said the other woman.

"Are you for real?" the man asked her in disbelief.

Valmiro took a cobra out of the cage, struck its head to make it bare its fangs and scare the tourists, then cut the snake's head off with the knife. He squeezed the blood out of the neck and into one of the cart's teacups, then offered it to them.

While the three made funny faces and tried the fresh blood, Valmiro hung the snake on a metal hook and ripped the skin off. He sliced the meat into big pieces, skewered them, and then carefully grilled the pieces over the charcoal fire.

After the Canadians left, it was quiet again. Nearly all of the blood was left in the teacup. Valmiro ran his finger through the liquid, then let the droplets sprinkle onto the red, glowing coals. He prayed to his Aztec god, remembering his dead brothers, sons, daughters, wife, and grandmother. When he'd emptied the teacup of blood this way, he used the grill to light another cigarette and returned to watching Mangga Besar.

Two Islamic women appeared like shadows from nothing, scurrying past Valmiro. They weren't wearing burqas that covered their entire bodies, just the headscarves that the Indonesians called *jilbab*. The way that they kept their eyes downcast as they hurried by spoke to the solemnity of the Ramadan period.

A month of fasting, Valmiro thought. *What a difference it makes in a city. I wonder if things changed like this in the Aztec kingdom.*

He'd seen wild festivals singing the praises of Jesus Christ in Mexico, but Ramadan here was not just some celebration. The people were fasting, sacrificing themselves for the sake of their god.

"Malam."

Valmiro was lost in thoughts and smoke when the brief greeting brought him back to the present.

There was a light-skinned Asian man in front of the cart. He was alone. Glasses, a white button-up shirt, knee-length pants, bare feet in loafers— it was the classic attire of a businessman working in tropical Jakarta. However, Valmiro sensed the scent of blood wafting from this man. It was an aura, something that had seeped into his soul and could not be wiped clean.

Chinese, I guess, Valmiro deduced, sizing up the guest.

"One cobra satay, please," the man requested in gentle Indonesian. "Surprised to see you're open, considering it's Ramadan."

"I'm a Catholic," Valmiro replied. "If I were a Muslim, I would be closed today."

As he removed the cobra's head, he reflected on the man's voice. The Indonesian didn't seem to have any hint of a Mandarin or Cantonese accent. Perhaps he was a Jakarta-born Chinese Indonesian.

Valmiro grabbed the writhing, headless cobra, held it upside down, and waited for the blood to drip out. When he placed the blood-filled shot glass in front of his customer, the man reached into his shirt pocket. Valmiro expected him to pull out a smartphone to take a picture, but that wasn't the case. The man retrieved a five-thousand-rupiah bill instead, folded it into a tube, and stuck it into the shot of blood sitting on the counter.

The "secret handshakes" indicating interest in a drug deal were a kind of shared international language. The man knew how to demonstrate that he wanted to buy drugs at Valmiro's cart. People didn't simply stick paper money into warm cobra's blood unless they were street magicians performing a trick or they really knew what they were doing.

Valmiro stopped peeling the snake and glanced at the slowly sinking bill, which was gradually absorbing blood. His expression remained unchanged, save for a dark light gathering in his eyes. He cast a piercing gaze at the Asian man.

He was past forty, his hair fashioned in an undercut. White peeked out here and there at the edges of his head, but he wasn't old yet. The black-rimmed glasses set before his eyes were high quality, and his lids were rather prominently double-lidded for an East Asian. He was about one hundred and sixty-eight centimeters, but sported a good build. No tattoos decorated the parts of his arms or neck visible beneath his business shirt. His short pants were crisply ironed, and his leather shoes shone.

Valmiro didn't recall seeing this man before, and he remembered *all* of the regulars.

The *kaki lima* was cheaply made, but Valmiro had a Japanese security camera installed under the overhang to catch the faces of every customer who came to buy drugs.

The headless cobra on the hook, skin only partially flayed, still wriggled. Valmiro gave the man a nod, then left the little cart behind and walked down an alley. Rats scurried away when they heard human footsteps.

"We've never met before," Valmiro said in Indonesian, leaning against the wall in the darkness.

The man noticed his accent, and replied, *"Mucho gusto. Por cierto, ¿puedo pagar con tarjeta?"*

"No," Valmiro said, grinning at the joke. Obviously, he wouldn't accept payment by card. He looked around swiftly—there was a possibility that this man was *encubierto*, an undercover cop.

The man returned the smile amiably. "Would you prefer to speak in Spanish? You have a Spanish accent. Indonesian is easy to understand, but we'd both still struggle a bit to communicate. Outside of my native tongue, I'm best at German. Then English, then Spanish. It's been a while since I've used it."

"Who told you about me?"

"Dai."

Oh, him, Valmiro thought.

Guiming Dai was a thirty-two-year-old Chinese man living in Jakarta. He was a member of 919 (Jiu-Yi-Jiu), claiming to be a lieutenant in the group. 919 was a Chinese *heishehui*, or "Black Society," and its name was taken from a bullet classification: the 9×19 mm Parabellum.

Dai was one of the customers who bought crack from Valmiro's cart. He had eighteen-carat-gold earrings and liked to wear traditional Indonesian batik shirts. He had his own nightclub on Mangga Besar Road, and he seemed possessed of adequate funds, but Valmiro didn't believe that he was a 919 lieutenant. That was a bluff. If he were, he wouldn't be buying crack from a cart on the street.

To Valmiro's eyes, Dai was someone starved for money and power, but whom the *heishehui* largely ignored, stranding him on the second or third rung of its pyramidal hierarchy. Crack was the drug that men like him took.

"I don't know what Dai told you," Valmiro said to the Asian man in Spanish, "but I don't have cocaine for a businessman like you. I don't have any at all. I only sell cheap rocks."

Valmiro bought freebase—pure base cocaine not acidified into hydrochloride—from a Malaysian dealer in Jakarta, then mixed it with baking soda or baking powder to create crack rocks about the size of pearls. He sold this in small quantities at his cart. Street-level dealers could easily get themselves killed if they cut their product without permission, but Valmiro gave 60 percent of his take to the Malaysian dealer in exchange for the right to adulterate his product.

Many dealers sold crack. It was much cheaper than powder cocaine and was a reliable commodity for quick, small sales within the overall drug market. If anyone in Jakarta was familiar with the name El Polvo, they would never have believed that he was selling crack. A narco who'd risen up to cartel lieutenant status didn't sink to being a crack dealer. It was akin to an oil baron selling candy on the street. But owning the cart and selling crack accomplished what Valmiro wanted it to do: obscure his identity.

"Crack is fine," said the man. "I'll buy it."

"If that's what you want," answered Valmiro. "You need a pipe? I've got good ones for sale."

The primary method of administering crack was heating it up in a glass pipe and inhaling the smoke. Valmiro went back to the cart, took out a box of pipes he kept hidden beneath the cobra cage, and returned to the alley. Only a third-rate narco hastened to end a transaction out of caution. You had to question a potentially dangerous person and actively glean more information from them.

"You're very dedicated to your business," the man remarked while examining the pipes on display. "I'll take this one."

"You Chinese?" Valmiro questioned, accepting payment for nine rocks and a glass pipe and counting the bills.

"I live in Jakarta," the man said. "What should I do the next time I come? Put a bill into the cobra's blood each time?"

"Get in touch. I'll have it ready," Valmiro responded, tucking the money into his pocket. He took out his smartphone and asked the man for his number. Then he called it and hung up as soon as it had rung once. "Just call that number. What do I call you?"

"You can call me Tanaka," the man replied.

"Tanaka... *Japonés?*"

"I've tried passing myself off as Chinese, but it doesn't tend to last." Tanaka smiled, pushing his glasses up the bridge of his nose. "My Mandarin is terrible. I quit doing that before the mobsters put a bullet in my head. Like you said, I am *Japonés*."

"Interesting. Japanese cars are the best. You don't happen to work for a car company, do you?"

Tanaka didn't answer that. With an *"Adiós,"* he headed west down Mangga Besar. Some police officers came walking by on patrol from the other direction. Drug crimes were punished heavily in Indonesia. Naturally, possession was a major felony. Yet Tanaka fearlessly strolled right past the police and vanished into the neon forest of night clubs with an odd confidence.

For as long as the man remained visible, Valmiro kept his eyes on him. A self-proclaimed Japanese buyer who smelled of blood and had something curious about him that did not belong to Latin American narcos or Chinese *heishehui* mobsters. A new type of Japanese mafia? Or perhaps he was an undercover cop.

Valmiro looked at his watch. Somehow it was four o'clock. He stripped the skin off a hooked cobra, chopped the meat, and skewered it. After grilling it over the fire, he stuck the skewers into a plastic container and took them to the durian cart on the west side of Mangga Besar Road. The Hindu man who ran it loved cobra satay. Valmiro sold it to him at a discount, and the man picked up some thick slices of durian.

"Hey, El Cocinero," he called, "take this. There's nobody coming by today."

Valmiro waved his hand to refuse the durian, then returned to his own cart.

16

caxtölli-huan-cë

Tanaka returned every three days. He did not order the cobra satay again and contacted Valmiro ahead of time to purchase crack in the alley a short distance away from the cart.

"It's important to smoke it with the pipe," Tanaka said in fluent Spanish, handing over the bills.

Valmiro took them and counted silently.

"If you keep snorting it, your nose will eventually melt," Tanaka continued gleefully. "I know someone whose *tabique nasal* dissolved. Supposedly, it cost a ton of money to get a black-market doctor to repair the cartilege. By the way, El Cocinero, are there any good Peruvian restaurants in Jakarta? I'd like to know a place I can take clients. I'm getting bored of all the Japanese and Chinese restaurants."

Valmiro had never actually heard the term *tabique nasal* before, but he guessed its meaning from context. He told Tanaka the address of a Peruvian restaurant he'd visited himself, then asked, "What kind of clients?"

Tanaka removed his glasses to wipe the lenses. He held them up to the sky to check that they were clear. With a smile, he bid, *"Hasta luego,"* and left.

The Japanese regular seemed to have taken quite a liking to the *kaki lima* owner.

Valmiro didn't think poorly of the other man, either. Seemingly true to the Japanese stereotype, Tanaka was unfailingly polite. He didn't light up the crack on the spot, and he always shared a little bit of conversation to help build trust. In addition to the crack he bought from Valmiro, he claimed to be a regular user of cocaine.

Cocaine users in Southeast Asia often maintained a functioning social life. They considered themselves to be cocaine aficionados, like people who enjoyed alcohol or cigars, and drew a line between themselves and drug addicts. They believed there was a difference.

The reason that Valmiro didn't deal in drugs with a bigger share in Indonesia, like heroin, amphetamine, and *hielo*, was because the clientele for those products were more likely to cause trouble. In comparison, crack customers were slightly more reasonable, and the cocaine market was considerably more mature. Market price for cocaine was high in Southeast Asia, and nearly all regular users were wealthy. These so-called cocaine aficionados with money and prestige were good at avoiding the minefield of drug searches. No matter how dangerous the territory was, as long as you didn't step on the pressure trigger, the game continued. Until, abruptly, it ended.

One day, after another crack purchase, Tanaka talked about his older brother.

"He was very smart," Tanaka said. "In nationwide mock exams, he scored within the top ten in every subject. But he died. And do you know why? He failed the national medical examination. That's all. He got food poisoning the day before, suffered from dehydration, and wasn't in any state to take the exam. He was so furious with himself that he jumped on a motorcycle and got into an accident. My brother was very smart but very unlucky. He's probably laughing at me from hell right now, though. Any brothers, El Cocinero?"

"No," Valmiro replied. He was thinking of Bernardo, his eldest sibling. *Abuelita* had given him the power of black Tezcatlipoca, and he had a tattoo of a sacrificial head on his left breast, and a beautiful *teocalli* on his back. The eldest Casasola brother was known and feared by the name El Pirámide.

It was always Bernardo's job to create the blueprints for Los Casasolas' next big business scheme.

When the month of Ramadan was over, the raucous celebration of Eid al-Fitr commenced, and on that July night, Valmiro had dinner at the Peruvian restaurant on Mangga Besar. It was on the first of a five-floor tenant building. Aside from a hookah lounge on the third floor, all the other spots were dedicated to the sex trade.

Valmiro was enjoying shrimp ceviche when he noticed Tanaka sitting at a table on the far wall. He was with another person, an Asian man in a necktie who was extremely drunk and wailing at Tanaka. Valmiro couldn't tell what he was saying, but it was probably in Japanese.

Eventually, the man passed out and dropped his head to the table. The impact bounced his plate up and onto the floor, where it cracked. Tanaka apologized in Spanish to the Peruvian waiter who came to scoop up the shards. The drunken man, who'd seemed completely unconscious, abruptly lifted himself and vomited onto the table. Then his head lolled downward again. Grimacing, Tanaka gave the waiter some money and apologized again, then propped up the sleeping man's vomit-stained face, loosened his necktie, and undid a few shirt buttons. Next, he squeezed the man's cheeks with his fingers to open his mouth and briefly shone a penlight inside.

Valmiro watched Tanaka's quick, economical work. It was the routing of someone familiar with how vomit blockages could suffocate. This was not an act of kindness or care but an emergency technician performing airway management.

Well, well. Valmiro's eyes narrowed. *Tanaka, the Japanese man.*

Tanaka leaned back in his chair, wiped his hands with a towel, and stretched his fingers like a pianist preparing for a concert, slowly curling them inward. He wiped sweat from his forehead and neck with a handkerchief and glanced around the restaurant. His gaze landed on Valmiro.

* * *

With some cold bottles of beer and an opener he borrowed from the waiter, Tanaka approached Valmiro's table. The two Bintang labels were aligned side by side.

"What a coincidence, El Cocinero," Tanaka greeted. "Or maybe it's not such a coincidence. After all, you were the one who told me about this place."

"It's a lot of work taking care of drunks," Valmiro said, eyeing the far table. "A fellow countryman?"

"I'd like to think I work to maintain the good reputation of the Japanese in Jakarta," Tanaka remarked with a laugh, "but this is ruining all my effort. I'm afraid that was quite a nasty scene."

They opened the bottles and began to drink without a toast. Outside, raucous voices sang in celebration of Eid al-Fitr. A Mexican passing himself off as a Peruvian and a Japanese man passing himself off as Tanaka listened to the revelry in silence, holding their beers.

The drunk Japanese man passed out on the table suddenly looked up. He gazed into nothingness with an expression of wonder, then limply squeezed his puke-stained tie, glanced around, found Tanaka drinking with Valmiro, and ambled over to their table.

"Oh, you found a new friend? Lucky you," the man said in Japanese as he came over. "You just sit there and chat, Tanaka-san. *I'm* gonna go have fun with girls."

The man had a map that displayed all the brothels in the Mangga Besar area. At these places, you could designate a woman to go out and about with you. Some of the businesses doubled as nightclubs or massage parlors, so you could have your fun there, too.

"Oh, yeah," said the man, who halted in his tracks and turned around. "How do you say 'Let's have sex' in Indonesian?"

"Mari jiki jiki," Tanaka answered, staring at the red star on the beer bottle.

The man lazily clapped him on the shoulder. "Nice," he leered. "And how do you say 'You're beautiful'? No, maybe 'I love you.'"

"Which one do you want?"

"Um, let's go with 'I love you.'"

"That's *aku cinta padamu.*"

The man fluttered off toward the door, muttering his newfound vocabulary words under his breath. Tanaka stood, paid the waiter, and walked off after his companion without waiting for change.

He seemed like an office worker forced to indulge his boss's drunken after-work exploits, or perhaps a pimp luring wealthy johns into doing business with his whores. But, Valmiro thought, neither of those likely hit upon Tanaka's true background.

He was hiding something. Valmiro needed to find out who his regular crack customer really was.

The next afternoon, Valmiro strolled through the city center of Jakarta, dressed in his best, and bought a copy of the English daily paper *Jakarta Chronicle* before heading to Plaza Indonesia, one of the most famous shopping malls in the city along with Grand Indonesia. After undergoing a security check, he entered a food court café and ordered an iced coffee and a quesadilla. The quesadilla didn't taste like one from Veracruz or Nuevo Laredo, but it still fit the definition of a quesadilla.

He opened the English *Jakarta Chronicle* and scanned through the public safety section.

"Indonesian National Police engage in firefight with heroin smugglers in Surabaya, kill one member of Chinese mafia"

"East Java police arrest internationally renowned English violinist in Bali cottage for possession and use of heroin"

"Joint BNN (Badan Narkotika Nasional) and Indonesian Navy search team seizes Filipino freight ship with one ton of methamphetamine off the coast of Batam"

"Jakarta police round up drug sellers lurking around Jakarta Kota Station, killing five suspects. One service member dies due to Pakistani-made grenade detonation"

A quick review of the morning edition while sipping his coffee was enough to make clear the immense heat of the drug business flowing under the country like magma.

Valmiro considered the contents of each article he read.

"Indonesian National Police engage in firefight with heroin smugglers in Surabaya, kill one member of Chinese mafia"

Was the slain mafia man from the Sun Yee On? They were the biggest Chinese criminal organization. Or maybe it was a 919 man. He'd met Sun Yee On people three times back in Mexico. Like the coyotes, they ran a business taking money from Chinese people who wanted to work in America and smuggled them through the Mexican border.

"East Java police arrest internationally renowned English violinist in Bali cottage for possession and use of heroin"

If a famous English musician was getting caught with heroin in this country, that was a sign of the quality of product that was available here. It had to be Golden Triangle heroin. Hip hop, rock, classical—whatever the genre, musicians big enough to go on world tours knew what the local delicacies were, in both drugs and food. The specialty here was cocaine, and across the border, it was heroin—that violinist had to be shitting bricks after getting caught in Asia. Had someone ratted him out? In any case, it was going to be a very costly vacation...

"Joint BNN (Badan Narkotika Nasional) and Indonesian Navy search team seizes Filipino freight ship with one ton of methamphetamine off the coast of Batam"

"Jakarta police round up drug sellers lurking around Jakarta Kota Station, killing five suspects. One service member dies due to Pakistani-made grenade detonation"

These two articles ought to be read as a set. A Filipino freight ship and Pakistani grenade painted a picture that even a child could understand. Islamic radicals were getting proactively involved in the Southeast Asian drug business, using it as a source of capital. Such groups were already well established in the Philippines, Pakistan, and the Indian Subcontinent.

Valmiro placed his tray on the return window and left the *Jakarta Chronicle* folded up over his partially eaten quesadilla. He departed the café and went down the escalator to the next floor of the shopping mall, thinking hard.

Indonesia was the biggest country in Southeast Asia, with a population over two hundred and sixty million—a tantalizing drug market. Cocaine made its way in from Afghanistan in West Asia, but it wasn't the finest quality. However, dealing in Latin American cocaine, given the transportation difficulty, would cause street prices to soar out of reach of most of that market and make stocking hard. It was a high-end good reserved only for a handful of wealthy enthusiasts.

Out of the biggest products—heroin, amphetamine, and *hielo*—the Golden Triangle's heroin was special. Poppies grown in Laos, Thailand, and Myanmar were treated to create morphine base, which was then refined into heroin. No. 4 was the finest heroin in the world and wildly popular. To get rich in the Southeast Asian drug market, you had to sell No. 4, but as the alternate name "China White" suggested, the Chinese *heishehui* controlled its flow. An unaffiliated lone wolf like Valmiro would never get to handle it. If he earned the trust of a Chinese triad, it might be a different story, but he didn't have time to work under the Black Societies and earn esteem the slow way doing dirty work. Valmiro wasn't Chinese, so they'd never trust him anyway. He would be ignored as soon as he walked in the door, leaving no greater impression than a fly buzzing around the room. But he also wasn't going to get any money unless he dealt with them in some way. It would take money to kill the Dogo Cartel. Money created power. He needed to find a new idea to earn.

As Valmiro reached the bottom of the escalator, the Oppo in his pocket rang.

The call was coming from an Australian in Jakarta who was getting dangerously hooked on amphetamines. Barry Grosse appeared to be a simple English teacher on the surface, but he was reasonably well known in the Jakartan underworld due to his great ability to perform personal background searches. Barry had worked for years as a private detective in Melbourne and sold his experience to underworld sources in exchange for a supply of speed. He had no moral compass, taking any job. He didn't care in the least if someone died as a result of his work, as long as he got his amphetamines.

"I've got your report on Tanaka," Grosse said in English. "He's been staying long-term at a business hotel. For at least a year. Doesn't seem to have any company housing or personal residence. The hotel isn't far from your cart. It's right along Mangga Besar."

"I see." Valmiro's voice was quiet, and he looked up at the EXIT sign as he walked. It wasn't particularly rare for businessmen to have long stays at hotels. The foot traffic outside Plaza Indonesia quickly swallowed Valmiro. "So is he, or isn't he?" he asked.

"He's not," said Grosse. "Not an undercover cop."

"You're certain?"

"I paid a new member of the cleaning staff to get into his room, and I waited for a reaction, but there was nothing. That means he's got no security cameras installed in there. An undercover man would never be that careless. I wound up with lots of footage of the room. I'll send you a video later."

"Good."

"And I went to great pains to get his real name. I can throw that in for another five thousand dollars' worth of bennies, as we agreed."

"I see," Valmiro replied. *Bennies* was a slang term for amphetamines.

"Okay. In that case, I'll make a deal with you for ten thousand dollars' worth of bennies."

"You're free to play hardball, but I haven't agreed to pay anything yet."

"Oh, but you'll buy what I've got. This is freshly caught primary information, straight from the source. I got the number of Tanaka's credit card and found the falsified name on his passport. From there, I made contact with a woman in the group that's counterfeiting passports and paid to have her look into Tanaka for me. All of this work costs me, you know, which is why my price has doubled. Honestly, I think it's worth three times as much, though. I cross-referenced with Japanese records."

"Send me the video first."

Valmiro hung up and waited for Barry Grosse's video to come through. It was a clip from the hotel cleaner's smartphone, searching tirelessly through the business hotel double room on Mangga Besar Road. A button-up shirt had been tossed in front of the mirror, German magazines were stacked on the nightstand, and a handwritten list contained the names of local prostitutes.

The camera went into the bathroom and found a glass pipe taped to the underside of the toilet tank lid. The pipe had soot marks here and there, evidence that Tanaka really was smoking crack with it. Unless he was trying to mislead a target in his presence, a police detective wasn't going to actively choose to get high. Dirty American cops were one thing; an Indonesian officer assigned to an undercover operation was extremely unlikely to betray his duties.

At the end of the video, Valmiro was convinced that Tanaka wasn't part of law enforcement. Beyond that, there was no reason for a Polda Metro Jaya officer to pretend to be a Japanese man. And if Tanaka were a detective sent from Japan, he would have no jurisdiction here. He couldn't act like he owned the place, the way DEA agents did when they stormed into Mexico from Texas to conduct operations.

Satisfied with the content of the video he watched on the Oppo, Valmiro took out one of his other phones, walked north toward Merdeka Palace, and called the young Javanese man who worked the cart for him

After receiving his instructions, the young man showed up on a motorcycle with a delivery bag for Mariking, a well-known local business. Inside the delivery bag was a plastic container with a fresh portion of cobra satay and ten thousand dollars' worth of speed.

Barry Grosse had a private room for English lessons near Sawah Besar Station. When the Mariking bag arrived, he checked everything inside it, then paid for only the cobra satay.

He waved at the bike as it sped off, then returned to his room. While chewing skewered Javan cobra, Barry Grosse encoded an English text file containing Tanaka's real name and personal history, then sent it to the email address Valmiro had given him.

17

caxtölli-huan-öme

Michitsugu Suenaga, who would never have guessed that his crack dealer knew his real name, passed through the crowds in West Jakarta.

He was dressed in his usual style—black-rimmed Effector glasses, a new half-sleeve buttoned shirt he'd just bought at the mall, coyote-brown short pants, and leather shoes with no socks. He carried a pair of neon orange sports shoes in one hand. Their laces were light green.

The throngs continued as far as you could walk, buzzing beneath the clouds of the rainy season. The population density here rivaled that of Tokyo. Through his lenses, Suenaga observed the traffic on Thamrin Road.

The three-in-one system intended to help ease traffic had only created a new street business called car jockeys, so it was promptly scrapped. Its replacement, the odd-even system, was based on the last digit of every license plate. Cars with plates ending in odd numbers could only pass through restricted zones on odd days, and even-numbered cars were permitted on even days.

Based on what he observed on Thamrin Road, Suenaga thought this new system was an improvement over the three-in-one scheme. Unlike the number of riders, you couldn't cheat your way without a different plate. Still, this method wasn't perfect. Some new issue was sure to arise eventually.

Suenaga turned his back on the road and headed down a one-way street. After a while, he spotted a three-wheeled *bajaj* coming his way. He held out the sports shoes, the sign to stop. In Indonesia, you didn't raise your arm to wave for a taxi or *bajaj*, you held it level.

He got in the *bajaj*, told the driver his destination, and started haggling over the price. When he first came to Jakarta, these drivers constantly took advantage of him, but now Suenaga had the upper hand. Compared to the black-market deals he'd seen many times, negotiating with drivers was just simple wordplay.

The *bajaj* trundled off, and Suenaga gazed at the passing people and vehicles. The seat was big enough that you could try to squeeze two people in, but it was really only meant for one. He breathed in a lungful of air mixed with exhaust, the breeze ruffling his shirt's collar and sleeves.

At last, I can extract the product tonight.

Reflecting on the troubles of the last week brought a sigh to his lips. Suenaga allowed the rocking of the *bajaj* to lull him into a quiet sense of release.

He was scheduled to remove the right kidney of a man named Yasushi Yamagaki. All the back-alley doctors in Jakarta who could remove the organ were booked, so Suenaga had to entertain Yamagaki, who'd flown in from Japan, until a surgery could be lined up.

The product couldn't be endangered. Suenaga should have forbidden Yamagaki from drinking and locked him inside his hotel room, but it was pointless to expect a man willing to sell his kidney overseas to respect a command to abstain from alcohol.

When Yamagaki got so drunk that he vomited in his sleep, Suenaga made sure that his airway didn't get obstructed and suffocate him. When he went out to enjoy the nightlife, Suenaga taught him dirty words in Indonesian.

An extremist Islamic terrorist organization in Indonesia was buying Yamagaki's kidney for the equivalent of one-point-six million yen, and they would sell it for more. Suenaga knew that the organ could command a maximum of four million at market. The profit would fund the organization's activities.

The fervor for organ selling in Southeast Asia was only growing, and Suenaga had seen much of it for himself. He'd witnessed filthy surgery rooms play host to illegal procedures and met the men who dealt with organ information on the dark web.

It cost less to get a child's kidney than an adult's. Impoverished children sold their kidneys to brokers without even negotiating the price. With the money they made from selling one of their two kidneys, the children could buy themselves a phone. It wasn't for games but to help them find work in the big city, which was impossible without a smart device. Selling an organ was the quickest way to buy one. If not that, they would hawk themselves to pedophiles.

Doctors who'd lost their licenses suddenly found themselves in great demand, and the schedules for black-market surgeries were as packed as those of big, legitimate hospitals. It was impossible to get around to all the procedures, and that had an effect on Suenaga's job as well. He'd been keeping Yamagaki occupied because there were no available surgeons.

The thought of the word *surgeon* made Suenaga laugh. It brought to mind the faces of the black-market doctors he'd gotten to know in Jakarta and their crude methods.

They aren't surgeons, Suenaga thought. *At best, they're more like* dismantlers. *I could take out a kidney if need be.*

Suenaga's job was to connect organ brokers in Japan to the Islamic extremists in Indonesia, using the darkness of Jakarta for cover. He considered himself to be an organ trade coordinator and strictly held himself to the boundaries of that position. He never, ever revealed to anyone that he was once a surgeon himself.

Cardiovascular surgeon. In the world of black-market organ trading, that title shone like a diamond. Suenaga knew quite well that if he let too much of his past come to light, others in the underworld would take a much greater interest in him. Terrorists, Black Societies, yakuza—the potential business partners in this line of work were all dangerous in their own way, and they wouldn't hesitate to abduct him the moment they learned of his background in surgery.

The "package" carrying the product around inside his torso, Yasushi Yamagaki, was a thirty-nine-year-old Japanese national, an accounting manager at a security camera manufacturer based in Tokyo's Minato Ward. Yamagaki had taken a paid leave and was staying at a business hotel on Mangga Besar Road.

Four years ago, when he turned thirty-five, Yamagaki first bought the synthetic drug MDMA on the dark web. He intended it to be a onetime thing, but it got its hooks in him. Pills, crystals—he took ecstasy in whatever form he could find it. The drug made him hear sound from all directions and feel like he was floating in space. Tripping became his reason for living, and he enjoyed getting call girls into his apartment and sharing E with them.

As authorities gradually cracked down on the market for synthetic drugs, the amount available dramatically decreased and the street price shot up. Yamagaki, who had become a heavy user, continued to spend his money freely on the drug, but at last his bank account went dry this year. He found cannabis to be a cheaper but unsatisfying replacement and decided that ecstasy was the only drug for him.

Instead of going into debt, Yamagaki's idea was to sell an organ. There were several people on the internet who'd sold a kidney to buy more MDMA. They said that it was better to sell a kidney than go into debt. It was a mindset that played into human desires. Once you thought to sell one of your organs for money, the notion elicited a kind of masochistic pleasure of death. Those who got off on fear found themselves reaching a natural high as the day of the surgery drew closer, although it still wasn't a replacement for actual drugs, if they had any.

In Yamagaki's case, it wasn't the pleasure that motivated him but the simple fear of debt. He didn't want things to get out of hand, and be forced to declare bankruptcy. He wanted to keep his job as an accounting manager.

He messaged a peddler he'd befriended and said he wanted to sell a kidney. After a few messages, the broker had determined that Yamagaki was serious, and said, "Fine, I'll show you to a back alley."

Yamagaki didn't understand the English term *back alley* until later, when he came to understand that it was short for "back-alley doctor," a surgeon who performed illegal operations. The broker pointed him toward a workplace in Kawasaki, a city in the Kanagawa Prefecture.

Most of the clients who visited the Kawasaki office of Kenji Nomura, a back-alley doctor connected to Michitsugu Suenaga, were junkies going through withdrawal or regular users on the verge of total addiction. Patients like that knew what drug tests or injection marks would reveal to a legitimate doctor and were afraid of being reported to the police, so they couldn't walk through the doors of a proper hospital.

Clients wary of criminal investigations might request a full blood transfusion—a frequent service. Nomura found it quite frenetic trying to stay stocked with blood packs.

He performed blood tests on clients who'd been shooting intravenously for years, did cardiopulmonary examinations, and executed lifesaving measures on people dragged in by friends after an overdose. Unlike when he was a properly licensed doctor, he had no nurses to help and was left to do everything by himself. And Nomura was not originally a doctor who saw patients individually.

Before he worked on the black market, Nomura was a doctor in the anesthesiology department as an associate professor at a university hospital in the Kansai area.

He abused his position to remove medical supplies and sell them in person to doctors at other hospitals for a little side income. The materials he peddled were used as drugs, so he was something like a dealer in the medical world. By the time the media was covering the dangers of fentanyl, Nomura had already used it several times himself and sold it to others in his profession. Fentanyl was an anesthetic used in heart surgery and was easy for a member of the anesthesiology department to acquire.

Once he'd sensed the danger of fentanyl, Nomura tried cocaine instead. The hospital didn't have a supply of that, so he had to get it from an actual drug dealer. He didn't pay cash, instead trading various chemicals he took from the hospital supply. The dealer was more than happy to exchange.

Many people used a rolled-up paper bill to snort cocaine. But in Nomura's case, he liked to cut a surgery schedule into strips and roll them up instead. Soon the powder had become a part of his daily life.

When the overuse of cocaine caused the collapse of his septum, he wore a surgical mask all day long to hide it. And when his nose grew even more misshapen, he had to visit a back-alley doctor, despite being a legitimate one.

On his day off, Nomura traveled to Kobe and paid a Korean doctor a large sum of cash for a septoplasty to reconstruct the cartilage between his nostrils.

It was October 2009 when Nomura was removed from the hospital. When his medical supply embezzlement was discovered, the hospital administration worked overtime to cover it up. It was a prestigious institution that worked on politicians and cabinet members, and they couldn't afford to lose their brand value. Nomura wasn't tried in court, and his activities were hidden from the media. Instead, the man was banished from the hospital; on paper, he submitted his own notice of resignation.

The name Kenji Nomura was put on a blacklist that silently circulated among the nationwide network of doctors, ensuring that he would never find work at a legitimate medical facility again.

The first thing that popped into his head was the Korean doctor he saw in Kobe. As he stared at his repaired septum in the bathroom mirror, he thought, *That fellow did good work. I bet he's gone through some stuff, too.*

Kicked out of the hospital, Nomura left Osaka behind and wound up in Kawasaki, Kanagawa, working as a black-market doctor. Not long after he started, a local yakuza member brought him a dead body. Nomura had made it clear to the gangsters that he was open for business, and he recognized the man who showed up.

"Doctor, take out his kidney," the yakuza member said. He looked at his watch. "Guy bit it two hours ago, so it should still be good."

Nomura looked at the fresh body. At first glance, it was impossible to tell if the death was a suicide, homicide, or accident.

"I was in anesthesiology," Nomura explained, "so I don't do surgery, as a general rule. At best, I can do a passable imitation of internal medicine."

"That's real good, Doc," the yakuza member replied. "You sound like you know what you're doing. Wouldn't guess that you'd just opened. Just charge us a special fee for it later."

He walked off, chuckling, leaving the body with Nomura.

With no other choice in the matter, Nomura put on a pot of coffee and stood there with a mug in his hand, gazing at the dead body. He was not ignorant of the organ market, of course. Sure, it was tough now, but if he was going to make good money as a black-market doctor, he'd have to work his way up to this sort of thing. Nomura had put together the tools he needed for that eventuality: scalpel, rubber gloves, stabilizers to hold the incision in place, a tray, and a wheeled tool cart. In addition to gathering the necessary items, he also perused German surgery websites with a drink in his hand, observing various methods of extracting organs. He'd been present for many extractions as an anesthesiologist and could tell what was happening on the screen even without an explanation.

If I just leave it here, it's only going to rot, Nomura reasoned, looking at the dead body the yakuza member left for him. *Maybe this is the best opportunity to take that first step.*

In order to preserve what little freshness he could, Nomura turned on the air-conditioning to lower the temperature inside. He removed the cadaver's clothes, then, on a sudden whim, checked for a pulse, inspected the pupils, and felt for breath. It was a slim chance, but Nomura would've felt terrible if the man were still alive. Once he was certain that the body was dead, he grabbed the scalpel, pressed it to the body, and performed a midline abdominal incision, severing skin and flesh.

The yakuza member eventually returned, wearing a fishing-tool-company hat and hauling a cooler over his shoulder. He stuck the two kidneys Nomura had removed into vinyl bags and inserted them into the cooler, which was lined with cold packs. "Hey, Doctor, do people like you dream of doing this sort of thing after reading *Black Jack*?"

"*Black Jack*?" Nomura said. "No, never read that manga."

"For real?" the yakuza member asked, aghast. "Have you read *any* of Osamu Tezuka's comics?"

"Only one," said Nomura. "When I was a medical student, I missed the last train and had to spend the night at a manga café. What was it called? I think it was *Gringo*."

"That's it? And that was the one he never finished drawing, too."

The yakuza member lifted the cooler, dropped an envelope with cash for the extraction, and left.

From that night on, Nomura removed kidneys from bodies brought to him. Additionally, he began experimenting with extracting corneas, which were also highly valuable.

When a seller introduced Yasushi Yamagaki, Nomura gave him a simple physical examination and didn't bother with anything else. He didn't have the surgical skills to remove a kidney from a living person, and in the Japanese organ trade, it was common sense that if a person could act of their own accord, it was best that they get the surgery done in Southeast Asia.

It was a simple matter of sending them out under the guise of an overseas vacation, then bringing them back when the organ was removed.

A major reason for this preference was that there were back-alley doctors in Japan like Nomura who could extract the organ from a donor (particularly dead ones) but almost none who were capable of transplanting the organ into a recipient.

The technical skills involved in extracting and transplanting were very different. Transplanting an organ was more difficult, and the organ trade required both ends of the business to actually make money. The organs were worthless without someone to pay to have them transplanted.

Southeast Asia was the place to find black-market doctors who did transplant surgeries. Rather than extract the organ and then go to the trouble of smuggling it to another country, it was much easier to just put the package himself on a plane to the source.

Nomura took Yasushi Yamagaki's passport, arranged a cheap flight, and contacted a coordinator in Jakarta, a man named Michitsugu Suenaga. He was a Japanese former cardiovascular surgeon who operated under the alias Tanaka, and he'd previously bought fentanyl from Nomura. Like Nomura, Suenaga had been kicked out of the Japanese medical world and was wanted by law enforcement as well.

Cardiovascular operations were the pinnacle of surgery, and when it came to carrying out a difficult procedure, the surgeon and anesthesiologist were an inseparable team. Nomura and Suenaga had belonged to different hospitals and never worked together legitimately. It felt like an ironic twist of fate that they found themselves linked in this way.

In terms of ability and future potential, Suenaga was far beyond Nomura. He was born to be a cardiovascular surgeon.

The *bajaj* carried Suenaga to a rock-climbing gym in West Jakarta. Suenaga paid the driver, opened the low door, and stepped out. It was just starting to rain.

The air-conditioning inside was pleasant. The gym was playing the popular Indonesian genre of dangdut over the speakers. The playlist was mostly new songs, broken up by the occasional 1970s sound and the voice of Rhoma Irama. He was a national star who came to prominence during the Suharto regime, popularly known as the "King of Dangdut."

The receptionist's head bobbed to Rhoma Irama's singing, and he smiled at the familiar Japanese visitor. Suenaga checked in with his membership (under a false name), and the receptionist already knew what size rental gear to give him. He changed in the locker room, put on the neon orange shoes, and tied the light green laces. You had to rent shoes here, which is why Suenaga brought his own. He forwent a simple Velcro set, opting for the laced kind that offered better fine support.

Rock climbing was growing popular in Indonesia, and there were many more members at the gym now than when Suenaga first enrolled. The holds were scattered across the wall face in colors that suggested paint splattered across a palette. Suenaga watched beginners yelp as they fell back to the mat while he performed some warm-up stretches and squeezed a chalk ball. He grabbed the vertical wall face with fingers dyed white with magnesium carbonate powder and lifted himself with pure arm strength, no legs. Using mostly side pulls, he reached the ceiling in less than a minute, then climbed back down with efficient ease—so practiced that it looked like he'd simply reversed a video of his ascent. Etiquette required him to move away from the wall, so he took a trip to the hydration area in the back corner. He waited for another part of wall to open up, then performed the same exercise, using only pinch holds to climb up, almost entirely on arm strength alone.

After his warm-up, he tackled the more difficult slab section and followed that with the overhang. The hundred-and-forty-degree angle was quite similar to the *dokkaburi* he tackled back home as a student. That was the term that Japanese climbers used to refer to an overhang on a cliff.

Once he'd conquered the *dokkaburi* and returned to the mat, Suenaga went back to the chalk ball, stared at his white fingers, and breathed deeply. Then he looked up at an even more challenging overhang on an adjacent wall. At the end of that slope was a hundred-and-eighty-degree world. In other words, it'd put you level with the floor. If you weren't stuck to the colored holds, it was nothing but a ceiling. Nobody in this gym attempted that wall, and naturally, there was no one waiting for it to open up, either.

Suenaga fought against gravity to get to the overhang, and when he reached the roof of it, his back was pointed directly at the ground below. He crawled along the roof with finger, arm, and core strength, dropping large beads of sweat. The staff and regulars at the gym called Suenaga "Laba-Laba," or "the Spider." Initially they called him "Manusia Laba-Laba," which was just Indonesian for "Spider-Man," but it was shortened to his present nickname.

Suenaga returned from the roof to the overhang corner, and carefully, methodically climbed back down. He was connected to ropes via a body harness, but Suenaga did not leave the wall to jump to the ground.

After a cooldown stretch and some toweling off, he went to the rest area on the third floor of the gym. He ordered a chocolate protein drink at the counter and added, "With water, not milk."

The staff member took out a plastic shaker, tossed in some chocolate-flavored protein powder with a measuring cup, then added chilled mineral water. He closed the cap on the container and began to shake it rhythmically.

While waiting for the protein to dissolve in the water, Suenaga tensed his quadriceps, touched his biceps, and shrugged to flex his traps. When that was done, he curled his fingers up one at a time and finished by moving them all at once in a game of invisible cat's cradle.

If he wanted to get back to where he used to be, it was absolutely crucial that he kept his finger sensation honed and his entire body strong enough to withstand extended periods of physical tension.

Being a cardiovascular surgeon was everything to Suenaga.

Such surgeries could sometimes last over ten hours. It was mentally and physically demanding, and a primary attending surgeon had to meet all expectations with unerring control to stave off death. The only thing that made this possible was powerful and delicate fingers. You needed core strength, too. If your muscles were screaming for relief, they were draining your concentration.

Suenaga refused to allow his condition to degrade to the point that he could never perform heart surgery again.

He'd stood at the pinnacle of medical surgery, preserved many lives that should have been lost forever, and received praise from everyone.

For his part, he felt no attraction to concepts like "saving lives" or "receiving the gratitude of patients." What Suenaga wanted was power; a different sort from politics or violence.

A person died when their heart stopped. The organ was a pump, powered by pulses from the sinoatrial node, which ran the circulatory system, keeping an organism alive. How was such a complex pump created? It had to be a miracle. Suenaga couldn't say if God existed or not, but at the very least, the perfection of the heart as a device was nothing short of divine design.

To understand the mysterious workings of the heart, remove its ailments, and keep the patient from death was akin to challenging God, in Suenaga's mind.

Exploiting his experience to fight battles in the surgical room made Suenaga feel that he was in close proximity to the sacred mysteries of the world. It gave him a sense of keen, peculiar power that resided only in himself.

He sat by the window in the rest area on the third floor of the climbing gym, observing the crowds of West Jakarta after the rain while drinking his protein shake. When he was finished, he poured some water into a paper cup and swallowed a creatine pill. He didn't bring his crack or cocaine into the gym.

Suenaga stared out the window. The many people were practically grappling with each other, all manner of ethnicities, genders, ages, each one with a visible *heart* in the middle of their chest. Repeating the cardiac cycle, as brilliant as the sun.

The blood that filled the lungs, left atrium, left ventricle, right atrium, right ventricle, red blood coursing through the body with no end, coronary arteries, carpal arteries, superior vena cava, mitral valve, tricuspid valve…

His eyes landed on a young man standing in the midst of the crowd, holding a smartphone to his ear. Looking down at the man, who wore a batik shirt that resembled a Hawaiian aloha one in style, Suenaga muttered under his breath.

"Will you let me extract your heart? Don't worry, I'll put it right back."

* * *

Smiling, Suenaga's eyes still pointed outside the window, but he no longer took in the sights. Instead, he focused on a shining scalpel in his mind. In his memories, he saw something only a cardio surgeon would: the cold illumination of the operating light shining upon the surgical field, where the entirety of fate was reflected, sewing with the finest of needles and thread, lulling Suenaga into a state of fevered bliss. There, he realized, *Whether this person lives or dies is up to me, the power is mine, I am face-to-face with this mysterious god.*

Suenaga had been chased out of Japan and sunk to being a coordinator for the black-market organ trade, but he still planned to return. He carried no intention of spending the rest of his life on the run around Southeast Asia, waiting to get buried. He had skill, so he'd go back—that was his conviction. The workplace of the cardiovascular surgeon was where he belonged. It was the only realm where he could sense his own power.

He wiped the remaining chalk dust from his fingers, unlocked his iPhone—a kind of status symbol in Jakarta—and called Yasushi Yamagaki's number.

After many rings, Yamagaki did not answer. He hung up, waited five minutes, and tried again. As the ringtone cycled hopelessly, Suenaga recalled the conversation he'd had with Yamagaki the night before.

"You got it? Your surgery is tomorrow night."
"I know," said Yamagaki. "You don't want me to eat anything."
"Right."
"But I can have a *little*, right? It's not stomach surgery."
"I'm not a doctor," Suenaga laughed, "so I won't tell you not to eat. You can go right ahead, but sometimes the contents of a person's stomach can come back up during anesthesia and block the windpipe. People have suffocated that way. As long as I get my product in the end, I don't care. What do you think? In exchange for getting to eat, we could play it safe and remove the kidney using local anesthesia instead. Want to try that?"

Yamagaki's expression shifted entirely upon the mention of local anesthesia. Suddenly, he didn't want to exchange his few remaining yen to enjoy the Jakarta nightlife. "I'll fast tomorrow," he promised.

Suenaga called and called, but Yamagaki never picked up. That hadn't happened at any point this week.

Something wasn't right. Suenaga left the rest area and headed down the stairs. He changed quickly in the locker room, then rushed out onto the street and hailed a motorbike taxi. The sunset cast a long shadow before the Honda bike driver.

Suenaga gave him the name of the business hotel on Mangga Besar. Yamagaki's hotel was across the street from Suenaga's.

"I'll pay you double," he told the driver. "Just make it quick."

18

caxtölli-huan-ëyi

Yamagaki was staying in a double room with two key cards, one of which was in Suenaga's possession. He inserted the thing in the reader slot without knocking and opened the door to Room 412.

Yamagaki, who should have been staying inside and fasting all day, was not there.

He ran out on me. It's not unheard of for people selling their kidneys to lose their nerve and run away when the moment arrives. But it's not all that common, either. These people are in this because they're desperate for money, after all.

Suenaga searched Room 412 thoroughly. He pored over the bathroom and closet and got down on hands and knees to peer under the beds. Junkies often squeezed themselves into tight spots.

The room hadn't been ransacked, and it seemed unlikely that Yamagaki had gotten into trouble.

Maybe he's gone off for a walk on his own.

Suenaga tried to call again from the hotel room, but Yamagaki still didn't answer.

He went to the front desk of the business hotel and introduced himself as Yasushi Yamagaki's personal lawyer and showed a picture of the man. Japanese lawyers weren't uncommon in Jakarta; in fact, they were increasing in number by the day. They stayed at legal offices and helped solve any issues involving Japanese companies in the city.

The receptionist didn't doubt Suenaga's story. She looked at the image of Yamagaki's face on the iPhone and said, "He left earlier. With another Japanese man, like you…"

Suenaga frowned. Japanese? Yamagaki had been with him until last night, and there shouldn't have been any other Japanese people in Jakarta that he knew.

"It's possible that he's being defrauded," Suenaga explained to the receptionist. "I want to know who he left with. It's a matter for the police, but he might be robbed if we don't act now. Can you show me any security footage?"

The receptionist accepted a hundred thousand rupiahs from Suenaga and went back to the security room. After sharing some of the money with the security guard on call, she got him to play back the video, used her smartphone to take a clip of the two men walking through the lobby, then returned. Suenaga couldn't hide his shock when he saw the footage.

Yamagaki was walking with Guiming Dai.

The man who fancied himself an important officer of 919, the powerful Chinese Black Society. Within the Jakartan underworld, nearly everyone knew he was a member of 919 but believed he was lying about being a lieutenant. He was an idiot who told stupid lies to preserve his ego, but he had money. Just another person with wicked leanings who was a little too stupid to be truly evil, the kind of person you could find in any country—any city.

Suenaga stared carefully at the video. Dai passed through the lobby with Yamagaki very casually; there was no sign that he was threatening him with a gun or knife. Dai probably told him he was part of the organ trade.

Based on this, Dai likely brought up the name Tanaka to convince Yamagaki to trust him, Suenaga thought. *But I never let Dai know I was an organ smuggling coordinator. Yamagaki wouldn't tell him, and he shouldn't have come into contact with Dai before this anyway. Why was Dai here? Was he prying into my affairs? When did he start sniffing around after me?*

If he had his glass pipe and a crack rock, he would have taken a hit to focus his thoughts. Powder cocaine would have done the trick, too.

There was only one reason Dai had lured Yamagaki out on this night, of all nights. Suenaga clenched his fists. He didn't want to believe it, but his product had been stolen out from under his nose. Dai knew everything and was going to sell Yamagaki's kidney to a different buyer. Perhaps he'd already sold it. If the transaction was already concluded, then it was all but game over. But the organ extraction schedules in Jakarta were completely jammed. It had taken this long just to line up a back-alley doctor. There was no way that Dai could find a surgeon to do the job after only just absconding with the goods.

A freezing line of sweat trickled down Suenaga's spine.

Whatever the truth, if he didn't get Yamagaki back tonight, he was going to be in breach of contract…

And then Guntur Islami will punish me.

They didn't accept excuses. They'd assume they'd been deceived; a wound to their warrior pride. Suenaga could offer them one of his own kidneys, but they'd never accept it. They'd say, "Shameless liar, give us your other kidney, too." In fact, they'd probably say, "Just give us *all* your organs."

Suenaga sat down on a sofa off to the side of the front desk, rested his chin on his fingertips, and closed his eyes. This had never happened before. He went through every possible remedy to the problem, but none of them seemed likely to help.

The tip of the Grim Reaper's frightful scythe was bearing down on his throat. There was no escape. Yet, in addition to the danger, Suenaga also felt curiously nostalgic, which mystified him.

After a few moments, he understood why. He was sensing something he'd experienced before—the extreme nerves that came just before going into an operation as a primary surgeon.

Feeling his past and present overlapping, Suenaga leaned back to look at the ceiling of the lobby. One man's face came to his mind.

After Tanaka contacted him, Valmiro walked to his *kaki lima* on Mangga Besar Road. The Javanese and Sundanese employees were dressing the cobras, beads of sweat on their foreheads, and placing the skewers on the grill amid the wafting smoke. The day's sales weren't bad. When Tanaka showed up, Valmiro gave him a bottle of Bintang and walked to the alley, like always. In the darkness, he sold Tanaka the number of crack rocks he wanted.

"El Cocinero," said Tanaka, handing him the money, "I want to hire you for a job."

Valmiro stared him in the face. The man didn't seem to have a clue that Valmiro had been snooping into his private business.

"I want you to recover something that was stolen from me," said Tanaka.

"I'd ask if I look like a fucking cop to you, but you seem too desperate for jokes," said Valmiro, taking a swig of beer.

"Dai stole a valuable product of mine."

"Dai... Guiming Dai?"

"I want the product back. When I say *product*, I mean *person*. A client of mine."

"A client, huh? Pretty sure I asked you about clients before..."

"If you help me, I'll make it worth your while."

Valmiro pulled a red pack of Djarum Super 16s out, popped a cigarette in his mouth, and lit it with an oil lighter. "What kind of client?"

"*Riñón*," Tanaka replied.

It had been years since Valmiro heard the Spanish word for *kidney*. He took a silent puff of tobacco. Barry Grosse's investigation had revealed Tanaka as an organ trader, but Valmiro pretended to mull over the information and exhaled slowly. "You an organ broker?"

"Not quite. A smuggling coordinator, to be precise."

"They're basically the same." Valmiro chuckled. "It's easy to find Dai. He shows up at his club every single night. You know that, right? He's the kind of guy who can't let other people handle his money. Go there and hash it out."

"You think a man who'd steal my client would admit it?"

"That's a good point," said Valmiro, putting on a straight face. "But why are you coming to me? I'm a food cart owner, a simple Peruvian who sells cobra satay and cheap crack."

"Your face popped into my head." Tanaka removed his glasses and wiped the sweat from his forehead. "It's a gamble. No matter how careful and thorough your planning is, it's impossible not to test your luck at some point. That's how life goes, doesn't it?"

"Very philosophical. So what are you betting?"

In reply, Tanaka grinned and ran his index finger level across his neck.

Valmiro fixed him with another stare. Someone who would offer his life without crying and wailing about it was worth teaming up with in the future. This was the kind of person he'd bought the cart and sold crack to find.

"What's your name?" asked Valmiro.

There was no more straightforward test of Tanaka's trustworthiness. Only one correct answer existed, and Valmiro already knew it.

"Michitsugu Suenaga," the man replied. "That's my real name. I'm not lying."

Beneath El Cocinero's dark gaze, Suenaga felt a strange, sudden fear that the man might just kill him, right here on the spot. It was a very odd and inexplicable intuition, but it was there. Suenaga did not pull his eyes away from the Peruvian's.

"Entiendo," Valmiro said, flicking the cigarette butt away. "Let's talk."

At a busy local Padang restaurant, the *narco y médico* sat across from each other. Valmiro knew who Suenaga was, but Suenaga still assumed the other man was from Peru.

Dai's nightclub didn't open until seven o'clock. Dai himself would show up an hour after opening. They needed to devise a plan before that point.

The Padang restaurant was run by Muslims and didn't serve alcohol, so Valmiro and Suenaga drank apple cider instead. After a bit, a waiter came by and simply placed the plates on the table. At this place, you ate what you wanted and paid for it at the end.

Valmiro washed his fingers in a little bowl of water with a thin lemon slice in it, then tore apart the fried fish, mixed it with rice on his plate, and added a heaping amount of *sambal*, a chili seasoning. Suenaga barely paid any attention to the food, nibbling at some thin fried shrimp chips and nothing more.

The *sambal* was so hot that tourists were guaranteed to gasp in agony, but Valmiro was unaffected by it. He was impressed with Suenaga, actually. Even if they were only little chips, it was notable that he could keep anything down at all. Plenty of people were sick to their stomachs all day once they knew their lives were in danger.

"Your client, your product," Valmiro said, dipping his fingers back in the water bowl now that they were covered with oil from the fried fish, "where did it come from, and where's it going next?"

"The product, or the product's *package*, was sent from the black-market doctor in Japan," Suenaga replied.

"As a living person?"

Suenaga nodded. "They came from a city south of Tokyo called Kawasaki. The Kawasaki doctors are under the orders of the local *mafia japonesa*. When the package arrived in Jakarta, I was supposed to handle it, find a surgeon, then hand over the *riñón* to the buyer and receive my finder's fee."

"If you lose the product, will the Japanese mafia kill you?"

"I can hide from them in Jakarta," Suenaga said, his voice low. "The ones who will kill me for breach of contract are the buyers. Guntur Islami."

Everything from this point on was new information that hadn't turned up in Barry Grosse's search.

Guntur Islami was Indonesian for "Thunder of Islam."

"Never heard of them," said Valmiro.

"Do you know a group called the Jemaah Islamiyah?"

"I know a little," Valmiro replied, but the truth was that was quite familiar. The cartels knew about the terrorist groups and vice versa. They shared at least one thing in common, which was a deep hostility toward the international activities and agencies of the United States.

Following the disbandment of Darul Islam, which sought to create an ideal Islamic state in Southeast Asia, Jemaah Islamiyah, which meant "Islamic Congregation" in Indonesian, was born in 1993. This new group was designated a terrorist organization by the American Department of Defense in late 2002.

Thanks to their training in the Philippines, their military power was considerable, and they committed many terrorist actions within Indonesia. The Jakarta bombings on July 17, 2009, which hit two luxury hotels, were the act of a faction within the group. They'd been lying low since 2009, but in 2014, their weapons factory was discovered and seized in Central Java, which led to the group's collapse.

That was everything Valmiro knew about them.

Apparently, Jemaah Islamiyah's former members had started a splinter group, Guntur Islami, which was new information to Valmiro.

"Have you ever met an officer of the group?" he asked Suenaga.

"No."

"Didn't think so."

"A man named Martono gets in touch with me."

"How do we contact him?"

"He calls me."

Valmiro scooped up a spoonful of gray soup. There was an unfamiliar kind of wild grass floating in it. "Does Dai," he asked, "know who your business partner is?"

"If he knew, it wouldn't have come to this. He made this decision on his own."

"You're certain?"

"I've checked with 919. There's nothing the Chinese *heishehui* or Islamic radicals stand to gain by fighting each other in Jakarta. If Dai causes business damage, I'm the one who'll pay the price for failing to handle the kidney."

Valmiro nodded, finished his apple cider, and asked the sale value of the kidney. When Suenaga told him, he then asked about the resale value. Suenaga told him. Both numbers were small by the cocaine business's standards.

Valmiro shrugged. "You said that coming to me for help was a gamble. What do you gain by winning this gamble? Surviving to see tomorrow? What is it that you hope for?"

After getting his medical license in Munich, Suenaga returned to Japan to work in the cardiovascular department at the Tohoku Cardiology Center, where he was a primary surgeon constantly on the clock.

He performed challenging operations, including simultaneous coronary bypasses on two separate patients due to an admissions error. Additionally, he completed an extremely rare heart-lung transplant on a patient with Eisenmenger syndrome.

Failure is not an option. It is absolutely unacceptable.

Suenaga dealt with the mental pressure that every primary surgeon labored under by taking cocaine. He was careful to hide any signs of his regular use. Aside from snorting it, he used a glass pipe, injected it no more than once every three days, and made sure to dispose of the waste among the medical center's trash, which was protected by stringent security.

Suenaga first used cocaine while studying in Munich; the dealer called it *schnee*, or snow. He went to a club that shook with the rattle of underground noise, and in the bathroom, all the kids were doing *schnee*.

Back home, Suenaga heard rumors about an anesthesiologist at a university hospital in Kansai. All the doctors who wanted an escape from pressure and were willing to buy fentanyl to address that need knew to go to Kenji Nomura.

Suenaga bought fentanyl at first as well, but after asking if Nomura had any cocaine, Nomura was able to arrange a source and sell that, too.

Street prices of cocaine in Japan were about four times higher than in

Germany, and when passed through Nomura's hands, those jumped to about six times. Still, it was much safer than dealing with street-level dealers.

When Nomura's medical supply embezzlement was uncovered, Suenaga was terrified. *What if he feels aggrieved about being caught and rats us all out?*

Contrary to that concern, Nomura did not reveal a single name from the list of doctors he sold drugs to. He chose to maintain his trustworthiness. The cheap supply of fentanyl, a controlled medical substance, was gone. But the doctors who bought the cocaine secondhand from Nomura, including Suenaga, continued their relationship with him afterward.

On the clandestine decision of the college board, the scandal was kept quiet, and Nomura was allowed to quit his position "voluntarily." Because of that, he lost his job but not his license. The incident was never on the books, so as far as the medical bureaucracy was concerned, nothing had ever happened. However, his name was on the hospital blacklist that circulated nationwide. He was banished from the legitimate medical profession.

Suenaga continued sending cocaine money into a fake bank account, but internally, he mocked Nomura's fate. It was all a big joke. He still had a legit medical license, but he was going to work like an unlicensed doctor.

Suenaga still received packets of cocaine from Nomura. He still boldly challenged the wall of cardio surgery, the same way one would attempt an overhang when rock climbing.

On Monday, April 29, 2013, his undoing came swiftly.

After a fourteen-hour heart transplant for a patient with dilated cardiomyopathy, Suenaga removed his isolation gown, showered, and went to the medical center parking lot to get into his car, a red Porsche 718 Cayman.

No sooner had he turned on the engine than he set down a line of coke on the dashboard and snorted it. He promptly hit the gas and left the parking lot to drive through Sendai. When he had to stop and wait at a light, he took another bump.

On Kakyoin Street, he hit a boy on a bicycle coming in from the left. It was 4:47 AM. The bike flew into the air and violently spun when it hit the asphalt. He thought he saw sparks fly.

Suenaga took his foot off the pedal, but the Porsche 718 Cayman followed the law of inertia and kept going. He never actually touched the brake. The next thing he knew, the boy and his bike were small in the rearview mirror. He sped up again.

The extreme exhaustion of an all-day surgery, the elation of the coke, the shock of the accident.

He fled Sendai in the middle of the night.

If I saved one life with a heart transplant, does that cancel out taking another? Probably not. Will I get charged with vehicular manslaughter? They'll certainly take my medical license away. Surgery is everything I have, but I'll never get to be a doctor again. In which case…

What do I even need to atone for?

The fourteen-year-old boy who died in the hit-and-run was crossing a green light on his way to go fishing.

The Miyagi Prefectural Police studied the traffic camera footage and placed thirty-eight-year-old cardio surgeon Michitsugu Suenaga on the nationwide wanted list. He was wanted for vehicular manslaughter, which, under the most recent law passed in 2001, carried a maximum of twenty years in jail.

Despite the outrage in the news, and the growing search by the police, Suenaga stayed loose and on the run. He reached out to his cocaine contact, Kenji Nomura, and got on a ship at Hachinohe heading for the Kanagawa Prefecture. In the port of Kawasaki, he met up with Nomura and passed him some cash, securing an escape route to Southeast Asia. Suenaga stowed away on a high-speed boat to Korea, then switched to a container ship that passed through Taiwan on the way to a country south of the equator.

My wish is to go back to being a heart surgeon.

When Suenaga revealed his desires to Valmiro in the noisy, crowded Padang restaurant, the other man made a show of being surprised by this knowledge, despite the fact that Barry Grosse had already told him about it.

Suenaga knew he couldn't go back to being a legitimate doctor. What he wanted was not to be some cheap, back-alley doctor in an inadequate substitute for an office, but to return to the finest possible surroundings, with the newest equipment, sticking his scalpel into the human heart. In pursuit of that, he used his experience as an organ trade coordinator in Jakarta to plan a big business move.

Valmiro wasn't the only one looking for an understanding, trustworthy partner. From the moment he first bought crack from him under the name Tanaka, Suenaga intuited that El Cocinero was a man who could be brought over to his side. And unlike Valmiro, Suenaga had a clear vision for what to do next.

The *médico* spoke, and the narco listened. The plan caused their fates to intertwine, locked in the promise of violence. It was a grand plan like none ever conceived before. Big business. *El mejor.*

The word *narco* was short for *narcotraficante.* But after joining in Suenaga's vision, Valmiro began to refer to himself and his new partner as *corazón traficantes* instead. Heart traffickers.

19

caxtölli-huan-nähui

When Dai's Jaguar XJ stopped in front of the nightclub on Mangga Besar Road, children came running out of the side alley and threw rocks at the back of the vehicle.

As Valmiro had instructed when paying them, the kids aimed only for the rear bumper and didn't hit the windows. He told them not to do that, because if they broke his rear windshield, Dai would assume he was being shot at and speed away in the car instead.

Hearing something hit his bumper, Dai swore and got out of the Jaguar. As usual, he had eighteen-karat-gold earrings in both ears and wore an expensive batik shirt. When Dai circled around the back of his vehicle, Valmiro snuck up behind him wearing a ski mask and struck him on the head with a sack full of rocks. Because the bag didn't reflect light, he never saw it coming, and the material absorbed most of the sound.

Valmiro promptly dumped the rocks out of the sack, then used it to cover Dai's head as he toppled forward. He used plastic restraints to bind Dai's arms behind his back and dragged the man out of range of the nightclub's cameras. Dai was lobbed into a Chevy Trailblazer off to the side, and the SUV sped off.

The Trailblazer had a false license plate. Since Jakarta instated the odd-even policy for easing traffic, the license plate–counterfeiting business had gone into overdrive, and it was easy to get them.

Suenaga kept an eye on Dai in the back seat, while Valmiro drove the Trailblazer to the southeast. They went down a back alley close to Jatinegara Flea Market and stopped the car there.

You could find anything for sale at the flea market. All kinds of goods, tools, and especially animals were for sale. Owls, rabbits, iguanas, ducks, and frogs were all watching the crowds from their cages, adding to the marketplace din with their own voices.

A black Toyota HiAce sat in the alley. A man stood next to it; a Malaysian dealer Valmiro was on good terms with, and he'd requested the HiAce as a transfer vehicle. Valmiro exited the Trailblazer, exchanged a few words with the Malaysian, then peered into the HiAce to see whether or not the tools he wanted were in there.

Satisfied, Valmiro paid the man, and he and Suenaga dragged Dai out of the Trailblazer and into the back seat of the HiAce. Under the burlap sack, Dai grunted a bit. He was coming to, if just for a bit.

Once in the HiAce, the trio traveled part of a mile east of the market. Suenaga marveled at El Cocinero's thoroughness in switching vehicles after the one with the faked plate.

The HiAce stopped at a warehouse that mainly stored junked home appliances. Valmiro typed a number into a keypad and opened the shutter, then drove the car inside.

With the sack over his head and his hands bound behind his back, Dai shouted and struggled as he was lowered from the HiAce. Valmiro punched him through the sack, smacked him on the nose, and violently dragged him out of the car. Dai scraped along the concrete, kicking his legs and shouting about something. The hard plastic of the restraints cut into his wrists and split the skin; blood oozed over the bindings.

Valmiro yanked Dai up and into a chair left in the warehouse, then used some industrial rope to quickly tie Dai's legs to the legs of the chair. A centipede hiding on the back of the scrapped chair crawled away quickly.

When the sack came off, Dai glared at Valmiro and Suenaga furiously.

"I'm gonna kill you both," he said in Indonesian. "I'll cut your families to pieces."

He also said the same thing in Mandarin.

Valmiro examined him coolly and asked where Yamagaki was in Indonesian.

Dai only smirked.

Valmiro put on some leather gloves and punched Dai in the face. Right, left, right. The corner of the eye, the nose, the cheekbone, the temple, the lips, the chin. Dai's cheeks split, and wet blood splattered around the chair. His right eye swelled until it was closed, and his nose was broken and bent at a strange angle.

Suenaga just watched. El Cocinero was pounding the man the way that he prepared cobra at his stand. It was something Suenaga couldn't do.

"We'll kill you," Dai menaced, spitting blood. "919 will tear you both limb from limb."

Even with his face beaten to a pulp, Dai remained defiant.

Valmiro paused in his torture, took off the leather gloves, and drank a Bintang he'd brought along. In Spanish, he said to Suenaga, "If he's not going to talk after this, he's not going to talk at all. I'm surprised."

"What should we do?" Suenaga asked quietly.

He was also surprised that Dai was holding out strong through such torment. Whether because of his gangster's wicked pride or something else, it was an impressive showing. If they hadn't looked it up beforehand, they might have thought that Dai genuinely commanded the might of 919. Dai's breathing was heavy. A sticky clump of blood from his nose ran over his broken lip, then down and off his chin, painting a bold new mark on his colorful batik shirt.

"Loosen up his right arm and nothing else," Valmiro instructed.

He handed Suenaga a box cutter and duct tape. Suenaga was initially confused by the duct tape, if not the cutter, but he quickly figured it out. If he just cut the restraints, both arms would be free and Dai would start swinging wildly. So he first tied down Dai's left wrist to the chair leg, then used the box cutter to cut the band holding both hands together.

Dai promptly and helplessly swung his right arm around.

Valmiro brought a desk forward from the back of the warehouse, dropped it in front of Dai, said, "Hold down his free arm," and returned to the HiAce.

Suenaga forced Dai's right arm against the desktop, ignoring his wails, and thought, *He's going to pull the nails off.* He'd seen that kind of torture in movies but never in real life.

Exhausted, face downward, Dai muttered, "I'll kill you. Don't even bother begging for your lives."

Guiming Dai stole a kidney that was meant for Guntur Islami.

If those words came from a simple Japanese organ trade coordinator, 919 would not pay him any mind. There was no evidence behind it. But if they heard it from Xin Nan Long, another major Chinese *heishehui*, they would have no choice but to sit up and take heed.

Xin Nan Long was a group of young Indonesian-born Chinese, established in 2011. They came up with new and creative ways to do their business and expanded their territory around Jakarta to the point that they began to rival Hong Kong triads like Sun Yee On and 14k in prominence. As proof of membership in the group, they all had tattoos of Komodo dragons. The massive lizards, which only lived on the island of Komodo in the East Nusa Tenggara province, symbolized the roots of the organization.

Xin Nan Long had a tight connection to the terrorist group Guntur Islami, also based in Jakarta, and they worked together on crypto-based drug and smuggling projects to raise funds.

Since becoming an organ running coordinator in Jakarta, Suenaga had to pay close attention to the activities of both groups. The more he sold kidneys to Guntur Islami, the more he learned about them, bit by bit. After carefully examining that information and tracing the connections, he eventually got to know Jingliang Hao, a lieutenant of Xin Nan Long. This was a major step forward for Suenaga.

The twenty-eight-year-old Hao was prized within the organization for his business talent, but before that, he had been a foot soldier with dozens of kills and led a combat team for the group. He liked mountain climbing, a common interest that Suenaga used to his advantage. Hao told him, "Climbing mountains made it easy to carry a body over one. You get what I mean?"

Suenaga had contacted Hao earlier and explained his problem. Hao then reached out to 919 and informed them of what Dai had done.

Hao had confirmed with a lieutenant of 919 that Dai's taking Yamagaki was a solo stunt and told Suenaga, "We'll have to abduct Dai to get our product back."

919 didn't trust Dai in the least, and if his proceeds from the nightclub dropped even slightly, they planned to use that as an excuse to kill him.

"919's our enemy," Hao told Suenaga after talking with the rival triad, "but now they owe me one. They don't want to wind up as targets of a suicide bombing, after all."

Unbeknownst to Dai, he'd been excommunicated from the group, and 919 had requested that Hao "clean up the situation in a way that doesn't leave any bad blood with Guntur Islami."

The responsibility for that part fell to Suenaga, which was why he'd reached out to El Cocinero for assistance. Such was the sequence of events leading up to Dai's capture.

Suenaga was determined to use this opportunity to carve out a position for himself between Xin Nan Long and Guntur Islami. That was the only way to bring about the business he envisioned.

And Dai, beaten and bloodied, held the key to that future.

I've got to take this gamble, he thought. *I have to make Dai confess where Yamagaki is.*

El Cocinero returned from the HiAce with a device very different from the nail-pulling implement Suenaga had envisioned. It was a long, thin canister, like an elongated fire extinguisher. The metal surface was green.

Valmiro dragged over the canister, which read LIQUID NITROGEN on the side. He was wearing a belt with an industrial steel hammer on it. These, too, were items the Malaysian procured.

He placed the canister of liquid nitrogen on the desk, just next to Dai's right arm. It sounded like a boulder rolling. He grabbed the hose, turned the valve, and brought the nozzle right up next to the arm.

"Stop!"

Dai bellowed with fear, but Valmiro's expression was unmoved. He sprayed the liquid nitrogen as calmly as if it were insecticide.

Negative-three-hundred-and-twenty-degree gas shot from the nozzle, creating an instant blizzard chill on top of the desk. Airborne particle matter froze white, and Suenaga had to release Dai's arm to keep his fingers from being severely frostbitten.

Dai felt as though his entire arm was being burned to a crisp; he emitted an unearthly scream. His eyes bulged, fixing on one empty spot and going still, creating the impression that they'd frozen like his arm. The affected limb lost all sensation and grew horribly discolored as the cells broke down and the blood and vessels froze within the flesh.

"Vigilalo."

Valmiro grabbed Dai by the hair and lifted his head. He pulled the industrial hammer from the belt and struck Dai's frozen arm with it. It made a strangely wet sound, like breaking a clump of snow, and from the elbow down, the arm simply crumbled to pieces. There was no time to spend slowly tormenting him.

After losing his arm in a manner of seconds, Dai tearfully admitted everything.

In February 2015—last year—a Japanese man named Daichi Motoki came to Dai's nightclub in Mangga Besar. Drunk and surrounded by women, he waited for his companion, Tanaka, to get up and leave for a minute before revealing to Dai, "He's involved in the organ trade."

Dai was already familiar with Tanaka to an extent, but this was new information.

Motoki, like Yamagaki, was a package that had been sent to Suenaga from Japan. As scheduled, Motoki lost a kidney, got his money, and went back home.

In other words, Dai had known of Suenaga's business for a year.

And tonight, Dai used Tanaka's name to earn Yamagaki's trust, then he lured him away in the hopes of selling the kidney to a wealthy Singaporean investor undergoing peritoneal dialysis. He intended to kidnap Yamagaki and take him to a back-alley doctor to get the operation done while the investor rode a high-speed boat to Batam. That was the idea.

But he hadn't considered how all facets of his plan fit together, and he'd completely failed to comprehend the depth of the darkness at his back. Dai was overconfident in his ability and believed he was intelligent, powerful, a meticulous planner, and an excellent businessman.

The Chinese proverb *ren wu yuanlu, bi you jinyou* meant, "He who gives no consideration to what is far off is sure to find trouble close at hand." This perfectly embodied the reason the organization did not trust Guiming Dai or his judgment and why Valmiro's torture had him within an inch of losing his life.

When Dai was done talking, Valmiro ripped the earrings out of his ears, checked the purity of the gold, and wiped off what little blood was smeared on them with Dai's batik shirt. Then he tied a towel around the stump of Dai's right arm to stop the bleeding and wrapped the elbow in a plastic bag to keep it from oozing all over the car. Lastly, the burlap sack went back over Dai's head; the same way he'd come in.

Suenaga helped Valmiro drag Dai back into the rear seat of the HiAce. Just to be sure, he asked, "We're taking him with us?"

"If it turns out he was lying," Valmiro pointed out, "the left arm is next."

He closed the sliding door, hunched down at the front bumper with a Phillips-head screwdriver, and started exchanging the license plate.

Suenaga watched the extremely thorough and cautious man work. He glanced back at the desk where Dai's arm had been shattered and saw a sherbet of blood, flesh, and bone rapidly melting in the hot, swampy air of the warehouse.

That's brutal, Suenaga thought. *Peruvian-style torture tactics? This man, El Cocinero, is as dangerous a viper as anyone in Xin Nan Long or Guntur Islami. What the hell was he doing before he wound up in Jakarta? I don't know anything about his past. And I don't have time to look into it. I just have to bet that he knows what he's doing.*

Valmiro finished affixing the new plate, then tossed the old one onto a pile of junked appliances in the corner of the warehouse. A high-pitched metal *clank* bounced off the walls, repeating a few times as the plate fell. Eventually, silence returned.

20

cempōhualli

The HiAce drove down the road from Kota Station to Jakarta Bay, stopping in front of a seven-story building. Valmiro and Suenaga went into Room 613, and just as Dai had told them, Yasushi Yamagaki was there. He was lying down on an old sofa, the cushioning poking out of rips in the old leather, looking worried.

"Took you long enough," said Yamagaki. "I haven't eaten a thing, and I was afraid I'd starve."

He sounded bemused and relieved to see Suenaga again, but when he noticed Valmiro behind him, his eyes bulged and he clamped his mouth shut. Valmiro had a black bandana around his face, leaving only his sharp, searching eyes visible. The business plan had already begun. Valmiro couldn't let Yamagaki see his face if the man was scheduled to go back to Japan alive after his kidney extraction. They'd met once at the Peruvian restaurant, but Yamagaki had been wasted and probably didn't remember. Valmiro had almost no interest in the man; he glanced quickly around the barren apartment instead.

When Yamagaki got into the back seat of the HiAce, his face blanched with fear. There was a man already inside the vehicle, and his right arm had been severed. Blood pooled in the plastic bag wrapped around the wound. And he recognized that it was the very person who'd come to see him at the business hotel.

"Tanaka, what is this?"

"Exactly what it looks like," Suenaga explained. "He's injured. We're going to the doctor now, and we're taking him with us. It's faster than calling an ambulance."

"Hang on, are you being truthful with me? I'm not in danger, am I?"

"Yamagaki-san," said Suenaga. "Do I look young to you?"

"What?"

"I asked if I look young to you. Just so you know, I'm your senior."

The sliding door slammed shut, and the HiAce drove away.

The doctor removed Yamagaki's right kidney, and the patient was moved to a bed by the window. Once he awoke from the anesthesia, the plan was for Suenaga to deliver him to the business hotel on Mangga Besar Road.

The doctor got up and left when the procedure was complete, but Valmiro and Suenaga remained. They weren't just waiting for Yamagaki to awaken; there was something else more important. The men privy to Suenaga's business plan had yet to arrive.

The surgery room was on the second basement of a brand-new tenant building, with a legitimately licensed dental surgeon and cosmetic surgery clinic on the ground floor. There was no secret passageway to get to the basement area; they just took the elevator down.

Someone else was lying on the operating table where Yamagaki had been just an hour before. It was the naked body of Guiming Dai, faceup, dead from blood loss after his arm was shattered.

The contact from Guntur Islami, Martono, arrived in the underground operating center, along with a man from the group's headquarters. His name was Zulmendri. It was the first time Suenaga had seen a principal member of Guntur Islami in person. Like Valmiro, Zulmendri was wearing a bandanna around his face.

Shortly after the terrorists' arrival, Jingliang Hao from Xin Nan Long appeared with a bodyguard. When he saw that both Zulmendri and Valmiro were wearing similar black bandannas, Hao smirked and touched his cheek. "I suppose I should have worn a garuda mask."

The garuda was a mythical bird from Indian mythology and was the centerpiece of Indonesia's coat of arms.

Valmiro, Suenaga, Zulmendri, and Hao stood around the dead body on the operating table. The others stepped back.

Their conversation took place in English. After speaking his turn, Suenaga left the room.

While waiting for Suenaga to return, Hao leaned closer to the gruesome stump of Dai's right arm and examined it with fascination. He said to Valmiro, "That's not explosive damage. What did you use?"

"Liquid nitrogen," he answered through the bandanna.

Hao was laughing loudly when Suenaga reentered. The organ broker was wearing a light blue cap, a surgical gown, latex gloves, and a surgical mask with head straps rather than ear loops.

In front of an audience of monstrous, dangerous men, Suenaga was going to exhibit his skill as a cardiovascular surgeon. He revealed his full name and told them his background in Japan. He even admitted that he'd received cosmetic surgery on his eyes and nose while in Jakarta. The truth was necessary to earn their trust and their investment. The final piece to gaining their confidence was showing what he could do.

He would've preferred to show them a high-stakes heart transplant, but he didn't have an anesthesiologist or perfusionist in a black-market scenario like this. Besides, Dai was dead. And he wasn't merely brain-dead, but completely expired—no bodily function at all. He wasn't breathing, and his heart was still. A stopped heart had no worth as a product.

Instead, Suenaga was going to demonstrate a simulated extraction using a cadaver. He wasn't just going to take it out but extract it for transplant use, as though Dai were not actually dead.

Suenaga reached out with a gloved hand and flicked on the LED light over the table. Although not a surgical light, it was still better than an incandescent one. He used a razor to shave the body's chest and spread a surgical sheet over it. Instead of the back-alley doctor's scalpels, he used a brand-new German-made one and cut a vertical slit in the chest. Then he used an oscillating saw to quickly sever the sternum vertically.

I see, thought Valmiro, watching the work carefully. *I always cut across the sternum with my knife when I took out a heart. But a professional surgeon does it vertically.*

This was the first time Valmiro had seen a cardio surgeon perform a medial sternotomy with his own eyes.

No nurses were handing over equipment. Suenaga was reaching over to a tray of steel instruments to get them by himself.

Retractor. Bone forceps. Tweezers. Muscle hooks.

The lack of help was not a problem. Even if this was just a simulation with a corpse, he'd finally taken a step back toward his old life. He cut open the pericardium, and when he saw the heart, Suenaga got goose bumps. He felt a kind of elation that even cocaine could not provide, and his hands worked faster than before.

Imagination. The dead heart beat powerfully, pushing the blood along. He could hear the blower keeping the surgical site clean of blood.

The tension. The heat.

Suenaga spoke in Japanese.

"Ligaturing the superior vena cava."

He did so quickly and efficiently.

"Clamping and severing the inferior vena cava in preparation for lung extraction."

Suenaga stopped the blood from flowing into the heart, checked a blood pressure monitor that didn't exist, and confirmed that the aortic pressure had dropped. He looked for where the ascending aorta and brachiocephalic artery split, placed his clamps there, and instructed the perfusionist to administer cardioplegic solution.

He treated it as a tense and serious simulation from start to finish, like a mock battle without live rounds that was still as close to actual combat as possible. When he was done, Zulmendri nodded with satisfaction, and Hao applauded.

They had found a real cardiovascular surgeon worthy of being a future business partner.

After Hao and Zulmendri left the operating room, Martono the messenger whispered into Suenaga's ear, "Brother Zulmendri has a message for you: 'I have some training in surgery. If anything you had done was unnatural in any way, I would have killed you on the spot and sold all of your organs.'"

It sounded like a bad joke but was likely the unvarnished truth. Suenaga laughed it off.

Only Valmiro and Suenaga remained at Dai's table.

Five minutes later, a new package selling another kidney was brought in. The Javanese doctor finished a Red Bull, popped a piece of gum into his mouth, and got to work extracting the unconscious woman's kidney.

After seeing Suenaga's earlier performance and comparing it to the man working with beads of sweat on his forehead, Valmiro could tell the enormous difference between the two, even without knowing anything about medical operations.

The heart Suenaga removed went into a basin.

"What is this liquid, water?" asked Valmiro.

"It's zero-point-nine percent saline solution. It's made to have the same osmolarity as human blood and tissue fluid. If the heart were alive, we would fill the basin with ice water to chill it."

Suenaga observed the way that El Cocinero picked up the heart out of the saline with his bare hand, as casually as palming an apple. It was a familiar motion for him.

He's not going to eat it, is he?

Suenaga frowned, but El Cocinero did something even more unexpected.

He placed the heart on Dai's face and began to mutter under his breath.

What he could hear was not Spanish. It wasn't English either, or Indonesian.

"What did you say?" Suenaga asked.

"I prayed to God," Valmiro replied.

21

cempöhualli-huan-cë

"The heart is the diamond of the body, El Cocinero.

"Blood capitalism.

"Of all the countless goods that flow through that red marketplace, the heart commands the highest price.

"A fresh heart sits atop that pyramid.

"Any doctor good enough to extract a heart and place it in another body can make millions of dollars on the black market.

"That's a person that the *heishehui* and terrorists would kill to get their hands on. If I were on their side, I'd want me, too. You seize a doctor like that, control him with violence, and make sure he does the surgeries.

"You've got a pair of kidneys, right? The difference there is that you only have one heart. One for each person. Nobody's born with two. When there's a heart transplant, it means that whoever's donating the heart is already dead.

"In the world of the light, hearts can only be removed from donors who have been declared brain-dead. A recipient in need of a new heart can only wait for a donor to show up. They have to wait for someone to go brain-dead. And there is a strict legal definition of brain death.

"Once all of the requirements are met, the heart doesn't just immediately come to you.

"For each donor, there is an endless list of recipients in waiting. They die in that queue. Happens all the time.

"However, El Cocinero, there are people in the world who resist the waiting game. The ultra-wealthy, for example. They hate delays. They despise the concept. After all, what is their wealth but a shortcut through every process?

"If their sons or daughters are guaranteed to survive with a heart transplant, the rich can't tolerate the thought of standing in line. It's impossible. They've always taken the shortest possible route. So they come to the organ brokers instead.

"'I want to buy a heart,' they say.

"But it's not easy to get a heart. It's much harder than getting a kidney, which you can extract safely from a living person.

"Someone's life has to be sacrificed.

"And you can't wait for brain death to be declared.

"You have to kill them.

"I've seen all kinds since becoming an organ trade coordinator. A father brought his son suffering from a heart disease to Jakarta for a transplant. When he witnessed the miracle of his child's survival, the man flew back home weeping tears of joy.

"He bought the heart of a child from somewhere in Southeast Asia.

"The people who sold him that heart made a whole lot of money.

"The organs they peddle come from kids in the slums, those unable to escape the cycle of poverty, living off theft and prostitution, selling drugs, even doing hit jobs.

"These kids get nabbed by adults even worse than they are. Then they're cut to pieces and sold as products in the blood-capitalism marketplace.

"Everything has a price.

"Hair becomes wigs, skulls are ornaments, and every last drop of blood has its use.

"It's the survival of the fittest out here. There's a death metal album called *Apex Predator—Easy Meat*. Yeah, death metal. Where it's nothing but growls and screams, and they play as fast as they can. You know what that is, El Cocinero? No, I didn't think you did.

"At any rate, the title is accurate. All the money in this world flows from the bottom to the top, like how aliens come to Earth on their spaceships and suck people up into them.

"The heart follows the same path.

"The business loop is perfect. No room for doubt in its workings.

"At least, that was what I thought for many years. But the truth is a little bit more complicated.

"Coordinating organ deals for so long has helped me see something I never noticed before.

"I mentioned just a minute ago that when it comes to the orphan organ trade, there's a class of elites who will buy the hearts of children from the slums of Southeast Asia in order to keep their own kids alive.

"You'd assume they'd have no complaints so long as their children survive. But they're never truly satisfied, El Cocinero.

"What do I mean? It's simple. There's a problem with the quality of the product.

"They're buying the organs of children who were involved in theft, prostitution, drugs, alcohol, and perhaps even murder for the sake of money.

"We don't have to tell these wealthy patrons the entire background history of the donors, but they're not totally ignorant. They know the products they're buying didn't come from perfectly healthy, happy homes.

"From their perspective, the organs are sourced from the human equivalent of stray dogs or sewer rats.

"Their beloved kids, carriers of their lineage, who will one day inherit all that wealth and take their family name to even greater heights, now have parts from dogs and rats in them. Naturally, the parents regret that.

"That knowledge sinks into their unconscious and puts down roots. It causes a persecution complex and fuels their anxieties.

"It's a type of biosentimentality.

"Biosentimentality is a kind of emotion that the transplant recipient and their family feel. They can't help but imagine the person who donated the organ and their background and life. It's especially easy to get sappy about heart transplants, because it comes at the cost of the donor's life. They unconsciously imagine what the original owner was like, because they never met them.

"Listen closely, El Cocinero. This is the first big key to my new business: the effect that biosentimentality has on a posttransplant client.

"The second is hidden within the issue of physical pollution.

"This is how the rich think: 'I bought the heart, but now all the effects of the drugs and alcohol the donor has consumed are going to show up in my child. Even if the donor child was never involved in those things, they grew up breathing smog in the slums all their life.'

"Atmospheric pollution is a huge issue that torments the minds of today's elites. Rich Chinese are particularly concerned with keeping away from PM2.5 pollutants.

"I once looked up the state of air pollution around the world.

"The results were shocking. There are only a handful of nations on earth where you can breathe good, clean air.

"You should really read a WHO report sometime. It'll make you laugh. It's so pervasive, they can't even put it in educational TV spots. Seven million people die from the effects of pollution every year. We're being exposed to danger on a planetary scale.

"Air pollution is relatively low in developed countries like in the EU and North America. In the more seriously affected areas like Africa and Asia, over ninety percent of lung cancer deaths and breathing ailments happen in areas with the densest pollution.

"But there's one exception in Asia.

"There is a country where atmospheric pollution is low.

"That's Japan, El Cocinero. My home country.

"As I read the reports and looked at the globe, a new business arrangement appeared before my eyes.

"Guntur Islami and Xin Nan Long haven't come up with anything like what I'm imagining yet.

"The important thing is biosentimentality and the quality of a product that has escaped physical pollution. It's a matter of sourcing.

"My wish is to do heart surgery again. That's all it comes down to. The money is secondary. But if I do it again, I want the best possible arrangements. I'm not going to use secondhand scalpels in some dingy warehouse while threatening men with guns observe. The doctors who have to do that are no better than part-time summer workers at a butcher shop.

"I'm beyond their level. It's why I've come up with my own business plan and have to raise funds to put my idea into practice.

"Creating a heart with regenerative cells?

"Yes, I've heard of that. But I've already answered that question for you, El Cocinero.

"The problem is, when does that tech finally become practical?

"Tomorrow? Next year? In a decade? What did I tell you earlier? Our customers hate the idea of waiting.

"Ahh, the research project to grow human organs within pigs.

"So you do check the science headlines now and then. What do you do, watch the BBC?

"At any rate, look at the menu of this restaurant. Do you see any pork? Of course not. The customers here are religious people. You don't need me to spell it out, do you? Human-sourced products will always be highest in demand.

"The heart will forever be the brilliant diamond at the top of the blood-capitalism pyramid. God created an electric pacemaker, and its value is rock solid. The possibilities of our new enterprise are endless.

"I know I've said this many times already, El Cocinero, but I repeat, you are the first person I've told about this. I trust you. This is a gamble.

If you're not the kind of man I think you are, then stab me in the throat and put me out of my misery right now, because I've already lost the bet. If I've failed, then I'm better off dead.

"You think I'm crazy for being so impatient?

"That's right. I'll fess up: I hate waiting, too."

22

cempöhualli-huan-öme

Light Kids Koyamadai was a licensed nursery school in Tokyo's Shinagawa Ward with a staff of nineteen, including eleven caretakers and eight full-time staff members. The establishment had an unspoken issue with over-time work that violated labor laws and a nursery director whose heavy-handed nature was unpopular with the staff.

One of the employees, tired of the abuse, confronted the director about his behavior. The woman who spoke out was an elementary school teacher who'd reached retirement age already, yet promptly returned to the workforce.

Outrage against the director grew among the staff, and while the director made various excuses and explanations, he did nothing to clearly demonstrate a desire to improve conditions. Fourteen staff members agreed to go on strike and demanded the director's resignation.

But it was only those fourteen who went on strike. Two staffers and three caretakers kept working.

Yasuzu Uno was one of the remaining caretakers. She'd moved to Tokyo from the Okayama Prefecture, far to the west, went to a vocational school, got a childcare license, and started working part-time at a nursery in Setagaya Ward. After her short seasonal program was up, she interviewed for a job with Light Kids Koyamadai. She got the position at the age of twenty. The work was hard, and she made many mistakes, but she stuck around for four years. The children loved her and called her "Miss Yasuzu."

Two days after the fourteen employees went on strike, a meeting called a "Caretaker Orientation" appeared on the afternoon schedule.

Yasuzu went to a 7-Eleven near the nursery school and bought some large bottled beverages for the parents and guardians who were coming to the orientation. She got mineral water, green tea, oolong tea, orange juice, forty paper cups, and a lunch salad and coffee-flavored gelatin pack for herself. It was a meager meal, but she wouldn't be able to keep down anything else.

On the way back from the 7-Eleven, she looked up at the clouds floating amid the blue. Despite their white brilliance, they looked dark gray and gloomy to her.

Naturally, the parents were angry.

As she carried the plastic bags full of drinks, Yasuzu thought, *I'm one of the people they'll blame, even though I'm working so hard for them.*

Yasuzu heard that the striking workers had told their entire side of the story to a weekly tabloid. If that was true, the uproar would get even worse.

There were thirty-two children under their care. If the media came sniffing around, the labor violations wouldn't be the only thing damaging the business's reputation but possibly child welfare infractions as well. There was no way all of the children entrusted to Light Kids Koyamadai would remain. On top of that, Yasuzu would have to watch over ten children, if not more, all on her own. The parents wouldn't all pull their kids out right away. They wouldn't find new nursery schools for their children in the course of a day.

One adult watching ten children was a dangerous situation, and the possibility of an accident was much higher. The sky looked even darker than before.

Back at the nursery, Yasuzu walked past the faculty office to a door marked ROOM 1. She lined up the plastic bottles from 7-Eleven on a desk by the door. Although normally raucous with the sound of children, Room 1 was presently silent, occupied only by rows of pipe-frame chairs.

Several hours later, the room would be filled with reproving glares and furious shouts from parents. Yasuzu sighed and ate her lunch of salad and coffee gelatin. She noticed that a piece of lettuce had fallen onto the knee of her black pants and picked it off in a panic. On the director's orders, she was wearing her interview suit in order to create as positive an image as possible to diffuse some of the impending disapproval.

Yasuzu didn't abstain from the strike out of a love for Light Kids Kiyamadai but a sense of duty to the children. She couldn't do much of anything. *I'm fine the way I am. This is best for me.*

Just as she expected, the orientation in Room 1 went off the rails. When the director included self-serving excuses among his apologies, it only further agitated the adults who trusted the nursery school to look after their children. They criticized the director's attitude as well as the abrupt drop in staff. Going from eleven caretakers to three, and those remaining having to sacrifice their days off to manage the workload, was cause for concern.

"This is all your fault!" "This is a crime!" "How do you expect us to leave our children in your care?" "I can't just pull my child out and get into another nursery like that!" "My husband and I have work!" "I had to leave early just to be here!" "What is your plan?" "How will you make this better?" "What are we supposed to do?"

When the shouting reached its apex, one mother got up from her seat and threw her cup full of orange juice at the director. But because she had swung her arm like a punch, her aim went off, and the cup smacked Yasuzu in the face instead, coating her hair with orange juice. All Yasuzu could do was look at the empty paper cup on the floor in shock.

The seventy-two-year-old security guard who stood at the gate had to help the other employees get the furious mother under control. When they held down her arms, she screamed, "Don't touch me!" After continuing to struggle and rage, she finally burst into tears and wailed, "Call the police." Room 1 was thrust into chaos. The papers that had been printed out and distributed to the parents wound up tossed onto the floor and trampled. Yasuzu could only observe the furor in a daze, orange juice dripping from the tips of her locks.

Why did I start this job anyway?

* * *

The version of herself who wanted to do this job for the children back when she was in vocational school seemed so distant now—a fading stain back on the horizon behind her. Yasuzu had a headache and felt sick to her stomach.

There would be another orientation at a later date. Yasuzu joined the other remaining staffers and saw off the disgruntled parents at the gate, bowing profusely. Her hair was sticky from juice and drying in strange clumps. None of the parents had a word for her. Even Masanori's and Erika's mothers, whom she'd been on good terms with, walked past without saying anything.

When the last parent had left, Yasuzu went into a bathroom stall and vomited. Once she had gotten everything out, she went to the sink and gargled.

Then she removed her jacket, leaned down to get her head close to the faucet, and washed her hair. She used a towel in her handbag to wipe herself off, then returned to the stall, closed the door, and locked it. Crying, she opened a compact mirror, doled out a pile of cocaine powder onto it, fashioned it into a line with her fingertip, and snorted the whole rail.

She closed her eyes and breathed deeply. She was sinking down, down to the bottom of the ocean, and then rose back up.

Her mood was elation. The worries were miles away. Alkaloids extracted from coca plants raised on the Central American sunlight and exported by narcos who won wars heavy with the wafting scent of gunpowder and blood traveled up the nasal membrane of the twenty-four-year-old woman and into her cranial nerves.

Learning about another world, another dream, and the route to reach it helped Yasuzu get through the difficulty of her life. She no longer ached at the difference between her ideals and reality or her inability to speak up about it. If she felt down, she just needed to get high enough to forget it. *The real me is here in this powder. There's nothing to worry about.*

23

cempöhualli-huan-ëyi

Through a tabloid, the staffers striking against the director of Light Kids Koyamadai told the world about the chaos unfolding at the nursery school in Shinagawa. The story was picked up online and soon made its way to the news entertainment shows on TV. It only had two appearances on television, but that was enough to make the nursery school infamous for its abusive ways.

Malicious packages started arriving. Whether falsified or not, the deliveries had addresses and names on them, and the school couldn't simply reject them without checking the contents. The employees had to open them up, whether they wanted to or not. There were letters with *divine punishment* scrawled in ink the color of blood, packages packed full of razor blades, and a box stuffed with black hair. The number of silent calls the school received grew by the day.

Yasuzu, who had to go out and lock the gate when work finished and the building closed for the evening, often found herself clamping down on her temples. Headaches were constant. She felt like there was a pain in her left arm, but she couldn't really tell. Her head definitely hurt, however, and she started to worry when the pain didn't go away after a week.

I wonder if it's because of what I did.

Mentally and physically exhausted due to the troubles at work, and in search of some change for the better, Yasuzu forwent her usual bumps and shot up the cocaine instead. She'd done that last Tuesday.

Using a needle and syringe she got from her dealer, she injected something into herself for the first time ever. The difference from snorting was immediately apparent; the needle worked faster and harder. Yasuzu was dancing in a field amid a cool, pleasant breeze. When she woke up from her blissful stupor, she noticed the dark blue mark on her arm and grimaced. Maybe she'd done it wrong.

Her headache had continued every day since then. It was a brand-new needle, and she'd made sure to sterilize it, so it couldn't have been an infection. But it was her first time, so maybe she'd missed something without realizing it.

I should have studied more, Yasuzu muttered to herself. *This is what I get for rushing into shooting up when I've never done it before.*

She tried to calm herself down and remain rational, but it didn't work. There was no one she could talk to for advice. The young woman just fell headlong into lonely anxiety and couldn't sleep. Her appetite waned. She was already fatigued from overwork at the nursery school—at this rate, she would die of exhaustion.

After a deep breath to calm her nerves, Yasuzu picked up her smartphone and called her dealer.

"No, definitely not," laughed the dealer, after she had explained her concerns. "The needle was brand new."

"But what if it wasn't...?"

The dealer continued chuckling but didn't bother to assuage her concerns any more firmly than that. Cocaine users gradually got more and more paranoid. This sort of thing happened regularly.

"Where do you live again?" he asked. "Ota? I can send you to a back alley nearby."

"Back...alley...what?"

"A doctor. Get an appointment and have him do a blood test. It'll cost you, though."

* * *

She got through the workweek (including a shift on Saturday) with no light at the end of the tunnel, and, at last, Sunday arrived.

It was difficult to climb out of bed, but Yasuzu managed to get ready, and took off on her 50cc Honda scooter. "Don't use a taxi, even if you feel bad," her dealer had cautioned.

Yasuzu took the Dai-ichi Keihin route south through Ota and crossed the Rokugo Bridge over the Tama River, which separated Tokyo from Kanagawa Prefecture. She then continued east along the river and into a neighborhood adjacent to the center of Kawasaki.

The street in Asahi-cho, Kawasaki, was full of warehouses for wholesalers. Stationery, swimsuits, nori seaweed, snowboards, toys for pets, oil lighters, e-cigs—beyond all of these other warehouses was one for medical supplies. The same wholesaler rented a three-story building next door, where they stored a huge number of products on each floor. Yasuzu parked her scooter in the lot for the medical supply warehouse as the dealer had instructed her, then gave her name to the intercom next to the warehouse shutter. A man replied, "Get on the employee elevator in the building next door and come to the second floor." Yasuzu obeyed and found herself walking down the hallway trepidatiously, past stacks of cardboard boxes with labels written in German, Korean, Chinese, and more.

A man in a work outfit opened boxes and checked the contents. Yasuzu wasn't sure if she was supposed to ask him for help. What if he had nothing to do with this...?

"Looking for the doctor?" asked the man. He had a Korean accent. Surprised, Yasuzu nodded, and the man said, "Then go down to the end of the hall and turn right."

Yasuzu had imagined the back-alley doctor's office would be dingy and ominous. She felt ashamed of her own lack of imagination but couldn't envision anything else. He would surely be bearded and unkempt, in a yellowed, tattered coat, with a stethoscope around his neck, grumpy and smoking a cigarette. Butts would be piled high in his ashtray, and the desk would be covered in scalpels and pliers, scattered about like pens and rulers. There would be an empty whiskey bottle on the floor, as well as a pile of bloody gauze sticking out of the trash can.*

Yet what Yasuzu saw when she opened the door was entirely different. Suddenly, she was in an examination room, as though having stepped onto a movie set. The walls, floor, and ceiling were white, and the whole place seemed utterly clean. There was no tarry cigarette smell or bloody gauze. A brand-new blood-pressure monitor and an examination table peeked through half-closed curtains.

The only qualities that Yasuzu had imagined correctly were the back-alley doctor's coat and stethoscope. But the coat wasn't tattered. The doctor did have a beard, but it was neatly trimmed.

Yasuzu's first impression of him was that he resembled a sharpened pencil. She thought of her brief time in the art club at her all-girls high school, and the many sketching pencils she'd been forced to sharpen after joining. The doctor's cheeks were sunken, and his chin was sharp, although maybe the goatee contributed to that effect. His head was shaved to about a tenth of an inch with an electric razor, which also made him seem pointier.

He was using a tablet at his business desk. Yasuzu sat down in the chair, but he did not take his eyes off the screen.

"What brings you here today?"

For a moment, Yasuzu thought she'd come to a real hospital. The timing of his question after she sat in the chair, the inflection of his voice, the gentle but clinical tone—everything was no different from the genuine article.

She knew this wasn't a legitimate hospital, however. This was undoubtedly an illegal examination room.

Yasuzu explained all of her symptoms, including the parts that she wouldn't be able to say at a real hospital. Merely talking about her issues helped her feel a bit better. There was no one else she could discuss these problems with.

It wasn't until he pressed his stethoscope to her chest that she felt nervous. She was all alone in this place, with the man who looked like a sharpened pencil. If he gave her any fishy commands or tried to feel her up...

"There's no need to take your top off," the back-alley doctor said. "Just enough bare skin for the stethoscope."

Yasuzu used both hands to pull the collar of her undershirt forward, allowing the doctor to slip his arm through and press the instrument to her chest. His face didn't change expression, and he didn't make any strange moves to fondle her. The doctor only listened for an abnormal heartbeat, then removed the stethoscope.

Next, he measured her blood pressure. Once he'd confirmed that her numbers were normal, he said, "I'll need to take a sample."

After wrapping the belt gently around her left arm, he asked her the frequency of her cocaine use. "Three times a day," she answered. "Only about a hundredth of a gram each time, I think."

He stuck a needle in her arm. Blood began to flow into a pack through a tube.

"Do you want to do more?"

"I..." Yasuzu wasn't sure how to answer at first, then decided to be honest. "I want to, but I'll run out of money. When I'm trying to make do, I just mix brandy and black coffee at home."

"Are things going well at your job? Lots of physical ailments are caused by daily habits and stress."

"My job..." Yasuzu trailed off. She stared at the blood going through the tube. Eventually, she responded, "Actually, I work at a nursery school. I love children. I do love them, but there's been a lot of trouble. In fact, it's a disaster..."

The doctor put the blood sample with measured serum, blood sugar, and blood count values into a storage case, and said, "Now let's run an EKG."

As he attached the electrodes to Yasuzu Uno, who was lying on the examination table, Kenji Nomura thought, *It's probably psychogenic, a general ailment brought on by stress. I won't know until I see the blood test results, but based on what she's said, the chances of an infection from shooting cocaine are almost nil.*

"Deep breath," Nomura instructed. "Relax your limbs."

Before he was an associate professor in the university anesthesiology department, Nomura was an intern, and that had given him enough knowledge to practice basic internal medicine, and he possessed a significant understanding of prescription drugs.

Nomura knew that the majority of medical activity worked on the placebo effect. For example, a patient that could only come to a black-market doctor might feel significantly relieved after merely having an EKG performed. The EKG and its results were real, but Nomura's purpose was more for the mental boost than the accuracy of the answers.

He looked down at the woman on the table; her eyes were closed and she breathed deeply. She was twenty-four, a nursery school worker, dealing with trouble at her job that had gotten tabloid attention. He'd heard all of these things from the dealer who sent her to him.

Maybe she'd be the right fit, he thought, staring at the monitor.

After a big surgery at a hospital, the first person to visit the patient once they'd been returned to their room was not the surgeon but the anesthesiologist. The purpose was to engage the patient in some small talk to see if anything was wrong with their condition. This anesthesiologist had to go in alone; the patient would think the operation was a failure if a whole team visited together. An experienced anesthesiologist needed a veteran detective's sharp insight.

Calling upon his knowledge, Nomura delved into the psyche of Yasuzu Uno.

He didn't need long. *She's got no confidence in herself,* he thought. *She struggles with her low self-worth and an inferiority complex toward others. But deep down, she thinks, "I have more worth than this. I should be able to do something else." She dreams of a different way of life and is angry over her unfair treatment at work. What makes her fun, though, is that she says she loves the children, but she hasn't said a word about the fact that she, a regular cocaine user, is responsible for others' kids. She possesses the desire to help others, law-breaking greed, and egotism all at once, without any apparent inner conflict. She was broken before she started doing cocaine. That's the best part. That's what we can use. We can give her a tremendous social cause and some more cocaine at the same time. She'll make a valuable hound. One that will come running back to us with our prey in her mouth. Only women can do this kind of job, after all. Men draw too much attention.*

A grand business swirled about Nomura. Suenaga had devised the idea over in Indonesia, and once Guntur Islami and Xin Nan Long got on board, Nomura got busy.

He had a certain inactive nonprofit from Ota in mind. Kagayaku Kodomo, or "Shining Children," was a certified NPO formed in 2009 for the purpose of child welfare. Since running into funding trouble in 2015, it had more or less ceased all activity. Inactive nonprofits were juicy targets for mobsters; such organizations were the perfect camouflage for criminal money flows. That made it worthwhile to invest in a charity, hijack the board, and take control.

The new acting director for Kagayaku Kodomo was a man named Reiichi Masuyama, a lieutenant of the Senga-gumi yakuza of the Korin-kai syndicate based in Kawasaki.

One of the duties the gang assigned Masuyama was sending the home-less or heavily indebted to Nomura the doctor, who would arrange for travel to Indonesia, usually to get a kidney removed in Jakarta. Like Nomura, Masuyama knew the organ trade business inside and out.

Once Suenaga had told Nomura his grand vision, the doctor passed the details to Masuyama with Suenaga's blessing. However you went about it, there was no taking part in the black-market organ trade in Japan with-out getting the yakuza's permission. Suenaga understood that well.

Masuyama reported back that he would reactivate Kagayaku Kodomo, of which he was the acting director, and use it to take part in this new organ business. The three patrons—Guntur Islami, Xin Nan Long,

Senga-gumi—would need to get together for a discussion on who held the initiative in the enterprise.

"But, Nomura," said Masuyama, "I'm impressed you managed to find a Japanese doctor willing to handle hearts for us. Did you track him down?"

"No, there was one in Jakarta," Nomura replied. He didn't reveal Suenaga's name.

Masuyama cast Nomura a piercing stare. It all seemed a little too convenient to him, but he couldn't discount the fact that both a terrorist group and a Chinese Black Society were involved. "Well, all right. For now, consider this an affirmative. I'll let the big org know what I can."

With the Senga-gumi on board, Nomura needed to find staff for the nonprofit. Unlike the board, which didn't need to be made public, staff positions couldn't be filled by blatant yakuza members.

The ideal fits were *katagi*, non-yakuza civilian, with gentle demeanors. People who fit Kagayaku Kodomo, who liked children, cared about children's rights, and wanted to do something to benefit society.

A week after her initial visit, Yasuzu returned to the warehouse in Asahicho, Kawasaki, to learn her blood test results.

The back-alley doctor had just put on a pot of coffee before she arrived. It was Mandheling coffee from the island of Sumatra in Indonesia. He offered her a cup, then sat down to speak.

"Yasuzu Uno, I got into this particular business because, when I was employed at a proper hospital, I discovered some dirty business the director was involved in and made the mistake of bringing it to light."

"Really?" she asked.

"Yes. I was fired and driven out of medicine. I'm certain you won't find any record of my employment anymore. As a matter of fact, there are many doctors with similar stories."

Yasuzu sipped her coffee and waited for him to continue.

"Still, I wanted to help people, and that's why I'm working illegally like this. Not everyone in a position like mine has ties to the criminal underworld. And some of those laboring to better society in legal ways understand the quandary people like me face. I'm on good terms with folks working for a few sympathetic groups."

"Groups…?"

"I'm not talking about religious organizations. I mean nonprofits, like foster care, for example."

Yasuzu nodded.

"There's one such nonprofit called Kagayaku Kodomo," the black-market doctor explained. "Their office just so happens to be in the Ota Ward, where you live. It's been inactive for years due to lack of funding, but an anonymous donation has recently made it possible for them to reopen. Unfortunately, it's so sudden that they're having difficulty recruiting staff. Honestly, I'm not surprised. Yearly salaries at a nonprofit are, at best, about one-point-eight million yen. Of course, every case is different, but that's no way to reel in a lot of employees. Fortunately, the anonymous donor said, 'In order to ensure we help these children, I'm willing to send along some extra pocket money to the staff for their living expenses.' These things sometimes happen in the EU, but it's almost unheard of in Japan. In terms of actual numbers, it's seven hundred thousand per person, per month. However, it can't go down as payroll. It's much higher than the average nonprofit salary, and it's hard to explain away numbers like that within the budget. Yet so long as there are adults willing to play along and seize that opportunity, children's lives will be saved. As it happens, I'm involved in that particular nonprofit myself."

Nomura paused there and looked at Yasuzu to gauge her reaction.

"I'll be direct with you. Here's our idea—we want someone trustworthy who is willing to accept this money every month for a benevolent cause: helping kids."

"Meaning…"

"Yes," Nomura confirmed. "Meaning you. Yasuzu Uno."

She let his words bounce back and forth inside her head.

"Yet so long as there are adults willing to play along and seize that opportunity, children's lives will be saved."

Seven hundred thousand yen a month paid under the table was much, much more than what Yasuzu made as a nursery school caretaker. She felt conflicted. "If I were to help this nonprofit, what would I be doing?"

Nomura picked up a fountain pen from the desk and gestured with it like a laser pointer as he outlined the specifics. The more he talked, logically laying out the responsibilities of the position, the firmer Yasuzu's resolve to quit Light Kids Koyamadai became. She already had no desire to remain working there. It felt like this was fate at work. The heavy fog that had shrouded her vision was clearing, bit by bit.

Nomura had finished his explanation of the nonprofit work, but Yasuzu was still in his office. He looked at his wristwatch; it was nearly time for the next patient to arrive.

"Is there anything you're unclear on?" he questioned.

"Uh, no," Yasuzu said. "I'm very grateful for the offer; it's quite wonderful. I think I understand the nature of the job, but you haven't told me the blood test results…"

"Ah, of course." Nomura reached for his file case and leafed through the papers. "You're healthy. Nothing turned up. I'm certain that your troubles were caused by the stress of your current workplace."

24

cempöhualli-huan-nähui

At that very moment, children were suffering from domestic violence, thrust into the depths of loneliness and despair.

As a nursery school attendant, Yasuzu was well aware of this deep-rooted issue. It tore at her heart every time she saw another case covered in the news. Poor, poor kids, controlled by the adults in their lives and victimized away from public notice.

Now she had a new job: saving those children.

The sheer breadth of the network Reiichi Masuyama, acting director of the Kagayaku Kodomo nonprofit organization, built astounded Yasuzu. Masuyama had the names and addresses of children who needed aid from every region of Japan.

Mothers and fathers alike were capable of domestic abuse, but Masuyama's database was overwhelmingly populated with paternal abuse.

From prestigious types such as business owners, executives, and city council members to the poor and unemployed, the network gathered information on any abusing their sons and daughters and sent Yasuzu out on assignment. From Hokkaido in the north to Okinawa in the south, she traveled across the country and made contact with the kids, getting evidence of their abuse on her digital camera, listening to their stories when possible, and sending the information to Masuyama. And just like that, the violence stopped. Terrible, wicked fathers divorced their wives and surrendered custody of their children.

Yasuzu didn't report anything to the city government or the police. She simply photographed the children's injuries and occasionally listened to their testimony.

What was actually happening? She didn't understand.

To sum up what the back-alley doctor had told her, Kagayaku Kodomo had a psychiatrist on staff recruited by the anonymous financial backer, who would analyze the father's personality based on abuse evidence, then call the father to discuss the matter with a clear direction and solution in mind. The psychiatrist was Japanese but had worked with the American military for years, successfully rehabilitating soldiers returning from Afghanistan with PTSD. He could improve matters without taking the lengthy time that a regular counselor did.

The doctor's story was bullshit, of course. Kagayaku Kodomo did not have any psychiatrists on staff.

As far as Yasuzu was considered, all she knew was that her work trips were saving kids. She felt fulfillment on a level she'd never experienced before and had newfound levels of self-confidence. The young woman cut her long hair to shoulder length and bought a black riding jacket. She wanted a big motorcycle but was afraid of getting into an accident, so she stuck to her usual scooter.

Blindly trusting the virtue of Kagayaku Kodomo, Yasuzu took new trips across Japan almost weekly. She consulted the filed photographs and found the children suffering domestic violence, made contact with them on the way home from school, and sometimes waited right outside their homes.

Yasuzu had no idea that the abusive fathers were later threatened by the yakuza, forced to pay large sums of hush money to keep the evidence out of official hands, and sometimes directly abducted and beaten.

Through the nonprofit, the Senga-gumi paid individuals working at children's consultation centers to hand over data about child domestic violence victims. It was a form of extortion preying upon the best of intentions. When the counselors became aware that parents were abusing their kids and the local police force wasn't helping, they reached out to Kagayaku Kodomo. Then a young woman in a motorcycle jacket would show up and stop the abuse one way or another. It was like magic. The counselors who contacted the nonprofit had no idea what happened. They only understood that the resolution was abnormal. But what use was the truth anyway? They didn't want or need to know. The result was everything. Kids were being rescued, and the counselors could go home without worrying they'd discover an obituary in the newspaper. Ultimately, they'd done a good thing.

As promised, Yasuzu received a salary from the nonprofit and a special allowance of seven hundred thousand yen a month. It was money that didn't exist in the system, and it meant she no longer struggled to afford coke. Yasuzu no longer had to conduct her drug deals in a park near the waterfront. Instead, she had the product sent to the doctor's office. Rather than seeing her dealer, she paid the doctor directly and received the cocaine from him. Additionally, the quality of the cocaine was much higher.

While Yasuzu had finer coke, she didn't dare shoot it up again. She'd rather go cold turkey than face that anxiety twice.

Yasuzu snorted cocaine and spent the rest of her time saving children in peril. The woman felt no conflict between these activities. *Everyone has their light and dark sides; nobody's a saint*, she reasoned. *Besides, I'm still better for others than a smoker. What I do doesn't create any secondhand smoke.*

In addition to homes where child abuse was present, Yasuzu also visited orphanages. Japan was home to roughly six hundred of them. Together, they supported twenty-seven thousand children.

The facilities were meant to be safe places for kids to live, but they had injustices, too.

Verbal abuse, hidden cameras, sexual harassment. Wrongdoing by orphanage staffers was difficult to spot from the outside, given the nature of the organizations. Well-meaning employees could report abuse internally, but there would be little action unless someone went to the police. The busy employees didn't have time to gather evidence like amateur detectives or the money to purchase recording equipment. Ultimately, they contacted Kagayaku Kodomo instead. Yasuzu listened to the well-meaning staffers and gave them the latest listening devices and hidden cameras, free of charge. The employees later sent the data they gathered to Masuyama.

After a while, the offending staffers nervously and hastily submitted their resignations. At times, their faces were bruised and swollen, as though someone had hit them repeatedly. A few had chipped teeth.

As she performed job after job for Kagayaku Kodomo, Yasuzu started to feel like she was akin to Batman or Spider-Man. She was rescuing helpless, innocent lives, and the rest of society was ignorant of it.

After visiting a number of orphanages, Yasuzu understood that sometimes the abuse happened between children, without any adult involvement. Kids raised in violent homes took it out on other kids the only way they knew how.

Is there no way to solve this problem, too?

She asked Masuyama, her director, for guidance on this matter, but he never gave her an answer. Yasuzu gave up on that line of thought and decided, *It's no use fretting over that. Nobody can save everyone.*

She never figured out Masuyama's reasoning for ignoring the question: There was no money to be gained from abuse between children. Kids had no status or economic power, and you couldn't extort them for any money.

After half a year of waking up every morning with a firm, bracing sense of purpose, Yasuzu's job duties changed.

Instead of solving domestic violence and abuse issues, Masuyama instructed her to take custody of the children herself. Essentially, she would be escorting children to the Kagayaku Kodomo shelter in Ota Ward.

Her targets were **undocumented children** not in school.

"Undocumented children?" she repeated to Masuyama over the phone.

"Yeah," he said. "Kids without legal documentation. You've heard of things like that before, right? This case involves a mother who was being abused by her husband. When she found out she was pregnant, she sensed that she was in danger and fled in the night. She hadn't filed for divorce yet; knew her man would kill her if she brought it up. She gave birth to a son in a little hospital in a faraway town, but she couldn't report his birth at the municipal office. Because the woman's still legally married, having her child officially registered is a risk. Her husband might find out where she's hiding and come after her. It's like being hunted by a monster. That's why her son never got a legal identity."

"We're going to separate her from her child?"

"Unfortunately, yes. She's raised the boy on her own but can't afford it anymore, and now she's turned to abusing him."

"Oh…I see…" Yasuzu sighed.

"She *wants* Kagayaku Kodomo to take her son from her, though. She wants us to help her before something worse happens to him."

The scenario Masuyama described for Yasuzu was only one of many. There were plenty of complicated reasons why a child went undocumented, and those kids had to survive without any way of proving who they were. They weren't Japanese citizens and didn't exist on paper.

Many were raised by single mothers in dire financial straits and didn't even go to school. It was not uncommon for them to be abused by stepfathers.

No one knew how many children like that lived in Japan. They weren't in the system and hadn't immigrated, so there was no paper trail for the government to follow.

It seemed right to Yasuzu that Kagayaku Kodomo prioritize taking undocumented children into its custody. Regardless of noble intentions, Yasuzu had no authority as a third party to seize children with legal identities and regular school records. She'd be investigated for kidnapping. *But I can save an undocumented child. I might not be able to save all the kids out there, but I can't let that get me down. I have to help the ones I can.*

Yasuzu found undocumented children who were underfed, abused, and uneducated and took them back to Tokyo. As Masuyama had said, their mothers already agreed to it. However, the women weren't informed where their children were going. If that information got out, it could expose the kids to danger.

At the request of the nonprofit's wealthy donor, the organization took boys and girls alike, but limited their scope to between the ages of three and ten.

Every time she visited a mother exhausted from trying to survive while a downcast, withdrawn child sat in the corner of the room, Yasuzu had to wonder where Masuyama was getting the information on these cases. The answer was very close, yet she didn't notice it.

The hidden link was drugs.

Various criminal groups bought information from dealers, who were in a position to know when one of their regular speed or ecstasy customers had undocumented offspring. Masuyama of the Senga-gumi in Kawasaki was known for paying a good price for that intel. Once he got a tip from a dealer, Masuyama sent the desperate single mother one to one-point-five million yen. That was all it took to buy a kid.

The undocumented children that Yasuzu "took into custody" first went to the back-alley doctor in Asahi-cho, Kawasaki, for a general examination. Yasuzu wasn't present for that, but from what the children said afterward, it consisted of tests like chest x-rays, MRIs, and CT scans. *But he didn't have those machines at his little office*, she thought. *There must be another room in there somewhere.*

After their exam, the children were sent to a safe shelter. It was not the nonprofit's office.

Kagayaku Kodomo only rented a simple two-room apartment on the second floor of a mixed-use building, a place not equipped to handle many people. The children were sent to a temple called Saiganji in the Ota Ward, the same area as the office. There was a living space in the temple's base-ment, which would act as shared housing for the children.

"Isn't it great?" Masuyama said to Yasuzu when he gave her a tour. "We get to use this space. The head monk at Saiganji originally built it as a shel-ter for women trying to escape domestic violence or stalkers."

"I'm surprised at how spacious it is," Yasuzu remarked. "I've heard of temples being used as a refuge for women, but I thought it was mostly just a rumor. This is more of a basement than a temple, though."

"They're still building it out. It's a slow and difficult process, since they need to keep it a secret. You catch my drift, Uno? We must keep this shelter absolutely confidential."

"I will."

"The children are coming here to be safe. We can't expose them to danger and despair again."

"I understand."

"I've known the head monk a long time," said Masuyama, and he began to describe the monk's nature. Yasuzu trustingly listened to every word of it. Almost all of it was lies, but it *was* true that Masuyama had known the man a long time. The connection between the Senga-gumi and Saiganji ran deep, and the monk was willingly involved in several shady business operations. The underground space had been constructed on Masuyama's behalf to serve as the base of a bigger project than anything they'd done before.

There were six shared bedrooms on either side of a hallway, a cafeteria, a meeting room, and a group bath, plus a kitchen. After some discussion between Masuyama and the monk, padded mats were placed in the meeting room to turn it into a play area. Instead of a storage chamber as planned initially, they turned one spot into a medical office by punching a hole in the wall for more floor space. The construction work was done in painstaking secret and was still ongoing.

Yasuzu had taken in three undocumented children: boys aged three and six and a seven-year-old girl. If there were many more, she wouldn't be able to take care of all of them. She couldn't be in the shelter all the time, of course. Her work demanded she go out and bring more kids in.

The response to her quandary was the arrival of a Chinese woman who would work in the shelter underneath Saiganji with her.

Masuyama introduced the lady, who said her name was Xia and claimed she had a child psychology degree. "I have experience working in places like this," she said. Her Japanese was strong. Although she didn't reveal her age, Yasuzu felt Xia was older than her. She had very short black hair and stood one hundred and seventy-four centimeters tall, with long, slender limbs, a petite face, and a sharp chin that bore her a resemblance to some famous actress. She didn't seem to wear any makeup and sported rimless glasses.

"It's a worthwhile job," Xia said to Yasuzu as the three kids cavorted in the playroom. "We must be the light that brightens the lives of these children."

Xia had a naturally thin expression with a cold beauty that could be a little intimidating, but she smiled while she spoke. Yasuzu nodded as she gazed at the children.

Undocumented, unsupported by the government, unable to go to school, and raised in abusive conditions. They were mistreated by their mothers, and in danger of being attacked by their fathers if discovered.

How unfair it all was. They'd done nothing wrong. There was more than enough reason to take custody of these children. *It's my job. My duty. I have no qualms. But still…*

There was one thing Yasuzu was desperate to learn.

"Masuyama-san," she asked, "how long will these children be here?"

He looked back at her, standing next to Xia, and replied, "We're looking for new families as hard as we can."

"Are they going to be adopted?"

"Sadly, there are cases in Japan of children being pursued by their birth parents and suffering tragic outcomes," said Masuyama. "So the plan is to find trustworthy homes outside the country, if possible. Once we've taken every step to confirm the background and trustworthiness of the potential foster parents, we'll proudly take the kids to their new homes."

I find undocumented children between the ages of three and ten and take them to the shelter. When I'm not out on assignment, I use my nursery school experience to help care for the children. It just has to last until we find them foster parents overseas, where their real future awaits.

A new chapter in Yasuzu's life had begun.

25

cempöhualli-huan-mäcuïlli

It was in juvenile detention that Koshimo Hijikata first learned the names of the seven seas of the world.

The correctional facility instructor's class was where he learned, for the first time, the location of his mother's homeland of Mexico. It was a country in the southern part of North America, with five times the land area of Japan.

"At one-point-ninety-six million square kilometers, Mexico is the thirteenth-largest country in the world," the instructor said.

The boys couldn't grasp how big that was, so they examined the globe the instructor brought, one by one, and compared the size of Mexico to the size of Japan.

"Japan is bigger on this," said the boy sitting in the seat ahead of Koshimo while examining the globe. He was missing his left ear.

Somebody snickered.

"Who just laughed?" snarled the boy with the missing ear, getting to his feet and glaring around the classroom.

"Be quiet," snapped the instructor. "Sit down. Pass the globe to the seat behind you."

The boy, red-faced with fury, did as ordered, passing the globe to Koshimo, who reached out with his long arm to take it and spun it to the right. On the third rotation, his index finger slid across Mexico. The sphere quietly stopped rotating.

The world Koshimo and all the other boys in the classroom knew was very small. Just the little neighborhood where they lived, the Tama River that ran between Tokyo and Kanagawa, the industrial area along Tokyo Bay, and whatever they'd seen in juvy. The entirety of their memories had been formed against those backdrops.

The message relaying the dinner hour played over the speakers, and Koshimo left the group dorm to line up in the hallway. The instructor looked up at him as he passed. Koshimo was taller than anyone else at the facility.

At fifteen, he was one hundred and ninety-nine centimeters, and he weighed ninety-eight kilograms.

Over two years had passed since July 26, 2015, when he killed his parents and was sent to Sagamihara Juvenile Detention Center.

When he first showed up at age thirteen, Koshimo was already one hundred and eighty-eight centimeters. That made him vastly taller than the average boy his age, and he'd grown several more centimeters since then.

When the other inmates saw how he was growing, a whispered rumor began to trickle through the group.

"Is there just way more nutrition in his food than ours?"

Koshimo sat down at his assigned seat in the cafeteria to eat his dinner. Unable to withstand their curiosity, three other youths snatched his tray away. They intended to taste his food to check.

They'd been sent to juvy after Koshimo, and they didn't know how furious he could get. That was their bad luck. Naturally, they'd heard stories, but the boys didn't take them seriously enough. Minors imprisoned for killing their parents weren't especially rare in here, and they believed Koshimo to be no different from all the others.

Assuming they were stealing his meal, Koshimo punched the boy who drank his consommé soup in the face and threw the one who took his spoon onto the ground, then stomped on his stomach. The kid gasped like a fish, writhing in agony. The leader who'd convinced them to take his food landed a hit first, but Koshimo grabbed his wrist to immobilize him, then stuck a thumb in his eye. He lifted the kid off the ground with one hand, then slammed him to the floor of the cafeteria.

The emergency alarms rang, and the detention guards surrounded Koshimo. The three boys were taken to the medical wing, where their wounds were dressed, and a report was made for the guards. All of the boys were seriously injured. The one who'd been punched had nose and facial fractures, the stomped boy had ruptured organs, and the one who got a thumb jabbed into his left eye and slammed on the ground suffered a concussion. They tested him after he regained consciousness and found that he was completely blind in his damaged eye.

Koshimo had already been likely to transfer from a Class-One facility to a Class-Two detention center for boys with more advanced criminal leanings, and the assault in the cafeteria only pushed that process further along, adding to his sentence. They even discussed sending him to a Class-Three center, which, under the old system, was called a medical juvenile reformatory. They couldn't, however, because he wasn't classified with a mental disorder.

At the Class-Two juvenile center, Koshimo was put into an individual room rather than a group dorm. They ordered him to repent for his assault, and from that point on, he was more or less in solitary confinement.

After five days, they allowed him to leave his room for educational lessons, life skills training, and vocational development. Two correctional instructors observed Koshimo at all times. Because he was one hundred and ninety-nine centimeters and over ninety-eight kilograms, they had special permission to carry stun guns to subdue him, if necessary.

Koshimo Hijikata has poor Japanese reading ability, shows almost no remorse for the crime of murdering his own parents, and

does not seem to possess the emotional depth that would allow him to express such a feeling. He is also prone to random violent outbursts.

Once he started fighting, he was completely out of control. The life skills lessons were doing nothing to make him more social.

Yet while it was anyone's guess when Koshimo would see daylight again, he scored well on the instructors' assessments. He was quiet, didn't make any noise after lights-out, woke up on time, and although he couldn't remember any kanji, he copied his writing assignments diligently and listened in class without dozing off.

Koshimo didn't attack any of the juvenile instructors in either the Class-One or Class-Two detention center. The only times he fought were when other boys messed with him. His biggest problem was that his retribution always went far beyond the realm of legitimate self-defense.

The instructors were impressed at his manual dexterity during the vocational development lessons. He was excellent at carving, and he picked up on how to use machines like lathes right away. He could carve pigeons and crows out of wood, and when the staff took the carvings to a charity event held outside the facility, they sold out immediately.

As his retirement day approached, one of the senior members on staff at the facility said:

"He's the greatest talent we've had here since the place opened."

Initially Koshimo was focused on birds, but after seeing a picture book of animals in class, he also started carving other creatures like tigers, jaguars, and crocodiles. These animals, too, sold out at another charity event.

And it wasn't just beasts. He was good at carefully bending bamboo into delicate frames for glasses.

Someone who bought one of his pieces remarked, "If he ever returns to society, I'd order something directly from him." The manager of a made-to-order furniture business added, "I wish I could recommend him to the workshop we're contracted with."

None of these buyers knew why Koshimo was imprisoned, and they quite possibly would have retracted their statements if they did, but all the same, the correctional instructors passed the messages on to Koshimo.

He showed no reaction, however.

The boy made the items to make them and was satisfied if they turned out well. He didn't quite understand why he should be happy if someone else complimented his work.

Dinner that evening was white rice, fried fish, vegetable stir-fry, and a Chinese-style soup with tofu and sesame oil. Once he finished his meal, observed by two instructors as usual, Koshimo stood and went to the instructor standing next to the wall to quietly proclaim, "I can't sleep at night."

It was against the rules to get out of your seat or talk in the cafeteria. The instructor was going to order Koshimo back to his chair but noticed the grave look in the boy's eyes and made the decision to take Koshimo to the medical room. They could hear what he had to say there.

Boys in the group dorms had to write in their journals after dinner, with free time following until lights-out at nine o'clock. Those in the private rooms, however, had to do additional math drills and spend time copying kanji. When inmates complained during dinner, it was usually an excuse to get out of their remaining daily assignments. Koshimo was not the type to make up lies like that, though.

"Did you sleep better at the Class-One detention center?" asked the instructor.

"No," admitted Koshimo. "I haven't slept well since I was there."

"When did it start?"

"A little bit before I fought in the cafeteria."

"When they held you for questioning there, did you tell the staff?"

"Yeah. They didn't do anything," said Koshimo. "If I can't sleep, I might fight again."

Insomnia.

The instructor wrote the word on his sheet gravely. "But it's not like you can't get a single wink, right?"

"What does it mean, a single wink?"

"It means to sleep for a little bit."

"I can do that," Koshimo replied, folding one long arm and scratching the elbow of the other with a fingertip. "After lights-out, I close my eyes. After a bit, I dream. Always the same dream."

"What kind of dream? Do you remember it?"

"Yes. It's a dark room, full of black smoke, hard to breathe. It seems like a fire, but not. Sometimes I hear talking. It sounds like Spanish but not. When I hear the words, I don't know them. Someone is on the ground in the black smoke, but I can't see the face. Someone stabs them with a sharp thing like a knife. More black smoke comes out of the stabbed person, so I can't see. Then I can't breathe, and wake up, and on the clock, it usually says one. Then I can't sleep. Even if I close my eyes."

Koshimo was usually reticent, but now he spoke with a fiery purpose. The instructor jotted down what the young man said, closed the notebook, and stared into Koshimo's big eyes.

"Now, listen closely," the instructor began. "In a sense, it's right for the people in here to have bad dreams. It's evidence that you feel guilt, and your heart is trying to move in the right direction. In some cases, we'd think this was a good thing. But not being able to sleep is very bad for your body. Unfortunately, I can't just give you medicine to help you sleep. We need a diagnosis first. If the same thing happens tonight, we'll have you see a specialist tomorrow."

* * *

After lunch the next day, a doctor from the Class-Three facility came to examine Koshimo, but he did not prescribe sleeping drugs. All he said was to drink lots of water, do regular stretches, and try to relax.

Koshimo's insomnia continued.

After a second visit, the doctor recommended that he write down the contents of his dreams every night.

"Sometimes, if you're able to externalize your dreams consciously, you stop having them."

Koshimo did as instructed and wrote down his dreams. It was always the same dream, so what he wrote was more or less identical each time.

Dream again today dark room ~~blackness~~ black smoke smokey coming out ~~voys~~ voice speaking what is is saying? I never herd it before someone is on the ground. smoke in spanish its humo

He awoke in the middle of the night over and over, tormented. Yet after roughly a month, he abruptly stopped having the dream. Koshimo was in no mood to celebrate, however. He wasn't free of the vision; he felt stuck inside it now. It was beyond him to explain the sensation to the specialist and instructors. Koshimo was sleeping soundly again, so that was all he told them.

He tried to recreate what he saw in the dream with a wood carving, but he couldn't give it shape. Drawing it proved impossible, too. Koshimo gave up and moved on to elephants and rhinos, which he hadn't carved yet. There were many more animals left in the picture book.

26

cempöhualli-huan-chicuacë

The domestic passenger plane departed from Soekarno-Hatta International Airport in Jakarta and made its way toward Sultan Hasanuddin Airport in Makassar, South Sulawesi. The trip from Jakarta on Java to Makassar on Sulawesi was close to a thousand miles, a flight over water that took about two hours and forty minutes.

Jingliang Hao leaned back into the first-class leather seat, refused the champagne the cabin attendant offered, and ordered an Indonesian coffee instead. The brand of beans he selected had a Komodo dragon on the label, and they were harvested from the island of Flores, where he owned a resort hotel.

Suenaga was sitting in the adjacent seat, separated by a partition. The other chairs around them were empty.

"Doctor," Hao asked him, "why didn't El Cocinero come with us?"

"He said he had work," Suenaga answered, flipping the page of the German medical journal he was reading.

"The cobra satay stand?" Hao questioned. "If he's not coming with us, does that mean he doesn't trust me?"

"I wouldn't say that," Suenaga replied. "He also said that in addition to his work, he didn't want to take a plane if he could help it. Perhaps that's the real reason."

"Scared of heights, huh?" Hao laughed. "What was his name again? Gonzalo?"

"Right," said Suenaga. "Gonzalo García. Back in Peru, he worked for a leftist guerilla group called Tanque del Pueblo, I believe…"

"He worked for them, eh?" drawled Hao. "As a *sicario*, no doubt."

The cabin attendant brought a fresh cup of coffee for Hao, and the two stopped talking. When the woman left, smiling, Hao took a sip and commented, "Such introductions are worthless, Doctor. If he says he's Peruvian, he's not Peruvian. Overly trusting people like you, who admit they're Japanese from the start, don't exist in our world. So, where'd he come from? Colombia? Mexico? Guatemala?"

"I don't know," Suenaga answered, lifting his head from the German medical journal, "but if he's lying, does it behoove our business not to have him around?"

"Now, now, let's not be hasty," admonished Hao, speaking to the older man as though he were lecturing his young son. "This self-styled Peruvian, Gonzalo García, who goes by El Cocinero—our business needs people like him. If there's a danger here, it's you, Doctor. You've got a face that screams 'undercover agent.'"

"Spare me the jokes."

"The thing about this Gonzalo is, though," said Hao, placing the coffee cup on a side table, "it's smart of him not to ride a plane. What do you think is the most efficient way to get rid of several people at once, Doctor?"

"I've never thought about that."

"You shove them into the cargo hold of a plane, fly to thirty thousand feet, and shove them out one by one. The bodies never show up. You do it when you're over the ocean, like we are right now."

Suenaga silently shook his head in a show of fear. Men like Hao were delighted when they scared people. Then he looked out the round window. The cloud layer was white and shiny, offering only the barest crack through which the Java Sea was visible.

After landing at Sultan Hasanuddin Airport in Makassar, a city on the southwest part of Sulawesi Island, Hao and Suenaga met up with four members of Xin Nan Long. The gun-toting men stood guard as they got into a helicopter and took to the skies again.

The helicopter took them north over Pinrang Regency and eventually to their destination. There was a vast holding along the Makassar Strait, like a military base. This was the Pinrang Shipyard, a place built on the heroin profits of the Chinese *heishehui* Black Societies.

When they got off the helicopter, Hao and Suenaga were given helmets with the shipyard's logo on the side. Workers operated electric vehicles that took them across the yard, past a variety of ships being constructed, and up to a genuinely massive hull.

Suenaga alighted and marveled at the sight before him. The steel bow looming before him was no less imposing than a rock slab hanging over a climber. The view was even greater than he'd imagined. When complete, this craft would offer its guests service that rivaled any three-star hotel.

In fact, Suenaga thought, gazing upward, *it's more than a three-star hotel. This is closer to a city on the water.*

Dunia Biru.

The massive ship, whose name meant **"Blue Earth"** in Indonesian, measured a total length of four hundred and ten meters, making it lengthier than the longest cruise ship, with a width of eighty-three meters and a gross tonnage of two hundred and thirty-eight thousand nine hundred tons. Its maximum passenger capacity was seven thousand five hundred and fifteen, spread across three thousand one hundred and twelve cabins and eighteen decks in total.

The floors on the cruise ship were called decks, so the *Dunia Biru* was somewhat akin to an eighteen-story building. Everything from Deck 3 to Deck 18 was considered a space for guests.

The Verulean Suites on Decks 11 and 12 were the largest on the vessel. In US dollars, they ran over eighty thousand per cruise. Including the main hall, there were thirty restaurants on the ship, eleven of which exclusively served halal food. There were fifty-four bars or lounges, eight theaters, four dance halls, three concert halls, five fitness gyms, a tennis court, a basketball court, a futsal court, a kickboxing ring, a Brazilian jujitsu mat area, an ice rink, library, meeting rooms, bathing areas, salons, a seventeen-meter climbing wall, and twenty-one pools for adults or children. A waterslide named *Air Terjun Garuda* ("Garuda Waterfall") ran thirty-two meters down from Deck 8 into a pool below.

Plans were in place to build a casino with AI-controlled robot dealers. But because gambling with cash was illegal in Indonesia, they would use tokens instead. In addition to the robots, human dealers would be present at every hour of the day and night, as well as regular stage shows with magicians and comedians.

If you got tired of all the water on your ocean cruise, you could walk through an interior park on the *Dunia Biru*. There were twenty-eight thousand trees in the open air and another four thousand in a greenhouse. You could easily enjoy your entire day from start to finish without even laying your eyes on the sea.

All of these features had been built into the ship over a three-year, six-month construction period, and with the addition of a state-of-the-art engine, it was nearing completion.

The rails set into the towering ceiling of the shipyard moved countless parts around on hooks, while forklifts raced around the floor. Welding sparks were flying everywhere. In addition to chefs and staffers inspecting the kitchen designs on each deck, there were brand managers for the shops, pool construction workers, landscapers and gardeners, interior contractors, and design engineers. All of them worked on their separate floors at the same time, like residents of parallel worlds. The construction site of a two-hundred-thirty-eight-thousand-ton cruise ship was at once a microcosm of the fanaticism of capitalist society, and a space teeming with sheer chaos.

A man in a yellow batik shirt appeared and exchanged a friendly handshake with Hao. His name was Haryanto Secioria, and he was the CEO of the cruise ship company and godfather of the *Dunia Biru*.

Through their four legitimate business fronts within Indonesia, Xin Nan Long was investing heavily in Secioria's cruise line.

"This is Tanaka," Hao said in English, introducing Suenaga.

"It's a pleasure," said Secioria. "Are you from Japan?"

"Yes," Suenaga replied.

The twenty-nine-year-old CEO was lithe and looked like a marathon runner to Suenaga. Perhaps he ran for fun. He was certainly a very young man to be taking the lead on this overwhelming cruise ship business. Perhaps that was a sign of modern Indonesia's momentum. *But how much does he know?* Suenaga wondered.

Under Secioria's lead, they filed into a work elevator and traveled upward.

The group found itself looking down at a device that resembled a whale's pectoral fin, jutting out from the middle of the lower part of the *Dunia Biru*. A crowd of engineers surrounded it. A site foreman noticed the elevator rising and waved when he saw Secioria.

Secioria returned the gesture and said to Suenaga, "They're tuning a fin stabilizer. Do you know what those are?"

"No," Suenaga replied.

"They help prevent rolling on massive ships like this. There's one on either side, and the computer keeps them coordinated. The system was designed by the Japanese. The Japanese are always good at whatever they do."

The three disembarked from the elevator on Deck 4 and were greeted by a man with a transceiver. He was the *Dunia Biru*'s hotel director, the manager in charge of all the customer services on the ship—the other captain who kept the seafaring city running. Once the boat was on the ocean, he was the one who controlled all the information about what was happening on board.

The hotel director took them to an infirmary.

"On deluxe cruise ships like this, we must be prepared for any and all emergencies," the director explained. "And health problems are the most urgent. We have a duty to provide the greatest possible service, not just for our elderly guests but anyone with any kind of disability or condition."

They stepped into the infirmary, which was expected to hold a regular staff of seventeen, including the doctors.

At nearly three hundred and sixty-five square meters, it was the size of six *Dunia Biru* suite rooms, sporting ergonomic beds, automated hand-washes made of artificial marble that used RO filtrated water, and two complete surgical systems from a German company as a result of a bidding war.

It was beyond a mere boat's infirmary—this rivaled any first-rate hospital facility. Suenaga turned on the overhead light above the surgery table and smiled. He was aware that there were more than two such tables on the ship.

Xin Nan Long, which was getting its hands into the luxury cruise ship business, had arranged to board several surgeons with Guntur Islami's help. The intent was to turn the great vessel itself into an organ marketplace. Their initial product offering was going to be kidneys, but after Hao heard Suenaga's pitch, they switched to heart transplants.

In order for Suenaga's business vision to become a reality, the *Dunia Biru* would have to leave Tanjung Priok, the largest port in Indonesia, and dock in the Kanto region of Japan.

There were six ports in Yokohama and three in Tokyo that could support ships over fifty thousand tons, and nearly all of those were container ships. **Kawasaki Port**, which Suenaga described as vital to his vision, did not have a single passenger terminal suited for a cruise ship. It offered only container terminals for loading and unloading goods.

However, the lead-up to the 2020 Tokyo Olympics changed all of that.

Based on the expected influx of foreign tourists for the Olympics, the Kanto region was at a deficit of up to fourteen thousand hotel rooms. The government's plan to overcome the hotel crunch was to introduce "hotel ships" at docks in and around Tokyo, pulling in as many high-capacity cruise liners as possible.

The government and public agreed: the docks should be as open as possible. One such candidate was Kawasaki Port. Despite its proximity to Haneda Airport, the port had never hosted a passenger vessel, so a large cruise ship would be test moored there in preparation for the Tokyo Olympics. The container terminal at the port's artificial island of Higashi-Ogishima was chosen as the dry-run site. The *Dunia Biru* would be the boat, once it finished its maiden voyage from Indonesia in 2019. The local media in Kanagawa Prefecture—especially within Kawasaki—was elated. The biggest cruise ship in the world, four hundred and ten meters long, eighty-three meters wide, and weighing nearly two hundred and forty tons, was coming to town.

"Hey, Doc," said Hao, walking through the spacious infirmary, gazing at the polished marble walls. "Words are such clever things, aren't they?"

"Words?" Suenaga repeated.

"The phonetic alphabet might not have the depth of Chinese characters, but it's still very ingenious. You're familiar, of course, with coronary artery bypass surgery. Patients with a coronary artery obstruction need proper blood flow to the heart, so you connect a different vein to a working part of the artery to provide flow."

"That's correct. You've done your homework."

"They call the vein that gets used in the bypass a 'graft.' I believe that word originally came from joining plants, or moving tissue, right? And it just so happens that it can be applied to bribery and corruption. It's the perfect name for both. You run a graft by bypassing an old artery with a new vein, bringing in fresh blood. Which is just what you and I are doing with *our* graft."

The CEO of the cruise line took them up to a lounge on Deck 17 when they were done viewing the infirmary. The lounge interior was still under construction, but there was a bartender there who made them cocktails anyway. They held a toast to the future of the ship.

That's all of human history, thought Suenaga. *Just an endless cycle of grafts. New blood routes, new sea routes, all making new business routes.*

* * *

When he returned to Jakarta from the boatyard on Sulawesi, Suenaga met Valmiro at a booth in a high-end sushi restaurant in the Grand Indonesia mall and told him what he'd seen on the giant cruise ship.

Valmiro drank a Bintang as he listened. He knew quite a lot about boats, in fact, but murmured with surprise as though hearing these things for the first time. When Suenaga finished describing the German surgical tables, Valmiro had a question. "Hao didn't ask about me?"

"He wondered why you didn't come along," Suenaga replied, pouring a bit of osy sauce. "He thinks you're a Latin-American *sicario*."

"I'm not a *sicario*."

Suenaga laughed. "You're not? What's the difference?"

"A *sicario* is like the knife that man's holding," Valmiro said, pointing at the sushi chef skillfully cutting tuna with a sharpened kitchen knife.

Like a tool, then, Suenaga thought. "When I'm around you, I always feel I'm being treated like a child."

"You're fortunate that you've got the opportunity to learn," Valmiro said. "There's no future for a novice who doesn't learn. Just look at Dai."

"I know that. But *you* did it to him." Suenaga ate a mackerel nigiri and washed it down with Bintang. "Why don't you ask the chef to cut that fruit for you?"

There was a woven basket full of salak in front of Valmiro. It was one of the traditional fruits of Indonesia.

"No," he said. "I'll eat them later."

There were stacks of dollars at the bottom of the basket under the salak.

While Suenaga had been observing Xin Nan Long's shipyard, Valmiro had taken his crutches of synthetic resin and liquid cocaine to the industrial city of Bekasi, east of Jakarta, and paid someone to extract the cocaine. Then he'd sold it to a Malaysian dealer for cash and carried around a portion of the money in his basket of fruit.

If he went to Japan with Suenaga, he would need big money on hand. That's why he'd decided to sell the crutches.

Valmiro grabbed a salak. "It's time to say good-bye to Indonesia. Won't be easy to eat these anymore. Here."

A salak rolled across the table toward Suenaga. The brown, scaly skin gleamed like a cobra's.

The sushi restaurant was packed with wealthy Jakartans and tourists. Fish soon to be prepared swam blissfully unaware in their tanks, and the lighting cast faint shadows on the diners.

Amid this colorful setting, Valmiro and Suenaga plotted a way to sneak into Japan as casually as businessmen might discuss work over beer and sushi.

III

El Patíbulo (The Gallows)

If I give my life to life itself to be lived and ruined
(I don't want to say, to mystical experience), I open
my eyes on a world in which I have no meaning unless
I'm wounded, torn apart and *sacrificed,* and in which
divinity, in the same way, is just a tearing apart or
being torn apart, is executing or being executed,
is sacrifice.

—Georges Bataille, *Guilty*

[We] went in two boats to the Island and we found
there a temple where there was a very large and
ugly idol which was called Tescatepuca and in
charge of it were four Indians with very large
black cloaks and hoods.

—Bernal Díaz del Castillo, *The True History of
the Conquest of New Spain*

27

cempöhualli-huan-chicöme

On Friday, June 23, 2017, Valmiro Casasola rode on a Garuda Indonesia Boeing 777-300ER in business class, from Soekarna-Hatta to Haneda, Tokyo.

It had been a year since he first met Michitsugu Suenaga at the *kaki lima* cart in Jakarta.

Valmiro had a fresh Indonesian passport whipped up for him so he could take the passenger plane out of Soekarna-Hatta, but Suenaga was wanted in Japan and wouldn't be able to enter the country directly, even with a fake name.

With the help of Xin Nan Long, Suenaga headed to Hong Kong after Valmiro left the country, then traveled to South Korea, kept his head down in Busan until July, and waited for a ship leaving for the city of Fukuoka. The boat he rode was a small and speedy craft owned by a Korean mafia affiliated with Xin Nan Long, which was used to smuggle methamphetamine to the shore of Shikanoshima, a small island in Hakata Bay right by Fukuoka. The Koreans didn't send the ship out until July because they were waiting for the Chinese to be ready.

An imitation fleet of fishing boats piloted by Xin Nan Long members invaded the coastal waters, drawing the attention of the Japan Coast Guard patrol. While the law was occupied, the smuggling ship raced in as quickly as possible. Local yakuza from Fukuoka who were buying the meth kept the Chinese alerted to Coast Guard activity. They bought off members of the Coast Guard and used their inside sources to get as much intelligence as possible.

The American DEA kept its Asian bureau focused on the heroin-producing Golden Triangle of Myanmar, Thailand, and Laos. It also watched the People's Republic of China, which held most of the profit from that triangle, and Vietnam, which was rapidly increasing its MDMA production. The DEA was reasonably cautious of Japan's organized crime, but in terms of charting out the great powers of drug capitalism, Japan was a minor player at best.

Japan was a buyer of drugs, not a producer or exporter. There were no international kingpins of the narcotics business in Japan. The DEA had no reason to interfere—just leave it up to Japanese agencies, Tokyo police, national police, the Ministry of Health, Labour and Welfare, and so on.

Japan's intelligence agencies had some understanding of infamous Mexican criminals, but they weren't keeping their eyes out more than they did for any other foreign country's wanted figures. Latin American cartels and narcos weren't getting involved in any land disputes or invading Japan's territorial waters, so as far as the domestic government offices were concerned, it was a problem that was, quite literally, an ocean away.

The safety inspectors at international airports were mainly there to seize drugs and weapons being brought in from outside the country; they weren't scanning for the faces of foreign fugitives. If you were guilty of major crimes back home, you could pass through customs with a smile and melt right into the big city. With the economic impact of inbound tourists growing by the year, global intelligence sharing was more urgent than ever for the country's intelligence agencies.

The DEA could have strengthened its cooperation with Japan's agencies, but it was held at bay by the CIA, whose activities in East Asia were based out of Okinawa. There was a longstanding rivalry between the two offices, and squabbles over who had the initiative during drug operations in Texas and Mexico City were regular. Who got to bust the kingpin, earn the president's praise, and be invited to the White House? That was a question with big implications for next year's budget.

DEA agents hated the CIA's members for being "dumb-as-bricks shitheels who chase their targets right through our operations like a dog tied to a loose chair." The less they saw or heard from them, the better.

Valmiro Casasola of the infamous Los Casasolas, "El Polvo," one of the most wanted men in the world, had already taken the Americans' power struggle and the Japanese lack of intel into account, and fell asleep in his reclining seat in business class, unconcerned with being arrested at Haneda Airport.

When he reached up to turn off the reading light and closed his eyes, he could sense that he was going to dream about his family being executed. It was one of those feelings he got.

The nightmare, which he had at least once a week, had been a constant long before the Dogo Cartel murdered his brothers, wife, and children in a drone bombing in Nuevo Laredo, Tamaulipas. It was something that had haunted Valmiro since he first became a narco as a young man.

In the dream, Valmiro's brothers and their families were apprehended by an enemy cartel, tortured, and killed. Over and over. Every horrible atrocity he could imagine played out. Of course, Valmiro couldn't tell he was dreaming when it happened. Heads were chopped off, bodies flayed and hung from hooks—all meat and bone, like cattle at a meat-processing plant. He couldn't tell it was a dream until he woke up, because every method of execution he saw was real.

If Valmiro had seen a psychologist, he would have heard that regular nightmares were a reflection of "fear and despair," and that they stemmed from "your past experience seeing your father killed by the cartel," or perhaps just summed up in a single statement like "It's PTSD."

However, Valmiro's thoughts about the nightmares were different. Throughout all the dreams, only two members of his family were spared: his *abuelita* and himself.

That it was only the two of them was a sign that the dream had some connection to his Aztec god. So Valmiro did not view the vision of his family being executed as an omen or a warning. If anything, it empowered him. The blessing of the god increased his resistance to despair and granted him the power to overcome his fear of death.

My brothers, wife, and children, bound hand and foot with wires, their eyes gouged out, dumped from the cargo hold of a plane into the Río Bravo—

Within the dreams, Valmiro carefully observed these horrible deaths and then woke up in bed, rising as though nothing had happened. He put on clothes, washed his face, brushed his teeth, ate a tortilla, and drank coffee. Then he rode in a bulletproof vehicle to the office in the Los Casasolas compound, sat at a desktop computer, eyed graphs of cocaine supply, and placed calls to Colombia and Guatemala.

He'd personally performed plenty of executions of important enemy narcos and their families. He'd killed wives, parents, sons, and daughters. And not just narcos. Politicians, judges, police officers, and journalists had seen the same fate befall their families. Los Casasolas had a death whistle. When they blew the *silbato de la muerte*, a pile of corpses appeared.

Valmiro told his subordinates, *"Esta es nuestra manera."* This is our way.

Still, no man was truly alone.

Even the narcos committing extrajudicial executions had families, and the *sicarios* they used to do their dirty business had relatives to support, too.

In fact, a person with no personal connections who acted entirely alone had no place in drug capitalism. No matter how bloodthirsty, every individual had to belong to a group, and their ability to understand human nature was heavily prized in the business. Humans understood humanity, and if you were human, you loved your family. Family was a source of strength and a reason to fight. However, it was also the greatest and most vital weakness.

Some narcos turned into shells of their former selves after their children were killed in the cartel war. And they weren't the only ones. Public prosecutors who gave bold speeches about wiping out all the drugs in Mexico would resign and flee to America the instant a cartel sent them a warning about their families.

A family could be the greatest of weaknesses.

Yet Valmiro had conquered that vulnerability. At least, that was how he felt about it.

My brothers, my wife, and my children were murdered. Every last one. And my cartel was shattered. Yet I never turned into a soulless husk, Valmiro thought. Looking back, he hadn't shed a single tear. It didn't matter whether his family lived or died. *What is family? It doesn't refer to the living. It's more like a paean to power. There is nothing beyond it. And the paean to power is built of words.*

Somos familia. **We are family.**

Los Casasolas built their cartel on the back of those words. They recruited narcos, trained *sicarios*, formed a hierarchy, and marched into an endless war. Through the battle of blood, money, and death, the strongest bond of all tied the four brothers to their Aztec god. Titlacauan, Yohualli Ehecatl, Tezcatlipoca—the holy names, the exalted names. *Somos guerreros, somos fuertes.* We are warriors, we are strong. Los Casasolas cut off the heads of their enemies and left them on the road to Nuevo Laredo, baking in the light of Tonatiuh, the sun god. In the arid heat, the cartel roared with victory.

"Somos familia. Somos familia."

With hair tidied from a trip to a barber, a Gucci bowling shirt in subdued colors, and sparkling, fine leather shoes, Valmiro easily passed through the customs gate at the airport.

He carried nine thousand dollars, just under the limit of how much currency you could bring into Japan without declaration.

His only luggage was a Gucci messenger bag he'd bought along with the bowling shirt at the Grand Indonesia mall. There wasn't much more in it than his wallet, a fraudulent credit card and passport, and his smartphone. In an era of more and more budget airlines with strict carry-on limits, a person traveling light didn't attract the same scrutiny they would have in the past. You could buy all your necessities at a convenience store. Tourists loved Japan's convenience stores.

It was raining outside. Droplets ran tirelessly down the windows of the international passenger terminal, clouding the view of the runway. Suenaga had told Valmiro that June was rainy in Japan, but strangely enough, this was not considered the rainy season, unlike Mexico and Indonesia.

"Japan doesn't have a rainy or dry season. It has four seasons," Suenaga had explained. "Although the boundaries between them are not as clear as they used to be."

Valmiro walked through the busy international terminal of Haneda Airport, observing the group tours and their rainbow of rolling suitcases and listening to the pleasant echo of the multilingual announcements. About the only thing that separated the airborne entry to Tokyo from Soekarno-Hatta Airport was the lack of Segways.

After converting his dollars to yen, Valmiro walked through the food court. There had been a number of Japanese restaurants at the malls in Jakarta, so the sight of Japanese-language signs was not particularly alien to him. Sushi and tempura were familiar concepts at this point.

He entered a steakhouse and ordered in English: a half-pound sirloin, well done, with a Kirin to drink.

While the kitchen prepared the meat, Valmiro drank the beer and looked at a map of the Tokyo area, confirming the route between Haneda and Kawasaki. He'd already done this on the plane, but the map of the Kanto region gave him a strange sense of déjà vu, despite having no past connection to the country.

The steak came out on a hot plate, so Valmiro folded up the map and picked up his knife and fork. He thought to himself as he cut the meat.

Have I seen this map somewhere before?

Nothing came to mind. While he chewed, he examined the steak knife in his hand. Faded stainless steel, marked MADE IN JAPAN, twelve centimeters long, cut from one piece of metal—an integral knife, blade and handle one piece, just the right weight.

When he was done eating the half-pound sirloin steak, he used the inside of his folded napkin to wipe his mouth and drank the complimentary cup of coffee. On his way to the register with his bill in hand, he reached for another steak knife at an unoccupied table, and, like a stage magician, deftly and instantly rotated the blade to hide it under his palm and wrist. Then he reached back to tuck it into his belt behind his back. The steak knife was hidden under the hem of his bowling shirt. This was the bare minimum of self-defense weaponry. As long as the knife came from a different table from the one he'd sat at, the staff wouldn't suspect him of anything.

He paid the bill at the register with cash and said, "Keep the change," then headed out the door past a group of four coming the other way.

It wasn't hot, but the humidity was higher than in Jakarta.

Valmiro walked along a covered path out of the international passenger terminal and toward a taxi curb, avoiding the constant rain. He would take a car, not the train. He wanted to see as much of the road route from Tokyo to Kawasaki as possible.

In the taxi area, all the cars lined up neatly and waited for customers; they didn't argue and jockey for better positions. You didn't have to worry about getting stuck with a bad driver, despite the busyness of the airport. Suenaga had told him about the taxis in Japan, but he hadn't believed it until seeing it for himself.

A driver over sixty hit the button to open the door automatically, ushering a genteel Indonesian man into the back seat before closing the door the same way. The driver knew enough everyday English to do his job.

Valmiro checked his watch as the taxi headed down Kampachi-dori Avenue. Someone else should have already checked into the Tokyo business hotel for a night under his Indonesian alias. When that man checked out in the morning (and collected his payment for doing so) the paper trail of the Indonesian man visiting Japan would come to an end.

Valmiro was supposed to receive a fake passport and residency card for a Peruvian man by the name of Raúl Alzamora from the doctor Kenji Nomura, who was waiting in Kawasaki. The identity's full name in the Hispanic style was Raúl Emilio Alzamora Misitich, with Alzamora being his paternal surname and Misitich his maternal surname. This was a different Peruvian alias from "Gonzalo García" in Jakarta. On paper, Raúl Alzamora had already been living in Kawasaki for over a year, a clever bit of construction to deceive the immigration office.

After a while, the taxi arrived at Rokugo Bridge, which crossed the Tama River. Valmiro gazed at the river separating Tokyo's Ota Ward from the city of Kawasaki in Kanagawa Prefecture and finally realized why he'd been getting that sense of déjà vu. He almost felt foolish for taking so long to figure it out.

The river.

He smirked.

An estuary that ran from west to east, forming the border between two cities in Tokyo and Kanagawa, then feeding into Tokyo Bay. On the map, the Tama greatly resembled the Río Bravo, that great river that started in Colorado, flowing west to east and forming the border between America and Mexico until it finally ended in the gulf. Water snaking west to east and generally southward, separating two worlds. All you had to do was cross, and many things would be abruptly change.

On both, the north side of the river shone with overwhelming capitalism. America stood to the north of Mexico, and Tokyo was north of Kawasaki.

So this will be my new Río Bravo.

Valmiro leaned back against the rear seat of the taxi and closed his eyes, smiling.

28

cempöhualli-huan-chicuëyi

He was a man of sharp features and sunken cheeks, just as Suenaga said. Very cautious and cold but with a manner and voice calm enough to disarm any wary conversation partners.

A man who seemed to fit the role of back-alley doctor perfectly. To Valmiro, Kenji Nomura appeared to be the same sort as the lawyers or accountants cartels hired.

In a hotel lounge in Horikawa-cho, Kawasaki, the two men pored over a catalog of air purifiers and conversed in English. Unlike Suenaga, Nomura could not speak Spanish.

Playing the part of a businessman and drinking his coffee, Valmiro asked about the source of Nomura's cocaine. He learned that the man's supply did *not* come entirely from the yakuza. He had his own, meager connection.

He's an interesting fellow, Valmiro thought, sizing Nomura up. *Or maybe it's just the* mafia japonesa *I find interesting? In the Mexican cartels, a lawyer or accountant selling even a hundredth of a gram of the cartel's cocaine is a dead man. Does he have more leeway because he's a back-alley doctor? Or maybe this Nomura has a knack for disguises.*

According to Nomura himself, he'd been smuggling cocaine from Taiwan since he was an active anesthesiologist. Valmiro envisioned a map of the drug world. After defeating Los Casasolas, the Dogo Cartel consolidated Eastern Mexico and now controlled the routes into America. As far as he knew, they weren't sending any product to East Asia yet. And the Sinaloa Cartel, which controlled Western Mexico, was focused on America and the EU. Thus, it was highly likely that the Taiwanese cocaine was coming from some new power in Michoacán or Jalisco.

Nomura's personal sales were strictly limited to the local area. Valmiro could have lent his wisdom and experience, but he hadn't come to Kawasaki to assist a Japanese man's small-time cocaine business. Besides, a true narco didn't grow his business as slowly as a farm raised marijuana and coca plants. It took time to build up an organization, but when it was time to expand the *enterprise*, you had to act as dramatically and explosively as a volcanic eruption, seizing your enemies' *plaza* as quickly as possible.

There was no real competition, only monopoly.

When a tech entrepreneur from Silicon Valley said something along these lines, Valmiro and his brothers laughed about it.

"We invented that line. Should we sue him for infringement?"

When monopoly and monopoly clashed, war was the result. Sometimes it could last for years.

Valmiro was here on this Asian island to build the funds he needed to launch another such war.

The gears were already in motion.

Blood capitalism. The red market. Valmiro and Nomura were flipping through the air purifier catalog, speaking English in hushed tones. A lounge waiter came to the table and asked, "Would you like some more coffee?"

The two men smiled and nodded.

In the month before Suenaga arrived in Japan, and the year before the cruise ship came to Kawasaki, he and his associates had a veritable mountain of tasks to get through.

Nomura bought an ailing workshop that made accessories in the Odasakae area near Kawasaki Port. Valmiro led the search for someone to manage the workshop and found a craftsman who was a mix of Japanese and Peruvian.

Valmiro and Nomura worked day and night without resting. Neither one slept more than four hours a day at the most. Adrenaline was constantly coursing out of their adrenal cortexes; they were the very image of modern entrepreneurs, quietly toiling away to build the bedrock of a new monopoly.

While they worked together, Valmiro had Nomura call him El Cocinero rather than his assumed identity of Raúl Alzamora. He called Nomura "El Loco," and Suenaga, who was still not in Japan, "Laba-Laba." The Cook, the Madman, and the Spider.

"Why a spider?" Nomura asked. Valmiro told him that it was what they called Suenaga at the rock-climbing gym in Jakarta.

Valmiro gave the orders. While Nomura performed his usual medical job, he entered the entire day's schedule into a standalone laptop with no internet connection. The files were password-locked and eventually deleted at the end of the day. However, the data itself was still recoverable, so they would destroy the laptop and its memory once the preparations for their business were complete.

- **Arrange purchase of a used vehicle**
- **Bug-proof the non–cell phone means of regular communication**
- **Observe restaurant created as a front**
- **Confirm chop shop that will outfit the car**
- **Collect intel about dealer-adjacent personnel**
- **Go to Saiganji, Ota Ward**
- **Cross Tama River on Rokugo Bridge**
- **Switch Toyota Alphard plate when leaving**

- Meet with head monk
- Meet with Xia (Xin Nan Long)
- Check on health of kids held at the shelter
- Double-check the shipping route of product

At the end of each of these breathtakingly busy days, Nomura cooked a low-sugar dinner in his home kitchen, drank plenty of mineral water, then moved to the couch in the living room and took a bump of cocaine.

Nomura believed himself a very diligent man. Ever since his days at the university hospital, he'd always kept on top of a very tight schedule.

And there was much to learn from El Cocinero, who'd likely been involved in the drug business in the past, although he'd never admit it.

Nomura heard that Latin Americans tended to treat time as a relative concept, but perhaps a certain looseness with time afforded them a greater sense of caution and intricacy when planning criminal activity. The yakuza were an excellent example of that property in reverse. Sometimes the Japanese propensity for fussy exactitude completely missed the point. There was perhaps no better example than the yakuza title *boryokudan*, or "violence group," which left nothing to the imagination.

Nomura found it quite thrilling to experience firsthand the difference in criminal sensibilities between the yakuza and a Latin American gangster.

- Confirm time of Laba-Laba's departure from Busan Port
- Destroy all cell phones, acquire new ones, change numbers
- Go to Saiganji, Ota Ward
- Cross Tama River on Daishi Bridge
- Switch Mitsubishi Pajero plate when leaving
- Meet with head monk, meet with Xia
- Go to accessory workshop in Odasakae
- Meeting about production of accessories and knives
- Select work machines (grinder, etc.) to acquire

- **Meeting about travel means at Kawasaki Port**
- **Monitor bayside industrial region**
- **Meeting with Jingliang Hao over satellite**

"Use this to buy an *escopeta*," said El Cocinero, who showed up at Nomura's office in Asahi-cho and tossed a wad of dollars onto the desk. "I want about four barracudas."

"What do you want me to buy on the dark web?" Nomura asked.

"*Escopeta* means *shotgun*. Not the cocktail. I want guns," El Cocinero replied.

There was no difference in his expression or tone, so Nomura couldn't tell if he was joking. That happened a lot with him.

"An *escopeta* with a silencer is a barracuda," El Cocinero explained. "You ever seen a barracuda? The fish."

"No."

"That's fine. All the *escopetas* should be Remington M870s—no Chinese-made. They must be twelve-gauges. Ever seen a wound from an *escopeta*?"

"I'm an anesthesiologist, not a coroner."

"Not in your old job, I mean now. You've never had a dead body hit by an *escopeta* brought in? It's so peaceful in Japan. An *escopeta* is meant for hitting your target at close range. Buy as much double-aught buckshot as you can. Double-O. Each shell has nine lead pellets inside, measuring a third of an inch across. Once we get the people together, we'll be making the shells ourselves. As for the silencers—"

"I thought shotguns—er, *escopeta* silencers—were just props for the movies," said Nomura.

"No. There's an American company called SilencerCo that makes them. We want the Salvo 12."

With that, El Cocinero left. Nomura looked up the Salvo 12 on the internet to confirm that it was a real product, then did a little research on the barracuda fish as well—it wasn't native to the area around Japan. He learned that they grew up to six feet long and were feared for their aggressive nature and sharp teeth.

Once the Jeep Wrangler for Valmiro was delivered, Nomura drove it himself to the chop shop in Nakahara Ward, Kawasaki.

The owner of the shop, Miyata, was an old drug acquaintance of Nomura's. While his current business involved breaking down cars for parts, he was previously known for doing custom work. He'd switched to dismantling because it was better money for the work, and there were more jobs.

"Bulletproof?" Miyata repeated. "I try not to do any jobs for the guys in black suits."

"It's not a yakuza car. I promise you that," said Nomura.

"In that case, fine. But it's going to take some time to get the glass."

"That's all right. Also, we want to put a trap on it. You know what that is?"

"Of course. Is this for a dealer, though? I don't think we've ever put a trap in a car before."

A trap was a secret compartment for holding drugs or guns. Following Valmiro's instructions, Nomura indicated that he wanted a double-layered dashboard and that it should open up with the following mechanism: turn the key in the ignition, switch on the hazard lights, and rotate the movable drink holders a quarter turn to the right.

Miyata listened to his first custom-order instructions in quite a while with great interest, double- and triple-checking each step, then drew up a quick diagram on the spot.

On the second floor of the Peruvian restaurant in Sakuramoto that had been made his headquarters, Valmiro booted up a desktop PC and watched footage of the Kanagawa Police performing counterterrorism exercises. Searching had led him to two types of videos online: training at a bus depot in Yokohama and training at a cargo terminal at Kawasaki Port. Firearms control forces and Special Assault Teams were present at both.

Valmiro poured mezcal into a tumbler and sipped it as he analyzed their gear. Most of them used 9 mm submachine guns. The H&K MP5 wasn't a bad weapon, but the type used in the training video was an electric toy model that shot plastic rounds. The videos had likely been sent to the media for PR purposes, but it was still a culture shock for Valmiro to see them using toy guns. It almost made him wonder, *Do those flimsy plastic bullets actually have some measure of lethality I don't know about?* In time, he learned the price of live ammunition in a non-gun-owning society like Japan. It was similar to how the street-level worth of cocaine here was miles above Mexico.

The special police seemed more like a rescue squad. When he'd finished watching, Valmiro took another swig of mezcal and muttered, "These aren't like the guys we fought in Mexico." Hao from Xin Nan Long had said that Japan's SST was tough, but that group was part of the Coast Guard. They wouldn't be clashing with the SST.

- **Live fire test (barracudas) at the chop shop in Nakahara**
- **Door-breaching test (barracudas)**
- **Drone piloting test**
- **Laba-Laba arrives in Kawasaki, time uncertain**
- **Meeting with livestock trader**
- **Arrange to buy one (fighting) bull**
- **Transport surgery table and lights to Saiganji**
- **Destroy all cell phones, acquire new ones, change numbers**

When Suenaga finally arrived in Kawasaki in late July, Nomura relayed the Peruvian boss's instructions once more: "No using real names in any communications."

Aliases were basic protocol to prevent anyone from being immediately identified.

Gonzalo García, a.k.a. Raúl Alzamora, a.k.a. El Cocinero, the Cook.

Michitsugu Suenaga, a.k.a. Laba-Laba, the Spider.

Kenji Nomura, a.k.a. El Loco, the Madman.

The head monk of Saiganji, a.k.a. La Cruz, the Cross.

Every other person involved in the business had a code name, and they were all forbidden from using any real ones in communication. La Chatarra (The Junker), El Barríl (The Barrel), La Cerámica (The Ceramics), El Taladro (The Drill), Nextli (Ashes), Malinalxochitl (The Sorceress). The titles were a mix of Spanish, Indonesian, and Nahuatl, which would surely help confuse any investigators or local mobsters who tried to identify them.

The ship had still not arrived.

But there were countless jobs left to be completed. Even if they succeeded at monopolizing a new market, hyenas would show up before long, following the scent of money.

Under El Cocinero's orders, Laba-Laba and El Loco worked tirelessly, day and night, across Ota and Kawasaki, under the assumption that there were already enemies out there threatening the operation's market dominance.

No matter how often Nomura offered, Valmiro refused to meet with Japanese gangsters. It swiftly grew difficult for Nomura to provide excuses for him.

Through Nomura, Valmiro gleaned quite a lot of information about what kind of man Reiichi Masuyama of the Senga-gumi was, but he continued to decline any in-person interaction. It was still too early for that.

"When the time is right, I will see him," Valmiro told Nomura.

The right time, in his opinion, was after he'd raised a local, here in this country, this city, to be his trustworthy and lethal tool: a *sicario*.

29

cempōhualli-huan-chiucnāhui

In the greenery along the Tama River, which had become a hidden buying spot for Kawasaki's drug users, a seller came knocking on the side window of a parked minivan. Inside the black Honda Stream was the manager of a host club, an affiliate of a quinary organization under the Senga-gumi. His girlfriend, a hostess, was present as well. They were familiar customers to the seller.

But that night, there was no response to the seller's knock. He pressed his forehead to the front passenger window to look inside. Both people were unconscious. They were dead, the seller intuited.

At first, he suspected they'd diverted the exhaust inside in a double suicide, but the engine wasn't on. That only left one cause for their deaths.

"Overdose," he muttered under his breath. They'd fucked up.

The seller's guess was more or less correct, although not in every respect. The two inside the car had done meth, and the woman had a bad trip. When she looked at her boyfriend in the seat next to her, she saw a crab that had been split in two. Her mother's bloodied face was trying to wriggle out of the tear in the middle. Her mother had died years ago, struggling beneath a mountain of inescapable debt. The woman strangled the man, her psychosis-aided fear giving her abnormal strength. Ultimately, the man couldn't overpower her and suffocated. Then the woman passed out.

When she awoke, she noticed her partner slumped against the wheel but did not call 119, Japan's emergency number. Instead of calling for an ambulance, she snorted all his remaining powder, enough to make her heart stop.

The seller contacted the Senga-gumi, who sent two men to recover the bodies and take them to their black-market doctor in Asahi-cho.

Nomura examined the corpses, particularly the compression marks on the man's throat, and picked up a smartphone with a number he'd recently changed—El Cocinero's orders. He placed a call to Reiichi Masuyama of the Senga-gumi.

"Hello, this is Nomura."

"You change your fuckin' number again?" Masuyama snapped. "I'm not gonna pick up the next time."

"It looks like the woman you sent to me overdosed," Nomura reported succinctly, "but she strangled the man first."

"Not the other way around?"

"No. The woman killed the man."

"Damn. Ain't that crazy," growled Masuyama. "Because of the drugs?"

"Presumably."

"Well, neither one's important, so go ahead and take out the kidneys."

"I understand the man is a member of one of your fifth-rung groups."

"And?"

"Do you need to hold a funeral?"

"Funeral?"

"I'm just asking if you need him in a casket or not."

Asking was a simple procedural formality. Nomura knew Masuyama's answer before he posed the question. A host club manager in a fifth-rung organization was a common brute, a freely disposable pawn.

"No, he doesn't need a fucking funeral," said Masuyama.

"All right. If you don't need a body afterward, I'll dismantle them both."

"Do whatever the hell you want." Masuyama chuckled. "You guys are sick, Nomura. You autopsy freaks."

Masuyama saw Nomura as a kind of highly educated psychopath, but he didn't call him "El Loco." He didn't even know the nickname existed. He didn't know a thing about El Loco, Laba-Laba, or El Cocinero.

Nomura placed a call to Suenaga, then contacted the boss, El Cocinero.

Valmiro had purchased the Peruvian restaurant in Sakuramoto, Kawasaki, and was living in the office space upstairs. The restaurant was called Papa Seca, after the beloved dried potato snack.

He left Sakuramoto for Asahi-cho in the outfitted Jeep Wrangler. Nomura and Suenaga were waiting for him.

Valmiro examined the woman's body on the examination table, then glanced at the man on the floor. Both were still clothed. There was only one table, so the ground was the only place to put him.

Crouching, Valmiro removed the dead man's leather shoes. He took a folding knife out of his shirt pocket and carefully cut off the toe of the shoe in his hand, revealing a tiny plastic bag tucked into a pocket there.

"Cocaine?" asked Nomura.

Instead of answering, Valmiro tapped the bag's contents onto the table, stuck his pinky into the powder, and gave it a little taste. Nomura and Suenaga did the same.

"That's *basuco*," said Valmiro.

Nomura looked to Suenaga, who just frowned. Neither had ever heard of it.

"It's cocaine paste, brick dust, and sulfuric acid," Valmiro explained, making a mixing gesture with his hands. "They sell it everywhere in Colombia. It's absolute shit, as cheap as hard candy. Can't believe someone's selling it here."

Nomura and Suenaga performed the kidney extractions on the two cadavers together, removing all four, and storing them in a cooler. Valmiro watched them work quickly and accurately and considered the current state of the business arrangement.

Once the kidneys have been harvested, the Senga-gumi gets ninety-six percent, and Nomura gets four...although it used to be as low as two percent. Still, four is nothing. The yakuza are going to demand the same for our heart business. We need to change their thinking on the matter in the near future... Need to seize the initiative...

"What now?" Suenaga inquired as he removed his bloodied rubber gloves.

"We dispose of them," Nomura stated.

"Can we do whatever we want with the rest?"

"They gave us the go-ahead."

Suenaga turned back to look at Valmiro. "Should we use them for target practice?"

He was aware that El Cocinero preferred having a real target to shoot at over a cardstock cut-out of a person. A real body helped train a proper *sicario*.

However, a target that was already dead meant nothing to Valmiro. At best, it might be useful for IED testing. He shook his head.

So Suenaga offered his idea. "In that case, why don't we take them to the shelter in Ota?"

Nomura had been thinking the same thing.

The surgery room under Saiganji was already set up with the latest equipment for when their business was ready to commence. The lights were installed, and there was far more equipment than Nomura could fit in his office.

Their future product was eating healthy food in the shelter, absorbing special artificial lights meant to mimic the wavelength of the sun's rays, and growing in the best conditions possible. It was too early to harvest them. They had to wait for the boat to come from Indonesia before they could start selling fresh hearts.

"The surgery room's been empty this whole time," Suenaga said. "If we have free bodies to use as we please..."

It was the perfect opportunity to test out the new facility.

Valmiro smoked a cigarette, his eyes dark with concentration. He nodded.

The two kidneyless bodies were slated for transport to Saiganji. But these were real human bodies, and it was too risky to simply toss them into a car and drive around, as the Senga-gumi did.

Naturally, the three men had a plan for how to deal with this issue.

They summoned the man code-named El Barríl to the doctor's office. The forty-nine-year-old Japanese man ran a private company selling propane gas in Takatsu Ward, Kawasaki. He loved gambling on horse and bicycle races, and he regularly bought cocaine from Nomura.

Valmiro gave the man his name based on the role he would play within the business.

The name El Barríl came from his propane canisters, the largest of which were fifty kilograms. El Barríl modified the biggest canisters, giving them larger interiors perfect for transporting bodies and organs.

If they happened to get pulled over for an inspection, no police officer was going to say, "Open up your propane canister to show me what's inside." They wouldn't even think it possible. The modified canisters might as well have been coffins on a hearse.

If there was one issue with them, it was the space. A petite woman could just barely fit inside the fifty-kilo canister, but a man wouldn't. That was an easy enough challenge to solve, though. Nomura and Suenaga severed the man's limbs at the joints to make him more compact.

El Barríl stuck the limbs into a smaller thirty-kilo canister that was similarly modified, loaded it among a bunch of ordinary tanks, and drove north along the national route, safely crossing the bridge over the Tama.

There wasn't a single body in the world that went entirely to waste. After at least ten hours since death, the most valuable part of the body—the heart—was no longer viable, but everything else could be sold, like poached elephant tusks from Africa.

A hundred thousand yen per eyeball, up to a million depending on the condition.

Five million yen for the pancreas.
Two million yen per gram of bone marrow.
Five hundred thousand per ligament.
Two hundred thousand for the gallbladder.
A hundred fifty thousand for an ankle.
Fifty thousand for a wrist.

Everything could go for a higher price. In the basement operating room at Saiganji, close to where the undocumented children slept, Suenaga gleefully cut into the dead bodies. Beads of sweat formed on his forehead as he worked the scalpel. It was common practice to stop the air circulation when performing surgery. Suenaga stuck to that rule, even when working on a corpse.

"It's too bad about the blood," he muttered, glancing at the empty blood packs.

Thirty thousand yen per liter of blood.

The blood in the bodies on the tables had stopped circulating the moment their hearts gave out, and livor mortis had set in.

"What will we do with the skull?" asked Nomura, who was sterilizing the bone saw and lamina spreaders in boiling water.

Suenaga removed his latex gloves, wiped the sweat from his forehead, and picked up his smartphone. He placed a call to El Cocinero, who'd returned to the office in Sakuramoto, and repeated Nomura's question in Spanish.

"¿Qué debo hacer con el cráneo?"

"Dáselo al artesano," Valmiro replied. *"A la Cerámica."*

Give it to the artisan. La Cerámica.

Using an oscillating surgical saw, Nomura and Suenaga removed the two heads, shaved the hair off, and peeled the scalps.

A hundred thousand yen per scalp.

"So, are we sending these right to the workshop?" Suenaga laughed.

"No, we should prepare them a little more," said Nomura. "I think we have some sodium carbonate in the supply closet."

"We gonna boil them ourselves?" asked Suenaga. "They don't even force medical students to make real skeleton models anymore."

"Not a model. Ours is an art piece," Nomura replied.

They set a large pot full of water and sodium carbonate over a stove and took turns boiling the two heads, carefully adjusting the heat level. When the muscle fibers softened up, they used surgical curettes and toothbrushes to scrub loose the material until they had bare skulls.

The rest would be up to the artisan.

If they removed the top of the skull and shaped it like a dish, polishing it to a fine finish, it could be sold for quite a lot of money in certain areas of Southern Asia. There was a time when the human skull and religious faith were tightly connected all over the world. There were still people today who worshipped the skull as a holy object.

La Cerámica.

The man's accessory workshop was very close to an ironworks, and Kawasaki Port was on the east side of the canal. For the moment, only one man worked there, where the salt was thick on the breeze.

La Cerámica's real name was Pablo Zaha; born to a Peruvian father and a Japanese mother and raised in the city of Naha on Okinawa. His full name was Kiyotake Pablo Robledo Zaha. Robledo was his father's surname, and Zaha was his Okinawan mother's surname. Pablo was the oldest, with a younger brother and sister following him. After their parents died, Pablo's siblings left Okinawa, and he hadn't seen them since. He had no idea where they were or what they were doing now.

When he was young, Pablo dreamed of being a soccer player, but he'd given up on the idea by the time he understood how poor his family was. He couldn't even get a soccer ball as a gift, much less cleats. He thought about stealing his friend's shoes, but he knew he'd be caught eventually. Since he couldn't join a local club, his only chances to play came from pickup games at the local parks and empty lots.

Going pro under such circumstances meant you had to show a gift for the sport as a child. Pablo understood that much. You had to be a genius, and he wasn't.

To help his parents, Pablo had to start working after his middle school graduation, the end of compulsory schooling in Japan. However, he didn't want just any old job. He had a new dream to replace the soccer one.

In his second year of middle school, Pablo saw a collection of folding knives at a friend's house. It was his friend's father's collection, in fact. While he'd envisioned that a knife collection involved many large and fearsome blades, all that he saw in the neatly arranged case was a group of pocket-size handles. Every one of the polished blades was tucked seamlessly into its grip, kept out of sight. The handles were made of various materials like wood and shell, and Pablo couldn't get enough of them. They were all single pieces, fashioned by the careful eye of the knifemaker. When the curved blades appeared from inside the handles, Pablo saw a perched bird on a tree branch spreading its wings. All it took for the weapons to become pocket-size again was folding the steel wing back in.

The idea was already in his head by the time he left his friend's house.

I want to be a knifemaker.

A company in Okinawa made and sold mass-produced, assembly-line knives, but if you wanted to make beautiful, single-piece custom ones, you had to apprentice with an independent crafter. If Pablo apprenticed, he'd have to work for essentially no pay for a while. That wouldn't support his parents, so Pablo took a job at the mass-produced knife company instead, and during his free time outside of work, he studied the art of knifemaking independently.

Pablo was good with his hands, and his efforts paid off. Sometimes he would visit the workshops of the more famous knifemakers. Most of them assumed that he was a spy for the assembly-line company trying to steal their secrets, and promptly banned him from their property, but a couple was impressed by the boy's passion for the art and spent some time with him.

Brian Toledo was the knifemaker most kind to Pablo.

Brian came to Okinawa as a Marine in his twenties and had never seen a more beautiful sea. He stuck around in Okinawa after leaving the Marines, married a Japanese woman, founded a knifemaking workshop in Naha, and had been working there for over twenty years. Brian had fans around the world. Twice a year, he went back to his home of Texas for custom knife events, where he would hold interviews with knife enthusiast publications from around the world. The pieces he brought with him sold out before noon, so the writers had to get their pictures the night before the event.

When young Pablo visited Brian Toledo's workshop, the older man stopped working, ground some coffee beans, and made them both a cup. Then he taught Pablo several invaluable knifemaking secrets.

At nineteen, Pablo entered his own folding knife into a contest put on by a Japanese knife enthusiast magazine and won with high praise from the judges. But because he was making a living at the knife factory, he'd submitted his work under his Spanish initials, fearing retribution from within the company. His craft was a rebellion against the company's style of mass-production; a betrayal to the employer. When the magazine asked for an interview after his success, the most he could do was a short phone call.

When the issue arrived at his apartment, Pablo opened it to the page with photos of his knife. He gazed at the caption that sat impotently below the pictures: *By P. R., company worker, Naha.* P.R. was Pablo Robledo.

He worked long overtime at his job and took part in the planning stages of many company products, but none of his work led to any savings. On his low salary, all of that money went back to his family.

As a middle-school graduate, Pablo didn't understand that the company was taking advantage of him. *I'm not the only one who's poor,* he thought. *Okinawa itself is struggling from the long, long recession. The only people who have it good are those from the main islands who fly down here to spend time at their vacation homes.*

Today, Pablo's parents were long gone, and he had a wife and two-year-old daughter to support instead. He needed more money to make their lives better. So Pablo summoned his courage and quit the company. He'd been working there nonstop since his middle-school graduation, but they didn't even give him a good-bye party.

Pablo left his wife and daughter behind in Naha and set his sights on Kawasaki in the Kanagawa Prefecture because he heard of a Peruvian community there.

However, it was challenging to find the right job in an unfamiliar place. The mass-market knife companies in Kanagawa were suffering, and they weren't looking to hire outside of the yearly hiring period. He couldn't become an independent knifemaker's apprentice, either—Pablo had no reputation in that world, and he was getting on in years.

Within the Peruvian expat community, he heard about an auto parts manufacturer and tried to get a job with them, but when he went for an interview, the office was full of foreign laborers from various countries, most of whom were turned away. The Japanese worker managing the line of interviewees asked Pablo if he had a residency card. He shook his head and quietly left the line. He didn't need a residency card. Pablo Zaha was a Japanese citizen.

To get more information on jobs, he started visiting a restaurant called Papa Seca in Sakuramoto, and spoke with the Peruvians living in Kawasaki. Some of them had done contract work with abusive companies out of desperation. One man couldn't find a job and went around collecting cans to sell until the local homeless community ganged up on him. Another person attacked and drove off a Bangladeshi drug dealer who hung out at the park where the Peruvians gathered. There was an American military base in Kanagawa, and the local Peruvians found themselves in fights with the soldiers more often than not. Hearing all of the stories of their struggles made Pablo realize that things weren't all that different from Okinawa.

Why did I even come to the main island? he wondered woefully one night over a bowl of canary beans. That's when Raúl Alzamora spoke to him.

"Oí que puedes hacer cuchillos." I heard you can make knives.

When he first laid eyes on Raúl, Pablo thought he was a factory worker with a cold. He was dressed like he'd come off a shift, wearing a khaki work cap and a white mask over his face that he never removed.

Raúl spoke only Latin American Spanish, which Pablo replied to with the Spanish he'd learned from his father. Raúl claimed that he was Peruvian, but Pablo didn't believe him.

Pablo had never lived in Peru himself, but it was clear that Raúl had even less attachment to the folk music coming through the speakers hung from the ceiling and the traditional Peruvian ceviche. You would expect a Peruvian who'd come here for work to feel more sentimental about their home country. When he learned later that Raúl was the owner of the restaurant, Pablo was shocked.

Raúl had money and bought Pablo a beer. He offered a cigarette, too, but Pablo didn't smoke.

While drinking the beer, Pablo explained his background. He took out the crumpled-up old clipping from the magazine to show Raúl the photo of the folding knife he made to win the contest at age nineteen. The man examined the picture and praised it with a quiet, firm voice. Pablo could sense that the comment was not flattery but an honest opinion. Emboldened, Pablo displayed photo after photo from his smartphone of the various blades he'd crafted. Raúl examined them all closely, praising each.

When a picture of Pablo's family popped up between the knives, Raúl asked, "Are you looking for work?"

"I have a wife and daughter in Okinawa." Pablo laughed guiltily. "It's time to stop sightseeing and start sending money back to them."

The second time they met each other at the Peruvian restaurant, Pablo noticed the darkness in the depths of Raúl Alzamora's eyes. He hadn't seen that the first time. Perhaps the man had cleverly disguised that part of himself.

Above the mask that covered half of his face, Raúl's eyes were as heavy as a blade made of tungsten steel. He didn't raise his voice or fly into a drunken rage, but Pablo had never met anyone who possessed such a terrifying aura.

Still, Raúl had money.

And he'd offered a job.

A job out of Pablo's wildest dreams.

"Call me El Cocinero," he said.

The job itself was greater than anything Pablo could have hoped for. It was at a workshop in Odasakae owned by Raúl Alzamora—El Cocinero—and his business partners. They had all the equipment. The main product was silver accessories, but Pablo was also permitted to make custom knives for sale.

They also gave him a living space and three months' salary to start off with. He sent part of it back home to his wife, then went to a barber for the first time in ages. After moving out of the cheap hostel and into the apartment, he reported to the workshop every morning.

Two Japanese men occasionally popped in, one nicknamed Laba-Laba, and the other nicknamed El Loco. Both were El Cocinero's business partners and co-owners of the shop.

One April evening, Laba-Laba sat down on the break couch in the workshop and brazenly lit up a joint. He gave Pablo a hit or two. This wasn't new to Pablo; Brian Toledo, the ex-Marine, had smoked around the back of his workshop as well.

Laba-Laba inhaled deep into his lungs, then examined the folding knife Pablo had constructed from handle to blade. "You made this yourself?"

"There was no one else to do it with me." Pablo laughed. "I got the steel stock and handle material and designed it myself."

"How did you make the blade?"

"First, I envisioned the overall form, then I cut it out of the steel along the marking lines. It's that simple. After that, it's just polishing."

"It's incredible work," Laba-Laba praised. "You could sell this for a lot. We gotta pray that you don't get too many collectors chasing after you."

Pablo's time at the workshop was like a dream come true.

He put his full effort into everything he created there, not just knives. He studied all he could from the Chrome Hearts brand—the "King of Silver"—and every silver ring and pendant he created sold like wildfire online. They weren't just copies of a more popular creator's works, either. Every excellent brand needed features that no other company offered.

The best hint came from his employer, El Cocinero. "You should use the ancient civilizations from Peru as a model," he suggested. "Incorporate designs from the Incan Empire."

In this way, Pablo's silverwork developed a unique style that could only be found at his little business.

He had no complaints about the treatment. He was getting more than twice the pay from his old company, and the sudden success was almost baffling. Once things settled down, he wanted to bring his wife and daughter to Kawasaki, but he suspected that would never happen.

The money was just too good. Something else was going on. Too many things hinted at a darker truth: the aliases that everyone used, the frightening depth of El Cocinero's eyes, even the casual comment that Laba-Laba made while examining his knife.

"We gotta pray that you don't get too many collectors chasing after you."

Who were these three men? Drug dealers? Just because Laba-Laba smoked weed didn't make him a dealer. And even if they were, they hadn't forced Pablo to sell anything for them. At least, not for now. He only went to the workshop, created silver accessories, and fashioned custom knives. His crafts were uncompromising and worth every bit his bosses charged. But even so...

Pablo could never dismiss the idea in the back of his mind that this was dangerous work. It wasn't the job itself, but the feeling that there was something more than met the eye to those three men. If Pablo was going to skip out on them, sooner was better than later.

But what other jobs are out there for me? Pablo asked himself. *I have no education. I can't feed my family washing dishes. The important thing is to provide for my girls and keep them happy. I can't do that without money, money, money...*

"I want you to make a custom piece for me, La Cerámica. It's an odd request, but I know that you can do it."

The afternoon after El Cocinero called him for a special job, the materials for the item showed up at the shop. A man from a propane gas company had a specially modified canister that stored real skulls.

Pablo had no medical education, but he'd worked with cattle shins to make knife handles before. The texture of the bones informed him these weren't props but authentic human skulls.

Where had they come from? Pablo couldn't imagine that El Cocinero would actually tell him if he asked.

The two skulls were different sizes and still fresh. They'd been attached to bodies in the recent past. There was a design chart for the custom order enclosed with the skulls.

Whatever Pablo was making and whoever bought it, these were not legal materials. He'd never worked on such a thing before. At this point, Pablo found it laughable that he'd been fretting over the idea his bosses would force him to sell drugs. That would've been preferable. He canceled everything on his schedule for the day and sat alone in the workshop, facing two fresh skulls from dubious, unknown sources.

Pablo wrapped them in newspaper to avoid touching them and placed them in a box for knife-handle materials. He turned out the lights, went outside, and locked the door. On the outside of the long, flat building was a sign that read RIVERPORT METAL. El Cocinero and the others had kept the name when they bought the workshop, so on paper, the company name was Kawasaki Riverport Metal, Ltd.

Pablo walked toward the port, listening to music on a pair of wireless headphones. He'd bought an MP3 player at an electronics store in Kawasaki, and filled it with nothing but Texas blues. That was all that Brian Toledo, knifemaker extraordinaire, listened to in his shop.

Brian had told him to always grind the beans for his coffee, so Pablo ordinarily never drank canned coffee. Today, however, he bought a can from a vending machine and drank it as he walked. He didn't mind the taste. He watched the smoke rise from the ironworks, he watched the sea, he watched the gulls, and he watched the container ships coming and going. He also looked at some photos of his wife and daughter saved on his phone. Allowing El Cocinero to see his family's faces felt like a fatal mistake. "What have I done?" he muttered to the ocean.

He'd have to turn down the job. Squeezing the firm steel can hard enough to crumple it, Pablo turned back to the workshop. He intended to call when he got back. He'd tell El Cocinero he couldn't do it. He repeated the phrase over and over, to convince himself as much as anything. *No puedo, no puedo, no puedo.*

Too late.

When Pablo unlocked the door to the workshop, he was greeted by the sound of a man speaking Spanish.

Sitting on the chair facing the workbench in the darkness inside was El Cocinero. With a cigarette in his mouth, he stared at the two skulls he'd retrieved from Pablo's box and placed them on the bench.

"Did you clear your head?" El Cocinero asked.

Pablo turned on the light and tossed the empty coffee can into the trash. He looked out the window. The branches of a cherry blossom tree, blossomless, wavered in the breeze. "El Cocinero, I'm sorry, but—"

"'Do whatever you can to make your money,'" Valmiro Casasola said, cutting Pablo off. "You can find people anywhere who will say something along those lines without a hint of shame. Any country, any city. Does having a low crime rate in an area mean that all the people who live there are saints? Of course not. But just because someone says, 'Do whatever you can to make your money,' doesn't mean they'll follow it with 'And I'll kill anyone who tries to stop me.' That's a different thing. If they get worked up, they might kill one or two, sure. You don't wanna go wild and kill ten people, though. That gets you thrown in jail, making it all meaningless. Normal people really don't know how to kill, but it's very easy for them to understand this simple motto: 'Do whatever you can to make your money.' Even snot-nosed college kids do it. However, they don't realize that it means the same thing as 'Kill anyone who tries to stop you.' It's the exact same fucking thing. That's capitalism. You see, La Cerámica, you're going to fashion those skulls. You don't have any other choice. You're going to grind out the top of the cranium with a metal rasp, polish it with some fine sandpaper, and get them as close as you can to the shape of the vessel on the chart. You do that, and we sell them somewhere in Asia for a lot of cash. You don't need to know anything more than that. Work here and make your money, La Cerámica. You want a car, right? You need clothes. You've got to put your daughter through college. Sure, you might have a little nightmare every now and then or wake up in the middle of the night in a cold sweat. But so what? That's it. Is that really worse than the hell of knowing your wife and daughter are starving to death? You don't wanna go back to being poor again. Poverty's there to stop you. And if you don't *kill anything that tries to stop you*, it comes right back. We put you in charge of this shop. We can tell at a glance who's fit for our work, no matter the language you speak, or the color of your skin or eyes. La Cerámica—Pablo Robledo—I chose you. You're family now. Got that? ***Somos familia.*** Don't think about anything else. If you ever have doubts again, do what you did today. Take a walk to the port and dump all those thoughts into the sea."

30

cempöhualli-huan-mahtlactli

Chatarra.

The nickname Valmiro Casasola originally gave Tohru Igawa was "La Chatarra," Spanish for "The Junker," but the definite article *la* had gradually been elided so that the Familia just called him Chatarra now.

At age thirty-one, one hundred and seventy-eight centimeters, and one hundred and fifty-four kilograms, he looked like a gentle giant at first, but his weight concealed a frightening amount of power. He could bench-press one hundred and five kilograms raw and lift two hundred and ninety kilograms in a bicep curl with either arm.

The total weight of his bench press was extreme already, but the one-hundred-and-five-kilograms bicep curl was truly extraordinary. Even massive sumo and pro wrestlers couldn't do that with one hand. It would be difficult to find anyone across the world who could match that feat. His grip strength was over one hundred and sixty kilograms, which would put Chatarra on the level of the world heavyweight arm wrestling champion, if not higher, in terms of arm strength.

Chatarra worked at an auto yard in Nakahara Ward, Kawasaki, where he reused the junk he was named after, and worked out on his own private training facilities in a corner of the weedy, unkept yard.

He made his own barbells out of old tires and driveshafts, built a bench for pressing with the remains of a reclining seat, and welded two metal pipes to the cabin of a scrapped truck to turn it into a machine for strengthening back and leg muscles.

The tools were practical but had all been fashioned out of junk. An auto-dismantling yard already had a dystopic look to it, and Chatarra's home-made training gym made this one look even more desolate. It was like an outdoor gym in a developing nation, with equipment cobbled together from various pieces.

The car parts the auto yard dismantled went into steel containers that were loaded onto a ship at the port and sent overseas to different markets. Some arrived in Russia, but the majority went to Southeast Asia.

No business could withstand its products being stolen before they could even ship them out, so the yard was surrounded by sheet metal walls and barbed wire, and several security cameras kept an eye out for burglars. Electrical current ran through the barbed wire in a few spots, supposedly to keep birds away.

Any place isolated and invisible from the outside world was a ready hot-bed for criminal activity. The auto yard in Nakahara was an easy hangout spot for a *bosozoku* motorcycle gang. Extortion, abduction, money fights—it became a center for all manner of illegal activities, and through the *bosozoku*, various unsavory types and street toughs were drawn to the promise of drugs and prostitution.

When he was first hired, Chatarra played the part of a bouncer who broke up skirmishes between the rowdy younger punks. However, it was rare that he intervened calmly. He typically erupted into extreme violence and beat the ruffians into submission. Any *bosozoku* biker or delinquent who tried to cause trouble in the yard would get smashed in the face, lifted up, slammed against the ground, threatened, and then hurt in even more explicit ways, if necessary, until they coughed up some cash as a penalty for their actions. He would do it to anyone. When they swore they'd kill him, he just smiled and laughed it off.

Chatarra paid attention to who came and went, remembering their names and faces and keeping track of their activities, until he reached the point where he was effectively running the show after hours. Even the company boss who hired him couldn't control him anymore.

Once they'd seen the power he commanded, the punks grew terrified of Chatarra. No sane person would dare pick a fight with him; only the junkies had the lack of self-awareness to endanger themselves that way.

Miyata, the owner of the chop shop, gave the *bosozoku* and street punks a place to conduct their business and collected a share of the proceeds. He also bought cocaine from Nomura the doctor, but he had a personal rule that he'd always kept: "No involvement in yakuza business." If he teamed up with yakuza, they'd take all the money he made from dismantling and shipping out auto parts. In Miyata's opinion, he'd made the right decision to keep his business separate from the yakuza.

If even a single yakuza tried to get into the auto yard, they would wind up causing trouble with Igawa, who'd beat them half to death. The kids in their teens and twenties behaved themselves because they were terrified of Igawa, but it wouldn't be that easy with the professionals. *If they ever set their sights on me, I won't be able to do this anymore*, Miyata thought.

Masakatsu Miyata was born in Kochi Prefecture and became a firefighter after graduating college in Yokohama. He met Kenji Nomura the back-alley doctor when he was fifty-four.

At the time, Miyata was working at a fire station in Tsurumi, Yokohama, and regularly buying meth from a local dealer. But when he learned that the drugs and firearms division of the prefectural police had his name on a list for investigation, he went to Nomura in Kawasaki and paid for a complete blood transfusion to pass a voluntary urine test. After that, he started buying coke from Nomura instead.

After retiring early from the fire department, Miyata moved to Kawasaki and started up a small car-repair shop because he liked tinkering with vehicles. At first, he used his knowledge of cars to repair and replace parts, but when he learned that exporting the parts to Southeast Asia was better money, he changed lanes. With his newfound success, he moved to a bigger location and became the owner of an auto-dismantling yard.

Unlike at his little repair and body shop, he had to hire more people for this place, but it was difficult to find good workers. All the young men he hired would start huffing and puffing after no more than rolling truck tires from one end of the garage to the other. Just watching the weaklings work made him angry, and he spent most days berating his employees.

His reasoning for bringing on Tohru Igawa, fresh off parole release for murder, was simple: his physical strength. Igawa was far, far stronger than anyone else he could find. It was like picking up a piece of heavy machinery for cheap.

The parole officer from the Ministry of Justice claimed Igawa was fully reformed and ready to reenter society. He was as round as a sumo wrestler, and his smile was pure and infectious.

Miyata had heard that Igawa's murder charge came after a string of severe workplace abuses from his old boss. In a sense, Igawa was also a victim. He was working hard to move past an event that he couldn't erase. If you didn't know what he served time for, you'd think Igawa was a gentle bear of a man with the strength to match.

Every day that Igawa showed up for work, he wore a Dickies safari hat. He had two of them, one khaki and one green.

"It's to hide a burn scar I got as a kid," he said, and he never, ever took the hat off in front of others.

Igawa was raised in the Naka ward of Yokohama, where he suffered at the hands of his father, a welfare recipient. The senior Igawa was an alcoholic who beat his son and put out cigarettes on his head. He did it so often that the younger Igawa developed permanent bald spots that gave him a mottled look.

Igawa plotted to murder his father but didn't get the chance to put his plan into practice because his father went to a psychiatric hospital. Half a year later, the man died of brain atrophy from alcoholism. Igawa's mother, who'd remarried years earlier, hadn't come to the funeral.

In Miyata's mind, since Igawa wasn't involved in customer service and merely worked at the shop all the time, there was no issue with him wearing a hat constantly.

Miyata bought him a brand-new Yokohama DeNA BayStars baseball cap as a present, but Igawa never actually wore it. The hat was still sitting in the office.

Miyata brought Igawa, wearing one of his safari hats, around to the front of a car he'd lifted with the hydraulic jack. He showed the big man exactly how to use the job's many tools during the prep phase and how the power shovel was employed to dismantle a car. Igawa didn't have a license for heavy machinery, but he could go and get one after learning the ropes here.

Although his personality had a few rough edges, Igawa learned quickly, and didn't take breaks longer than the designated time. Best of all, he liked Miyata.

Miyata remembered his father back in Kochi, who'd kept Tosa fighting dogs and keenly felt that blood in his veins. Tohru Igawa was a man out on parole after committing murder, blessed with unfathomable strength. *And only I can tame him, like a fighting dog*, Miyata thought. To Miyata, who was a bachelor without a family, Igawa was the closest thing he'd ever had to a son.

Four months later, Miyata was terrified of Igawa, regretted ever hiring the monster, and cursed the parole officer who'd lied out of his ass that Igawa was "fully reformed."

The cars that came into the chop shop were often stolen from Tokyo or the surrounding prefectures. These thefts weren't done by individuals but by groups that worked in tandem. Some of them preferred to do business quickly and discreetly with text messages or emails, while others came into the office to loiter or harass Miyata like wannabe yakuza, trying to squeeze as much value as they could out of their ill-gotten goods.

On one particular day, the leader of a vehicle theft group was taking up space in the upstairs office. Igawa asked him, "Have you seen the Chevy I ride?"

He lured the car thief to the garage downstairs, then beat him to death with a wrench. When the man's subordinate followed, Igawa ran him through the stomach with a metal pipe that had been sharpened on one end with a grinder.

The two car thieves never came back after leaving the office, so Miyata eventually got suspicious. When he asked Igawa what happened, the man replied blankly, "Them? They're gone."

Miyata learned the truth the next morning.

When he arrived at the shop, he found Igawa in the corner of the yard with a drum can over a fire. The man had a gas mask on his face and a driveshaft in his hands, stirring the liquid inside the barrel. He wore his safari hat like usual and looked as though he were making a big meal for a camping group.

"What are you doing?" asked Miyata.

"Stirring," Igawa replied. "I wouldn't get too close. This stuff emits gas."

"Stirring...what?"

"Sodium hydroxide, boiling water, and human remains," Igawa said. "I'm melting down those guys from yesterday. Couple of small-time car thieves trying to act like they're important. Their clothes and shoes are over there. I'll give them to the collectors later. They can sell both in Southeast Asia."

Miyata was speechless. He stared at the bubbling liquid inside the drum can.

A crow cawed overhead. Igawa looked up at the clear sky, rolled his head left and right, then let go of the driveshaft. He took a few steps backward, removed the gas mask, and lit up a cigarette. "It's been boiling for a while now," he said. "When you do it this way, only the teeth remain. Last time I did this, I crushed those in the press."

"The last time...?"

Igawa looked at Miyata and smiled, then exhaled smoke. "You gonna turn me in? Go right ahead. But I can kill you before they send me back to prison. I'll kill you, and then your friends, and I know where you live. When I decide to do it, I do it. Nothing personal, of course. I'm just killing, that's all. Oh, by the way, Boss, I forgot to thank you for the fire department barbecue you took me to last week. It was great. I liked the microbrew there, too."

The steel nerves to murder two people and remain utterly nonchalant about it, the total lack of any conscience—Igawa wasn't reformed in the slightest. He was just playing the role of a friendly, gregarious man. To Igawa, other people were nothing but targets to be hunted as he saw fit.

He'd killed people right here at the shop, melted their bodies in a barrel with sodium hydroxide, and admitted it freely to his boss—it was all insane. Miyata was utterly overwhelmed by Igawa's ruthlessness. He couldn't turn the man in or fire him. It was clear who among this pair standing by the bubbling drum can was in charge.

Miyata couldn't get Igawa's words out of his head.

"I'm just killing, that's all."

Tohru Igawa had once been a cameraman for a film production company in Yokohama. The eleven years between leaving that job and getting hired at the chop shop in Kawasaki was time he spent in prison serving a sentence for murder.

Igawa dropped out of high school to become a contractor for the production company, where he started learning how to film. The company made its business by subcontracting for a local station, and a lot of what they did was put together materials for news programs.

When there was word of a traffic accident or house fire, the company rushed out in the place of the station's busy camera operators to get footage from the scene. The subcontractor's job was to get the shots, even if it necessitated speeding violations, using scanners, or trespassing. As long you didn't get caught, it was fair game.

It was a mentality shared with tabloid photographers, but all of the workers at the company thought of themselves like stringers, in the American sense. Stringers were independent cameramen who sold images and videos of notable incidents to news producers, most of them working in teams at night. If they negotiated to sell a piece of video to one station and the deal fell through, they'd offer it to a competing channel instead. Igawa's company, however, had an exclusive deal with one station, and re-upped their contract every six months.

A stringer was a freelancer, but Igawa's company was a subcontractor. And in the TV world, being a subcontractor meant eating as much shit as those in charge wanted you to eat. If your picture lacked oomph, the director would berate you, hurling ashtrays and half-finished soda cans at you. If you weren't producing enough for the company to justify keeping you around, they would cut you loose without a second thought.

"If they're about to snap, let them beat on you. Then they'll keep you around," was the motto at Igawa's work. Employees were just an outlet for a director's stress. The only way to survive was to understand the structure of the show-business pyramid.

Under the wing of the chief cameraman, who had the grandiose title of "Video Strategist," Igawa lugged a video camera all over Kanagawa Prefecture.

As a matter of fact, he had almost no interest in TV shows or the telecommunications business, but he did like seeing the aftermath of traffic accidents. The more spectacular and gruesome, the better. A car wrapped around a telephone pole to the point of being barely recognizable, the approach of ambulance sirens, rescue workers sawing the body apart to pull the critically wounded passengers out, carrying them on a stretcher toward the emergency vehicle, all happening with a front-row view, stepping on pieces of shattered windshield strewn across the asphalt—Igawa loved every bit of it.

When he saw the body of an elderly woman who'd been run over by a large truck making a left turn, Igawa felt his stomach lurch with hunger. He bought a pastry at the convenience store and then returned to the scene to eat as he watched. From that point on, it became his habit to eat something at the scene of every accident he visited.

As it turned out, getting up-close-and-personal footage using a high-quality professional camera rather than just ordinary smartphone cameras, especially when you had a press badge on, was the perfect job for Igawa.

He always had a smile on his face when he got video of an accident scene with a company camera. His right eye was perpetually closed, with his dominant left eye pressed to the lens. Pretending he was squinting and focused helped conceal the fact that he had such a huge grin on his face.

When the company's footage appeared on the news, mosaics were used to blur out the blood, the agony of the injured, and the faces of the dead. But there was nothing like the rush of seeing all those things through Igawa's own lens in person. And he got *paid* for it. There were no scheduled days off or overtime pay, and virtually every new hire quit soon after starting, but he didn't think it was all that bad.

Igawa wasn't bothered when the senior employees chewed him out, and when the station director tried to smack him, he felt nothing but pity for the blow's complete ineffectuality.

However, there was one person—just one—he couldn't stand.

The company's chief cameraman always scolded Igawa for eating bread or rice balls at accident scenes. "Stop eating!" he'd shout. He even tried to grab a piece of bread away from Igawa once or twice.

In Igawa's mind, this qualified as workplace abuse. The man was trying to take away his right to eat.

He should shut the fuck up.

May 22, 2006, just so happened to be Igawa's twentieth birthday.

At ten PM, on the Tsunashima Highway near the Tsurumi River, a large truck collided with a passenger vehicle. Igawa intercepted the fire department call on the scanner at the company building and headed out with the chief cameraman to get video.

Igawa drove the company's SUV, a Mitsubishi Outlander, well over the speed limit, honking his horn and executing a number of dangerous take-overs on the way to the scene. In the passenger seat, the chief cameraman criticized his reckless driving, and the two got into an argument.

Eventually, Igawa let out a big sigh.

I'm hungry today. I'm in a bad mood.

He switched on the hazard lights and pulled the Outlander over to the shoulder of the highway, not bothering to turn off the engine.

Igawa removed his khaki safari hat and placed it on the dashboard, exposing his damaged scalp. Then he undid his seat belt and casually placed his left hand on the chief cameraman's neck, as though he were going to put his arm around his shoulder for a picture. He quickly pressed the passenger seat belt button with his other hand, then tensed his left arm and smashed the man's face into the passenger-side glove box.

It sounded like a chunk of concrete falling off a building. The impact shook the car, and the passenger airbag deployed.

Igawa laughed loudly and heartily. The chief cameraman's face was buried in the airbag. He did not move.

Using the flat-head screwdriver for adjusting the camera tripod, Igawa ripped the inflated airbag open, pulled the cameraman back into an upright position, and clicked the belt back in place. He then proceeded to drive to the site of the traffic accident on the Tsunashima Highway, got out of the car with his camera and his press badge, and shot footage like he always did.

He was hungry. On the way back to the office, he stopped at a convenience store and used cash from the dead cameraman's wallet to buy four yakisoba buns, two chicken katsu bento lunches, and three Monster energy drinks.

Igawa returned to the office, utterly calm, and got to work editing the accident footage. Another employee getting video of a different accident came back after three o'clock and spotted the chief cameraman sleeping in the Outlander in the parking lot. The shape of his face seemed weird. The employee wondered if the lights were playing tricks with shadows. They were not.

Suddenly, there was a lot more noise in the middle of the night. One employee burst into the editing room.

"You took the Outrider, didn't you?" he asked Igawa, his voice trembling. "What the hell is that in the parking lot?"

Igawa had just handed off his finished edit to a bike courier. He chuckled and replied, "Did you see it? It's exactly what it looks like: a traffic accident."

An open depressed skull fracture, brain lacerations, cervical spine dislocation and fracture, and a glove box door so warped by the impact that it could no longer open.

The examiner determined that the chief cameraman had died instantly. The Kanagawa Police had no prior record of a person smashing another person's head so hard into a glove box that it was immediately fatal *and* deployed the airbag.

By the time Tohru Igawa was sentenced and imprisoned, society had forgotten all about him. He'd beaten his work superior to death, but there was nothing more salacious than that to the story.

Other facts in the case—his use of unbelievable arm strength to smash his victim's head into a glove box and activate the airbag and that he proceeded to drive to the scene of an accident to take footage with the victim's body sitting in the car—were kept quiet by the TV station's executive staff. The day that Igawa committed the murder, footage that he took of the traffic accident aired on the news, a damning fact that the station dearly wanted to keep from going public.

That Igawa continued driving to do his job with the corpse in the car after the murder was judged harshly, contributing to a nineteen-year sentence. However, once in the system, Igawa was a model prisoner. He gave carefully constructed statements about his regrets, kept a journal, earned high marks with the prison guards, and on May 31, 2017, eleven years into his sentence, he was released on parole.

Once integrated into society, Igawa was pleased with his new workplace overlooking a pile of junked auto parts. He learned how to use the power shovel to dismantle cars and proactively studied for the test to get a heavy machinery operating license.

The Peruvian calling himself El Cocinero arrived at the chop shop in the winter of 2018.

He had a Japanese man with him nicknamed Laba-Laba, which sounded like a joke. The man was interpreting for the Peruvian, who only spoke Spanish.

Initially, Igawa thought they'd come to exact retribution of some kind.

Many Peruvians worked in Kawasaki, but he couldn't remember crushing any of them in a fight.

El Cocinero kept most of his face concealed behind a black bandanna. Only his eyes were visible. Igawa thought he was some kind of practical joker.

He reached out with an arm built like a log to rip the bandanna off the Peruvian's face. The man merely stood in place, staring at Igawa. Something felt off, eerie. Ultimately, he decided not to grab the bandanna.

Igawa's brow creased. He'd never experienced a stare or bearing quite like this before. There'd been a few foreign prisoners in jail, but none of them had the same intensity as this man.

"I like your background," Laba-Laba said, translating for El Cocinero. "The bit with the airbag? Classic."

Igawa chatted with these strange guests and showed them the garage, trying to get a feel for what they wanted. There was a 1977 Chevrolet Chevelle SS in there now. He liked the garage for many reasons: It was a great place for violence, to relax, and to concentrate on work.

The three of them examined the carefully tuned vintage car.

"That's a nice ride," Laba-Laba said for El Cocinero.

The Peruvian knew his American cars. They discussed automobiles for a few more minutes, and when that had run its course, the time for business had come.

To his surprise, the job request was to take care of a puppy. When Laba-Laba translated the phrase into Japanese, Igawa thought it was some new euphemism or code word for a criminal act he hadn't heard of yet. But he was wrong.

They literally wanted him to take care of a puppy.

Initially astonished, Igawa threw back his head and laughed until tears came to his eyes. No one else was chuckling.

"Who sent you?" Igawa demanded. "Why would you think I'd look after a dog?"

"It's not just any mutt. It's a dangerous one," Laba-Laba replied.

"A pit bull?"

"A pit bull can't handle this thing."

"It's bigger? That reminds me, the boss here said his dad kept Tosa fighting dogs."

"When this one grows up, it'll be even stronger than them. It's the greatest hunting dog in the world. Can even kill a puma."

"Whatever you say. You're better off asking the boss, not me. I've never had a dog."

"You're going to take care of it. You'll be its boss, La Chatarra."

"What's Chatarra?"

"That's you. We're going to call you La Chatarra."

"Yeah, but what is that? What is *this*? Who the fuck are you people? Is this a joke?"

"We're hiring you for a job. That's what we've been telling you, La Chatarra. You're going to give the puppy a name and feed it. We'll pay you. Plus some money up-front."

"That's all you want?"

"That's all."

The animal was a Dogo Argentino, something Igawa had not heard of until today. A large white dog hopped out of the Jeep Wrangler Laba-Laba and El Cocinero had taken here. Igawa waited for a puppy to come down after it, but there was no other dog. That was the puppy.

Igawa didn't have to discipline the dog like a trainer; his only responsibility was to feed it meat and help it grow. And for that, the Peruvian would pay him good money.

The Dogo Argentino puppy was already abnormally powerful. Igawa put a leather collar around its neck, buried a driveshaft deep into the dirt, and tied the leash to it.

That was only the start of the very odd job. He walked the dog around the shop in the morning and evening and tossed it hunks of beef on the bone.

The puppy quickly took to Chatarra.

After a month of care, the dog already weighed over twenty-five kilograms. Its rippling musculature spoke to its nature as a hunting animal, and Chatarra had to switch from a nylon leash to a chain one.

El Cocinero told him to give the dog a name, so Chatarra called it "Lanevo." It was a common nickname among car enthusiasts for the Mitsubishi Lancer Evolution, which he'd driven years ago.

Chatarra liked hearing the sound of Lanevo crunching through the bone of the meat he fed it. He would've loved to feed the dog a live cow if he could. Watching it fight the vicious pumas that prowled Argentina's forests would have been magnificent.

Lanevo understood very well that Chatarra was the boss. Like any good hunting dog, it had two very distinct sides: it was openly hostile to anyone it didn't know, but it never bared its fangs at its chubby master in the safari hat.

If any of the other employees, *bosozoku*, or street thugs tried to hold the leash, the ferocious Dogo Argentino dragged them through the dust. When the dog managed to get on top of them, they screamed in terror. If the beast didn't have a leather muzzle on, it would have easily bitten them to death. When the men wailed and yelled for help, Chatarra just clapped his hands and laughed.

Another month later, El Cocinero finally returned to the chop shop with Laba-Laba. He was holding a paper bag in one hand.

He made his orders very simple.

"Dispara a ese perro."

Chatarra didn't speak a word of Spanish, but he had a vague idea of what he'd been told.

El Cocinero handed him the paper bag. There was a pistol inside. It was not a Philippines-made counterfeit but an authentic German Walther Q4 with a silencer attached to the muzzle and a SureFire tactical light on the underside rail.

"When it's done, come and speak to me. I'll be in the office."

Laba-Laba translated the message from El Cocinero and left Chatarra to wonder if this was a test of some kind. Were they seeing how cold and cruel he could be, asking him to kill the dog he'd been raising? *The bastards are testing me. No wonder the pay was so good.*

Chatarra held a gun in his hand for the first time in his life. He didn't like that he'd been tested, but realized that, strangely, he wasn't all that angry with the Peruvian. El Cocinero was a kindred spirit. He was quiet and said only what he needed to. He wasn't like the antisocial chatterboxes in Japan that Chatarra hated so much. And beyond this test, Chatarra could smell much more money and blood.

He didn't know what kind of trial it was, but something big was waiting for him.

Chatarra stared at Lanevo, chained to the pole ten yards away.

The *sicario* profession was born in the slums of Colombia.

About four hundred kilometers northwest of Bogotá, in the Comuna 13 area of the city of Medellín, nearly half the population struggled with devastating poverty. Twentysomethings there recruited a bunch of teenagers to start their own gang, which was the beginning of the *sicario* hitmen. Some of the members were as young as eight years old.

Born into a desperate fate and offered no better options, the way they treated one another was a reflection of the cruelty around them. Friendship and sympathy were weaknesses. Softness was a liability in the fight for survival.

Those wishing to join the group had to pass a test set up by the leader to prove they were worthwhile. One part of the trial was particularly notable.

"Crush a little bird that you raised on your own, or shoot your friend dead."

Eventually, adults became aware of the presence of these "child villains" in the slums of Comuna 13. They were perfect for getting dirty jobs done cheaply, and they were much better at it than most adults who pretended they were tough.

The legendary drug kingpin Pablo Escobar led the Medellín Cartel to seize control of the criminal underworld, amassing a fortune large enough that it had implications for the financial world—and he made the most out of the accursed power of the youth of Comuna 13.

Those in the group who were shown to be the most vicious and clever were chosen to kill the enemies of the Medellín Cartel. After crushing their pet birds or shooting their friends dead, the boys possessed unparalleled cruelty, proving themselves to be far better hitmen than adults in the same situation, who would panic and spray gunfire when they cracked under pressure.

As the drug war swirled around its kingpin, the boys treaded into deeper and darker places. The few who survived grew into adults and took on new jobs for the cartel. Eventually, it wasn't just boys from the slums but former special forces from countries like Mexico and Guatemala who joined the *sicarios*.

The system of hitmen working on the cartel's orders spread beyond Medellín, beyond Colombia entirely. Soon there were *sicarios* in Mexico to the north, and Brazil and Argentina to the south.

The demand for the *sicario* never faded. For as long as the narcos had cocaine to transport, they needed agents of murder who could be counted on to deliver death and despair to their enemies.

31

cempöhualli-huan-mahtlactli-huan-cë

Boys without homes.

Boys who had homes but no family who wanted them.

When such people were about to leave a juvenile detention center, they fell under a category called "specially adjusted."

The specially adjusted needed a place to live and a job for income. For convicted minors to return to society, they needed the help of a support center to make all manner of adjustments—hence the name.

Between the severity of the murder of his parents, the lack of remorse on his part, his low Japanese comprehension, and the assault he committed during detention, Koshimo Hijikata's release had been put off several times. At last, in April 2019, he was permitted to leave, but because he had no place to live, he was moved to a rehabilitation facility in Sagamihara, then transitioned into life as a specially adjusted individual.

Koshimo was seventeen.

Seven companies were willing to hire him based on his uncanny ability with woodworking

A minor's prior record was wiped once he'd been granted conditional release from the detention center, but potential employers had the right to know about the boy's past. When interested businesses heard about

Koshimo's crime and the assault he committed in juvy, they immediately changed their minds.

There was only one man who still wanted to hire Koshimo: the president of a coating company. He had discussions with the rehabilitation facility, and eventually, Koshimo was granted a conditional release. The staffers at the rehabilitation facility were relieved at first, but when they noticed some gradual changes in the president's attitude, a foreboding gloom crept over them.

Sure enough, the coating company president eventually informed them, "The staff does not share my opinion, which makes hiring the boy nearly impossible."

Koshimo had a small shoulder bag filled with the minimum of daily necessities in preparation for his discharge. He took the items out of the bag, arranged them on his desk, and returned the empty pack to the staffer.

When a boy's conditional release was abruptly retracted, the rehabilitation workers had to keep an eye on him. Anyone would grow self-destructive after having freedom denied. Yet Koshimo didn't cause a fuss or commit any violence. He stretched out his long limbs on the tatami floor and stared silently at the ceiling.

Wake up, roll call—the usual morning routine. *There's nowhere for me to go*, Koshimo thought. *I can't get out without a place to go.*

"You're probably going right back to prison."

That's what one of the boys getting out on conditional release before Koshimo told him as they ate in the cafeteria. The boy was scheduled to leave the rehabilitation center an hour after breakfast. Koshimo looked down at him; the boy's expression was serious, not joking or mean. If anything, he seemed to be pitying Koshimo.

After breakfast, there was a morning physical activity period, then a lesson on personal savings in the afternoon, followed by a vocational development exercise. It was quite similar to life in the juvenile detention center.

Koshimo was using the electric saw in the workshop, crafting a lizard out of a single board, when a staffer carrying documents stopped by. "Come with me, Hijikata," he said.

In the office, Koshimo sat in a chair while the man broached the topic at hand. "We've found another workplace that would like to interview you for a job. It's a workshop in Kawasaki that makes accessories and knives, although the knives are for collector's displays only. Do you know what that means—*display*?"

Koshimo shook his head.

"It means you don't use it as a tool," the man explained, "you only look at its beauty."

"Like decoration?"

"That's right."

"The knife can't cut?"

"I'm not sure," the man admitted. "I think it does have an edge, but you're not meant to use it that way. You've shown you're capable of handling various blades safely during lessons here. You're good with your hands, and I think you'd do well at a workshop. It's in Odasakae in Kawasaki, near the port. Are you interested in taking a job interview with them?"

Koshimo sat there in a daze. Eventually, he bobbed his head.

"Use your words."

"Yes, sir."

"All right. The person conducting your interview isn't a worker at the shop but an NPO employee helping coordinate your employment situation."

"Enpeeoh. What is it?"

"Nonprofit organization. It's a group that doesn't work just to make money. The NPO is called Kagayaku Kodomo, and they'll be sending a woman named Yasuzu Uno to us in the next few days. Good luck with your interview. I hope you do well. There's an apartment near the workshop they rent for use as an employee dorm, so you won't need to worry about a place to live."

A week later, after an odd interview in which his hiring seemed all but predecided, Koshimo walked down the hallway of the rehabilitation center with an employee and out the firmly locked door into the open air. It was not a courtyard or an exercise area but the true outdoors. Conditional or not, freedom was ahead. Yet Koshimo felt no particular emotion.

The sky was clear, and the air was filled with cicada cries.

It was Wednesday, July 31, 2019.

Hair close-cropped, Koshimo bowed to the employees of the rehabilitation center, his home for three months after transferring from the Class-Two juvenile detention center in Sagamihara. After his good-bye, he turned his back and walked away.

A white Toyota Alphard awaited the seventeen-year-old.

A woman leaned against the front door, watching Koshimo approach.

She had come to the center twice for their interviews. Koshimo muttered her name under his breath. "Miss Uno. Yasuzu Uno. Enpeeoh. Kagayaku Kodomo."

It was the first time in Koshimo's life that someone had come to get him.

Yasuzu had her long black hair woven into cornrows. Ignoring the summer heat, she wore a leather jacket over her T-shirt. It caught the sun and took on a bluish hue where the light reflected off it.

"Now that you're finally out," she said to Koshimo, "I'm sure there are a bunch of places you'd like to go…"

She handed him a bottle of mineral water.

Koshimo took the plastic bottle and considered her words. Did he want to go anywhere? He thought about Todoroki Arena, where he'd gone to see basketball games, but he didn't have any money to buy a ticket.

"However, we're going to the workshop in Kawasaki, as scheduled," Yasuzu added. "All right?"

She looked up at the young man. He was incredibly tall. The Alphard van was at least one hundred and ninety centimeters, but the boy's head still rose above it.

Koshimo ducked down to enter the passenger seat and awkwardly put the seat belt on. He'd never been in a "normal" car before. After getting arrested, he hadn't bothered with the seat belt in the police car, and the minibus that took him from the Class-Two detention center to the reha-bilitation facility didn't have seat belts at all.

The light turned red, and Yasuzu stepped on the brake pedal of the Alphard. Without taking her eyes off the road, she inquired, "Do you remember the name of the workshop?"

"Yes," Koshimo replied, nodding. "Kawasaki, river, port, metal... lima-ted."

"I guess that counts as a correct answer." The woman smirked. "Can you write it?"

Koshimo thought he could, but as soon as he started thinking about the kanji, he grew confused and gave up, shaking his head. His mouth clamped shut, and he said nothing more.

I think I might have hurt his feelings, Yasuzu thought with her hands on the wheel. She started to blame herself. *It doesn't matter if he can't write it. Why did I even ask?*

The Alphard reached National Route 16 and continued on it for a while.

Koshimo's eyes were locked onto the view through the windshield. It made him dizzy. Everything was just so *straight*. He felt like he was dream-ing. Something was spiriting away his mind to a distant location. The juvenile detention center and rehabilitation facility had offered no sights like this.

"Are you feeling carsick?" Yasuzu asked.

Koshimo's eyes were locked forward. He said nothing.

"Want me to open the window?"

Koshimo nodded silently.

Yasuzu pressed the power window button to lower the passenger win-dow, ushering a blast of hot, humid July morning into the air-conditioned car. She looked sidelong at Koshimo. The young man remained quiet but seemed to have regained his poise. It reminded Yasuzu of the undocu-mented children at the shelter, and she felt as though she were interacting with one of them. *His body might be big, but at heart, he's still a child. He's much younger than seventeen*, she mused as the wind buffeted Koshimo's cheek.

As the Alphard passed under a pedestrian bridge, Yasuzu said, without preamble, "Oh, about my name—"

"Miss Uno. Yasuzu. I remember," said Koshimo.

"Thank you," she replied, smiling. "But I have a nickname, another name. And at the workshop where we're going, all the workers use it."

"Nickname..."

"They call me Malinal."

"Mali..."

"Ma-li-nal," Yasuzu repeated, sounding the syllables out. "It used to be longer: Malinalxochitl. But that's too long and weird, right? And it has no connection to Yasuzu Uno."

"What language?"

"I don't know."

"What does it mean?"

"I'm not actually sure," Yasuzu admitted with a chuckle. "Someone at the nonprofit came up with it and gave me the nickname. It's weird, right?"

Koshimo watched the silhouette of birds crossing in front of the radiant clouds and lifted the bottle of mineral water to his lips. He murmured Yasuzu's strange nickname to himself.

Malinalxochitl.

It was Xia who gave Yasuzu the name, in the shelter under Saiganji. In reality, it hadn't originally been her idea, of course. Xia was just passing along the name that El Cocinero had told her to say.

"Is that Chinese?" Yasuzu asked, but Xia didn't respond.

Malinal came from *malinalli*, "grass," and *xochitl* meant "flower." The Nahuatl name belonged to a sorceress from Aztec history who took the form of a human woman, but was actually the sister of the war god

Huitzilopochtli. Her name was the basis of the city Malinalco, southwest of Mexico City.

As she drove, Yasuzu noticed something like a pale blue gear held in Koshimo's fingers. It seemed to be made of plastic. Where had he gotten it? Was it one of his possessions from the facility?

The empty bottle of mineral water was sitting in the drink holder beside Koshimo, but there was no cap on it. Yasuzu recalled the color of the cap: pale blue.

"Is that…," she began while they were waiting at the light. "The thing in your hand, was that bottle cap?"

Koshimo nodded.

"Could I see it?" She took the cap from Koshimo, her eyes wide. The bridge of the cap had been flattened so that the sides were extended straight outward and split, as even as a casino chip. "How did you do that?"

"Fingers," he replied, moving his index finger and thumb.

Yasuzu felt how hard the plastic piece was. Her jaw dropped upon recognizing the sheer power of Koshimo's finger grip.

The woman didn't even notice when the light turned green and only pressed the accelerator pedal after the car behind hers honked four times. Her attention was utterly captivated by Koshimo's crushed bottle cap.

Could a normal person do this to a plastic bottle cap with just their fingers?

The roof of the workshop was painted blue, and the wooden exterior walls were made of red-hued larch.

The RIVERPORT METAL sign was rattling slightly in the wind. The previous owner liked to ride in a canoe for fun and kept it hung on a hook from the rafters, but now it and its two paddles were resting on the dirt out in the open, exposed to the rain and sun.

Yasuzu went for the doorknob, but Koshimo reached out from behind her with his long arm and opened it first. She felt keenly aware that the young man she thought childish had just treated *her* like a kid. More importantly, however, Yasuzu was pleased that Koshimo was being considerate to her.

Inside, the air conditioner was running at such a low temperature that it felt cold.

A worker in a red-and-black-checkered flannel shirt was on the other side of a stack of cardboard boxes near the door. Between the goggles, beard, and work apron, he looked like the owner of a mountain cottage. He was standing at a machine, grinding metal.

"Hello," Yasuzu greeted. "I've got the kid here."

The worker turned around, then stopped the machine's motor and removed his goggles.

Koshimo stepped over the boxes and walked right up to the man to examine the tool he was using without so much as a greeting. The workshop at the juvy center didn't have one of these.

Pablo—La Cerámica—stood next to the fascinated boy in silence. Eventually, he said, "It's a belt grinder. Costs a lot of money to buy one. I use this to fashion the blade for a knife."

"What's a blade?"

Pablo reached for a nearby folding knife, undid the lock, and opened it up. The polished stainless-steel item shone like a freshly caught sweetfish.

"And you use this machine to…," Koshimo remarked.

"Just for the basic stage. The sharpening is separate. Check that work rest over there. I was just grinding the blade out of 440C."

"Four forty… What is this line?"

"That's a marking line, same as woodworking. You cut it out along the line. I've heard you're pretty good at that sort of thing. "

"I've…never done it with metal."

"Of course not. You can't cut through steel with a fretsaw."

Koshimo did not budge from his spot by the belt grinder.

Pablo put his goggles back on, held the ends of a piece of 440C that already had the required holes punched into it, and began to grind the edge.

Sparks flew, and the section of metal, far harder than any wood, was suddenly reborn as a smooth blade right before Koshimo's eyes.

Pablo turned off the grinder and patted Koshimo on the back. For the first time, the boy tore his eyes off the machine and looked at the man.

"I'm Pablo," he said. "They call me La Cerámica, but here you can call me Pablo. Only in this workshop."

La Cerámica? Koshimo thought. It was a strange nickname, like Malinal. As best he could see, there were no plates or vases in the workshop that might correspond to that name.

Koshimo looked back at Pablo again, and something the correctional instructor had taught him suddenly passed through his head.

"When you meet someone for the first time, introduce yourself. When you're at your job and dealing with someone who'll be looking after you, make sure you say your name, and be polite about it."

He abruptly straightened his back, bringing his head much higher than Pablo's, then bent over and stated, "I'm Koshimo Hijikata."

"Mucho gusto," Pablo replied.

"Pablo—Pablo-san—are you Japanese and Mexican, too?"

"No, I'm Peruvian and Japanese. My father was born in Lima, and my mother's from Naha. That's why I can speak Español, like you."

Yasuzu, who'd been observing the pair's interaction, was alarmed to hear the knifemaker openly discussing his parents, of all topics. She observed Koshimo's expression carefully. But despite her concern, Koshimo didn't seem bothered at all.

"You're damn huge," Pablo continued. "How tall are you?"

"The last time I measured, I was two hundred and two."

"Two hundred and two centimeters?"

"Yes."

"What about weight?"

"Wheyt?"

"How many kilograms?"

"One hundred and four."

"You're over one hundred?"

"Yes."

Pablo glanced at the ceiling fan moving quietly just above Koshimo. "Just watch your head, okay?"

After Yasuzu left, Pablo and Koshimo were alone in the workshop. Koshimo was so busy gazing at the many custom knives that he forgot to say good-bye to Yasuzu as she headed out the door. She said she'd be back to check in at a later date, so Koshimo knew he'd see her again.

Pablo ground some Colombian coffee beans, brewed some hot coffee in the pot, and poured it into two mugs.

"Two kinds, straight kind and pointy kind," said Koshimo.

"You mean the edges?" Pablo asked, sipping the coffee. "The straight ones are called normal-edged knives, and the pointed ones are serrated-edge knives. There are names for each other part of the knife, too. This is a ricasso, this is a quillon, and this is a bevel stop. On this sort of knife, this area is called a double hilt. Isn't that interesting?"

"You made all of these, Pablo?"

"There's nobody else here to do it."

"That's amazing, Pablo. You're really good," the boy praised.

Pablo smiled awkwardly. "Drink the coffee. It's very tasty."

Koshimo said nothing and didn't touch the mug. His gaze had been stolen by a beautiful blade with no handle attached. It was a Damascus edge with complex patterns on the surface, like smoke wafting through air. Koshimo was entranced by it; the more he stared, the more it exuded a mysterious power. It reminded him of the pictures of different galaxies he saw in a book. *This is metal? It's so beautiful. How do you make it?*

The most important thing to Pablo, more than trading a bunch of words in conversation, was that Koshimo was completely fascinated by the knives on his first trip to the workshop. If you weren't drawn to the craft, you couldn't perform good *shigutu*. That was an Okinawan word, the equivalent of *shigoto*, work, in standard Japanese.

"The handle's important, too," he said. "You don't have a good knife unless the blade and grip are as one, with perfect balance."

Koshimo examined the handle materials stacked up on the bench. Some were wood, and others were not.

"This one..." Koshimo picked up a piece of material.

"Guess what it is from the texture."

"Bone... Animal?"

"That's right. It's a cow tibia. The shin bone. It's called jigged bone—you dry it out, carve some patterns into it, and then make it look like stag. Stag means antler material."

"So this is a fake?"

"If you want to see it that way. Jigged bone was a material they developed in the West for when they couldn't hunt deer, and they've been producing it ever since. Some collectors are crazy about those handles. Differences in the carving and dyeing can make them feel quite different."

"And this is jigged..."

"Yeah, that's jigged bone, too. See how different they are? Red, green, amber. The ones without any carving are called oiled bone, which maximizes the texture of the bone itself."

The workshop was a wonderful place. Koshimo could have inspected it for hours and hours: the finished knives, the blades, the handles still in progress. Somehow it was already past noon. Very belatedly, Koshimo remembered his mug and drank the cold coffee. Then he went back to staring at the knives and asking Pablo the occasional question.

An overflowing crowd flooded the cargo terminal of Kawasaki Port, waiting for a ship to arrive.

When the vessel from beyond the Equator arrived, the people waiting on the man-made island of Higashi-Ogishima cheered until they forgot how hot it was. Photographers, both professional and amateur, peered through their finders as they searched for the perfect shot.

Seagulls perched atop the breakwater in the bay took flight as one when the shriek of the ship whistle pierced the air.

One little boy perched atop his father's shoulders pointed past the sparkling waves and shouted, "Is that the door beer? It's so big."

"It's not door beer," his father said. "It's the *Dunia Biru*. That's the name of the ship."

Dunia Biru. Indonesian for "Blue Earth."

Total length: four hundred and ten meters.

Total width: eighty-three meters.

Gross tonnage: two hundred and thirty-eight thousand nine hundred tons.

Maximum passenger capacity: seven thousand five hundred and fifteen.

Total cabins: three thousand one hundred and twelve.

Number of decks: eighteen.

The world's largest cruise ship had left the Port of Tanjung Priok to make its test voyage to Kawasaki. Now it loomed as tall and foreboding as a cumulonimbus cloud, escorted by a vessel from the Coast Guard. The patrol boat looked as tiny as a Jet Ski in the *Dunia Biru*'s presence.

As the *Dunia Biru* got closer to the port, the sunlight reflected off its body grew stronger, making the waves sparkle. The cobalt blue body featured white outlined letters on the side that drew the eye of the crowd.

DUNIA BIRU

Maritime signal flags fluttered in the Pacific breeze, and up on the open deck, the passengers waved to the port, tiny compared to the ship on which they stood.

32

cempöhualli-huan-mahtlactli-huan-öme

Anyone was capable of drawing out their innate sense of aggression and turning into that monster that lurked in the abyss. Those who underwent *sicario* training lost something that made them human. There wasn't the slightest shred of guilt in the cold, stony gazes of those killing machines.

No one but El Cocinero would have devised the idea of using the auto yard in the middle of Kawasaki as a shooting range.

When Nomura and Suenaga heard the suggestion, they were nervous. Did El Cocinero understand that this was not a gun-owning society?

But they soon understood that the auto yard was actually the perfect spot for a secret shooting range. It was protected by security cameras, steel sheet walls, and barbed wire.

However, they couldn't shoot whenever they pleased. High-quality silencers and a lot of dismantling noise to cover up the sound were both absolute requirements.

Before he even learned how to say hello and good-bye in Spanish, Chatarra learned El Cocinero's particular instructions.

"Trae una barracuda." Bring a barracuda.

With that simple command, the shotguns were pulled out from under a pile of parts and prepared for use, transforming the chop shop in the middle of Kawasaki into a firing range.

El Cocinero called the Remington M870s equipped with Salvo 12 silencers "barracudas."

When he gave the order, bringing out the barracudas from their hidden metal case was the job of El Taladro, the Drill—one of the chop shop workers.

He was nineteen years old, a fourth-generation Japanese Brazilian. El Taladro admired Chatarra's strength and looked up to him like a brother. His real name was Flávio Kuwabata. He could speak Portuguese and Japanese and a bit of Spanish.

El Taladro had experience shooting guns in the backstreets of Rio de Janeiro. He'd lived there until his mother brought him to Japan at age fourteen. If Chatarra got to shoot at the chop shop, then he would, too, he decided. The only issue was that El Taladro was so nearsighted that he had difficulty seeing in the distance even with contact lenses. And the young man was nowhere near as vicious and violent as Chatarra.

His role, according to El Cocinero, was to prep the barracudas, use heavy machinery to cover up the noise, and ensure that the silencers kept the gunshots as quiet as possible. It was a very, very important task.

The Salvo 12, as the name suggested, was a twelve-inch silencer. Yet unlike the cylinder most people imagined when they thought of silencers, this one resembled a long, extended box. The object was made of aluminum and stainless steel with a matte black finish that did not reflect any light whatsoever.

Chatarra did as El Cocinero taught him, loading shells into the tube magazine, pulling the foregrip back, then pushing it forward. After that, he just had to put his finger on the trigger.

The Salvo 12's ability to cut down on sound was tremendous, although the amount of smokeless powder used also played a part. The silencer absolutely cut down the higher frequencies when firing, lowering the decibel range to the level of a nail gun firing into a board, a common enough sound on construction sites. Naturally, you could fire something like that without earmuffs.

While firing practice took place, El Taladro used a power shovel to dismantle scrapped cars noisily. With that racket going, they could use submachine guns, and nobody outside the auto yard would be capable of identifying it as gunfire.

Chatarra blasted the human silhouette target full of holes at a distance of thirty feet, pulled back the foregrip, and ejected the empty shotgun shell that had been relieved of its double-aught buck pellets.

It was Las Casasolas who introduced the barracuda to Mexican shootouts. Before them, no one thought to put a silencer on a shotgun. They attached silencers on both types of shotguns—those with longer shoulder stocks, and those with shorter pistol grips. They slapped on flashlights for use in darkness, prioritizing the elimination of targets at close range. They called the crude-looking guns with their boxy silencers by the name of a fearsome carnivorous fish, but to the Casasola brothers, the shape of the gun reminded them of an Aztec weapon their *abuelita* told them about: the *macuahuitl*.

Out of all the people who patronized the hotbed of criminal activity that was the chop shop, two were chosen as potential *sicarios*, went on to pass the Dogo Argentino puppy test, and were allowed to take part in Valmiro's shooting lessons. Their nicknames were El Mamut, the Mammoth, and El Casco, the Helmet.

El Mamut, real name Daigo Nakai, was twenty-nine, stood one hundred and ninety-one centimeters, and weighed one hundred and twenty-three kilograms. He reached the national finals in boxing twice in high school and worked as a firefighter in Kawasaki after graduating. Although Nakai was an alum of the same high school as Miyata, the shop's owner, he'd never met the other man in person.

When El Mamut was twenty-six, he was arrested on suspected possession and use of marijuana, discharged from the fire department, and given a six-month prison sentence. After getting out, he worked his way into a loose criminal group in Adachi, Tokyo, making a living by extorting high-earning club hosts.

El Casco, real name Akira Ohata, was twenty-six, standing one hundred and seventy-seven centimeters, and weighing seventy-nine kilograms. He'd formerly led a *bosozoku* motorcycle gang in Sagamihara and started working with sheet metal once he moved on. He was drinking at a pub with some work friends when he got into a fight with another patron and seriously injured three, including one who was an experienced full-contact karate practitioner. One of the men died from his injuries twelve days later, and El Casco was given a six-year sentence for manslaughter. Once back out, he earned money as a bookie for the fights held at the chop shop and paid a third of his income to Chatarra, whom he idolized.

El Mamut and El Casco were both good with tools, learned quickly, and displayed a talent for gun handling, although they weren't quite as proficient as Chatarra. While he looked fat, Chatarra could run about the yard faster than they could, and he truly loved shooting guns.

Instead of the usual concentric circle target, the silhouette targets they used for practice displayed vital zones that would result in a fatality if shot, like the brain, heart, lungs, and liver. On Valmiro's orders, Suenaga and Nomura drew up diagrams of the organs, and then El Taladro copied them and stuck them to the targets.

Once they'd shot at dozens of stationary targets, they moved on to old tires. The worn-down ones with exhausted treads would be rolled in various directions to approximate a moving target. Anyone who couldn't kill a person on the run was worthless as a *sicario*.

El Cocinero grabbed a barracuda for himself and joined in the exercise to instruct the trio.

"When you're lowering your gun to hide behind cover, make certain the muzzle is held out in front of your legs. People accidentally fire them and blow off their own toes or knees."

* * *

"Always keep track of how many times you've shot. Bullets are vital to your survival. Lose count of how many you have left, and you'll die like the stupid dog you are."

"Don't just stand there like a stiff while you're shooting. This isn't a game. Never stay in the same spot. Imagine those old tires are special forces. Be prepared to hit your target from any position."

To minimize the powerful recoil of the shotguns, El Cocinero taught them the push-pull technique to enable faster shooting.

He pushed out with his hand on the foregrip and pulled the stock back to his shoulder. By extending the gun body front and back, he minimized recoil and fired with better accuracy at high frequencies.

Chatarra, who was left-handed, had to do it in reverse. When he tested out the push-pull method, he no longer needed to use his considerable arm strength to hold the muzzle in place and was able to shoot at the rolling tires with significantly better accuracy.

This is so much fun, Chatarra thought. He grinned as shotgun shells flew out of the corner of his eye. Wiping away the sweat, he pushed the foregrip for another round.

Shooting the barracuda reminded Chatarra of the time he spent as a cameraman for the video company. In English, getting footage with the camera was also called shooting. There were many shared features between the two actions, and that gave Chatarra an advantage over El Mamut and El Casco. He didn't need to think about which of the two was more exciting. Filming gave him the chance to see dead bodies but firing a gun *made* them.

After performing maintenance on the barracuda, it was time to bathe. But this wasn't an ordinary bath. Three bathtubs were set up in the garage, full of cow's blood, entrails, and lukewarm water. El Cocinero called the tubs *estofado*. His three trainees would dunk their entire bodies, heads and all, into the stew, becoming one with the smell of blood. Then they would hum some Spanish songs he'd taught them. They didn't know what the lyrics meant, only that they were *narcocorridos*, songs of praise for narcos.

The sight of men covered in blood from the tubs was a bracing sight. El Taladro, who was tasked with preparing the *estofado* in the garage, vomited several times during the process.

A man living on the street was brought in to be their target.

A live target meant practical lessons. They had no quarrel with him. He was just unlucky.

They shot and killed the man, who begged and pleaded for his life, then they stood around the corpse to observe the destructive effects of the double-aught buck on the human body. Their victim had gunshot wounds with characteristic "rat-hole" markings on his chest and stomach. His head had blown up like a shattered watermelon.

Chatarra, El Mamut, and El Casco had all shot the same way, so why did only the man's head explode? El Cocinero explained.

"It's the skull. When the pellets get into a tightly enclosed space, it creates a shock wave. The internal pressure causes the skull to burst like that."

The next day, all three men were ordered to undergo a three-day fast. They were locked in the garage and forbidden to go outside.

They spent the night in sleeping bags, smoked cigarettes, and swatted at mosquitoes and flies. They were only permitted to ingest fluids. Chatarra and El Mamut got up many times to drink huge amounts of water. El Casco just read manga he'd downloaded to his phone.

The morning after their three-day fast, they were let out of the garage and into the rain. Strutting around the muddy auto yard was an animal as large and solid as a boulder.

A deal with a bullfighting broker in Shimane had brought in a live four-year-old bull. The beast weighed nearly nine hundred and fifty kilograms.

The listed price for the animal was four million yen, but Nomura had haggled on Valmiro's orders, and with some coke and ecstasy from Taiwan to sweeten the deal, they got it for two-point-five million instead.

El Cocinero gave the starving men their orders.

"Kill and eat the bull. But you can't use the barracudas."

The one-ton black fighting bull was given a stimulant, and each man received a bowie knife with a seven-inch blade. They stared at the animal's raised shoulders and the jutting horns on both sides of its massive head.

Following the psychological test of shooting a pet dog, this was an entirely new and more desperate kind of task—hunting an angry bull armed only with a knife after three days of fasting.

Valmiro lit up a cigar and carefully watched the three men approach the bull with their blades.

Whether you had experience with murder or not, the ritual of hunting *el toro* built bonds between you and your fellow hunters. When he was fifteen, Valmiro and his brothers teamed up to kill a bull in an empty lot in Veracruz. The creature weighed over a ton, and the older narcos gathered to enjoy the illegal bullfighting show. The boys weren't armed with guns or matador *garrochas*, just machetes.

That fight had been four against one. Valmiro had thought his men would be at a disadvantage, since there were only three of them. To even the odds, this bull was smaller.

"Vamos!"

Valmiro's command sparked more anger in the bull than in the three men. Thus began a mad hunt in the rain. The muddied men desperately tried to avoid the black bull's fierce charges; El Casco, the lightest, clung to its back and jabbed the bowie knife into its side wildly. Blood gushed from the wounds, splattering onto the damp ground.

Chatarra stood in front of the charging bull, jabbed at its forehead with the knife, and attempted to split the beast's thick skull.

The bull snorted like an engine spitting exhaust, shook its head, and lifted Chatarra, who was still holding the handle of the knife stuck into the animal's brow. The over-one-hundred-and-fifty-kilogram man felt his feet leave the ground.

El Mamut lunged from the left and stabbed the side of the bull's neck. It severed the artery, and the blade made it all the way to the vertebrae, but the creature still did not relent.

All three of them clung to the bull for dear life, trying to keep it from throwing them off. Rain rinsed away the blood that decorated their faces, only to give way to more blood. It was a bullring without cheers, occupied by struggling amateur matadors.

Under dark storm clouds, a battle from the Stone Age played out in the auto yard. Starvation, the hunt, the blood of their prey—deep, timeless instincts were being channeled, giving birth to a special kind of kinship. *If we combine our abilities, we are stronger than this massive beast. We are special. We are family.*

Somos familia.

The spell El Cocinero taught them, short as it was, gained a magical power when fused with the blood of the sacrificial bull. It etched itself into the deepest parts of their consciousness. This was also the source of the Aztecs' greatness, offered to the gods with human hearts atop the *teocalli*.

Chatarra released the bowie knife stuck in the bull's forehead and grabbed its horns. "Give me your knife," he said to El Casco, who was still hanging on to the bull's back. The moment the knife came to him, Catarra grabbed it with both hands, and like swinging an ax, he drove the tip into the fighting bull's head with all his might.

La Cerámica's fine bowie knife, made at his workshop in Odasakae, split the thick skull and destroyed the cranial nerves. The charging bull promptly stumbled and fell. El Casco would have been pinned beneath the animal if he hadn't leaped off.

The bull went still. Three men coated in blood and mud stared up at the rainy sky, limbs splayed, and took great, heaving breaths. Blood from the animal pooled on the ground, staining the moist earth red.

Chatarra was the first to laugh, and the other two promptly followed. The droplets got bigger and bigger, cascading onto the piles of scrap in the yard and turning the bare dirt into sludge. Then the storm truly began.

33

cempöhualli-huan-mahtlactli-huan-ëyi

The boy went from his nearby apartment to the workshop at seven thirty for his shift every morning. Pablo used a device he made from an old tool motor to grind coffee beans and carefully brewed a pot. In addition to his stock of Colombian beans, he had Mandheling and Guatemalan, too—five kinds in all.

Koshimo's first job was to make toast. He put a half dozen pieces of bread in the toaster oven, heating them until lightly browned, then added butter and put them back in, removing them for good once the residual heat had melted the spread. He was also tasked with cutting the bacon while the bread was toasting. There was always a slab of bacon in the workshop's little fridge. He used a cutting board, savoring the slice of his mentor's handmade knife each and every morning. Even if they were meant for display, Pablo refused to sell a customer a knife that couldn't cut.

"Listen up, Koshimo. Knives aren't beautiful because they're art. They're beautiful because they're tools. Don't ever get that wrong."

They ate breakfast at a table in the corner of the shop. The toast and bacon alone weren't enough to satisfy Koshimo's hunger, so he also ate a steamed, seasoned chicken breast he bought at the convenience store. The light, healthy food, known as salad chicken in Japan, was sold in vacuum-sealed packs. Koshimo had two packs at a time initially. But as the days went on, he ate more and more. Now he could handle ten. The salad chicken was piled high on his breakfast plate, and by the time he cleaned up the dishes, it would all be gone.

Pablo's job was to teach his apprentice, and Koshimo's was to learn from his mentor. The knife was the oldest tool in human history, and the body of knowledge the ancestors had built about it was both deep and vast. The possible combinations of blade and handle were infinite, and a knifemaker dedicated to his craft could pursue perfection endlessly.

Koshimo learned about the various kinds of sheath knife blades. Sheath knives were also called fixed-blade knives because the blade and handle didn't collapse together. These were easier to make than folding ones, because you didn't need to design the folding and unfolding mechanism. Sheath knives were called such in Japan because they had to go into a sheath in lieu of safely folding shut. Elsewhere, most countries just called them fixed knives.

When showing Koshimo blade materials, Pablo always took them out of the handles, so he could see what the whole part looked like.

Straight point.

Drop point.

Spear point.

Tanto blade.

Fillet blade.

Crooked skinner.

Guthook skinner.

Koshimo stared closely at each type of blade, all honed with a diamond sharpener, copied their forms to paper, cut the shapes out, pasted them to steel sheets, and used a pencil-type scribing tool to mark their outlines. Unlike his writing, which was clumsy and childish, Koshimo's lines were powerful, delicate, and precise.

Pablo gave Koshimo a strict instruction.

***

"Make sure the blade is shorter than a hundred and fifty millimeters."

The regulation limit for a knife blade in the Japanese retail market was a hundred and fifty millimeters, or fifteen centimeters. Many of Riverport Metal's custom knives were sold internationally, but Pablo started Koshimo on the domestic standard.

As he sipped rich black coffee and watched Koshimo dedicate himself to the work, Pablo thought of Malinal. She would disapprove of this. That woman had been adamant that Koshimo shouldn't be a knifemaker. Given the boy's past, she had a point.

The first person to tell El Loco about the kid in the rehabilitation center named Koshimo Hijikata was El Casco, an employee at the auto yard in Nakahara. One of El Casco's former *bosozoku* friends who'd come out of a rehabilitation center told him about a two-meter-tall mixed-race kid who was really good with his hands. From there, El Casco informed El Loco.

Soon after, El Loco brought Malinal, Yasuzu Uno the nonprofit worker, to Pablo's workshop, to see if he would be interested in taking on a new employee.

Pablo was surprised by the attitude and vocabulary of the Japanese woman who went by the name Malinal. It seemed as though she didn't know what was happening under the temple in the Ota Ward. From what Pablo could tell, she genuinely believed she was performing a valuable service for the sake of undocumented children. Was she brainwashed, like some kind of cultist? That was Pablo's assumption, but he couldn't ask about it in El Loco's presence, and if she were truly brainwashed, then questioning her about it wouldn't do any good.

While Malinal was on board with putting a boy from the rehabilitation center to work at the shop, thereby giving him a proper place in society, she was consistently against him getting involved in knifemaking.

"It's dangerous," she insisted. "This boy killed his parents, and you're going to have him work with blades?"

"Setting aside what he might do for me," Pablo interjected, "I want to see what he *can* do first. Do you have any samples?"

"I do," Malinal replied. "This is a bit of his woodworking that I bought from a charity event."

She produced a small carved jaguar. The moment the woman placed it on the table, the look in Pablo's eyes shifted. His accumulated experience working with his hands allowed him to glean quite a lot from the finished product.

Malinal, who'd bought the item, thought it was a male lion, but Pablo instantly recognized it as a jaguar. Although it lacked the characteristic spots, and its exterior was simple, unfinished wood, there was no way Pablo could mistake the look of the majestic carnivore, lurking under the shade of the leaves and watching its hapless prey.

The boy who created this wouldn't commit an act of violence without reason, Pablo thought instinctively. Wood, clay, plaster, metal—whatever the material, modeling was an art that required great patience. A person couldn't truly finish a piece without control of their emotions and the ability to grasp the full image in their mind. However, if Malinal was right, and the boy was dangerous, then the men who were trying to hire the boy through her—El Loco, Laba-Laba, the people at the chop shop, and most of all, El Cocinero—were far *more* dangerous.

If the boy left the system and came here, he'd be inducted into a new, a much greater, sin.

Pablo wanted to refuse, to send the young man away for his own good, but El Loco's mind was already made up. There was no choice in the matter now. All Pablo could do was pity the unfortunate boy for not having a better place to go.

Koshimo liked looking at the stockpile of handle materials in the workshop.

The jigged bone made from cattle tibia; oiled bone; bone slab; sambar stag made from the antlers of a large Indian deer; mastodon ivory, which served as a replacement for illegal elephant ivory; and walrus ivory, which had been on the market before it was regulated. In terms of natural wood, there was ironwood, cocobolo, bocote, greenheart, and African blackwood. For shell, options included pearl oyster, abalone, and black pearl. Koshimo was even interested in artificial materials like acristone—rock fixed in acrylic resin—and Micarta, a laminate of linen compressed in phenolic resin. Koshimo inspected them all enthusiastically, and learned how to fashion them with Pablo's help.

Once he'd grown accustomed to the fundamentals of knifemaking, Koshimo's first completed piece was a sheath knife made with a straight point blade cut from a steel called CrMo7 and a handle crafted of hard cocobolo wood from Mexico. He even used a sewing machine to finish the leather covering to hold the knife.

By the time he put the finishing touches on the blade with an American general-purpose file, the sun had set, and it was dark outside the shop.

Pablo stayed with his apprentice the entire time to supervise.

Koshimo got up from his chair to show off the completed knife, but Pablo held up a hand to stop him. "Did you finish sharpening it?" he asked.

"Yeah. I used the Nicholson file."

"Then put it in the case and bring it here," said Pablo. "We'll check the edge with our dinner. If it can't cut, you can't call it a knife."

Koshimo put his new sheath knife into a black, ABS resin case and closed the lid. All of a sudden, he felt a pang of hunger. He'd been so focused on his work that he'd forgotten to eat lunch.

Boss and employee got into a Citroën Berlingo with Kawasaki plates. Pablo drove it to a pay parking lot in Oshimakami-cho near the workshop, then took Koshimo across the street to a steakhouse.

At a table inside, while Chuck Berry played over the speakers, Pablo ordered two one-hundred-and-fifty-gram sirloin steaks. "One very rare, the other very well done," he instructed.

The waiter turned to leave, but Pablo stopped him. "That was just for me. He hasn't ordered yet."

With the blessing of his employer, Koshimo ordered a three-pound steak off the special menu and added a large side of rice, plus a soup and salad.

When the meat came out on the heated iron platters, Koshimo tapped the edge of the metal with his fork, listening to the sound.

"You're going to get used to doing that working with steel every day." Pablo laughed. "All right, let's see that knife," he said, his face stern once more.

Koshimo opened the plastic case and handed over the sheath knife. Pablo examined its blade under the restaurant lights, then used it to cut the very rare sirloin. It severed the red meat like it was melting butter. Pablo placed the slice on top and cut again. He repeated the process until the blade went through four layers, then stared at the flecks of blood on the edge.

Next Pablo cut the very well-done steak, which lived up to its name. As with the rare steak, he cut the pieces, stacked them, and cut them again, slicing through fat and tough sinew, trying to see if he could do it without needing to use his fork for support, as the iron platter was slick with melted fat already.

After quietly wiping off the blood and fat with his napkin, Pablo held the knife by the endpoint and the bolster so he could closely examine the marking on the ricasso.

Koshimo y Pablo

Koshimo and Pablo. When writing on paper, the boy's letters were clumsy, but when carved into metal, they were flawless. The finishing on the knotty heartwood of the cocobolo handle and the leather sheath was perfect.

"This is good work," said Pablo. "Keep it up."

Internally, he thought Koshimo was a genius. Could anyone else have created a piece this good after just three weeks of lessons? Blade, handle, sheath—every part was perfect. Pablo couldn't even complain about the sharpening.

Koshimo didn't show any outward happiness from his teacher's praise. He was too busy eating. The three-pound steak was gone in less than ten minutes, and he finished the extra-large rice, salad, and soup as well.

Pablo didn't touch the meat he used in the test cut; he let Koshimo have it. Still not satisfied, Koshimo ordered an extra one-pound steak and a mashed potato side.

"What do you usually eat on your own?" Pablo asked.

"For dinner?"

"Yeah."

"Boiled bird. That's the only thing I can cook."

"You just boil it? No salt?"

Koshimo shook his head.

"You were eating that chicken this morning, too. The kind from the convenience store. How many packs of those?"

"*Diez*," Koshimo replied.

"And chicken for dinner, too?"

"Yeah."

"You need vegetables, man. And blueberries. They can be frozen, that works, too. They're good for your eyes. Eyesight is really important to this job."

"Okay."

Pablo took a sip of the restaurant's iced coffee and winced at the flavor. He exhaled, then muttered, "I guess we've been so focused on knives, we haven't had any conversations like this."

"Yeah," Koshimo agreed. "I have a question."

"What is it?"

"Do you watch basketball?"

"Basketball? The sport?"

"Yeah."

"I dunno. I guess I do; when I have time. Basketball, soccer, bicycle races, horse races, you can see them all around here. There's also American football. You like basketball?"

"Yeah."

"You played?"

Koshimo shook his head. He asked Pablo about the team from Kawasaki he'd rooted for years ago.

"That team's not around anymore," Pablo answered. "They're gone."

"They're gone...?" Koshimo repeated. His hands stopped working at his food, and he gazed dully at Pablo.

"Well, they changed," Pablo explained. "Oh, right, you don't know. While you were on the inside, they created this thing called the B. League. That's the new professional league. The team you were following was reborn there."

Pablo took out his smartphone and searched for an image to show Koshimo, who stared with great interest at the little screen. Red uniforms. Kawasaki Brave Thunders.

"Are they tough?"

"They're a good team."

"The best in the world?"

"Are you including other countries in that question?"

"Yeah."

"You come up with some weird questions, kid. Okay, listen. The Brave Thunders play in a Japanese domestic league called the B. League. The best basketball team in the world wins the NBA championship; that's the North American pro league. Have you even seen an NBA game before?"

"No."

"Didn't think so," Pablo replied. "You gotta subscribe to some satellite channel to see them."

"Who's the toughest in the Enbeeay?"

"This year it's the Toronto Raptors. They won the 2018-to-2019 season. They're based out of Toronto. That's in Canada, not America."

"Raptors..."

Pablo smirked a bit at the sight of Koshimo struggling to absorb so much new information. He took another sip of the bad iced coffee.

The **Koshimo y Pablo** engraving on the ricasso of the knife caught his eye. He imagined Koshimo, whose handwriting was so awful, painstakingly carving each letter, when he could have stopped at just his own name. The thought of Koshimo being unknowingly dragged into the workshop's other work brought tears to Pablo's eyes.

He dabbed at them with a napkin and said, "Don't walk around with the sheath knife you made today. If the cops stop you for questioning, you'll get thrown right back in jail."

"Okay."

The sound of sizzling meat, dinner guests in conversation, Chuck Berry, the smell of the smoke, and the scent of seasoning. Koshimo just kept eating and eating at the steakhouse table under the soft orange lights, while Pablo leaned back in his chair and gazed out at the night through the window.

Having gained Pablo's trust, Koshimo was given a key to the workshop, and he started showing up even earlier than seven thirty.

Cattle tibias had been left boiling the night before in a stockpot, and Koshimo used a toothbrush to polish each one. Each was fifteen to twenty centimeters long and very thick and firm, to support a cow's weight.

When the shinbones were fully washed, he took them to an air-conditioned storage building behind the workshop, hung them up on wires, and dried them at a low temperature. The pressure of the air-conditioning breeze made the line of thick bones sway and clack wetly in the dark room, turning the storehouse into a stone-age cave dwelling.

Four of five of the tibias would be left behind and placed in a box, not fashioned into jigged bone for knife handles. Pablo had explained that one of his friends who ran an auto yard in Nakahara Ward had a big hunting dog that needed chew toys to relieve stress. The dog's jaws were so powerful that it would bite through cattle shinbones in no time, and so it required a regular supply of them.

In addition to the cattle tibias, there was another kind of bone they boiled in the workshop. They were about as long as the cow ones, with little bits of blood and flesh still stuck to them, but they were softer on the surface, lighter in color, and just generally looked weaker.

It was always the same man who delivered these mystery bones, not a delivery service. The only things in the back of his truck were propane gas canisters.

Under Pablo's tutelage, Koshimo learned how to sign the slips for the steel and handle materials when they were brought to the shop. Thankfully, he could just scrawl something unreadable, and it would still be accepted. The man who drove the truck full of gas canisters never asked for a signature, though. He didn't have any paper slips to begin with.

"Don't boil those with the cow ones. Treat them very gently."

Those were Pablo's instructions. Koshimo had asked what kind of bones they were, but never received an answer. Whenever the topic of the mystery bones arose, Pablo's expression grew dark, and his eyes refused to meet Koshimo's.

One day, Pablo finally told him the name of the bones. Typically, he referred to the bones as "those" or "them" to Koshimo. Perhaps he'd grown tired of being so vague.

C-bones.

Knowing the name didn't help Koshimo understand them any better. He thought they might have been calf bones, but if so, Pablo's instructions didn't make sense. He'd said not to boil them with the cow bones.

So they weren't from cattle. What had they come from?

34

cempöhualli-huan-mahtlactli-huan-nähui

A major typhoon swept over the Tokyo region, turning the grounds of the
chop shop to muck and leaving a sludgy pool behind.

El Taladro had to use the power shovel to clean up all the car doors
and roofs cast about by the storm. When he was done, he returned to the
upstairs office, and on Miyata's orders, he placed a call to an appliance rental
place for a drainage tool. Their power shovel was designed for dismantling,
with a grappling-style arm attachment, and wasn't suited for removing
water.

When done with the phone call, El Taladro glanced at the calendar.
Technically, he wasn't looking directly at it, but at the reflection through
a mirror on the opposite wall. If he stood in the right spot, a small mark
made in purple marker on the mirror overlapped with today's date on the
calendar. There was nothing actually marked on the calendar itself.

The purple dot on the mirrored date indicated a police inspection.
Miyata was paying an investigator under the table, so the chop shop employees knew about the visits before they happened.

The steel sheeting, barbed wire, and security cameras were imposing.
The various business yards of Japan—from cars and home appliance
dismantlers to material storage—sometimes boasted security more impressive than what could be found in yakuza offices. Additionally, their
closed-off nature made them breeding grounds for crime. Local police

departments all over the country performed regular inspections on suspicious private lots like these. They were warrantless investigations, but if an owner refused, it invited further scrutiny from the cops.

To someone in Miyata's position, keeping things calm and friendly with the law was paramount. He'd been on good terms with the police before he hired Chatarra. Ever since, he'd had to be more cautious than ever not to attract unwanted attention from the authorities.

Miyata always held an operational philosophy that even if he skirted the line of the law, he would never touch traditional yakuza business. Yet now the auto yard he owned was run by people more dangerous than yakuza. Chatarra killed people and melted their bodies in the most cavalier manner. A black-market doctor brought in an unidentified Peruvian. The Peruvian brought dogs, ordered some of them shot, and allowed others to live. They'd fired thousands of shotgun shells in the yard, and there was a bathtub full of blood and viscera in the garage. His business had turned into a charnel house of nightmares, and most frightening of all to Miyata, he had absolutely no idea what was really going on behind all this horror.

An unmarked car from the Kanagawa Prefectural Police stopped in front of the auto yard. The silver Subaru Impreza carried two members of the International Investigation team from the Organized Crime Department: Assistant Inspector Toshitaka Ozu and Patrol Chief Kazumasa Goto. They were following a lead on a group selling stolen cars overseas.

Ozu was a highly experienced investigator and information source, and young Goto had no idea that Ozu was known in the underworld as a man who would play ball. Goto idolized and trusted his superior. The Ukrainians running an illegal casino in Kawasaki and the Koreans with the secretive, members-only prostitution club all knew that Ozu was a dirty cop. Only Goto, who spent every day working with him, was in the dark.

The heavy sheet-metal front gate of the auto yard opened automatically, and the Impreza drove onto the grounds. Ozu and Goto spied El Taladro's back, small in the distance, as he used a drainage snake to remove the huge pond of muddy water that had formed. He seemed to be the only person outside in the spacious lot.

The unmarked cop car rolled slowly through the muck to where Miyata awaited them, smiling.

Ozu leaned back against the couch in the office, sipped the cup of green tea offered to him, and asked, "You got an ashtray around here, Pops?"

Miyata promptly found a round copper ashtray and placed it on the table.

"That rain yesterday was somethin', wasn't it?" Ozu remarked. "Wish it was a little stronger, so it could wash this goddamn trash heap away."

"Let's not tell jokes, sir," Miyata winced, looking from Ozu to Goto. "Your tires are all muddy, aren't they? We have a pressure washer that you can use to clean them off before you go."

"No thanks," Ozu replied. "We go back lookin' too clean and shiny, and they're gonna ask where we got the car wash. If there's no receipt, there'll be hell to pay. Turns out you were offering us a gift, then the department'll *really* bring the hammer down."

"I hear that in the past, anti-mob agents would go to the yakuza offices and get the youngsters there to clean their unmarked vehicles."

"That's right. It was a hell of a time."

Ozu exhaled, pulled a hundred-yen coin from his pocket, and tossed it up into the air. He'd explained to Goto earlier that if the coin landed on heads, they'd look at the east side of the lot, and west for tails. The auto yard was as spacious as the construction site of a major apartment complex, so they had to pick and choose where they'd search if they wanted to be done by the end of the day. Officers couldn't spend the entire day on a warrantless search.

"Looks like east today," Ozu told Goto, slapping the coin against the back of his hand. He hadn't actually looked at the coin. The decision to search the east side of the yard wasn't a random decision, either. It had been relayed to Miyata beforehand.

"I'll go look first," said Goto, rising from his seat. He had a list with the makes of all the stolen cars in the prefecture and a digital camera for taking evidence.

"I'll be right after ya," said Ozu, pulling a pack of cigarettes from his inside his suit pocket. "Just let me have a smoke first. Can't do it in the car."

Oblivious, Goto descended the stairs outside the office. When his footsteps faded, Ozu lit up the cigarette with an oil lighter. As he exhaled, he glanced at the colorful pack he'd set on the end of the table. Natural American Spirit Gold, 0.8 mg nicotine, 6 mg tar.

The veteran agent, faithful to his office and always ready to dispense advice to a subordinate in need, suddenly wore the face of a man who'd sold his soul for cash.

He puffed on the smoke blissfully, certain that he understood what was really going on behind the auto yard's closed gate. However, times had changed, and Ozu knew less than he had before. He could never have dreamed that a narco from Mexico was raising hitmen here, training them in a paramilitary style.

Ozu ground the butt against the ashtray and peered into the pack of Natural American Spirit. There were still a few left, but he asked, "Pops, you got any spare smokes?"

Miyata handed him a pack of the same brand, but there were no cigarettes inside, only folded-up ten-thousand-yen bills, fifteen in all.

Ozu tucked the pack into his suit pocket and slowly rose from the couch. "Times do change, don't they?" he said. "People are so into e-cigs these days, folks like me feel left out in the smoking sections."

"To be honest, I bought one, too," Miyata confessed, smiling apologetically.

"Well, I'll be damned." Ozu clicked his tongue. "By the way, what kind of dog you keep around here? What's it called?"

"It's a breed called Dogo…"

"You're giving it rabies shots and all that, right?"

"Of course…"

"Don't you dare let those things run loose. If it gets out, it'll kill two or three people."

"I understand."

"Make sure your boys know that."

"I will, sir."

Once the two policemen finished their inspection and left the yard, El Taladro headed for the piles of old tires on the west side of the grounds to return the guns he'd placed there back to the pile of scrap on the east side.

He moved the old tires off the top of the heap, dragged out a heavy wooden chest, and then stuck it into a wheelbarrow. He pushed it along through the mud, wearing rubber boots for better stability. However, he stopped partway along and stared at the box he was hauling. Inside were the Remington M870s that the other guys called barracudas.

He wanted to shoot one of those shotguns with a boxy silencer himself. El Taladro had only just turned twenty, and burned with desire for a chance to use the guns, but he was never allowed. It would've been one thing if only his hero, Chatarra, got to use the firearms, but El Mamut and El Casco had come to the chop shop after El Taladro. It wasn't fair that they got to shoot, but not him. He couldn't beat them in a fistfight, but firing accuracy had nothing to do with arm strength. He had talent of his own, surely.

El Taladro knew that El Cocinero's reasoning for not letting him shoot was his innate nearsightedness. But he was tired of being forced to accept a mundane reality that would never change. He wanted to make a name for himself somehow. El Taladro had no idea what the shooting practice was actually for, but that didn't matter to him. He wanted the respect of El Cocinero and Chatarra, and he wanted to join El Mamut and El Casco. He wanted to be a genuine member of the gang.

After hiding the box back in the pile of scrap on the east side, he tossed cattle tibias into the empty wheelbarrow and jammed a can of A&W root beer in the back pocket of his jeans. It wasn't cold, but he didn't care. El Taladro pushed the wheelbarrow again, this time to the south side of the auto yard, where the hunting dog was.

Of all the Dogos Argentinos they'd bought for the *sicario* tests, one had been left behind as a guard dog, and it was now bigger than any of the other hounds they'd kept.

El Taladro gave it the name Músculo, Portuguese for "muscle," and no one else looked after the dog, so no one could complain about the moniker.

As he got closer, the powerful Dogo Argentino lifted its head up off its front paws and yawned lazily; it was chained to a metal pole and had nothing to do. El Taladro tossed it a shinbone, then cracked open the A&W and watched the dog gnaw. It was the world's strongest guard dog, a breed known for killing pumas before total physical maturity. While its face was similar to a bull dog's or pit bull's, its legs were much longer, and its body was bigger.

Bred to be strong enough to hunt an apex predator, the dog was naturally fearless, and as it grew to adulthood, it almost never barked. It devoured its meat, chewed on the bones, lapped up water with its thick tongue, then shook its head, jangling the thick chain, and glowered darkly at people across the yard.

El Taladro felt nervous when he was close to Músculo, and found his palms getting sweaty. He could only imagine what would happen if the chain came loose. At this distance, a gun wouldn't save him. But Chatarra and the other two had unleashed their dogs and killed them while they were free. It was remarkable that they hadn't faltered in the face of the beasts. However…

Weren't the dogs Chatarra and the others shot smaller than the one I've been raising?

Upon realizing that, El Taladro knew he had the right idea for garnering esteem. *The boss and Chatarra will be happy with me after this. It's a great idea.* He couldn't get it out of his head.

With the sound of Músculo cracking the cow bone in his ears,

El Taladro looked up at the sky, so blue and clear that last night's storm might as well have never happened. He downed the A&W in one go.

Koshimo spent the majority of his time in the shop working on handles. That was an important part of being a knifemaker, especially for folding knives. Handles were the face of those pieces. Bone, wood, shell, fossil: Koshimo carved the various materials into different shapes and combined them with Pablo's blades. Eventually, he was permitted to add the final touches.

The workshop took in materials from all over the world.

Those cow shinbones he boiled just about every day came from America. The deer antlers were from India, the mammoth tusk fossils were Russian, the mastodon tusk fossils were from Canada, and the hippo tusks, which were listed under Appendix II of the Washington Convention, came from South Africa.

"Poacher items like elephant tusks and rhino horns," Pablo explained to Koshimo one day, "will get you a much higher price for a knife. But I don't use them. A real knifemaker doesn't use black-market goods to try to squeeze a higher price out of his items."

Koshimo was reminded of what a correctional instructor had told him at the juvenile detention center.

"If you do something right and good, be proud of it."

Curiously, Pablo's mannerisms seemed far from that axiom. His features looked terribly sad, his eyes wandered, and he seemed like a man who was living a lie. When Koshimo asked him about it, Pablo said he was going for a walk and practically fled the workshop.

Left all alone, Koshimo continued working on a handle. Eventually, he got hungry, so he put the last piece of delivery pizza from earlier into the toaster oven.

35

cempöhualli-huan-caxtölli

On a cool afternoon in early October, Pablo laid out a railway map of Kawasaki on the worktable so that he and Koshimo could examine it together.

He used his fingers to trace the stops where Koshimo would need to switch lines, but the boy's lifeless responses made him nervous. *Will he actually be capable of reaching the destination?*

Koshimo had never taken the train on his own, nor had he ridden a bus or taxi. Naturally, he had no driver's license. Pablo crossed his arms and frowned. A man well over two meters tall, lost in town, would stand out. *Maybe I should just go with him, like I've been doing.*

He was about to say as much when Koshimo remarked, "I know this area." His long finger pointed at Musashi-Nakahara station, the stop closest to the auto yard that was his destination.

"You know it?" Pablo asked, surprised.

"The basketball arena is around there."

"Yup," Pablo said. As Koshimo noted, Todoroki Arena was in the direction of the Tama River. "Oh right, you like basketball. Have you ever been there?"

"Yeah. On my bike."

"Your bike," Pablo echoed. "Of course. That's an option, too."

They were going to take extra cattle tibias not used for knife handles to the auto yard in Kamikodanaka. All Koshimo had to do was hand over the future dog chew toys to the worker there, and then he'd be done.

For this simple errand, Pablo went and bought Koshimo a second-hand bicycle. It had a rusty basket and rack, and the brake wire was hideously warped. Pablo straightened out the wire, oiled up the chain and gears, changed out the tire tubes, and pumped them up until they were tight.

Before he tied the cardboard box with six cattle tibias inside to the rack, Pablo opened the container and tossed a bag of dog food inside. That way, if a police officer happened to stop him during the trip, Koshimo could convincingly explain that he was transporting dog food and bones.

"Turn the light on when the sun goes down."

"Okay."

"Don't do anything with the guys at the yard. Once you deliver the box, come right back."

"All right."

Koshimo worked the creaking pedals, riding toward the sun in the west. Flocks of birds flew into the distance, and cloud trails floated overhead.

As he got closer to the Tama River, Koshimo could tell the breeze was changing.

Wide wind.

There were many kinds of wind: wide, narrow, round, sharp, angry, laughing, crying. Sometimes they combined with one another, forming an infinite variety of patterns, like a knife blade and handle.

As he pedaled, he wondered how long it would take to get there. Koshimo had a watch from Pablo on his wrist, but he'd never looked at the face. Soon, the young man started thinking about the concept of **time**.

Koshimo had a peculiar philosophy regarding time. Naturally, he didn't think of it as philosophy, and he wasn't well-spoken enough to convey his thoughts to anyone else.

He'd been scolded when he said, "Time is in the bath," to a correctional instructor at the juvenile detention center. "That's wrong," the instructor had chided. "The proper way to say it is, 'The time in the bath.'"

The same thing happened during a conversation with Pablo. When Koshimo remarked, "Time is setting in the sun," Pablo carefully corrected his syntax. "You mean, 'The time the sun sets'—right?"

Koshimo didn't think he was incorrect in either instance. He'd described time naturally and properly, as he experienced it.

To Koshimo, time was not a container for a subject or thing, but life itself. Time *was* the subject. He believed time was experiencing the world. This was the inverse of how others saw it, like a film negative version of the typical conception of reality.

Once Koshimo realized that his way of thinking was unique to him, he refrained from discussing the subject of time around others.

It was already dark when he reached the auto yard.

He dismounted the bicycle in front of the barbed wire fence with the security cameras above it, and pressed the button on the intercom. "Good evening," he said. "I'm here to deliver the bones."

There was no answer. Koshimo went to press the button again, but the steel gate began sliding open first. He took in the expansive yard before him, lit by floodlights, and walked his bicycle inside.

The young man who showed up out of the darkness wore a backward baseball cap and dirty work gloves. He was chewing gum, and tattoos were visible on parts of his neck and left arm that his T-shirt didn't cover.

"Are you fucking kidding me?" El Taladro gaped. "How goddamn tall are you?"

Pablo set down the C-bone handle he was working on and glanced at the clock on one of the shop's walls. It was eight o'clock. Koshimo still wasn't back. He tried calling the smartphone he'd given the boy, but there was no answer.

He took off his work spectacles and rubbed at his eyes. There were shavings all over the workbench. C-bone shavings. A sight from hell.

Of all the products he made on assignment at the shop, the most valuable material for custom knife handles after real skull was C-bone. All Pablo made with it was small folding knives, hardly ever crafting sheath knives from it. Pablo believed C-bone wasn't a sturdy enough material to serve as the grip for a medium or large blade.

While he let Koshimo help with prepping the material—boiling and drying—Pablo never let him carve the C-bone itself. He didn't even show him how it was done. He did all of it himself. Pablo etched the patterns into the C-bone, sanded it with paper, and oiled the surface. All the while, he lamented the cruelty of the world and begged for forgiveness.

When the finished product was placed in a sealed box, the label didn't mention C-bone anywhere. It had a more generic description.

Kawasaki Riverport Metal Ltd.
Custom Display Knife / Steel / Cow bone (Jigged bone, oiled bone, bone slab)

Pablo put his glasses back on and resumed carving the high-priced handle, which was being falsely sold as cattle bone. He worked with the chisel, occasionally glancing at the clock. Anxiety was building.

It had been a mistake to send Koshimo to the auto yard alone. What was he doing? He wasn't answering the phone. If he couldn't perform an errand like this on his own, he'd never be a respectable man in his own right.

Immediately, Pablo felt a pang of self-mockery at this stray thought.

Respectable? That word only exists for people who have upstanding jobs. No, what we're doing at this workshop—what I'm doing is...

El Taladro's time in Brazil until he was fourteen had taught him that very tall men were called *montanha*, mountain, in Portuguese.

Aside from the fact that the guy who showed up to deliver the cattle tibias was a shocking *montanha*, everything was going to El Taladro's plan. In fact, it was even better for him that a new person had made the delivery. The middle-aged La Cerámica would've been wary, and the plan might have failed.

Upon talking to the *montanha*, El Taladro learned that the guy was actually younger than him, and he didn't even have a nickname yet. El Taladro believed that a lack of title was proof that El Cocinero saw him as useless. Poor sap—all that size and nothing to show for it.

In truth, Koshimo had never met El Cocinero, and didn't even know the man existed.

El Taladro was one hundred and sixty-eight centimeters, and Koshimo was at least a thirty centimeters taller than that. Silhouetted against the auto yard's floodlights, they might as well have looked like father and son.

The smaller man crunched gravel underfoot, walking beside Koshimo and his bicycle, and muttered:

"Don't blame me, *montanha*. You were just unlucky."

El Taladro took Koshimo to the south side of the yard and stopped next to Músculo. He never approached like this, even when caring for the dog.

Koshimo stared at the chained animal, which was resting on the dirt. It looked bigger and more powerful than any dog he'd seen in Kawasaki. It was covered in short white fur, except for a black spot around its right eye, which gave it the appearance of wearing a pirate's eyepatch. This was a relatively common genetic pattern for Dogo Argentino, and the men who took them on boar and puma hunts in Latin America called them *piratas*.

El Taladro peered into the cardboard box Koshimo brought and lifted out the bag of dog food. "What is this?" he asked. "He doesn't eat this shit."

He tossed the bag onto the ground, then told Koshimo to stand in place holding the box full of cattle tibias. Then El Taladro snuck over to the sleeping Músculo. Once at an angle where Koshimo wouldn't see, he began undoing the lock that connected the dog chain to the metal pole.

A large dog suddenly breaking free, bursting from its cage due to owner negligence, and attacking unlucky bystanders was the sort of thing that happened all the time, all over the world. It was a tragedy no different from an auto accident. Even animal trainers at zoos got attacked and killed by the lions they cared for. Accidents happened with deadly animals. *New guy shows up to deliver the cow bones, and the Dogo Argentino goes wild and attacks. Nothing surprising about that*, El Taladro thought.

The guard dog gets loose somehow. The guy from the workshop gets attacked. El Taladro has no choice but to shoot the dog to save him.

That was the scenario he envisioned. He would show himself to be brave, team-focused, and a good shot. It was the only way to convince El Cocinero and Chatarra that he was worthy of them.

The problem was the amount of time it would take to run over and grab the barracuda hidden on the east side of the yard. If he already had it out, it would draw suspicion. So his only option was to rush over to grab it once the emergency occurred. The only thing that could buy him enough time was another person for the guard dog to attack. God alone knew what would happen to the *montanha* when Músculo went for him

Once he had the lock undone, El Taladro quietly let the chain dangle to the ground, cognizant of its considerable weight in his hand.

Músculo stared at the undone leash in wonder, then leaned over to sniff at it. Eventually, the beast rose to its feet and yawned, exposing thick canines. It shook its head, which then rippled into a full-body shiver. The dog was one hundred and twenty centimeters long, stood sixty-eight centimeters tall, and weighed fifty-two kilograms.

In the floodlights, the dog's white fur shone like snow, unfittingly slender compared to its blocky head. It shook again, then glared at the nearest person.

Koshimo sensed a change in the wind, a violent one. It was like a whirlwind had just passed through the auto yard without making a sound. *Time is going into a rage.*

To El Taladro, it stood to reason that Músculo would approach the unfamiliar man holding the box full of cow bones when freed. However, that's not what happened. El Taladro was already rushing over to the east side when he heard faint steps behind him, and turned to see Músculo tearing after him without so much as a warning bark. Terror gripped the young man.

Why me? I'm the one who takes care of you.

He was knocked down in an instant and heard the sound of his own cheekbone being crushed between powerful jaws. He cried and pleaded, but the beast's hot breath was the only response. Out of the corner of his eye, El Taladro spied the *montanha*, still standing in place with the box in his hands—and then he could no longer see through the blood. His face was utterly destroyed. To a hunting dog capable of killing big cats, a twenty-year-old human male was no more than a kitten.

The Dogo Argentino lifted its head from El Taladro, who was convulsing on the ground, and gave a tremendous tongue-lolling shake that cast warm blood, flesh, and spittle all around. Fragments of skull were mixed with the saliva.

Overjoyed at the chance to satisfy its genetic instinct to hunt, the dog pointed its red snout at the next target. It stared with dark intent at Koshimo, who hadn't moved. The Dogo Argentino was smart enough to know there were chewy cow bones in the box. But tonight, it had a much more enjoyable toy to play with.

Late that night, Pablo got a call from El Cocinero.

He was waiting for Koshimo to return to the workshop, but the boy never came back. Eventually, he gave up and went home, turned on a basketball game on the TV, and drifted off to sleep. The last thing he remembered was the middle of the second quarter.

When he awoke to the sound of the phone, Pablo turned off the TV, which presently displayed a still pattern of colored bars, and answered. It was an unfamiliar number. Intuitively, he guessed it was El Cocinero or

El Loco. They changed their numbers just about every day and often called in the early morning or late at night without a care for his needs.

"La Cerámica," said El Cocinero, speaking in Spanish. "The kid you hired is at the chop shop. Koshimo, I think? Go get him and bring him to my place."

Pablo said nothing. Koshimo was still at the auto yard? He couldn't think of what to say at first. Eventually, hesitantly, he asked, "Did Koshimo do something?"

"Can he make knives, too?" El Cocinero replied, ignoring the question.

"I taught him the ropes and let him make a few..."

"I want to see them," El Cocinero stated.

He ended the call there. Pablo had been contacted in the middle of the night a few times before, but he'd never been summoned to El Cocinero's, the Peruvian restaurant in Sakuramoto. The echoes of El Cocinero's deep voice in his ears frightened Pablo. His pulse quickened, and his T-shirt felt unpleasantly damp from soaking up sweat. He cradled the phone in his hands and stared at the picture of his daughter on the lock screen. All he could do was stare at her little smile, clinging to its warmth. Everything around it was steep darkness without a bottom. Eventually, he tore his eyes away from the smartphone.

Something was up. El Cocinero wanted to see him, and he wanted Koshimo, too. What happened at the auto yard? Pablo closed his eyes. He wasn't a religious man, but his father had been a devout Catholic. Like his father had done so many times, Pablo kneeled at his bedside and prayed of his own accord for the first time in his life. "Dear God..."

36

cempöhualli-huan-caxtölli-huan-cë

Each time he saw the steel gate of the auto yard, Pablo thought of the American military base in Okinawa. When the way opened, he pressed the pedal and rolled the Citroën Berlingo into the lot.

The headlights caught the power shovel used for dismantling; it was as menacing as a monster in the night. He stopped the car in the eerie quiet, closed the door, and headed up to the office above the garage.

The door to the office was already open. Pablo saw Koshimo and Miyata, the owner of the yard. They were sitting on the sofa used for meetings. Koshimo's head was hung, and there was blood on his shirt.

An exhausted Miyata noticed that Pablo had arrived. "I was hoping to give him a change of clothes, but nothing fit him."

"What happened?" Pablo questioned.

Miyata took a puff from his vape pen. "Our employee got bitten by the guard dog. Although *bitten* might be the wrong word…"

He didn't come out and say, "And he's critically injured and possibly dying."

"Bitten? By…that dog?" Pablo asked quietly. "Koshimo, did it hurt you, too?"

Koshimo didn't reply. Pablo noticed that the boy's shirt was stained with dirt in addition to the blood.

"Did the guard dog get away?" Pablo inquired.

"Guard dog," Miyata repeated scornfully. "You know that's no guard dog. It's a monster. When I quit the fire department, I wanted a quieter life. And look where it's led me. I'm surrounded by monsters. Can't get a decent night's sleep. It's even worse than before."

Again, Pablo asked, "Where's the guard dog?"

"It's gone," Miyata said. "That kid of yours killed it."

They drove through Kawasaki in the middle of the night.

Pablo tried to keep the Berlingo moving as slowly as possible on the trip from the auto yard to El Cocinero's restaurant, Papa Seca. When a traffic light was approaching, he'd slow down well before reaching it. He needed time to think. Pablo's mind was in chaos. He hadn't exchanged a single word with Koshimo.

In an alley off the side of an intersection, some boys were gathered in a cipher, freestyling. There was a population of Koreans in Kawasaki who'd grown up in Japan, not unlike Pablo and Koshimo. Some of them spoke the Korean of their roots, and some knew English, but others couldn't speak anything but Japanese. Pablo cracked open the window while waiting for the light to change, so he could hear their flow. Japanese rapping, Korean rapping, English choruses, beatboxing, clapping, stomping.

Within the rhythm, they were free. The kids were of the same generation as Koshimo. The light turned, and Pablo stepped on the gas pedal.

When they reached Papa Seca, he turned off the Berlingo's engine, then the headlights. There was a CLOSED sign on the door, but light shone through the windows. Pablo glanced at the parking lot: a Jeep Wrangler, Range Rover, and an imported Toyota Tundra.

Something struck the window next to him. There was a man with his finger bent to tap on it, peering through at Pablo, who still had his hands on the wheel. Pablo had seen this Japanese man at the auto yard before. He knew his name—El Mamut. Pablo opened the door.

"What are you doing?" said El Mamut. "Get out already."

The two did as he demanded. El Mamut was a huge man at one hundred and ninety-one centimeters and one hundred and twenty-three kilograms, but even he laughed when he saw Koshimo standing upright. He had a plain, heather-gray T-shirt, size 8L, in his hand. "Put this on for now."

Koshimo dipped his head, took off his bloody shirt right there, and donned the new one.

El Mamut opened the door with the CLOSED sign on it. The biceps bulged out of his black tee, and tattoos ran down his forearms to his wrists.

Pablo walked into the building, which was full of raucous shouting. Koshimo made to follow him, but El Mamut held out an arm to block the way. "You're going upstairs. Come with me."

Pablo could only watch Koshimo go, his expression hard. The door to the restaurant closed in his face.

Koshimo followed El Mamut up the outside stairs to the office. The way was barred by a steel door and watched by a security camera. The door was locked from the inside. It opened, and El Mamut prodded Koshimo to send him through. Then he turned around and went back downstairs to continue his meal.

The room was pitch black; Koshimo couldn't see a thing. It was even darker than the private rooms in juvy after lights-out. He heard the door lock itself after closing, but he couldn't take a single step without knowing what was around him.

Despite being surrounded in darkness, Koshimo sensed that someone was watching him carefully. Out of nowhere, he remembered a night when lightning had flashed, but there was no thunder.

"It takes time for your eyes to ease into the darkness," a man said in Spanish. "You'll be able to see eventually."

He struck a match and lit something. After a few moments, Koshimo smelled something bizarre, like a mixture of sweet nectar and gasoline.

"What is that?" Koshimo asked, also in Spanish.

"*Copalli*," the man answered. "That's the Nahuatl word for resin before it turns into amber."

"…Nahuatl…"

"Copal smoke is a crucial part of Aztec culture."

"…Aztec…"

"How tall are you?"

"Right now, I'm…" Koshimo tried to remember what the number had been the last time he used the tape measure at the workshop. He'd grown four-fifths of an inch since he first met Pablo, so he was close to two hundred, four centimeters. *"Dos y cuatro."*

"Looking at you," the man remarked, "reminds me of Rafael."

"…Rafael…"

"Rafael Contreras. They called him El Yeti. I met him once in Nuevo Laredo. He was over two meters, too. But from what I can tell, you're bigger than him."

Koshimo still couldn't make out the man in the dark. The name put a thought into his head, though, so he asked, "Was Rafael a basketball player?"

"Basketball?" The man lit another match, but this one did not go to a piece of *copalli* but a joint in his mouth. "No, he's a narco. A very famous one. Probably still in prison."

Valmiro always waited in total darkness when he summoned someone to visit. The only times he kept the lights on throughout were with Nomura and Suenaga.

He had a stun grenade hidden in the drawer of his desk, a throwback to his Mexico days. That way, if an enemy came charging in with night-vision goggles, he could instantly rob them of their sight.

"Is your mother Mexican?" Valmiro asked.

"Sí," Koshimo replied. He was starting to see the contours of the man's face.

"Where was she from?"

"Sinaloa."

"Sinaloa," Valmiro repeated. He exhaled thick smoke. "Did she tell you about her home?"

"No," Koshimo replied. *"Madre* didn't talk about Sinaloa. She talked a lot about Mexico City—the fireworks at El Zócalo. *Viva Mexico."*

"Ah, for Independence Day. The big celebration," Valmiro stated. "Did your *madre* tell you what's buried under Mexico City?"

"No."

"There are pyramids under the ground there. Temples. Mexico City was built atop the glory of Tenochtitlan. Everything the Aztecs had was destroyed and now sleeps beneath the city."

"Who are the Aztecs?" Koshimo asked.

Koshimo never told jokes when speaking with others, but when he asked very direct questions, the other person sometimes burst into laughter. Koshimo had the feeling that the man in the darkness was going to do the same. Yet he didn't so much as chuckle. He was content not to answer the question, either.

"Koshimo," said Valmiro, "I am almost never surprised. But when I heard that you killed the Dogo with your bare hands, I was surprised for the first time in a long while."

"…Dogo…"

"The animal you killed at the auto yard."

Koshimo bit his lip. "I'm sorry." He lowered his head and kept it there. Miyata, the president of the auto yard company, had told him that the dog belonged to the owner of a Peruvian restaurant. The animal was already gone, and the man it attacked was dying. Maybe he was dead by now, too.

"Keep your head up," Valmiro told him. "Do you remember what happened?"

"*Sí.*"

Everything was caught on a camera hidden in a location El Taladro didn't know about. El Taladro's actions were nothing short of betrayal. He freed the Dogo in an attempt to sic it on an outsider. Traitors deserved death. But to Valmiro, the Brazilian-born kid's treachery was nothing compared to what happened after.

Before Valmiro met Koshimo, he'd watched the entire spectacle on the security video Miyata sent to him.

The Dogo Argentino came back into the frame, snout bloodied after nearly killing El Taladro. Koshimo tossed the box aside, spilling the cattle shinbones onto the ground.

Five seconds had passed.

The Dogo Argentino didn't spare a glance for the bones. It set its sights on Koshimo and charged. The boy stood his ground and reached out with his long right arm. He grabbed the snarling dog's face and caught the beast in midair, slamming it to the ground. He made a fist with his left hand and brought it down against the side of the dog's head.

Ten seconds had passed.

The strongest hunting dog in the world was convulsing, tongue lolling, and then stopped moving. The force of the blow caused one of the animal's eyeballs to pop out. It looked like a special effect from a movie. From his seat, Valmiro felt a chill run down his back. How much arm strength, how much grip force, was necessary to accomplish such a feat? It wasn't a matter of power alone, either. The agility to time the counterattack, the cold-bloodedness to eliminate the enemy—this boy had them in spades.

"I'm not angry that you killed the Dogo," Valmiro explained. "But Koshimo, killing that creature with your bare hands is going to bring a big change in your life. Now that you've met me, it already has."

Am I going back to juvy? Koshimo wondered. *I bet Pablo and Malinal will be angry at me.*

"You've been chosen. You stand before the pyramid," Valmiro said, exhaling more smoke. "Once you're there, the only place left to go is up the steps to the sun and moon. The priests are waiting at the top to cut out hearts. You will be one of them."

Koshimo had absolutely no idea what the man was talking about.

"It's not your problem that the Dogo is dead," Valmiro went on. "You only did what was natural, Koshimo. You fought like a warrior, and you vanquished the beast. But what about El Taladro? All of this is his fault. El Taladro betrayed us, his *familia*. He didn't listen to us, and chose to unleash the Dogo. It's only because you bravely fought the Dogo that he still breathes, despite losing half his face. Now that he's shamed himself, his life will come to an end soon. El Taladro must be punished for his actions. He betrayed the *familia*."

"...*Familia*..."

"Koshimo, from this day on, you are our *familia*. You will be there to watch us offer El Taladro to God. But before that, go downstairs and eat. Meet with Chatarra, El Mamut, and El Casco. Do you understand me, Koshimo? From now on...

"Somos familia."

37

cempöhualli-huan-caxtölli-huan-öme

El Patíbulo. The Gallows.

That was what El Mamut and El Casco called Koshimo when he came downstairs after meeting with El Cocinero. They were used to calling people by Spanish nicknames.

They knew the nickname El Cocinero had chosen for the boy before he did—he was still trying to process what was happening. An unforeseen accident resulted in El Cocinero's praise and a prompt position on the list of *sicarios*. The other two welcomed Koshimo into their group, but he had no idea what it meant.

El Mamut and El Casco called him to their table. The two men sat on either side of Pablo, who looked small and miserable. They'd been feeding him pisco, a Peruvian brandy, even though he'd driven here. He stared silently at the table, his face dark.

"I hear you can make knives. That right?" El Mamut asked Koshimo, flexing his fingers. "It's a great skill to be good with your hands. Guys who are good with their hands are good at squaring up, too."

"You punched that thing dead? That's crazy shit. Right, Pops?" El Casco clapped Pablo on the shoulder, but the knifemaker didn't look up.

These men had raised their own Dogos Argentinos at the auto yard and shot the dogs dead, so they understood what a feat it was to kill one with your bare hands. When El Cocinero told them about Koshimo, their eyes had lit up with excitement.

"By the way, what'd you do to get locked up in juvy?" El Casco asked.

"I—"

"We already know," the man cut him off, laughing. "Don't actually say it out loud. There are other guests here."

The CLOSED sign was out front because Papa Seca was rented out for the night. Over ten well-built men feasted on empanadas, pisco, and cocktails of pisco and ginger ale with lime called chilcanos.

The men carrying on were Mexican luchadors who'd just finished an event at a venue in Yokohama. They were a mixture of *técnicos* and *rudos*, faces and heels, who'd been flown over by a Japanese promoter. Some of them had taken their luchador masks off, while others remained in full costume.

"*Quiero comer sushi!*" someone yelled drunkenly. None of them could have guessed in their wildest dreams that a cartel narco in exile was on the floor above them.

Drunk on pisco, they gathered around a table to bet on impromptu arm-wrestling matches. They placed coasters on opposite corners of the table—if the back of your hand touched one, you lost. They were betting three thousand yen per contest. The largest of the luchadors was still only one hundred and eighty centimeters or so, but each man's neck was as thick as their profession demanded. Every one of them was rippling with muscle along the shoulders, biceps, and forearms.

The arm wrestling was pitched and competitive, Spanish insults flying. A drink spilled on the thousand-yen bills, and the men all screamed and laughed, sweat beading their foreheads.

"Do you know who they are?" El Mamut inquired.

Koshimo looked over at the men. One had his head entirely covered in glittering red cloth, while others wore purple or green. The fabrics were beautifully embroidered, and Koshimo would have liked to see them up close, but he was too busy eating the Peruvian food served to him: empanadas, octopus ceviche, a stewed mix of potatoes and tripe called cau.

"Are they *familia*, too?" Koshimo asked, savoring the acidity of the lime and the spice of the *aji amarillo* peppers.

"No, they're not. They're pro wrestlers." El Mamut laughed.

"Don't call them pro wrestlers. You're supposed to call them luchadors," El Casco snapped. "El Patíbulo, you speak Spanish, right? Pro wrestling is *lucha libre* in Spanish, right?"

Lucha libre. Koshimo chewed a mouthful of octopus and considered the words. "I don't know it."

"You've never seen pro wrestling?" El Mamut was incredulous.

"I told you; it's called *lucha libre*," El Casco reiterated.

"It doesn't fucking matter," El Mamut snapped. He put his hand on Koshimo's shoulder. "Watch this, new guy. That one over there is gonna take all these fools' money."

When Chatarra offered to join the arm-wrestling competition, the luchadores praised the Japanese man in the safari hat. They thought he was just a regular at the restaurant, or perhaps a fan of professional wrestling.

But when the matches started, no one could beat him. The luchadores were like children challenging a grown man. Chatarra slammed their hands against the table without mercy. Each time, the impact bumped a bottle or glass off the surface to smash onto the floor.

Koshimo ate as he watched Chatarra's victories stack up. The man was short, but extraordinarily thick, like a balloon that had sprouted limbs and a head. His arms were undeniably broader than the Mexicans'.

The luchadors grabbed the edge of the table with their left hands for extra leverage, pushing with all their weight, but Chatarra was so firmly in control that he could take a shot of tequila with his free hand.

The thousand-yen bills piled up in front of Chatarra. One man who'd been drinking tequila at the bar as he watched finally came over to the table to try his luck. He was tired of seeing his fellows humiliated by this amateur.

The man's black mask had a goat's head and a Satanic circle sewn onto it, symbolizing black magic. He was a popular *rudo* by the name of El Veneno. His fighting style was ruthless and attracted the crowd's ire, but he was also keenly observant. You couldn't play a good *rudo* unless you were smart.

He'd had some experience with arm wrestling before becoming a luchador. He did his own training program and even placed third in the ninety-kilogram right-hand category in an international arm-wrestling competition in Mexico City.

The fat Japanese man beating all the luchadores certainly possessed arm strength, but as far as El Veneno could tell, he lacked technique. He won using the top roll method every time, and probably didn't even realize he was doing it. Competitors who won via top roll regularly had trouble with the hook technique, which wrapped around the wrist better. That was basic knowledge in arm wrestling. If a strength-first top roller met with a hook grip right from the start, there was no escape. El Veneno knew that an amateur didn't stand a chance against the explosive power of an experienced competitive arm wrestler.

When El Veneno put his elbow down on the table, brimming with confidence, Chatarra turned to the Japanese promoter, who was acting as judge, and said, "How about all the money I've won against his mask?"

Instantly, the mood among the luchadores changed. Chatarra's suggestion riled them to the core. The mask wasn't just expensive; it was a symbol, the mark of the professional. It wasn't a Halloween prop.

Yet El Veneno accepted the wager, albeit with chagrin.

He immediately attacked with the hook, but nothing he did could get Chatarra's arm to budge. In moments, his right arm was being overpowered in a way he'd never experienced before. He sensed that it was going to break. El Veneno let go, pulled his hand out of those fingers like anaconda jaws, and backed away.

"The coward ran," Chatarra remarked.

Sensing that their compatriot had been insulted, the luchadors promptly discarded their entertainers' personas and looked ready to scrap. They grabbed beer bottles and smashed the ends, surrounding Chatarra. The restaurant was suddenly deadly silent except for the Peruvian Criolla music.

Under the table, El Mamut and El Casco undid the safeties on their guns, watching carefully. They could kill the luchadors at any moment, but they didn't want to hurt anyone in the restaurant. Plus, the wrestlers were El Loco's guests.

"Go on over," El Mamut said to Koshimo without warning. "Our brother's in trouble. Stop the fight."

Koshimo had been watching the whole scene as he ate, so he understood the situation. With El Mamut's encouragement, Koshimo rose uncertainly to his feet. The luchadors had been partying and carrying on for over two hours, so they hadn't noticed when Koshimo arrived. Startled by his height, they all looked up at him in alarm.

Only a bouncer would approach a situation like this. The luchadors with broken bottles tensed up, preparing for a scuffle, but Koshimo's next action took them by surprise.

"I'll go," he said in Spanish. He pushed El Veneno aside, who was shaking his numbed hand, and approached the table.

Chatarra, already taking another shot of tequila, knew who the giant boy was. El Patíbulo. He looked up and said, "You want to arm wrestle me?"

"Yeah."

The other men had been cut off just before they could fight. They stood around awkwardly, holding their broken beer bottles. Back in the corner, El Mamut and El Casco clutched their sides with laughter.

"You're a funny guy," Chatarra chuckled. "What's your dominant hand?"

"Left."

"Mine too. Let's go with the left, then."

They set their left elbows down on the table and faced off. Their arm lengths were quite different, and so were the angles of their elbows.

El Veneno, who'd disqualified himself out of fear of Chatarra's strength, whispered into the promoter's ear, requesting the chance to play judge. It was partially to calm things down before it turned into a melee but also because he wanted a chance to see the match up close.

Koshimo and Chatarra clasped hands. El Veneno placed his fingers on their wrists to adjust the angle, and said, "Wrists straight." Then, since Koshimo could understand Spanish, he advised, "Don't take your eyes off your own hand. You'll get hurt real bad."

Once the signal was given, Koshimo's fingers tensed. Neither arm budged. Chatarra was trying to crush Koshimo's hand with his grip, rather than push the arm down. He wasn't going to break the bones, but if he made the boy scream, he could show where each of them sat in the pecking order.

As for Koshimo, his first thought was, *So this is how this game works.* He'd thought it a contest of strength to see who could push the other arm down to the table, but apparently, it was actually a contest of grip strength to see who could crush the other's fingers.

With that in mind, Koshimo squeezed back. Python-like veins bulged in his arm, and his muscles rippled. It was grip on grip. The smile vanished from Chatarra's lips. He looked deadly serious and puffed out his cheeks. There was a dark look deep in the eyes of both contestants.

Aha, thought Chatarra. *No wonder he was able to kill the Dogo Argentino with his bare hands.*

The door to the restaurant opened, and El Loco appeared. He was carrying a duralumin case containing goods that the luchadors had requested for their three-week tour of Japan: painkillers and muscle builders. The painkiller was fentanyl, a substance permitted to pass through Narita. The muscle builders were Dianabol, which was legal in Japan. There were no doping restrictions when it came to entertainment, so they had nothing to worry about there.

The luchadors crowded around El Loco and his case, handing over cash for the amounts they'd need during their stay. They had lost all interest in the arm-wrestling contest. "Time's up," said El Mamut, placing his hand over Koshimo's and Chatarra's. "El Loco's here, so we've got to go."

Chatarra smiled and let go. The three *sicarios* under El Cocinero's tutelage headed for the door with Koshimo, the new guy. Pablo was still sitting at the table, surrounded by beer bottles and Koshimo's empty plates. No one paid any attention to him.

As Chatarra and Koshimo made to leave, El Veneno called out to them in Spanish, having finished his Dianabol purchase. "You guys are both monsters. It gave me chills just watching you. What do you do for a living? You ever feel like giving wrestling a shot?"

38

cempöhualli-huan-caxtölli-huan-ëyi

Koshimo stepped through the door of Papa Seca and gazed up into the night.

The crescent moon glowed dimly. He couldn't sense any expression in the wind blowing on his face. It was neither laughing nor scowling. The floating clouds, illuminated by the moon, were silent.

"Get in the car," El Mamut said. Koshimo climbed into the Toyota Vellfire belonging to El Loco, the back-alley doctor named Nomura.

Chatarra took the lead with the Tundra pickup (its steering wheel was on the left-hand side), followed by Valmiro's Jeep Wrangler, then Nomura and Koshimo in the Vellfire van. The three vehicles maintained an even distance, their headlights forming a single line that wove as it followed the road.

While waiting for the gate of the auto yard to open, the cars turned off their headlights and switched to fog lights. The glow from the vehicles only faintly illuminated the dust rising from the ground in the darkened lot. The three *sicarios* got out of the Tundra and headed for the garage. Nomura hit a quick rail of coke in the car, then told Koshimo to get out of the back seat. Valmiro stepped out of the Jeep Wrangler. The sky was as cold and black as obsidian, and he stared evenly at the sliver of moon.

El Taladro was lying on top of the dismantling worktable in the garage, awaiting his execution. His bloody clothes had been removed, leaving him in nothing but a pair of Calvin Klein boxers. The crotch was stained dark where he'd pissed himself.

The Dogo Argentino had torn the right side of his face, and his arms and legs were in a similar condition. The bleeding had stopped, but he couldn't turn over on his own now. He was still conscious, however. El Taladro stared at the garage ceiling and breathed weakly. His mandibular joint was broken, so his mouth hung open. Occasionally he groaned, but was unable to utter any intelligible words.

Suenaga looked down upon the dying man. The morphine he'd administered was easing the pain, but it had worn down over time, and was about to run out. El Taladro shivered in anticipation of the torrent of agony that awaited him. He blinked rapidly, moving his eyes, beseeching Laba-Laba for help.

Despite the young man's pleas, Suenaga didn't intend to give him any more morphine. He put the syringe and bottle of painkiller back in his bag and took out a chocolate-flavored protein bar to nibble on. When the cars pulled into the space around the garage, he gazed at El Taladro from head to toe and recalled what El Cocinero had told him.

"We will remove the corazón of the traitor to the familia with our own hands."

Privately, Suenaga griped, *We could actually make money if I dissected him myself.*

He didn't know if this was a Latin American execution method or some ancient custom, but it seemed like a stupid game. However, when the boss gave clear orders, he had no choice but to obey. Suenaga considered calling Hao from Xin Nan Long for advice, but the structure of the heart trade they were building was child-focused. Extracting El Taladro's heart before he died and finding an urgent adult patient within the four-hour limit for transplants would only disrupt the direction of their business. If you wanted to monopolize a particular market share, it meant occasionally leaving profit on the table.

But surely the lungs could still be sold. Suenaga stared at El Taladro's bare chest longingly. Then he sighed. It wouldn't work. If an amateur tore out the heart, he would ruin the lungs and bronchial tubes. Nothing of his cardiopulmonary system would be salvageable.

Men came into the garage: Chatarra, El Mamut, El Casco. Then Nomura, followed by the seventeen-year-old they hired at the workshop in Odasakae. When he saw Koshimo, Suenaga's only thought was, *Monster*. El Cocinero had a natural knack for attracting monsters. He smirked. *I guess that makes me one of them.*

Suenaga crumpled up the finished protein bar's plastic wrapper and jammed it into the bite wound on El Taladro's leg.

When Koshimo walked into the garage and saw El Taladro lying faceup on the workbench, the first thing he felt, even more than the dying man's terror and despair, was a violent, seething hatred. It looked like an invisible vortex of black smoke to him. The dark, choking emotion was coming from Chatarra, El Mamut, and El Casco. They called the dying man a traitor many times. Koshimo didn't know what kind of betrayal the wounded man had committed. *Was it that bad to let the dog go? I was the one who killed the dog, so I should be punished, too,* he thought. In the juvenile detention center, the instructor would have scolded and disciplined him, so it was bizarre that everyone here praised him instead.

The spacious garage was filling up with a dark, nasty emotion, streaming from the mouths of the three men standing over El Taladro like ink squirted by octopuses or squids. Koshimo had never felt such hatred and fury before. It made him dizzy and left him short of breath. It reminded him of that dream he'd had, the one that plagued his sleep and caused him to wake up every night.

Chatarra held down El Taladro's left arm, while El Mamut and El Casco took care of his legs. Only the right arm remained, making it Koshimo's job to secure it.

"What's wrong?" Chatarra asked. "Hurry up, or he's going to die first."

Koshimo had no choice but to hold down El Taladro's right arm. He had no idea what he was doing anymore. Were they condemning the misfortunate person attacked by the dog, or trying to save him? The vertigo and breathlessness were terrible.

El Taladro didn't need four powerful men to keep him from moving. There was no strength left in his body. However, he could still feel pain and had enough consciousness to be terrified of his gruesome, imminent execution.

Valmiro finished smoking his joint and gazing at the moon over by the Jeep Wrangler. He quietly made his way into the garage. The hideous hatred and murder in the air thickened. Valmiro brushed El Taladro's chest with his fingertips; the helpless man's eyes welled with tears. When Valmiro spoke, it was in a mixture of Nahuatl and Spanish.

"Yohualli Ehecatl, Necoc Yaotl, greatest of gods. I offer this betrayer's yollotl to you, Titlacauan."

Valmiro placed a piece of charcoal on El Taladro's stomach and lit it with a lighter. When it was burning red, he added a few drops of some amber material: pieces of copal incense. The resin melted in the heat and joined the smoke, filling the garage with an odd scent: a mixture of sweet flowers and gasoline. It was the same odor Koshimo had smelled upstairs at the Peruvian restaurant a few hours earlier.

El Taladro's eyes were as wide as they could go. The capillaries in the whites were engorged like bolts of lightning.

When he saw the blade El Cocinero drew, Suenaga couldn't help but shake his head. It was a primitive stone knife, with a blade made of natural volcanic glass. He'd seen its like before: an obsidian knife. The tip was sharp, and so was the edge, but it was nothing next to a good surgical scalpel. It hadn't been sterilized, either. It looked like a relic from a museum. *Why would you choose a Stone Age tool to cut open a person?* Suenaga thought. *You're the craziest one of us all, El Cocinero.*

He adjusted his glasses and glanced at Nomura. The other man did not meet his gaze, keeping his eyes on the table.

Valmiro plunged the obsidian knife into El Taladro's chest. When he pulled out the knife, droplets of blood sprayed on the men holding the limbs down. El Taladro screamed with all the strength he had left. His voice was hoarse. The knife went up and down, over and over, separating flesh with the sound of a beaten sandbag. When Valmiro severed the sternum, it added a grinding and cracking to the mix.

The incense filled the garage and went as high as the ceiling. Through the veil of the smoke, Koshimo could see the beating heart.

Why? Why are we doing this?

His mind was racing with confusion.

El Taladro convulsed, wracked with horrific torment deep in his chest, and continued screaming with what little voice he had. Thick red lava trickled inside his rib cage, filling his body with burning agony. His throat and tongue burned, his ears were ringing, and he couldn't see through the tears. There was no feeling in any of his limbs anymore. Blood spurting from his chest landed on his face, and the cruel warmth of it devastated him. It was a worse death than being shot. He couldn't remember a single memory. Not his parents, not Rio de Janeiro. His only desire was swift release from the hell befalling him.

I'm dreaming, Koshimo thought. The maelstrom of sickening black hatred filling the garage gradually ebbed, pushed out by the crowding of the incense smoke. If he closed his eyes, it might have seemed like the smoke had cleansed the garage, but the only thing cleansing the scene was El Taladro's dying flesh. The phenomenon transcended Koshimo's imagination.

A living human sacrifice brought a fanaticism and ecstasy that worked to dispel the vortex of hatred and violence. The *copalli* smoke was nothing but a piece of set dressing to adorn the horrific miracle.

Valmiro severed thick arteries and pulled out the still-beating heart. He thrust his fist upward, drawing all eyes up. Their furious, black emotions were concentrated on the bloody organ, which turned it all into shining radiance to Koshimo's eyes.

El Taladro was dead. His extracted heart was absorbing, sucking up all the garage's sickening atmosphere. Like sunlight focused through a magnifying lens, the dark, scattered power was drawn into one brilliant point. An accursed purification, a ritual of blood practiced since ancient times, the foundation of a hidden civilization.

The whirlwind of darkness had vanished, and the dead man's heart shone as brilliantly as a star. Even his body, gaping hole in the chest, seemed wreathed in a wondrous rainbow of color.

Koshimo was present for something he could not describe in words. Valmiro did not attempt it, either.

Just as humanity worshiped the solitary sun and solitary moon, the burgeoning impulse of violence had been transferred into the body of a solitary sacrifice. The spilled blood and excised heart swallowed the chains of hatred, neutralizing them. The priest overseeing the ritual fabricated a form of order for the living, built on the cost of the dead, in the name of a god. **Sacrificio.**

Valmiro pointed at the heart he held aloft, then at the garage ceiling.

Koshimo's sight gave way to illusion. The blood dripping from the heart disobeyed gravity, falling upward, tearing through the high roof. It was sucked into the crescent moon in the night sky. El Cocinero gave the obsidian knife to Chatarra, who used his brute strength to cut off El Taladro's left arm. The limb closest to the heart would also be offered to the god.

Valmiro placed the still-warm heart atop El Taladro's face, silent and wide-eyed. Suenaga, who was leaning against the wall as he watched, recalled when Valmiro had done the same thing in Jakarta.

As he'd done back then, Valmiro gravely whispered the holy words his *abuelita* had taught him.

"In ixtli, in yollotl."

39

cempöhualli-huan-caxtölli-huan-nähui

Journals (Children)

Write down something fun that happened today!

[Name ☞ Yuji]
I studied in the morning. Docter taught me letters, it was fun.
After lunch I played on the trampoleen.
Mitsuhiro got ~~hurt~~ a sprain, and I helped him. I'm glad he's ok.

*

Write down something fun that happened today!

[Name ☞ Keisuke]
I can't believe we got a Playstation like I wanted   three of them,
plus three TVs they are so loud we played them together I waited my
turn   everything is really fun here

*

Write down something fun that happened today!

[Name ☞ Emiri]
They showed cockroaches on the news on TV. They were causing

problems. There were cockroaches at my old home, but not here. Doctor said, "There isn't a single cockroach here, because we keep it clean." I'm glad I get to live in a clean place now.

*

Write down something fun that happened today!

[Name ☞ Ryoji]
h a m   *w a ʑ*
            b a ϼ e r   *g u d*

*

Write down something fun that happened today!

[Name ☞ Shihoko]
7:20 I got to take a bath again today. I get a bath every day. When I was with Dad, I couldn't get one. He sprayed me with the shower head. It was cold. I got out of the bath at 7:40 today.

*

Write down something fun that happened today!

[Name ☞ Akari]
If all I eat is snacks, Doctor will be sad. I should eat more rice and be healthy. I ate some vegetables at dinner. I had broccoli.

*

Write down something fun that happened today!

[Name ☞ Tadashi]
What happened today was Doctor looked at my broken finger that Mom hit a long time ago. It's my right pinky. Also, I played with balloons.

Teacher brought a bunch of balloons. Everyone blew them up. After my nap, I went on the running machine.

*

Write down something fun that happened today!

[Name ☞ Michiru]

I had a birthday party today It's a goodbye party Tomorow I will go to a new home Today I ate birthday cake for the first time

IV

Yohualli Ehecatl
(Night and Wind)

Only for a brief moment,
The flowers, for a moment,
we have readied them:
Already, we carry them to the god's home,
To the home of the Fleshless.

—J. M. G. Le Clézio, *The Mexican Dream, Or,*
The Interrupted Thought of Amerindian Civilizations

40

ömpöhualli

It was just after two o'clock in the morning. Suenaga had just finished extracting the heart of a nine-year-old girl in the surgical room of the shelter beneath Saiganji temple.

The one-hundred-and-fifty-gram heart went into a drainage bag along with a liter of preservation solution and was then placed in an icebox.

The heart had to be delivered within a four-hour window. It left the shelter on a truck that made its way over the Tama River into Kawasaki, guarded by the *sicarios'* vehicle all the while. It passed through the underground tunnel to the artificial island of Higashi-Ogishima.

Heart, solution, icebox. They unloaded the nearly two-kilogram package at the cargo terminal and attached it to a Chinese-made drone that was waiting for them.

No one was going to notice a single drone with an infrared camera on board flying through the stiff breeze over the breakwater at three thirty in the morning. The drone's AI pilot lifted its cargo to the top open deck of the *Dunia Biru*, which was over seventy meters up, discounting what was under the water line.

Men lurking on Higashi-Ogishima's cargo terminal scrutinized the footage the drone's infrared camera sent back, exchanging wireless messages with their plants among the ship crew. If anything went wrong, they were ready to switch over to manual control at the drop of a hat.

The drone landed on the open deck, its rotors buzzing so softly they were nearly inaudible. Crew members promptly secured the icebox, and the drone lifted off again and melted into the night.

They took the icebox down to Deck 7 to give it to the medical team waiting there. The current atmospheric pressure reading was the code word greeting. Once they'd confirmed the contents, a medical staff member responded, "Be careful, the floor's slippery," spoken in English. Finally, the icebox was placed on one of the carts carrying replacement bedsheets and wheeled to the employee elevator going down to Deck 4, where the medical office was located.

A separate room stood at the back of the fully outfitted, state-of-the-art infirmary. A seven-year-old girl suffering from an enlarged heart was anesthetized and sleeping there.

Even the ship captain didn't know of her presence on board.

She wasn't listed on the passenger manifest, and she wouldn't be surreptitiously disembarking at a port of call.

The girl's father was a Singaporean investor. Upon a visit to a semiconductor manufacturer in the Chinese special economic district of Shenzhen, he came into contact with a man from a *heishehui*, who told him about the secret of *choclo*.

The Singaporean investor paid a total of eight million Singapore dollars— roughly six hundred and forty million yen at the time—for his daughter's new heart and the surgery, given to the Japanese man nicknamed El Loco, who was the *choclo* contact. That was over twice the cost of a heart transplant at a hospital in medically advanced countries like Germany or America. But her father didn't think it was too expensive. In the world of heart transplants, where no donor might ever be forthcoming, you paid whatever it took to ensure there was an organ. And despite being arranged illegally, this was not the heart of a child raised in the squalid, polluted slums but one raised to be healthy and strong in Japan. The man would have paid more and not regretted it.

An Indonesian team handled the transplants on the *Dunia Biru*. The cardiovascular surgeon, anesthesiologist, perfusionist, cardiologist, and nurse—everyone on the team—had a close connection to Guntur Islami. When the icebox landed on the top deck, the recipient's chest X-rays had been finished, and the immunosuppressants had been administered. The team had cleaned the recipient's skin and depilated even the fine hair. Preparations for the surgery were complete.

Choclo.

The term they used for the juvenile hearts, shipped from the shelter in Tokyo over to Kawasaki Port, was *choclo*.

Choclo was originally the word for an enigmatic type of corn grown in Peru. For some reason, it had kernels twice as big as the more common corn varieties. It only grew in the highlands around the Incan capital of Cusco, at elevations of three kilometers, and would revert to normal-size corn if grown anywhere else. It couldn't be reproduced with genetic engineering, either.

Valmiro had chosen the name of this corn to represent the hearts his business peddled because of its rarity due to its exclusive location and the inability to imitate it through scientific methods.

It was Xia, dispatched from Xin Nan Long, who was responsible for managing the undocumented children under the shelter's "protection." She had a staff under her wing, including a Chinese pediatrician and Yasuzu Uno. Some working in the underground facility knew the full scope of the business, while others didn't. Yasuzu was one of the latter. Those in that category understood the shelter to be a place to protect children from violent parents, and out of respect for that mission, they didn't reveal its existence to anyone else.

With the facility's secret safe, the children were linked with foster parents overseas by the nonprofit agency, and then "sent home," never to return.

These were not slum-raised hearts but quality products, authentically made in Japan.

When setting up the new enterprise, Suenaga went to the shelter in Ota Ward to meet Nextli.

Nextli, "Ashes," was the Nahuatl nickname Valmiro ascribed to Xia.

Much like a presurgery conference between doctor and patient, Suenaga gave the shelter director a comprehensive orientation of the process.

"I want you to have them write journals. That's right, journals. That might seem strange as far as eliminating evidence is concerned, but the idea is that I want you to have the children at the shelter keep a record of what good things happened each day.

"When I was in Jakarta, I read a book on organ transplants written by an anthropologist—*Strange Harvest* by Lesley Sharp. Her studies found that organ recipients and their families often want to know more about the donor. A life-prolonging transplant is not a simple, forgettable experience. It has a deep and complex emotional resonance.

"What kind of person was the donor? The recipient and their family desire to know, much like a child seeks to know about estranged parents. But the medical companies keep the two sides apart to avoid unnecessary trouble. Particularly in the case of heart transplants: The donor is, by definition, dead. There's always the possibility that a relative of the deceased will hold a grudge. This pattern holds true in Japan. The two sides never meet.

"I've taken part in many heart transplants, and I'd never really considered the question of what would happen if the donor and recipient were brought together.

"Sharp actually witnessed this happen. She wrote that there was an upswell of joy and celebration when they came together. I was honestly shocked by the reactions she reported in her book. I'd imagined it would be a much darker scene, but it wasn't.

"This mutual understanding and sharing of emotions between strangers, which seemed so odd to me, Sharp described as biosentimentality.

"In other words, an organ isn't just a part but a symbol of a person's entire existence. When it continues existing in another person, it becomes a separate soul. And that's where the sentimentality arises. A heart transplant will undoubtedly exacerbate that emotion.

"You see what I'm saying? This is the first key to the success of our *choclo* business. The second is the localized branding. These two things form our original sales pitch and must be upheld.

"We have to be open to the customer and tell them, 'The children at the shelter were abused by their parents in the past, but we offered them a helping hand.' That's the appeal of the business. Kids abandoned by the world, left to die by cruel, uncaring parents, were given a chance to experience stability. They were nurtured and restored to pristine health, and they entered a long sleep after the most pleasant memories. Following that, their souls will live on in new bodies.

"We need to provide all of these ingredients to paint a picture for the rich people buying these hearts for their kids. To help them imagine that happy story for themselves.

"The information we give our customers will fulfill their sense of biosentimentality. It will absolve them of their sins, and probably get a few tears from them, too. That emotion will then be extended to the child they bought the *choclo* for. Everyone wants to be a good person—especially the outrageously wealthy.

"The journals we give the customers are a new kind of Japanese-style psychological aftercare. They must be real words written by real children in their clumsy, authentic way. These people are going to bawl their eyes out when they see those scribbles, even if they don't understand them. We'll translate them, too, of course. English, Chinese, Arabian, Indonesian—we'll adapt our service to any language on Earth.

"So buy a bunch of journals and pencils. Buy crayons and let them draw pictures, if you want. That's all up to you to decide, Nextli."

The ultrasecret news of a new heart transplant business, aimed at children rather than adults, on a gigantic Indonesian cruise liner made its way through the worldwide elites like the ripples of an earthquake underground.

Within the vicious blood-capitalism market, *choclo* became a one-of-a-kind brand. It had totally carved out the market for youth heart transplants.

Based on orders brought to Xin Nan Long, the shelter chose a child of the same weight as the recipient. That was considered the most crucial requirement to get a heart of the right size, more than sex or age.

Once the aptitude test was cleared, the donor child was told that a foster family had been found for them in another country. They said goodbye to their friends and were ushered away in total ignorance. The kids never set foot outside the shelter. They walked down the hall to the hidden surgery room at the other end of the compound, where their short lives ended on the table.

The child would lie down on the bed as instructed, at which point Nomura administered the anesthetic. When the child was unconscious, Suenaga performed a medial sternotomy and removed the fresh heart himself. There was no process to determine brain death. The child was put to sleep while alive and never woke up.

After extracting the heart, Suenaga and Nomura collected the other viable parts: lungs, retinas, kidneys, and tendons.

"That reminds me, El Cocinero said something funny the other day," remarked Suenaga to Nomura, while removing a femur that would go to the workshop as material for handles. "He said we're '*corazón traficantes.*'"

"Heart traffickers?" Nomura replied, placing a bundle of removed muscle fibers onto a stainless steel tray. "Like drug traffickers?"

Suenaga just beamed back at him.

There was sweat on their foreheads, but they continued dismantling the body parts regardless. Blood capitalism. A sawing noise filled the room.

41

ömpöhualli-huan-cë

Familia. The new men who appeared in Koshimo's life beyond the work-shop. Chatarra, El Mamut, El Casco. Group shooting practice at the auto yard. In the same way that he practiced and honed his skill at knifemak-ing and got the most out of his tools, Koshimo learned how to use a bar-racuda, breathed in smokeless gunpowder, and blasted the vital zones of his targets with double-aught buckshot pellets. They accepted Koshimo, praised him, instructed him, and he absorbed the tools of the *sicario*. Since he didn't have an automobile or motorcycle license, they taught him how to drive a trike. Like a buggy, it had a low profile, and its tires were much fatter and more stable than a scooter's. He didn't need a helmet when rid-ing on public streets.

El Loco paid for women to come to the garage. They wore heavy makeup and perfume that wafted everywhere. They were very happy to receive cocaine in addition to the money, but they also had to put up with Chatar-ra's insults.

Before she left, one woman took off her clothes again in front of Koshimo and snorted a line of cocaine. "What's that fat piece of shit's problem?"

The prostitute was Bolivian, and spoke Spanish. She called the powder *polvo de oro.* Koshimo merely watched in silence as the naked woman sniffed the line of white powder she laid out on her wrist.

"Don't you want some?" she asked, putting her arms around Koshimo.

Koshimo didn't really understand the difference between *polvo de oro* and *hielo*. The image of his mother drifted into his head, but it vanished just as quickly.

He ate breakfast and lunch at the workshop with Pablo and had dinner at the table with all the *sicarios*. Koshimo never paid for it. It was usually steak, and Koshimo had a three- or four-pound slab of beef every night. He grew even taller and put on weight. The huge intake of protein helped him add muscle. At eighteen years old, he was two hundred and six centimeters, and one hundred and eighteen kilograms.

Seeing the tattoos all over El Mamut's arms, Koshimo decided he wanted some ink, too. He asked for the artist's contact info and thought about the art he wanted while eating his steak. He drank water, ate steak, sipped soup, and had more steak. They didn't drink any alcohol. Koshimo had only seen Chatarra drink once—the night they killed El Taladro. No one had imbibed since then. They kept to El Cocinero's rules. He'd been very clear.

"I'll let you hunt very soon. Keep yourselves in shape so you're ready to go as soon as I call."

"Hey, El Patíbulo," said Chatarra, pulling a dish of vanilla ice cream closer now that he'd finished with his steak, "when you were in juvy, even the bad guys were afraid of certain things, right? I saw that in prison. Guys scared of a spider or caterpillar and raising hell about it. I always laughed at them, but now I see it differently. It's a *good* thing to be frightened of some stuff. That's what I think. If you are, you think about it, don't you? If you're not afraid of anything, it's boring. You're better off being scared. I never had anything to be afraid of before this. But now? I'm scared of El Cocinero. Your *padre*. It keeps me on my toes."

The others could tell that the boss viewed Koshimo as special, and it wasn't just because they both spoke Spanish. El Cocinero was the only one who didn't call Koshimo "El Patíbulo." Instead, he called him El Chavo, the Kid. He had Koshimo call him *"Padre"* in return—a *familia* within the *familia*. El Cocinero should have been a father to all of them, but it was obvious that he only treated Koshimo like a real son.

However, the men weren't jealous that Koshimo was El Cocinero's favorite. They'd sworn loyalty to El Cocinero, but were also deathly afraid of him. It was a fear none could describe adequately. They would do anything to avoid what Koshimo did, going up to the office on the second floor and speaking with him in the dark.

"Do you see ghosts?" Chatarra asked out of nowhere, eating his ice cream. "Sometimes I see the ghost of a guy I killed. At a distance of about that wall over there, wearing clothes, just standing there. It's not scary at all. He's just standing. I mean, I'm the one that killed him—if anything, he should be afraid of me. You gotta be one sad, stupid *pinche cabrón* to be freaked out by me after you're already dead. But your *padre*, he's haunted by a ghost on a different level than that. It chills me to the bone. What the fuck is that thing? Even in the dark, it hides in an even darker hole. I don't think I could take that thing in a fight. Just thinking about it—look, see the goose bumps? He's always calling you up there, right? Don't you see it? Don't you feel it?"

Koshimo didn't answer. Even among the *familia*, he couldn't just say whatever came to mind. Truthfully, his experience was no different: he felt like he saw things he shouldn't be able to see, and touched intangible things. Chatarra impressed him in that way. Maybe someone who'd killed many people developed special abilities. Koshimo believed that the thing Chatarra described wasn't a ghost, but a god—a terrifying Aztec god. The one his father served. A great deity, sometimes called Titlacauan, sometimes called Yohualli Ehecatl, and sometimes called Necoc Yaotl.

The one who transcended even the war deities. Silently Koshimo repeated that god's true, hidden name.

The smoking mirror. Tezcatlipoca.

The sharp incense and sacrificial hearts were all for him. He was the one who received El Taladro's heart. As Chatarra said, he lived in a hole, like the fundamental root of darkness, that existed in the core of the dark. But it wasn't a hole, it was a mirror. A mirror of obsidian. At the very base of the world beyond human comprehension, even deeper than the land of the dead where the gods of death dwelled, there lay the dark Aztec mirror that existed from the moment the world began.

Once a week, Koshimo received a summons from Valmiro, and he went to the office above Papa Seca.

In the darkness, Valmiro lit copal incense and sparked up a cigarette or cigar. Oftentimes he smoked marijuana. But he never did cocaine. A narco only tasted *polvo de oro* to determine its quality, nothing more. A first-rate sommelier didn't get drunk in the kitchen, and a true narco didn't become an addict.

Valmiro would light an oil lamp just as Koshimo's eyes adjusted to the gloom. He propped his elbows on the table over a skull decorated with fine mosaics of obsidian and turquoise. The shining black and greenish-blue combination was so beautiful that it looked like an artistic model, but it was a real skull. It was El Taladro's, in fact, fashioned by Pablo on Valmiro's orders, offered up to the great god.

On the night of the sacrifice, Koshimo watched Valmiro cut the man's head off. After severing the neck, he flayed the skin. Everything had a reason, and each action tied him to the power of the gods that dwelled beyond the universe.

The orange ring of flame in the lamp, the gleaming skull, the drifting smoke of the *copalli*…

Each time Koshimo visited, Valmiro told him about the Aztec kingdom. He removed the bandanna he normally wore over his nose and mouth, exposing his face to Koshimo.

Never before in Koshimo's life had a single person gone to such lengths to tell him something. Pablo was his knifemaking teacher at the workshop, but Valmiro spoke about the wider world, the gods, and the arts and rituals of the lost *indígena* civilization. All of them had a profound effect on Koshimo's thoughts and sensibilities. He listened, enrapt.

Valmiro brought in scholarly materials about the Aztecs and showed him the diagrams and pictures. It was like an archaeologist instructing his beloved son about the wonders of history. However, Valmiro didn't teach El Chavo about history or wonder, but rather the Aztec mentality itself.

The books and their combination of Nahuatl and Spanish words were so enthralling to Koshimo that he forgot his hunger. He could have stared at them for hours and hours.

The diorite bowl for holding the sacrificial hearts was carved with fine representations of eagles and jaguars. The *tecpatl* knife for carving out the heart was decorated with corn and arrow symbols. The Aztec artisans did beautiful work with carved shell and gemstone ornamentation. Koshimo couldn't get enough of the common motifs: flowers, birds, corn, arrows, maguey thorns, cactus thorns, skulls, and animals. Even the war equipment was beautiful. The grace of the shields covered with quetzal feathers was incomparable, and they shone like burning stars.

Once, Koshimo talked to Valmiro about time.

Koshimo consistently felt that time was not a container through which all things passed, but that time itself took many forms, and had its own expressions.

"That's how it feels to me," Koshimo said in Spanish. "So in this room with the copal smoke around us, time itself is flowing as the smoke."

When his explanation was over, Valmiro didn't correct Koshimo's syntax, unlike the detention instructors or Pablo.

"Your senses are correct," Valmiro said. "It was the same for my *abuela*. When traveling to a distant town, she would often say, 'It'll take one sombrero,' or, 'That's a two-sombrero trip.' She could see time in the form of sombreros. The amount of time it takes to weave a sombrero, therefore, is the god that resides in the sombrero. The shape of the sombrero already existed in the world of the gods; it was human labor that allowed it to manifest outside. There is a god even in a sombrero, yes. That is Aztec time. Things are not just collections of their materials. The order of the gods exists in them. Also…

"All of the gods live by eating human blood and hearts. If we did not give them blood and hearts, even the sun and moon would cease to shine."

Valmiro made a show of opening up a drawer and pulled out a scalped human face, gazing at the trophy. It was El Taladro's skin.

Suenaga had skillfully sewn up the part that had been bitten by the Dogo Argentino. The top of the head had been clawed as well, and the sides were damaged where his ears had been taken off and shrank as they dried.

The repaired face reminded Koshimo of the luchador masks he'd seen earlier. Flashy, glittering fabric that covered the head. There was something similar in the skin of the deceased El Taladro. *Should this skin be worn in the same way and allowed to shine like those masks?* Koshimo wondered.

Valmiro exhaled smoke, sending it through the eye, nose, and mouth holes.

"Put this on, El Chavo," he instructed out of nowhere, gazing at the skin.

"The face?"

"That's right. Fit his face over your own."

Koshimo took the carved-off skin; it was chilly and soft against his fingertips. He recalled the luchadores again and tried to slip the dead man's mask over his own head.

"It's not working, *Padre*," said Koshimo. "It's too small."

The man's face had already been torn by the dog while he was alive. If he kept going, it would be ripped again after death.

"Too small? You're too *grande*. Forget it, give it back," Valmiro said, snatching the face out of Koshimo's hands. "It's been ages since I did a Tlacaxipehualiztli, so I wanted to try a little one out. Can't be as extravagant as the real thing."

"Tla...capesh..."

"Tlacaxipehualiztli. It's a festival to celebrate the Flayed One, Xipe Totec. That doesn't mean he actually walks around with his flesh exposed and shining red, no. Xipe Totec always wears the skin of the dead. His eyes are always closed, and he brings all kinds of illness, especially afflictions of the eyes. Those who suffer from blindness and other ills must be sacrificed to Xipe Totec. Are your eyes healthy, El Chavo?"

"They see good."

"Then there's no problem," Valmiro replied with a shrug. "Before I tell you about the great Yohualli Ehecatl, I'll teach you about Tlacaxipehualiztli. Once a year, in the second month of the *xiuhpohualli* calendar, the Aztecs held a flaying ceremony to honor Xipe Totec. Sacrifices were brought before a roaring flame, and their hair was pulled out. For the twenty days of the festival, the hair would be carefully stored. Once the sacrifice's heart was removed at the top of the *teocalli*, the body was pushed down the steps, at which point the skin was diligently flayed. Not just the face; the entire body. The *tlamacazqui* priest removed the heart, but it was the *tolteca* artisans who did the flaying. They used obsidian knives, skillfully removing the flesh from dozens of sacrifices. Young men chosen for the festival would come together and don the skins taken from the bodies. This was fresh skin, of course, not boiled into leather. Only the fast and strong were chosen, not the most exalted jaguar warriors or the hot-blooded eagle warriors, but mighty men nonetheless, because they had to be on the move all day long. These men would play the role of Xipe Totec, chasing the populace around. The fearful people needed to calm Xipe Totec by giving his representatives food or gifts. Eventually, those who were afflicted with diseases would come as a group and bring offerings to placate the god who was the source of their illness. The men playing Xipe Totec would sometimes hold fierce mock battles. Many people would come from far around to witness these fights. Blood and fat ran from the holes for the eyes and noses, and the elbows and knees where the skin ripped. Like I said, the skins were not boiled and cleansed. One whole month in the *xiuhpohualli* is twenty days. The men playing the role of Xipe Totec were not allowed to remove the flayed skins until the final day, when they were stored at the *teocalli*. No bathing allowed. They had to wear the skin for all that time, as it rotted with blood and fat. That is how Xipe Totec appears. That is Tlacaxipehualiztli."

Koshimo had never considered the idea that wearing the skin of a dead person could make you a god. When Valmiro's story was done, El Taladro's skin suddenly seemed much more special, and he really wanted to put it on. He wanted to see the world from the inside of the dead man's face. What would it look like?

"Don't," said Valmiro, reaching over. "Your head's too big. I'll wear it instead."

He stretched El Taladro's face and fit it over his head. Koshimo no longer saw Valmiro's features. He looked like clay with holes poked into it.

Valmiro popped the cigarette back into his mouth and turned on the selfie camera of his phone to see himself, then burst into laughter, shoulders shaking. El Taladro's skin was nearly about to split. "Worst Tlacaxipehualiztli that's ever been done," he cackled.

He kept chuckling, to the point that a smile formed on Koshimo's lips, too. Valmiro tried to take off the face, but it got stuck over his nose. That made them laugh again.

Koshimo watched Valmiro struggling by the light of the oil lamp. This was the first time Koshimo had ever laughed over the same thing with someone else. He was experiencing something he never had before: time spent laughing with his father. Time was laughing with *Padre*. Everything was like a dream.

42

ömpöhualli-huan-öme

After a long day of watching over the undocumented children at the shelter under Saiganji, making them write in their journals, checking on their health, and recording her own data, Yasuzu left another staff member in charge and departed from the facility.

Three types of biometric scans were needed to enter or leave the premises: facial, print, and retinal. The security was no joke—not a single mouse could get in. The strictness was necessary to keep the monstrous, abusive parents away from the children. That was what she was told by Xia—who went by the nickname Nextli in correspondence—and Yasuzu believed it.

She hadn't revealed the shelter's existence to anyone. In her private life, she never talked to others, period. She traveled from aboveground to below, and, when ordered to do so, brought children into the group's custody. That was her entire life at this point. She was saving children in secret and doing cocaine in secret. It wasn't easy to manage the ever-growing group of kids, but with the power of the all-encompassing mission and her little white friend, she got through it.

From what she could tell, the boy she'd interviewed at the juvenile rehabilitation center, the one who became a knifemaker's apprentice, was doing well without any incidents. He was still working at the workshop in Odasakae.

Light still shines in the shadows, Yasuzu thought. She took pride in what she was accomplishing. That boy, the children hidden at the shelter, their futures—everything shone brightly. *Thanks to my help.*

Yasuzu walked up the stairs to ground level and got into a rental car parked at the temple. They'd given her a black Toyota Aqua. She put on the seat belt, started the engine, and put the gear in drive. As the tires crunched over gravel, she turned on the headlights.

Driving a different rental each day was for the children's protection. After all, a wicked parent could still change their mind and come chasing after a kid after giving them up. Xia had explained that, even if the shelter's location was a secret, using the same car with the same number every day wasn't secure.

Yasuzu's daily rentals all came from a car service that helped sponsor Kagayaku Kodomo's activities. She would have liked to meet company representatives in person to thank them, but she never did. Xia simply handed Yasuzu the key, and she drove it away.

She returned to her apartment in the Setagaya Ward, filled up the tub, and washed her hair. When she was done bathing, she put on a robe and used a hair dryer. She took a can of beer out of the fridge, sat down on the couch, and placed a twelve-point-nine-inch iPad on the table. When placed at an angle on the stand, she saw herself in the reflection of the darkened screen. She only used it to watch movies on Netflix—nothing else. Yasuzu didn't often buy things on the internet, and she didn't use social media.

She popped the tab on the beer and started up a Marvel movie. The heroes were fighting to save the world.

As the scene jumped and cut through a thrilling car chase with sparks flying, Yasuzu suddenly thought of one of the children at the shelter who'd written a troubling journal entry. The boy was one she'd taken into custody personally.

He'd written a single line on the paper.

They'll kill us all.

The boy's life at the shelter was quiet. He wasn't being picked on. Yasuzu wondered if he was still afraid of his parents, but he'd never met his father, and his mother was already dead. Before coming to the shelter, he'd been in the custody of one of his mother's friends. She was cold enough that it could be considered child neglect, but there had been no signs of physical abuse.

Who did he think was going to kill everyone? Or did he just feel like writing that?

Yasuzu wasn't going to figure out the answer by mulling it over endlessly. Xia would eventually give the boy counseling if he kept writing things like that. Yasuzu pictured Xia, with her round, rimless glasses and her facial features without makeup, like a pretty primary school teacher.

Yasuzu put the idea aside and drank her beer. When it was empty, she turned it upside down and tapped a hit of cocaine onto the base of the aluminum can. Then she leaned over, snorted it, and focused on the movie again.

The night Valmiro taught Koshimo the name of that god in the office above Papa Seca, he acted differently. Normally, Valmiro spoke to Koshimo about the cruel and sometimes ridiculous Aztec gods with the occasional wry chuckle, but on this occasion, he didn't so much as smile. He spoke as though he were describing an austere monotheistic religion, not a looser, more welcoming polytheism. Valmiro lit incense for the great deity, pricked his earlobe with an imported Mexican maguey thorn, and sprinkled his blood over the smoke. He commanded Koshimo to do the same.

With each flick of the blood into the smoke, Koshimo sensed a terrifying presence spreading throughout the room. It was the thing cruel Chatarra had been so frightened of, the entity he'd warned Koshimo about.

"Titlacauan," Valmiro whispered. "We Are His Slaves." The dark office on the second floor of a Peruvian restaurant in Kawasaki turned into

Mexico, into the memory of Los Casasolas, into Veracruz, where the brothers gathered in their *abuelita*'s bedroom.

To Valmiro, the young man who had come to him in the Far East was a gift from his *abuelita* and his god's will. He knew from the moment he first saw Koshimo. *This boy is a jaguar warrior. Once he has the power of Yohualli Ehecatl, my* sicario *team in this far-off Asian country will at last be complete.*

But it was no simple thing to speak about this god. Valmiro couldn't just start up a conversation about it, as though recalling a story from the past.

Beneath the hanging incense smoke, Valmiro placed Pablo's twelve-centimeter obsidian mirror and Koshimo's wooden jaguar onto the desk. He'd commissioned the items from them. The mirror went on the left edge of the table, and the jaguar on the right. Between them, he laid a dish, upon which he rested a rooster's heart. He dusted the tiny organ with smoke, and prayed that the god would forgive him for what he was about to speak. He added that if his tongue spun lies, he should be cursed.

"Jaguar y espejo, ocelotl tezcatl," Valmiro intoned, the words for jaguar and mirror in both Spanish and Nahuatl. "There is nothing in common between the two. Their color and shape are different. Yet both are forms of the same god. Do you know why, El Chavo? Don't be misled by their looks. Their color and shape are different. Still, they are the same thing. They are forms of Tloque Nahuaque, the greatest of all gods. My god is also called Titlacauan. And what does that mean? He is so dreadful that the oaths of obedience to him *became* his name. My god is also called Yohualli Ehecatl, Night and Wind. What does that mean? The night is dark, and the wind has no body. In other words, he cannot be seen or touched. That is the greatness of Tezcatlipoca, the Smoking Mirror."

"Tezca…tlipoca…"

Valmiro had shown Koshimo the alien image of Tezcatlipoca pictured in the Spanish-language edition of the Codex Borgia. It had looked like neither human nor animal to Koshimo, but a kind of fantastical machine envisioned by the *indígena* artist. It was fearsome and combative; there was a face and limbs, but it didn't seem to be a living thing. Tezcatlipoca was equipped with all twenty of the day symbols: *Cipactli* (Crocodile), *Ehecatl* (Wind), *Calli* (House), *Cuetzpalin* (Lizard), *Coatl* (Snake), *Miquiztli* (Death), *Mazatl* (Deer), *Tochtli* (Rabbit), *Atl* (Water), *Itzcuintli* (Dog), *Ozomahtli* (Monkey), *Malinalli* (Grass), *Acatl* (Reed), *Ocelotl* (Jaguar), *Cuauhtli* (Eagle), *Cozcacuauhtli* (Vulture), *Ollin* (Movement), *Tecpatl* (Knife), *Quiahuitl* (Rain), and *Xochitl* (Flower). Through this image, the native artists depicted Tezcatlipoca as a being that transcended time, existing beyond the calendar.

"The strongest beast in the Aztec lands was the jaguar. It speeds through the forest, swims underwater, and even catches and kills snakes and crocodiles," Valmiro explained. "None can match the jaguar's power. Do you know how strong a jaguar's jaws are, El Chavo? That Dogo you killed would be no match for one. Not even a wild puma could hold its own. The jaguar's jaws are over twice as strong as an African lion's. It crushes the skull of its prey and drags it down into the darkness. The mightiest beast of the forest became another form of Tezcatlipoca. In the sky, there is the eagle. Nothing is stronger than the eagle among the creatures of the air. So that bird became the form of Huitzilopochtli, god of war. But Huitzilopochtli himself is not an eagle. His name means Left Side of the Hummingbird.

"The strongest Aztec fighters join the jaguar warriors, while the inexperienced but bloodthirsty join the eagle warriors. Listen closely, El Chavo. My ancestor *led* the jaguar warriors in the days of the Aztec kingdom.

"I heard the story years and years ago. I was just a child at the time, but I still remember the first question that popped into my head. I thought, 'The jaguar warriors are stronger than the eagle warriors. So Tezcatlipoca is stronger than the god of war. Why is that?'

"In order to understand, you must know why Tezcatlipoca is considered Tloque Nahuaque, the greatest of all gods.

"Like I told you before, in the great Aztec city of Tenochtitlan, there was a grand pyramid, which is now called the Templo Mayor. The front of it faces west. At the top of the long staircase are two *teocallis*. The temple on the south side honors Huitzilopochtli, god of war, and the one on the north side honors Tlaloc, god of rain. Beneath the war god's *teocalli* is a rack of skulls called a *tzompantli*. And below the rain god's *teocalli* is a statue called a *chacmool* with a basin for holding blood and hearts. The god of war and the god of rain. The Aztecs prayed to these gods at the Templo Mayor and offered sacrifices to them.

"If wars are lost, the country will fall to ruin. If the rain does not fall, the people will die of starvation and thirst. War and rain—both important things. However, the mirror is more critical than both.

"Do you understand, El Chavo? Listen with your heart. There is a deep, deep secret of the world there. Before winning wars, or receiving the rain's bounty, *the nation must be a nation*. For that to be true, *men must not kill their brothers*. It means *somos familia*. If we kill each other, the people will all die, to the very last man, before an enemy country can destroy us, and before the plants wither away without rain. Human beings are a herd with no cohesion. When one is killed, they kill another in revenge, which leads to another murder, which demands more lethal responses. The people fall like dominoes. In the herd, violence is contagious. If you cannot contain the cycle of hatred and quell the violence with force, there will be no victory in war, and the blessing of rain will go to waste.

"That is when special sacrifices are made. Offering a heart and its blood to a single black mirror binds the shards of our individual hearts into one. It's not praying for victory or for rain that does it.

"They pray to remind themselves that Tezcatlipoca rules over all. Titlacauan, Yohualli Ehecatl, Necoc Yaotl. Tezcatlipoca does not have any fixed home, and goes freely between the heavens and the Earth. Even the gods of the afterlife obey his word. The mirror is greater than the god of war, so it is natural that the jaguar, which is stronger than the eagle, is his earthly form.

"You see, El Chavo, in order for the human herd to survive, they must offer sacrifices to the god. These ignorant modern people say, 'The Aztecs were a barbaric, uncivilized people who thrived on violence,' as though they understand. They are hopelessly stupid. Just look at the world. Herds of people always desire sacrifices. That is what our god wants. If humanity stops giving offerings to the black mirror, the violence will spread before that day is done. They will start to kill their own kind. There will be no more friends and allies. Sacrificial blood is not just blood; the hearts are not just hearts. They are tied to the secrets of the gods. The Aztecs knew that better and more deeply than anyone else."

Koshimo listened to Valmiro's story, looking as though he had wandered into a dream he couldn't escape. He tried and tried, but he couldn't understand. He thought back on the story of Tlacaxipehualiztli, the festival of our flayed master, Xipe Totec. He believed he understood Xipe Totec after hearing about the festival back then. If he heard more about a celebration, perhaps he would also comprehend Tezcatlipoca a bit better.

"Padre," Koshimo said, "did Yohualli Ehecatl—did Tezcatlipoca have a festival?"

"I was getting to that, El Chavo," Valmiro replied.

43

ömpöhualli-huan-ëyi

"Listen closely, El Chavo," said Valmiro. "I will tell you about **Toxcatl**—the fifth of the eighteen months in the *xiuhpohualli* calendar, and the name of the festival held in Tezcatlipoca's honor. Toxcatl means 'dried thing.' It falls right around the month of May, too. The fifth Aztec month is at the end of the dry season, the hottest part of the year. The sun is blazing, and hot winds blow even at night. The earth dries up, and the plants wither.

"Aside from the night when time ended, which only happened every fifty-two years, Toxcatl was the greatest celebration for the Aztecs. The conquistadors and their accursed Catholic priests wrote that it rivaled the Lord's Easter Day.

"The preparations for the festival lasted an entire year. When the fifth month of that year's *xiuhpohualli* ended, the next year's preparations began, and when that was over, the next year's started, and so on.

"One boy had to be selected for Toxcatl, a healthy boy. Not a slave with his ears cut off, or a wounded enemy prisoner. A boy with no injuries would be selected for each Toxcatl, and even if he were born of the lowest possible station, he would be given the finest of clothing and jewelry, and move into a great mansion as opulent as any palace. He ate delicious feasts, slept in a luxurious bed, and a *tlamacazqui* taught him how to speak properly, like a *tlatoani*. A *tlatoani*, El Chavo, is an Aztec king.

"The boy would not cut his hair. Servants in charge of looking after him would comb it every day. It would go down to his waist, black and shining like an obsidian mirror.

"The boy learned songs from famed singers known throughout the land and studied the flute under a noted musician.

"He would bring a festival atmosphere just by walking through the city. He wore a large feather headdress, carried flowers from the garden, and led a large procession of servants around. It didn't matter if a different festival from the *xiuhpohualli* was taking place already. He was uniquely special. When the people saw him, they fell to the ground and worshipped him. Nobles and chieftains were no exception. Jaguar warriors would kneel in his presence. The leader of the warriors would place his hands on the dirt in humility. They did this, El Chavo, because the boy was the living image of Tezcatlipoca. In the case of the other gods, this role was played by a warrior or dancer in costume, but only one boy could be Tezcatlipoca in an entire year.

"But now there's a major contradiction, El Chavo. Think hard about it. This god was **Yohualli Ehecatl**. Remember what I told you about him? The night is dark, and the wind has no body. He cannot be seen or touched. Why is this god taking the form of a child?

"This contradiction was solved a year later in a most stunning way. The celebration ended very differently from the festival of Xipe Totec. You'll understand what I mean by the end of the story, El Chavo.

"The boy didn't simply live a life of total opulence. It was important to exercise. Eternally youthful, Tezcatlipoca's living image couldn't afford to overeat and look like Chatarra. He would stay in shape by playing *ulama* against his servants in the arena. That's a game in which you try to put a ball through a ring made of stone. It doesn't involve the hands, like soccer, but you don't kick it. You strike the ball with your hips, wearing large leather waistbands. Imagine you're hitting someone with a hip check.

"Finally, the fifth month arrives. The city is enveloped in baking heat, and when twenty days remain until the Toxcatl festival reaches its zenith, four girls are sent to the boy. They were raised only for him and are dressed in dazzling outfits.

"The day the four maidens visit, the boy's clothes are exchanged for a more sacred dress. His long hair is cut short, like the captain of the jaguar warriors. One year of the greatest food, sleep, and exercise will have turned the boy's flesh into that of a young, strong warrior. The boy then mates with his four wives. He does this for twenty days, until the end of the festival. They spend every moment together.

"Five days before the end of Toxcatl, the boy and his four wives take the servants and make a public appearance. There is a grand feast, with roaring fires, and pulque and tortillas for all. The air is full of flutes and drums. Slaves tied along a single rope are arranged in a circle to dance around pillars. Royals and all other powerful figures of Tenochtitlan attend the banquet.

"On the day of the ritual, the boy is taken to the place of the flute, Tlapitzahuayan, where he will bid farewell to the four girls who have accompanied him for those twenty days.

"For the first time in a year, he is alone. He plays the flute there, the last song of his life.

"Then he heads to Tlacochcalco, the holy place. That, too, is a *teocalli*. He climbs the steps, holding a bag that contains all of the flutes he's used in the last year. He takes out a flute on each step and breaks it with his foot.

"One flute for each step. And just as he has run out of flutes to break, he is at the top of Tlacochcalco.

"Five *tlamacazque* are waiting for him there. The boy walks right up to the sacrificial altar and lies down. Four priests hold his arms and legs, and the fifth, the highest *tlamacazqui* of them all, cuts out his heart with an obsidian knife.

"Do you understand what happened, El Chavo? The boy was the embodiment of Tezcatlipoca. He spent a year in that form, absorbing peoples' prayers at all times. But the god is Yohualli Ehecatl, and cannot be seen or touched. So when the god's time of transience is over, he must return to being Night and Wind.

"Tezcatlipoca sacrifices his own blood and heart to himself.

"This is the stunning end of Toxcatl, El Chavo. The most beautiful of Aztec festivities. In most cases, the body is simply thrown down the steps of the pyramid after the heart has been removed, but this is not the case for Toxcatl. It is carried carefully down from the *teocalli* by the priests themselves. Back on the ground, they cut off the head and skewer it on the *tzompantli* with all the others.

"And from that moment, the preparations begin for the next year's Toxcatl. Another boy will be chosen to play the role of the great and mighty god."

44

ömpöhualli-huan-nähui

Koshimo cut through two kinds of hard wood at the shop.

He had a piece of 76-by-19-centimeter rosewood and a 90-by-20-centimeter piece of cocobolo, both two centimeters thick.

He lined them up on the floor, blew off the sawdust, and then peered at the worktable diagram. Koshimo had drawn a full-scale diagram of the weapon he was about to make.

The *macuahuitl* was an Aztec warrior's weapon. *Ma* meaning *hand*, and *cuahuitl* meaning *wood*. It was meant to be swung like a machete to slash at a target, but after hearing Valmiro's description, the shape Koshimo drew up looked less like a machete and more like the canoe paddles that had been left outside the workshop.

Pablo watched Koshimo work, his expression dark. To him, his apprentice's design was identical to a cricket bat, to the point that he wondered if that's what the young man was actually making. However, the material wasn't right for that. The rosewood and cocobolo Koshimo had selected were far, far harder than proper cricket bat woods like Kashmir willow and English willow.

He did not stop his apprentice from undertaking the bizarre project, for he lacked the right. El Patíbulo was El Cocinero's favorite pet, and one of the fearsome men of the auto yard now. Koshimo was enthusiastically crafting a tool for murder, probably something Aztec in nature. Every time

El Cocinero summoned him, Koshimo returned with his head full of nightmares from that ancient kingdom.

Koshimo sliced the boards along the marking lines, and the contour of the *macuahuitl* took shape. The rosewood board was fifty-seven centimeters long, with the remaining nineteen centimeters cut into a narrower shape for the handle. The cocobolo was now sixty-seven-point-five centimeters with a twenty-two-point-five-centimeter handle.

Once he had carefully polished the wood, Koshimo carved the twenty symbols of the *trecenas* in the center of the boards, arranged across four rows.

Crocodile   Wind   House   Lizard   Snake

Death   Deer   Rabbit   Water   Dog

Monkey   Grass   Reed   Jaguar   Eagle

Vulture   Movement   Knife   Rain   Flower

Only the mightiest of Tezcatlipoca's warriors had the right to carry a *macuahuitl* carved with all of the symbols at once.

When he finished his carving, which was every bit as skilled as Pablo's by now, if not greater, Koshimo used a fretsaw to work fine grooves in the two-centimeter sides of the boards. He blew out the sawdust and checked the depth of the cuts.

Then he started on the obsidian blades.

Owing to his expertise with stone knives, Pablo had taught Koshimo the technique of cracking. To make a thin blade out of natural, glassy volcanic rock like obsidian, you couldn't use polishing tools as with mirrors or ornaments. You had to prepare a large chunk of obsidian that would be your core, identify the natural lines in the material, and strike a wedge into it along the seam. The Aztecs used antlers and copper tools to do it, but Koshimo employed steel the way Pablo had shown him. The wedge left a crack in the obsidian core, breaking off little shards from the edges. Those smaller pieces of black glass would become blades that could cut human and animal tissue, and help strip hide. Koshimo cracked the core again and again. The obsidian had been mined on Onbasejima, one of the Izu Islands.

Koshimo attached five obsidian blades, each ten centimeters long, to the grooves on either side of the rosewood board's edges. Eight of the same were stuck to the cocobolo board. He used the natural adhesive *chicle*, a favorite material of the Aztecs, along with pine resin to affix the volcanic glass firmly in the grooves. He chewed the leftover *chicle*. It came from the boiled-down gum found in Sapota tree resins, and was primarily known in modern times as an ingredient in chewing gum.

After the final coat of varnish had been applied, Pablo examined the indigenous weapons Koshimo had spent four days creating. He felt nothing but fear. They weren't knives or axes. What was the boy going to do with them? Pablo didn't want to know the answer, so he didn't ask.

To Pablo, Koshimo's very existence was so pure, lonely, and pitiable. But above all else, knowing that he would do nothing but watch as Koshimo slid into a life of sin and crime filled him with wretched self-hatred.

Tears formed in Pablo's eyes as he examined the weapons again. The wood was hard enough to split a man's skull, and now it was lined with black glass blades like goat's teeth. The simple beauty of the mysterious symbols Koshimo had carved into the side of the boards gave the weapons an indescribably wicked aspect.

El Mamut drove Koshimo to the auto yard in the Tundra. There, the boy pulled the two modern recreations of the *macuahuitl* out of his bag. The other men were performing maintenance on the barracudas, and when they saw the strange weapons, they grinned. Not in mockery, but out of respect for Koshimo's brand of madness.

"This is brilliant," said Chatarra, examining the row of black blades lining the sides of the boards.

"Someone comes charging at you with one of these, it's going to look like a horror movie," El Mamut remarked. "What are they called?"

"Macuahuitl," Koshimo answered. "The rosewood one is for *Padre*, so I'll use the cocobolo."

"You're gonna use this…?" El Casco said in disbelief. The former *bosozoku* lifted the cocobolo one, which was heavier than he imagined. "You really gonna hit someone with this? That's crazy. I've seen my share of fights with aluminum bats, but this…?"

"If you want one, I can make it for you," said Koshimo.

El Casco shook his head without a word, still holding the *macuahuitl*. The obsidian edges shone under the garage lights.

El Loco showed up as the sun went down, retrieved all of the iPhones they were using, and gave them burners with new numbers, registered under false names.

"You need to install Hidelamb on those," El Loco instructed.

Their new phones were Chinese-made with an Android-based OS. They did as he instructed and installed the app. Hidelamb 2.0 was an Indonesian-developed app for encrypted communication, prized among the Asian criminal underworld for its security. The server was in Jakarta; the Japanese police couldn't trace or analyze the data.

"Wait here; you'll get a message soon," El Loco stated, turning to leave with their iPhones.

Chatarra yawned and stopped him. "I'm gonna fall asleep while I wait. You can't leave a few baggies with us?"

El Loco stared at him for a moment. Quietly, he replied, "You think I walk around with drugs in my pocket? If you want some, you have to come to the car."

"I'm kidding," Chatarra laughed. "As long as we get a job to do, I don't need coke. The natural adrenaline will wake me right up."

45

ömpöhualli-huan-mäcuilli

The Japanese mobsters maintained a firm negotiation stance regarding the international heart-smuggling business.

The Indonesian cruise ship had already docked in Kawasaki three times, and the *choclo* business had turned a profit of seven billion yen. The Senga-gumi syndicate of the Korin-kai was demanding twenty-five percent of that.

Reiichi Masuyama, the acting director of Kagayaku Kodomo and executive director of the Senga-gumi, sat at the negotiating table of the hotel meeting room in Omiya-cho, Kawasaki, for the second time, reading a prepared statement off a sheet to reiterate his side's previous claim.

"We offered you the space underneath Saiganji in Ota Ward, Tokyo, and we have provided you with the information to gather the products you've assembled there. The entire *choclo* business does not have a leg to stand on without our help…"

The Chinese Black Society Xin Nan Long had wide reach in Southeast Asia, and Guntur Islami was a powerful militant Islamic group. Masuyama was aware of their strengths, but he knew that even they wouldn't have the same access to information about undocumented children within Japan. They needed the Senga-gumi's data network, and Masuyama repeatedly reminded everyone of that fact during negotiations. It would take Xin Nan Long and Guntur Islami a long time to build that level of comprehensive intelligence. They needed local collaborators if they wanted to keep the business running.

"Without the Senga-gumi, your supply of hearts dries up," Masuyama threatened. Surely a 25 percent share of the profits wasn't an unreasonable cost to keep things running.

At the third negotiation, the Senga-gumi party included, for the first time, the group's leader, Tadaaki Senga, and his second-in-command, Masaru Tanimura. Senga's expression was dark from start to finish, and he puffed on his vape pen incessantly. It wasn't so much the lack of progress in the discussions as the choice of partners that angered him.

Masuyama proposed a twenty-minute recess, providing a welcome respite from the never-ending discussion, and both sides left for separate rooms.

After a brief call with the Korin-kai parent organization, Tadaaki Senga pulled Masuyama from his study of the negotiation sheet. He hissed, "Have you *always* been talking to fuckin' nobody kids like them?"

Masuyama had no good answer. Their negotiating partners were Kenji Nomura, Suenaga, and a Chinese woman named Xia. Nomura was nothing but a black-market doctor who came up as a local contractor for Senga-gumi, and Suenaga was in the same business. Suenaga had the kind of benign face that so-called intelligentsia yakuza possessed. They were the sort tasked with running the mob's public fronts. Thirtysomething Xia was there as a proxy for Xin Nan Long and Guntur Islami, and she seemed totally out of place—just an ordinary girl. Hao from Xin Nan Long was absent, and there was no word of him coming to Japan. The Senga-gumi were here arguing for their continued existence, yet their partners were totally mocking them with this lineup of flunkies.

Sensing that the third bargaining session was going to break down, Nomura called El Cocinero as soon as the recess started.

A strategy was already in place if the Senga-gumi refused to budge on their 25 percent cut. The plan was to give them a lifeline. In order to get them to relent and take less of the *choclo* profit, El Cocinero's people would offer money from a different source.

The keys were *hielo* and *plaza*.

Suenaga had taught Nomura what those Spanish words meant. *Hielo* was ice, crystal meth, and *plaza* was the word for territory, where you sold your product.

Hielo was the Senga-gumi's primary source of income. But in recent years, their business had dried up to almost nothing. The problem was that the *plaza* where they made the lion's share of their profits—the southern part of Tokyo and their home of Kawasaki—had been taken over by rivals who undercut their prices. Without the same cash flow from drugs, the Senga-gumi had to make up that loss elsewhere, and it made them desperate in the *choclo* negotiations.

El Cocinero had a simple answer.

We can simply eliminate the competitors selling *hielo* in their *plaza*.

Nomura thought it was a good point. If the Senga-gumi's meth sales recovered, the group would quickly give up on their ridiculous attempt to squeeze 25 percent from the *choclo* business.

That meant getting rid of competitors that even a yakuza group couldn't eliminate, however.

Nomura was more nervous than he'd ever been. The time had finally come to unleash El Cocinero's monsters, and let them exhibit their Latin American–style violence. His hitmen were vicious without compare, and Nomura couldn't imagine what this might bring.

Sure enough, when El Loco called to report that the third negotiation meeting wasn't going well, Valmiro placed a call to Chatarra, who was on standby at the yard. He gave the order to begin the hunt.

A criminal gang called Zebubs started out in Kawasaki but pushed north over the Tama River into Tokyo. They were classified as "semihard" because they weren't part of any designated violent mob groups. Thus they enjoyed freedom from onerous police and public safety oversight for the most part.

They had two main advantages: Vietnamese connections to the Southeast Asian underworld and particularly violent members for a non-yakuza gang—most of them coming out of street fighting rings.

In July 2015, the Kawasaki burglary ring RKG, comprised of Vietnamese and Vietnamese Japanese, decided to expand their operations by teaming up with a Japanese group that had been operating an illegal martial arts club. Such was the origin of the Zebubs.

The current leader was a twenty-seven-year-old Vietnamese Japanese man who'd been a principal member of RKG. He went by the alias Tham Hoa, which was Vietnamese for *disaster*.

Like RKG, which he named after Soviet antitank grenades, the Zebubs name was also his invention. Back in his mother's home country of Vietnam in 2011, they discovered a new species of bat and named it Beelzebub. The actual scientific title was *Murina beelzebub*. So he named the group after the demonic creatures.

The group of Vietnamese, Japanese, and Vietnamese Japanese criminals had been rivals with a Korean street gang until they overpowered the competition and expanded from there.

They chose to rise not through burglary or underground fighting, but the drug trade, following personal connections to dealers in Hanoi and Ho Chi Minh City. They sold their product in Kawasaki and the Setagaya Ward—high-quality meth, ecstasy, and nitrous whippets. Vietnamese-made meth acquired a reputation for quality. The biggest boost to the Zebubs' cred came from a French backpacker traveling the country. Before he was arrested in the Philippines, the man posted on the dark web that "Zeb has the best crystal you can buy in Tokyo." More and more foreign customers flocked to the group, which led to a change in Japanese buyers.

With all the momentum on their side, the Zebubs expanded beyond Setagaya into Ota, Shinagawa, Meguro, and Minato. All of these wards, which made up the southern quadrant of Tokyo, had previously been the Senga-gumi's meth territory. There had already been clashes between the two sides, but the latest wrinkle stacked things in the Zebubs' favor.

The Senga-gumi's North Korean meth couldn't compete, and their business was destroyed. It was so bad that one dealer got himself arrested after fighting with a buyer who laughed at his inferior product.

The first to attack the Zebubs in place of the yakuza was an Iranian smuggling group furious over the loss of their ecstasy market. They kidnapped and beat a dealer, but the Zebubs led an armed assault on them in response, killing two. They didn't use the typical street weapons of Japan like metal bats or brass knuckles, but SMGs and pistols that fired 9 mm bullets. They also possessed assault rifles and military bulletproof vests, all of which had been smuggled in from Vietnam. Completely overpowered, the Iranians fled from South Tokyo and lay low.

The Zebubs were young and knew about the latest means of communication, and with the help of some complex encryption, they kept their location secret from the police and yakuza. Even if they happened to run into the Senga-gumi in the seedier parts of town, the former MMA fighters enjoyed the opportunity to scrap. Some wore mouthpieces at all times, just in case of a fight. To young, bloodthirsty brutes, a sloppy yakuza was just a human sandbag that shouted a lot. They broke noses and teeth, stripped their opponents, and forced them to beg for forgiveness on the street.

Sensing danger, the Senga-gumi lieutenants looked into other former MMA fighters around Osaka and Nagoya to hire as personal bodyguards. When Tham Hoa and his cohorts found out about this, they laughed to the point of tears. The Zebubs hacked into the social media accounts of the syndicate's members and sent them messages like *Muscle for hire, looking for work, inquire for details*, then roared with laughter again.

Having built up a war chest with sales of Vietnamese meth, the Zebubs considered expanding into crypto-based investment. Like amateur fighters angling for a contract with a major organization, a group of non-career-criminals has no choice but to travel upward from the underground to the surface—from the dark of night to the shadows, and then into the sunlight. Crypto investment was part of that process.

They were scheduled to meet with a Vietnamese investor and get a private lesson on this new enterprise, but things went south when one of their members, Nakaaki Morimoto, didn't show. When they realized they couldn't contact him at all, the situation got serious.

The twenty-six-year-old Japanese man was the group's dispatcher, the number-two man after Tham Hoa, responsible for building the Zebubs into what they were today, and he had vanished without a trace.

46

ömpöhualli-huan-chicuacë

Nakaaki Morimoto was a supremely cautious individual, not the sort of man to get captured by an enemy organization because of his laziness. Tham Hoa named him dispatcher because of the great care he took in everything. The Zebubs spread out to search for Morimoto, but they found no clues to his disappearance.

Four days later, they learned of his death.

A cardboard box without any postal markings was placed outside the home of a Zebubs member. Inside was a severed left arm packed in dry ice. It was tattooed with a skull wearing a crown of thorns, just like Morimoto's. The wolf's-head ring on the pinky belonged to Morimoto, too. There was also an unopened can of Dr. Pepper next to the arm. It was his favorite soda, and everyone who'd spent time with the man had seen him drinking it before.

The Zebubs had twelve different hideouts, so they gathered all the senior members at one of them.

Tham Hoa waved away the flies drawn by the stench of decay and stared at the cut where the arm had been severed. It wasn't the clean laceration of a blade, but a hideously messy wound resembling the work of a car tire. The flesh and bones were a mangled mess. Discolored skin revealed burns in places. It had likely been removed while Morimoto was still alive.

Who did it? Tham Hoa had to think.

Probably not the Senga-gumi.

The unopened Dr. Pepper sent with the arm was Morimoto's favorite. The yakuza were too humorless to come up with a sick twist of the knife like that.

All Tham Hoa knew for certain was that an unknown enemy had appeared on the scene.

Uncertain of who his people were up against, Tham Hoa brought in his eight best men and sent them out with briefcases full of weapons and transmitters to an area in Okawa-cho, an industrial section of Kawasaki, which they code-named 4C. The name referred to four canals—Keihin Canal, Shiraishi Canal, Sakai Canal, and Tanabe Canal—which surrounded Okawa-cho. The Zebubs had purchased a warehouse there under a false name from a soy sauce company.

At two o'clock in the morning, Tham Hoa and his men, hiding in the cargo space of a four-ton truck painted to look like a shipping van, followed a black Nissan Elgrand 350 Highway Star minivan to their 4C warehouse.

They'd just passed the American Navy base oil tank storage on the west and crossed the Shiraishi Canal, putting them in sight of their destination, when the truck carrying the Zebubs' leadership was attacked.

Chatarra's barracuda blasted double-aught buck through the front door of the vehicle. The driver died instantly. The Elgrand in the lead stopped immediately, but a tricycle was bearing down on it, each of its three wide tires squealing from friction. The trike had been in the bed of the Tundra. An unlicensed Koshimo was driving the three-wheeled motorcycle. He yanked on the throttle, his long hair blowing in the wind, while the Tundra did a U-turn and approached the four-ton truck.

Koshimo leaped off the trike in front of the Elgrand 350 Highway Star and raced like a jaguar, smashing the windshield with the *macuahuitl* in his left hand. The volcanic glass blades shattered the glass, scattering shards that glittered under the moonlight that illuminated the industrial zone. With his other hand, Koshimo stuck a barracuda through the hole in the windshield and shot the driver in the side of the head before the man could duck out of the doorway. The buckshot was so powerful at close range that the man's head essentially vanished.

The five in the rear seat had no choice but to get out of the car now that their driver was dead. They opened the powered sliding door and jumped out with SMGs—right into the line of Chatarra's shotgun pellets. One of them survived by crawling under the car. He rolled to the other side and got up once he was clear, only to see Koshimo the giant waiting for him. Koshimo kicked his submachine gun away, leaving the man no choice but to leap on the giant in a suicidal rush. The man was a former welterweight champion in an underground fighting league; he had great confidence in his left straight, but his best punch didn't even stagger the huge brute.

Koshimo put his right hand on the man's back, almost as though reassuring his opponent after the failed attempt. It looked a bit like a Mexican side hug, except that he grabbed the man's forehand with his free hand. Using his palm on the back as a fulcrum, he pushed the man's neck backward until the cervical vertebrae snapped. The Zebubs member's head now faced directly upward. With dull eyes, he stared at the sky over the city for a few seconds, spittle dribbling from his lips. Ultimately, he collapsed like a lifeless puppet.

El Mamut stood before the rear door of the stopped four-ton truck, barracuda at the ready. It wasn't loaded with buck but a single-shot door breaching shell. He blasted the latch off, and the door promptly opened, gunfire erupting from the darkened cargo container. That was Tham Hoa and his men retaliating with AK-47s they'd acquired from Hanoi. Yet there was no one in their line of fire. When they briefly stopped shooting, El Casco tossed a stun grenade into the container. The resulting sound and light inside the enclosed space robbed the men of sight and hearing. El Mamut hurried in with night vision goggles and shot the three bodyguards in their necks and chests with a pistol. He had no qualms about killing the Zebubs, but he did feel like it was a shame. A lot of valuable blood and organs were being wasted. Perhaps the black-market doctor's frugal mindset was rubbing off on him.

El Casco made sure to hit the leader, Tham Hoa, in the shoulder. It was much harder to shoot to disable than shoot to kill, because it required more focus and decisive action. El Casco's pistol was loaded with hollow-point rounds designed to expand within the body; Tham Hoa's left shoulder was torn apart like an old, soft piece of fruit.

Chatarra charged into the container, still filled with white smoke from the grenade, and kicked Tham Hoa in the face as he attempted to aim his AK-47. After taking the assault rifle, Chatarra leaned over Tham, grabbed his left wrist, and twisted the arm past what the shattered shoulder could take, breaking the wrist.

The *sicarios* were careful not to shoot out the tires of the enemy vehicles so that once the fighting was over, they had no trouble commandeering their opponents' cars. The only issues were dealing with the drivers' dead bodies and the blood and glass on the steering wheel and seat.

As a former firefighter, El Mamut had experience handling large vehicles. He took the truck, while Chatarra claimed the Elgrand van. El Casco drove the Tundra, and Koshimo got back on the trike. They went to the warehouse where the Zebubs' leader had intended to hide and closed the shutters from the interior.

Valmiro was waiting inside already; he'd been watching the assault as it happened. He applauded the execution. Between the brevity of the attack and the total lack of mercy for the enemy, the job was close to perfect.

Chatarra dragged the Zebubs' leader out of the truck's container and tossed him onto the concrete floor like a trash bag. Tham Hoa grimaced from the agony of his gunshot wound and broken bones, but managed to spit, the projectile flecked with blood. "Who the fuck are you?" he demanded in Japanese.

"We're the volunteer neighborhood watch, *pinche cabrón*." Chatarra grinned. He started humming the melody of "I Love Kawasaki, City of Love," which got a laugh out of El Mamut.

"Kill me," said Tham Hoa. "What are you waiting for? Just get it over with."

Chatarra slapped him on the head and jabbed a thumb over his shoulder at Koshimo. "Come on, don't be in such a rush to throw away your life. How about this? If you can beat him in a fight, you get to walk out of here alive."

Slowly and painfully, Tham Hoa got to his feet. He looked up at Koshimo. The young man had just removed his T-shirt and was beating out the many little pieces of glass that had gotten stuck in the fabric.

Sensing eyes upon him, Koshimo stared back at the bloodied Tham Hoa. The leader of the Zebubs had very short hair, tanned skin, and diamond studs in both ears. His left shoulder was torn apart, and his left wrist was broken at an ugly angle.

"Do it, El Chavo," Koshimo heard Valmiro say, and he had one more command.

"It's the *xochiyaoyotl*."

In order to gain prisoners for sacrifices, the Aztec warriors fought a ritual war among themselves called a flower war, or *xochiyaoyotl*. The Aztec kings chose not to subjugate the neighboring state of Tlaxcala for generations, maintaining a formal hostility that would ensure they could dispatch fighters to claim sacrificial prisoners whenever needed, in times of floods or droughts, or to prepare for major festivals in the *xiuhpohualli* calendar. It was a war fought for pleasure and treated like a game, a manhunt on a national level, and the perfect opportunity for inexperienced fighters to learn about practical combat.

Koshimo tossed aside his glass-strewn shirt and grabbed the cocobolo *macuahuitl*. There were fresh tattoos all over his arms. When he went to the artist on El Mamut's recommendation, he asked for Aztec designs. The twenty day symbols dotted his forearms, and he was getting a stepped pyramid *teocalli* done across his broad chest. Koshimo thought the incomplete line art of the tattoo looked like the marking lines he drew on metal and wood when cutting it.

The sight of him, well over two meters tall, with long hair and mysterious tattoos, plus the strange flat board weapon in his hand, seemed pulled from a nightmare. It was so bizarre to Tham Hoa that he actually smiled.

Valmiro tossed him a bowie knife of Damascus steel. Tham Hoa stared at the blade at his feet, spinning like a top. When it came to a stop, he reached down to pick it up with his good hand. The blade was covered in a swirling pattern and measured a good twenty centimeters or so, but it seemed wholly inadequate against the monster before him.

His mind was reeling from the loss of blood and the pain. But Tham Hoa was going to stand and fight. No matter how eerie his opponent was, he carried too much pride to crawl and flee for his life.

Tham Hoa took as deep a breath as he could manage, summoning all of his strength to leap at Koshimo, but the *macuahuitl* split his functioning forearm. He'd managed to raise it to protect his head in time, but now his right arm wouldn't budge. The bladed weapon struck his right shoulder next, then bit into one of his sides, breaking his collarbone and ribs. Tham Hoa withstood each blow's incredible impact and remained conscious against all odds. Through hazy wits, he thought of all the men he'd killed. He wouldn't beg as they had. *Why am I still alive? Is that giant going easy on me? He probably is.*

Koshimo dropped his hips and swung the *macuahuitl* level, close to the ground. It took out Tham Hoa's feet and utterly destroyed his calf muscles.

The man collapsed and landed hard on his back on the concrete, kicking up a layer of dust. He twisted as best he could, turning onto his front and crawling, leaving a trail of blood, trying desperately to stand again. Through the window of the warehouse that had once belonged to the soy sauce company, he saw the power plant on Higashi-Ogishima Island across the canal. The shadows of the structures illuminated by the distant lights and the soft, glittering dust floating within arm's reach intermixed, surreally dreamlike.

Koshimo stared at the bloodstained cocobolo *macuahuitl* in mute surprise. He'd swung with all of his strength many times, but his opponent yet lived. *I messed up*, he thought. *I built it wrong. It's not a proper warrior's weapon.*

Blood dripped from the obsidian blades he'd stuck to the edge of the board with *chicle*. There was also a faint gleam of oil on them. Koshimo's face was reflected in each obsidian stud.

"No, this is good," Valmiro assured, planting his foot on Tham Hoa's head as the dying man tried to crawl away. "The *macuahuitl* serves a purpose that swords and spears do not. It's not meant only for killing—although with your arm strength, he's about ready to die any moment now. A *macuahuitl* is a weapon for hurting the Aztec's enemy so he can take him prisoner and escort him back to the *teocalli*. In the *xochiyaoyotl*, if you kill your opponent, you don't have a sacrifice for your god. How will the heart of a dead man beat? This is very important, El Chavo. The heart of your sacrifice must beat. Our god is the one who eats that heart, not us."

Tham Hoa's eyes ran red with blood, robbing him of sight. He could just barely sense the shadow of an arm reaching toward him, and he closed his eyes. He was ready for the final blow. But after waiting and waiting, nothing happened. A much, much worse end was in store for him.

The men set up a camera on a tripod and started recording.

No faces were visible aside from the sacrificial victim's. The *sicarios* held down Tham Hoa's limbs, while Valmiro jammed an obsidian knife into his chest and pulled out his heart. Screams, gouts of blood, and a look of terror on Tham Hoa's face as he died. Koshimo swung down the *macuahuitl* with all of his strength on the man's neck; the second swing severed it. The follow-through brought the weapon down upon the concrete below, loudly chipping the obsidian blades.

They paused the camera at that point, then went to the Tundra's cargo bed to take out the equipment they'd brought.

The primary piece was a three-meter steel pole with a white polycarbonate board and ring attached to the top. The ring was about forty-five centimeters across, and an open net hung from it. When the pole was stood up straight, it became a basketball hoop.

They started recording again. On Valmiro's instruction, Koshimo picked up Tham Hoa's severed head and tossed it toward the hoop. It went through and fell to the concrete. Chatarra picked it up and shot again.

Valmiro took a pull off a joint and watched the footage through the LCD monitor on the video camera.

The clever leader of the Zebubs, who had evaded all attempts at an ambush, wound up having his heart excised and his head removed on camera. Men wearing bandannas over their faces used the skull as a basketball.

When the Senga-gumi received the gruesome footage as a present, they were speechless.

The DVDs were sent to the private homes of the Senga-gumi boss and all of his lieutenants. As a bonus for Reiichi Masuyama, his package also contained Tham Hoa's ears. The diamond-stud earrings were still in the lobes.

Now that the Senga-gumi had full control of the meth market in South Tokyo, their business partners had a new proposition: "How about we agree on *seven percent* of the *choclo* profits?"

The situation left no wiggle room to refuse or demand a fourth negotiation meeting. The Senga-gumi received no explanation as to who had destroyed the Zebubs, whether Xin Nan Long or Guntur Islami. Regardless, the footage was sent to the gang's highest-ranking members—to their homes, no less.

It was a warning. The men who killed Tham Hoa were sending a message with the recording of their demented execution.

"We can do this to you, too, whenever we feel like it."

47

ömpöhualli-huan-chicöme

Half a month after the *corazón traficantes* demonstrated their strength to the Senga-gumi, the *Dunia Biru* made its fourth visit to the port of Kawasaki.

The world of 2021 was very different from 2019, when the massive Indonesian cruise ship first visited. Back then, it was a media sensation, showered with glowing descriptions like "the symbol of Asian evolution" and "a city of dreams at sea." Diet and city council members went on publicity tours of the ship, and crowds came to see the *Dunia Biru* each time it came into port. But just two short years later, it was the center of fierce debate, a taboo on social media, and the target of scorn across the country. The cause of this controversy was not the cruel *choclo* business coming to light, but the virus that turned into a pandemic.

SARS-CoV-2, the novel coronavirus that caused COVID-19. In early 2020, an English cruise ship anchored in Yokohama Harbor was racked by COVID. The media reported on the unmoving ship for many days, causing a diplomatic scandal with England and the American cruise line and casting a pallor over the national mood.

The *Dunia Biru* was the fifth major cruise liner in the world to resume activity. Its crew took every countermeasure they could, leaving Tanjung Priok in Jakarta with just a fifth of the maximum capacity of passengers, but that did nothing to quell the tide of criticism.

Before the pandemic, the top decks were lit in fantastical blue shades at night—*Blue Earth* being the translated name of the ship. The sight drew lines of cars through the tunnel to Higashi-Ogishima. But in 2021, the only people who visited were protesters and the media members who came to cover the protests. Lines of socially distanced people carried signs and posters demanding that no cruise ships dock.

The crowds could only come within five hundred meters of the container terminal where the *Dunia Biru* moored. The police cordon kept them from getting any closer, manned by Kanagawa riot police and Coast Guard members with masks and face shields.

"Send all the passenger ships away!" "So, the government chooses the economy over human lives again!" "Get the Chief Cabinet Secretary down here!" the people roared. Someone shouted, "Please don't raise your voices!" so another began blowing an emergency whistle instead.

Three activists within the crowd dropped an inflatable raft off the side of the dock and attempted to hit the side of the ship with flares to light it on fire. They succeeded at shooting the craft with bright pink smoking flares, but a few police officers on a boat caught them immediately while a news helicopter circling overhead captured the whole thing on camera.

The cloud of pink smoke over the water climbed to where the seagulls cawed and screamed, until it eventually dissipated on the wind.

Xia played back all of the security camera footage in the shelter, hoping to review a particular problem child's actions. He was a nine-year-old boy. In the time since Yasuzu brought him to the shelter, three other children had been selected for surgery and successfully processed.

Bedroom, cafeteria, hallway, bathing room, playroom, classroom, and the "outdoor" yard with grass and a sandpit under artificial sunlamps. Kids ran about and played with the toy cars that rolled on the grass at low speed. There were four of them, and the one made to look like the

Batmobile was the most popular, to the point that even the girls wanted to ride in it.

Nothing seemed out of place from what she observed on the camera. It didn't seem like the boy had seen anything he shouldn't have. He couldn't get to the surgery room Laba-Laba and El Loco used. There was absolutely no way the boy knew what was happening.

So why...?

Xia opened his journal.

Write down something fun that happened today!

[Name ☞ Junta]

They'll kill us all.

Xia stared hard at the page, then removed her rimless glasses and took a sip of coffee. He'd written the same thing yesterday and the day before that.

Yasuzu was worried about his mental state, and asked Xia if everything was all right. That question alone was a bad sign. The shelter's management system was airtight, and there couldn't possibly be any information leak. However, once someone got worried, they'd start searching for their own answers. Yasuzu might stick her head somewhere it didn't need to be and see something she ought not to.

Staffers like Yasuzu weren't the only thing to worry about. Negative thoughts were strongly contagious. If the other children started mimicking these words, it would have a major influence on the journals that were key to the Japanese-style aftercare offered with the *choclo*. Laba-Laba would be furious about that.

Xia could already imagine what he'd say.

"What the hell are you doing? To ease the customer's biosentimentality, they need to know that the children were happy right up until their final moment. It's crucial."

* * *

Xia took a drag on her e-cigarette. Junta was clearly not improving. They had a bug on their hands, and she would have to tell Laba-Laba.

When she was done with her vape, Xia quietly finished her coffee, closed the journal, and returned it to the file case. Then she put her glasses back on and performed maintenance on the gun that was always present in the shelter. The H&K G36 assault rifle was a familiar tool from Xia's police days, as was the carbon steel baton.

The men in the Senga-gumi looked down on Xia for being a woman, but before she joined a Black Society, she'd worked for the Hong Kong Police. She built up experience working at the Juvenile Crimes desk, passed a harsh test with a low success rate, and was admitted into the prestigious Special Duties Unit.

Xia's parents were both elementary school teachers. When she received a doctorate in child psychology in graduate school, they assumed their daughter would follow in their footsteps in education. Instead, she joined the police force and made her way into an elite tactical squad.

During an operation invading the hideout of a group of pro-independence activists, Xia shot and killed two men who resisted arrest. A metal pipe and ax sat on the ground, but they hadn't been reaching for them. She could have easily taken the men in without firing her weapon.

The families of the deceased claimed that it was an extrajudicial killing. In court, Xia insisted that she was warranted in firing her weapon, but the circumstantial evidence worked against her in every regard. She really, really didn't want to go to prison.

In Xia's moment of greatest need, the Black Society Xin Nan Long worked behind the scenes for her. They won her a not-guilty verdict through clandestine means, and she escaped a jail sentence, as she'd hoped. The woman quietly resigned from the police force, got facial surgery, changed her name, and started working for Xin Nan Long. Her first duty in Jakarta was defending Jingliang Hao, a high-ranking member of the group. She was given a Type 03, an assault rifle used by the People's Liberation Army, and killed a half dozen or so members of rival groups with it. Xin Nan Long recognized her skill as a hitman and allowed her to get a Komodo dragon tattoo. She'd been aware of her homicidal impulses before she joined the police. Life in a Black Society suited her very well.

After dismantling it, Xia put the G36 back together again, then went out on her nightly patrol of the shelter. She didn't take the gun, but the carbon steel baton and a folding tactical knife stayed on her person. She strode down the long hallway lined with rooms of sleeping children, hearing nothing but the echoes of her footsteps. Using the same kind of flashlight she had as an officer, she illuminated the darkness.

The gods came to Koshimo in his deepest sleep—into his dreams. The kingdom of the vanquished *indígena*, enormous *teocallis*, a city on the lake buried beneath Mexico City. Both the *tlatoani* and the *tlamacazque* knelt in fear.

The gods came one after the other, seeking the blood and hearts of sacrifices captured in the *xochiyaoyotl*.

Huitzilopochtli, god of war, wearing cotinga feather earrings, a waistcloth dyed the color of the clear blue sky, a fire serpent mask slung over his back, and bells tied to the rings around his ankles that rang as he strode forward...

Tlaloc, god of rain, with a crown of heron feathers, an emerald necklace, a face black with soot and decorated with dots of kneaded amaranth, a coat of mist, sandals of froth, and green and white banners woven from reeds...

Mictlantecuhtli, god of the underworld, king of Mictlan, with a skull face spattered with blood, an owl feather headdress, a necklace made of the eyes of sacrifices, earspools of carved bone, and a hellhound for a pet.

Occasionally taking the form of a flying bat, and sometimes crawling along the ground as a spider...

Quetzalcoatl, the feathered serpent, with turquoise mosaic earrings, a green hood drawn with a wind-summoning spiral shell pattern, and a necklace of the ribs of human sacrifices...

Xipe Totec, our flayed master, wearing the skin of the dead, a wig of feathers, his face painted with vertical yellow stripes, wearing golden earrings, a skirt of sapodilla leaves, and holding a shield with a red ring painted on it, exuding the stench of death, and dripping blood...

Then the goddesses came. They show up one after the other for the blood and hearts.

Teteoh Innan, mother of gods, goddess of childbirth and divination and sweat baths, wearing a skirt lined with glittering shells, and a *huipil* decorated with eagle feathers, holding a turkey leg in one hand and a broom in the other...

Cihuacoatl, the snake woman, goddess who weeps eerily in the night, wearing obsidian earrings, holding a weaving stick decorated with a turquoise mosaic, capable of sensing the signs of imminent war about to break out...

Chalchiuhtlicue, the one who wears the jade skirt, goddess of the water who drowns humanity, with blue lips, a face as yellow as a sunflower, a crown of quetzal feathers, a *huipil* with a golden circle upon it, and holding a shield painted with a single water lily and a musical instrument of mist...

Cihuapipiltin, the noblewomen, represented by five identical women, five as one, an alternate form of the goddess Tlazolteotl. Each had a white face that mocked humanity, a *huipil* of paper with obsidian points drawn upon it, sandals decorated with macaw feathers, a naturally twisted face and mouth, and they possessed the ability to curse their victims to an ill fate...

Tlazolteotl, the goddess of sin and lust, wearing nothing but a fearsome expression, listener to the secrets of men through *nahualli* sorcerers, learning of the worst sins and greatest shame...

Coatlicue, the one who wears a skirt of snakes, mother of the god of war, whose head is two serpents facing each other to form one face like an illusion, appearing even more fearsome than her son Huitzilopochtli...

More and more gods appeared.

The Aztecs had a religious pantheon that was as broad as it was deep.

Eventually, once all the gods had come and gone...

"We are his slaves," said the king. Titlacauan.
"The night and wind," said the priest. Yohualli Ehecatl.
"Enemy of both," said the sorcerer. Necoc Yaotl.

Silence descended abruptly, and Koshimo was alone. There was no longer any drumming or flute playing. The *teocallis* vanished, leaving only Koshimo, standing alone in the desert at night with the arid wind all around.

Only a black mirror floated nearby. A massive circular slab of obsidian.

Tezcatlipoca.

Koshimo was mystified. It was just the mirror. There was no god in human form anywhere to be seen. No feather headdress, no crown, no sandals. He didn't see the warrior of endless youth as depicted in the Codex Borgia. Just a silent mirror.

Everything about this was strange.

For one thing, Koshimo still didn't really understand what it meant to be a "smoking mirror." *Padre* had been teaching him about so many things, but this god, the most important, was still a mystery.

A mirror that smokes. A mirror spits out smoke. What does it mean?

As Koshimo pondered this question, the black mirror reflected the face of a sacrifice. Two eyes pleaded with Koshimo for salvation. He felt a terrible pain, as though it were *his* chest the knife had sunk into, and he sat upright, yelping.

The room was dark. Where was he? Not the chamber at the detention center. This was a proper bed, not a blanket set up on the ground. He stared at his long legs that stuck out over the edge of the bed. Then he exhaled and realized that he was covered in sweat.

He closed his eyes and lay down but could not sleep.

Eventually, Pablo gave up and got out of bed to open the window. An unusually powerful breeze buffeted the curtains, and something inside the room fell to the ground. Pablo stood in the darkness for several moments. Eventually, he headed to the desk, sat in the chair, and started scrolling through the pictures on his phone.

Dozens and dozens of images of his daughter, sent by his wife back in Okinawa.

He slid his finger across the screen, scrolling through the list, but his fingers felt only the texture of the **C-bone** he'd been working on earlier that day. Now that finger was touching his daughter's smiling face. He felt an overwhelming horror settle on his shoulders. The devil's crooked digit touched his daughter. He wanted to shout, to scream, "Stop!" But the finger was his own.

Pablo set down the smartphone and buried his face in his hands. He did not move for minutes. Finally, he turned on the small reading light on the desk and glanced at the little bookshelf ahead of it. The few possessions he'd brought with him from Okinawa were there.

The first custom knife he made by himself at nineteen, the knifemaking notebook he no longer needed to open, the portrait of him his daughter drew on his birthday, a cactus-headed doll his wife bought him. Behind all of them rested a single book.

A Spanish Bible.

The Bible had been on a longer journey than Pablo's first knife, having traveled much farther. Its deerskin cover was bent and tattered. Pablo had never read it himself, and he wasn't a religious person. It was his father who read from the book until the deerskin was properly vintage.

The father who was born in Lima, Peru; the father who came to Japan for work and labored until he died; the father who lived in such poverty his whole life that he couldn't buy his son a soccer ball. He was the descendent of Afro-Peruvians persecuted for their skin color.

Pablo didn't want to live like his father. He'd always been desperate to stay out of poverty, but lately, he found himself thinking of his father multiple times a day. Occasionally, he wished to see him again.

Pablo made far more than his father did. He was able to buy his family the things they wanted. In a few years, they might actually be able to afford a house. However, Pablo knew what he was doing to earn that money. He understood where this good living for his family came from.

Lately, when he returned from the workshop, Pablo found himself gazing at the Bible in the back of the shelf. The man was aware of the change in himself. The book had previously been of no interest, just a memento of his father, something he kept around as a courtesy, a tome whose contents held no appeal. Now it was a mirror that reflected his own sin back at him, the only thing in the lonely room that would meet his gaze.

Pablo rose from the chair and reached for his father's keepsake. He brushed off the dust and opened it up under the light of the reading lamp. There were dark fingerprints on the yellowed pages; marks left behind by oil-smudged fingers after shifts at the harbor. Pablo didn't read anything. He just flipped page after page after page.

He stopped when he reached a certain one and found a paper bill used as a bookmark there. It was a two-hundred-nuevo-sol bill, which probably wasn't even used in Peru anymore. A portrait of St. Rosa of Lima adorned the front.

Pablo carefully picked it up, feeling at it like an archaeologist, and whispered a word he hadn't said for decades. A word that Koshimo called El Cocinero regularly.

"*Padre.*"

Pablo could feel his father's presence. Toiling at the dock for meager pay, sitting by himself during the lunch break away from everyone else, nibbling on scraps of bread and drinking water, concentrating hard as he pored over the Bible. Pablo could see the image clearly in his head.

The bill was tucked into a page in the **New Testament: Matthew 9**. Pablo decided to read what was printed there. Then he did so again, and again, and yet again. The light outside the window brightened until the sky was as blue as a freshly honed blade, and Pablo was still reading that single page.

48

ömpöhualli-huan-chicuëyi

Yasuzu was carrying a load of children's laundry to be washed when she happened across Suenaga in the hallway. The shelter under Saiganji was large enough that it was only the third time this had ever happened.

She didn't know his name, or even his nickname, Laba-Laba. Xia had only told Yasuzu that he was a doctor, like El Loco. The man was an excellent medical professional who cared for the children.

Each time she saw him, Yasuzu thought that if he was the same as El Loco—Nomura—then he had to be another criminal doctor who couldn't work at a legitimate establishment for some reason. However, he didn't look like someone who'd get into trouble.

To her eyes, this doctor was anything but criminal. He fit the part so well that she could practically see the white coat on him, even though he wasn't wearing one. Black-rimmed glasses rested on his face, and he sported a crisp haircut on the sides with a seven-three part. His eyes shone with confidence. He walked with firm, direct purpose, and wore a faint, gentle smile. He didn't meet Yasuzu's eyes as he walked past, on any occasion.

Suenaga monitored the state of the shelter himself, going about it like someone would for a farm. He walked past the nursery for three-year-olds and the medical room, then opened a door at the east end of the hallway. Only Xia and a few others could get past its security system. There was an office on the other side where they managed all the children's information, and beyond that was the surgery room for heart extraction.

The journal in question was sitting on the desk of the empty office. Suenaga sat in the chair and booted up the computer to confirm the information on the child who would be given to the customer.

Name: Junta
Sex: M
Age: 9
Blood Type: O
No preexisting conditions

This boy came from a single-mother household. She was a resident of Chiba and a meth addict, and she had been neglecting her undocumented son. Her money went to drugs, to the point that she couldn't pay the bills to keep the lights on, and she ended up dying of dehydration inside during a heat wave. His mother's last name was Onogaki, but that information was not relayed to the customer, only the given name "Junta." He had type O blood, meaning his heart could be sold to any recipient with A-, B-, or O-type blood.

While he waited for Xia to arrive at the office, Suenaga looked through Junta's diary. As he'd been told, the nine-year-old's entries were full of despair and curses, written in a child's clumsy handwriting.

Write down something fun that happened today!

[Name ☞ Junta]
They'll kill us all.
These people are stupid.
This is an awful place.

Xia came across Yasuzu moving the laundry into the dryer and asked if she'd seen the doctor.

"He went that way," Yasuzu said, looking toward the east side of the shelter.

"I see," replied Xia. "Thank you."

"Don't you think," Yasuzu added, "he looks like Cary Joji Fukunaga?"

"Who?"

"The film director. He's Japanese American..." Her voice got quieter.

"He does?"

"Yes. Um...sorry, that doesn't have anything to do with anything."

"Why are you apologizing? By the way, today's the day to check on the lighting in the garden."

"I know. I was planning to head over there after I finish this."

The garden was what they called the indoor play area for the children. At the start of every week, it was Yasuzu's job to use a device to measure the artificial sunlamps' luminosity to make sure the children were getting the right amount of light.

Xia rushed down the hallway, passed the security system on the door at the end, and entered the office.

Suenaga was reading Junta's diary.

"You can see it right there," Xia told him. "We still don't know why he's writing like that. I've looked through every bit of security footage we have, but there's nothing..."

"And when you ask him if he's talking about this shelter, he won't give you a straight answer?"

"That's right."

"Then there's nothing else we can do," Suenaga grimaced. "This isn't a child-psychology research facility. If this Junta senses fate, then we're talking about some sixth sense, precognition shit. That's beyond me, I just do operations. Nextli, didn't the Hong Kong Police have experts in that stuff? Premonitions, x-ray vision. I bet the police in the PRC have folks like that."

"No," Xia said flatly. "They don't."

"I'm just kidding." Suenaga smirked. "On the other hand, Junta's got some very convenient blood. Type O means we can transplant his organs into any blood type."

Xia nodded without a word. They needed to be ready to harvest Junta's heart at any moment. And not just him; all of the *choclos* needed to be ready to transport to the *Dunia Biru* on a drone at any moment. That was Suenaga's instruction, and Hao, Xia's boss in Xin Nan Long, had told her, "Do whatever Suenaga says."

For now, Junta's diary was the only bug in the system. Otherwise, his health management was proceeding optimally.

If only his diary weren't so awful, she thought.

Suenaga took a string out of his pocket and wrapped it around his fingers, crossing the threads like he was playing cat's cradle. The material was suture thread that he'd personally selected. He wanted to be sure of the monofilament's feel before using it in the next extraction. He tied a square knot, granny knot, and surgeon's knot of each size he would need: 3-0, 4-0, 5-0. These were standard knots that every surgical student had to practice every day.

After placing the third knot on the desk, Suenaga said, "We are committed to our aftercare. The boy's diary will have to be written by someone else."

"By a different child?" Xia asked.

"No, an adult."

Although she didn't let it show, Xia was troubled by this assertion. Requesting a staff member mimic the writing of a nine-year-old child who hadn't been to elementary school was a big ask. Spelling mistakes and missing letters were common, and children sometimes wrote mirrored letters by accident. If they did a poor job of faking one, and a particularly skeptical customer took it to a handwriting specialist, they would easily tell that it was done by an adult. And if their fakery came to light, it would do massive damage to *choclo* business's trust.

"I didn't say we'd get a staffer to do it." Suenaga laughed, sensing Xia's consternation. "I know just the person for the job. His writing's awful, and he can't do kanji at all. He'll be the perfect replacement. But I'm sure he'll claim he can't write a diary for someone he's never met before. He'll want to meet Junta once or twice. I'll talk to El Cocinero about it."

Xia's calm expression finally slipped a bit. She'd never considered this possibility.

He's going to let that young sicario *write the journal?*

Once Xia had gone back to work, Suenaga left the office, passed through an even more stringent security system, and headed into the surgery room. He surveyed the empty room and breathed in perfectly purified air, courtesy of their filtration system. The underground surgery chamber's air system had a positive pressure mode for ordinary surgeries, a negative pressure mode to prevent viral contamination from spreading outside the room, and could even raise the exhaust flow to the point that the lower oxygen concentration made the room a partial vacuum. It was designed to be as finely sealed as an experimental pathology lab.

Suenaga approached the surgery table and tapped out a line of cocaine on his wrist. It reminded him of when he'd worked at a legitimate hospital as a cardiovascular surgeon.

In the post-op observation period after an eleven-year-old girl received a heart transplant successfully, Suenaga heard her talking about the ten-year-old boy who'd been her donor. That was impossible, though—he sort of thing that could only happen in a movie or a book. Yet somehow, she knew that he'd gone braindead after a traffic accident, and accurately described a number of other facts about the day that it happened.

The boy had been walking with his mother on the sidewalk when a minivan jumped the curb and hit him. It was just outside a park close to his house. He'd been carrying a handheld game console in his left hand, and wore orange Adidas sneakers with black stripes. And so on.

A hospitalized recipient couldn't know these things about the deceased organ donor while they were in the hospital. It was simply unthinkable for the girl to have heard such a detailed account of the accident.

Her descriptions were so accurate, in fact, that the hospital staff suspected someone involved in the transplant of leaking private information. They conducted an internal investigation, and even called in Suenaga, the primary attending surgeon. He was chagrined at the whole process. Suenaga didn't know a thing about the donor aside from his age, sex, blood type, and the fact that the boy was dead. A heart transplant surgeon didn't have time to fill his head with any facts beyond that.

As he snorted the line of coke, Suenaga ran through his recollections of that incident. People had unexplained abilities. The concept of biosentimentality suggested as much. In Japanese, the word for the organ could be read as "guts of the heart"—if the heart sent some kind of signal, then a particularly receptive child might interpret it as voices or visions…

Is it possible that Junta wrote those things in his journal because he can sense the extractions we're conducting?

Suenaga reclined on top of the surgery table, as though resting on his own bed at home. He looked up at the unlit surgical lights and envisioned the name *Junta*. He had to sneer at the irony of it. Koshimo might not understand, but El Cocinero would. When read with a silent *J*, it became a military takeover.

A coup d'état, huh. As Suenaga snickered over his observation, the unlit surgical lights began to shine. The cocaine was working. *Yeah*, he thought. *This is good shit.*

He felt himself ascending with bliss, resting atop the very table upon which he'd spilled juvenile blood, removing their hearts while they were still alive.

"El Chavo," Valmiro said, "have you ever written a *diario*?"
Koshimo asked him if he meant in Spanish or in Japanese. The reply came through the wafting incense smoke: "In Japanese."

He had done that before. The juvenile detention center had journal time after dinner, which the correctional instructors insisted was mandatory.

"I see." Valmiro nodded. "Then you're going to write one again. But it's not your diary. It's one for a boy in the shelter. He's having trouble writing what happened during his day. You should help him."

As a member of the *familia*, Koshimo felt that he grasped the nature of the task given to him.

The shelter was a modern-day *teocalli* in Tokyo's Ota Ward across the Tama River, where children chosen for a modern-day **Toxcatl** were kept. They lived in peace and happiness. The children would give their hearts to Titlacauan, also known as Yohualli Ehecatl or Necoc Yaotl—the greatest of all gods, Tezcatlipoca. Koshimo's job was to uphold the Aztec celebration and protect *Padre* and the *teocalli*. It was even more important than his responsibilities at the workshop.

However, he had no idea how he to write a diary entry for a child he'd never even seen before, much less met. It seemed more difficult than creating custom knives and *macuahuitls* or killing people with barracudas.

"I'll let you see him," Valmiro said, exhaling heavy, thick smoke. "But don't say a word about **Toxcatl** to him. Got that? The only one who can tell the sacrifices about **Toxcatl** is the *tlamacazqui* preparing the festival. Even the jaguar warriors are not allowed. And the *tlamacazqui* has not visited this boy yet. You're going to visit the shelter, listen to what he has to say, and write his diary for him. It doesn't have to be important. Just write when he went into the bath, what he ate for dinner, and things like that. Don't make up stories. Don't draw a picture. Your art is much too good compared to your writing. Kids can't draw the things you can."

As he left the office, Koshimo heard Valmiro say that the boy was nine years old. While descending the stairs outside in the dark, he realized that he'd forgotten to ask the boy's name.

49

ömpöhualli-huan-chiucnähui

Wednesday, August 4, 2021, was the day of Six Rabbit (Chicuace Tochtli) in the week of the House (Calli) according to the Aztec calendar as Valmiro had taught Koshimo. He had explained about all the other months in the *xiuhpohualli*, but Koshimo couldn't remember them all.

Early on the morning of Chicuace Tochtli, an electric Honda car came to the workshop in Odasakae, and Koshimo ducked low to get inside.

The car drove quietly north up the Dai-ichi Keihin route and across the Rokugo Bridge over the Tama River, from Kawasaki into Ota, Tokyo. Koshimo had grown up on that side of the river, always gazing across to the other side, making this the first time in his life that he'd crossed the river into Tokyo. He could have easily walked across the bridge at any time, but it had never occurred to him as a thing he might want to do.

Koshimo looked at the woman silently driving the car. She wore rimless glasses and was in no hurry to speak. He'd seen her a few times at the auto yard. She was a member of the *familia* they called Nextli.

The flow of traffic continued north toward the center of the capital, but the electric car made a left turn and proceeded west along the river instead.

It's just like Kawasaki, Koshimo decided. He looked up at the sky through the windshield. The vast blue seemed to continue forever. Against that backdrop, passenger jets slowly made their way toward Haneda Airport.

Koshimo followed Xia onto the Saiganji grounds. Just as he'd never been to Tokyo until today, this was also his first visit to a Buddhist temple.

A gravel parking lot, a stone path, a stately tile roof building, a water trough with wooden ladles for handwashing, and a vending machine selling candles meant for offering light to the statue inside. Koshimo understood that the place where the rectangular stones with kanji on them and the wooden Sanskrit boards stood was the graveyard. Under his breath, he muttered, "Buddhist graves."

He reached out and touched one of the smooth, shiny stones. It was made of hard granite, and someone had placed incense before it. He traced the posthumous Buddhist names carved on the side of the stone, guessing that they were done by a machine. Eventually, he recognized a sound like Nahautl spells being chanted from the main temple building behind him. He listened closely, tuning out the buzzing cicadas.

"On kakaka bisanmaei sowaka, on kakaka bisanmaei sowaka..."

The temple monks chanted the mantra of Jizo Bosatsu, the patron saint of deceased children.

The modern-day *teocalli* where the Toxcatl children lived was located directly below the graveyard on the temple grounds.

The kids didn't leave once they'd been taken underground. They only emerged in the form of a *choclo* being shipped to a new owner.

Koshimo bent over so that his head didn't hit the ceiling of the stairway down to the shelter. There wasn't much light, the passage was narrow, and the air was cold. It felt like he was descending into a terribly frigid place, where snow fell despite it being summer.

If this took him below the graves where the dead slept, then it had to be at the very bottom of the Earth, far beyond death. Koshimo was reminded of the Aztec god who ruled over Mictlan, the underground realm: Mictlantecuhtli. When the Christian conquistadors saw his frightful depictions in art and sculpture, they saw Lucifer and Death. The god's epithet was Tzontemoc, "He Who Falls Head-First," so Koshimo was careful not to slip on the stairs. The name Tzontemoc reminded him of *tzompantli*, the wall of sacrificial skulls. That was beneath Tenochtitlan's *teocalli* of Huitzilopochtli, god of war.

These thoughts eventually brought back one of Koshimo's frequent wonderings. *Why do Mictlantecuhtli and Huitzilopochtli always seem so much stronger than the exalted god that Padre worships?* The Tezcatlipoca who appeared in Koshimo's dreams took the form of a round obsidian mirror. It didn't make sense that a lone black mirror was more powerful than the skull-faced king of the underworld or the god of war with sharp eagle claws adorning his feather headdress. *He's kind of scary, but he doesn't seem like the strongest.* Despite being plagued by this question, Koshimo was unable to bring it to Valmiro's attention. Guilt kept him silent.

Instead, he issued himself a reminder.

You can't do that. You have to respect Padre's god most of all. Somos familia.

Xia and Koshimo reached a door at the bottom of the stairs.

Koshimo's face, retinal pattern, and fingerprints were already registered. The security system authorized him to enter, and the door opened. The first area was a darkened sterilization room. Koshimo washed his hands and walked over an adhesive substance that grabbed all the dirt and dust off the soles of his boots. Then he was subjected to a powerful air shower from head to toe that knocked loose all the microparticles stuck to his hair and clothing.

Nomura had a testing machine delivered from China to run PCR tests on Koshimo for COVID-19 before he visited the shelter. They tested him four times to eliminate the possibility of a false negative, and each test was indeed negative.

Two sets of doors opened, revealing a brightly-lit hallway. Night had turned to day, completely eradicating Koshimo's fear that he was venturing into a frigid place. There was actually a pleasantly temperate breeze. The wafting air felt as cleansing as the riverside at dawn. There was none of the darkness and dankness of Mictlan here.

Doors lined both sides of the hallway. One of the rooms had playground rings hung from the ceiling like handholds on a train, with some of them being low enough to the floor that children could reach them.

The detention center where Koshimo spent several years was regularly cleaned, but it was nothing compared to this place. Everything in the shelter appeared brand new, and between the balmy breeze and light, Koshimo forgot that he was underground where the sun couldn't reach.

He heard children shouting. They were high-pitched screams, but those of delight and laughter. The kids were playing in the inside yard beneath the artificial sunlamps.

Junta was already in the medical office that was being used as a meeting room, wearing a yellow T-shirt and waiting for Koshimo.

He was nine years old, one hundred and thirty-one centimeters, and twenty-six kilograms. When Yasuzu brought him to the shelter, he was only twenty-two kilograms, about six under the average nine-year-old. While living with his mother, he typically had only one meal a day. That didn't change after she died and one of her friends took him in. Junta still didn't have a legal identity, didn't go to school, and thus didn't get regular lunches.

Junta was the type of child who never changed expressions. He didn't even cry when given an injection. But when Xia brought Koshimo through the door, his eyes filled with fear.

At nineteen, Koshimo was two hundred and eight centimeters and weighed over one hundred and thirty kilograms. El Loco calculated his body fat percentage at just 8.8 percent, making him one solid mass of muscle. His black hair came down to his collarbone, and from his black shirt sleeves to his wrists, his thick arms were covered with tattoos of Aztec symbols.

An anti-droplet clear acrylic stand was placed in the middle of the desk in the medical office. Koshimo sat in the chair, smelling a vague whiff of chemicals, and faced Junta through the transparent board.

Xia considered whether or not she should be present, then decided to do as planned, and left the room to watch on the monitor from next door. Junta wouldn't say anything to her; that much she already knew. She didn't think that Suenaga's plan to try things this way would have any better results, either.

Even I would be intimidated sitting across from a man like him, Xia thought. Would a mere child open up to someone that frightening...?

Between her police days and time in a *heishehui*, Xia had seen many criminals in her time. However, she'd never seen anyone whose physical presence held as much force as nineteen-year-old El Patíbulo.

Junta didn't say a word, and neither did Koshimo.

Fifteen minutes passed without either opening his mouth. Conversation was forbidden between them. They almost seemed to be waiting for someone to arrive and get them.

Koshimo looked up at the security camera on the ceiling.

In the spherical cover over the lens, he saw the small reflections of the boy and himself. He stared at them for thirty seconds. Then he looked at the child. His eyes were empty, and his face resembled a wooden mask. No expression colored his features. Was this really a sacrifice chosen for the glory of Toxcatl? It seemed odd to Koshimo. The kid wasn't wearing clothes decorated with jade. His hair wasn't grown out. He had no obsidian earplugs and no flutes.

Was the child really leading a life of luxury here?

This isn't at all the life of a sacrifice that Padre *described.*

"I know your name." Koshimo was the first to break the silence. Xia had told him what it was. "You're Junta, right?"

Junta didn't respond. Silence filled the chamber again.

Xia sighed in the monitoring room next door and glanced at the clock out of habit. She was reminded of when her father used to play long, long games of Go.

Koshimo yawned, opened up the blank notebook Xia had given him, and started to draw. Valmiro had warned him not to draw any pictures, and he hadn't forgotten that command. But there was no harm so long as he didn't leave any drawings in the diary entries he was writing for the boy. He could just tear this page out.

Koshimo first thought of drawing the mother of the god of war, the beastly Coatlicue, or the earth monster Tlaltecuhtli. However, it was wrong to call forth terrifying gods merely for fun. Instead, Koshimo drew the symbols of the days. Today was Six-Rabbit day in the Week of the House, so he sketched a house and a rabbit, and marked ⁑ next to the rabbit. He tore out that page and handed it to Junta over the top of the acrylic board. When Junta didn't reach out to take it, he stretched farther and let it drop in front of the boy.

"Can you tell what this picture is?" Koshimo asked.

Junta didn't react at first. Eventually, he picked up the piece of paper and stared at the strange symbols.

"A rabbit," said Junta.

"That's right."

"And this one…"

"That's a house. It has a roof. I have the same thing on my arm."

Koshimo pointed at two symbols inked on his left forearm. Calli and Tochtli.

Junta looked at the tattoos, then at Koshimo. He turned the piece of paper upside down, then back upright. Then he looked up at Koshimo again. He said something under his breath. Koshimo had keen hearing, but failed to make it out.

He leaned forward, sticking his ear to the clear board between them. Junta opened his mouth and repeated the words.

"Did you come to kill me?"

This time, it was unmistakable. Koshimo looked at the boy in surprise. Did he already know about Toxcatl?

That couldn't be true. Only the *tlamacazqui* preparing the festival could tell the sacrifice about Toxcatl. And *Padre* had said that the priest had not yet visited the boy.

Koshimo couldn't help but ask Junta, "Why do you think that?"

There was no answer. Another silence came over the pair. Koshimo could hear the air-conditioning blowing, and he smelled a faint whiff of chemicals. Junta stared at the drawing, and Koshimo just sat there.

After more time had passed, Koshimo got to his feet without warning, startling Junta.

"Just tell me one thing," Koshimo said. "What time did you take a bath yesterday?"

When Koshimo left the medical room, he was taken through the stringent security system to the office. Xia ensured that none of the other children encountered the giant.

He was given a fresh notebook there, and wrote Junta's diary for him. On the entry for two days ago, August 3, he did as Suenaga instructed, and scribbled down a message.

Write down something fun that happened today!

[Name ☞ Junta]
Yest today i took a bath at six

50

ömpöhualli-huan-mahtlactli

It was the adults' naive expectation that if Koshimo met the boy once or twice at the shelter, he would come to imagine other journal entries on his own.

If Koshimo hadn't met Junta, he wouldn't have been able to write a single sentence in the diary. He couldn't record even the tiniest bit of text without hearing it from the child directly. All Koshimo could do was write by proxy. After reporting as much to Suenaga, Xia went to pick Koshimo up from the workshop every morning.

Koshimo and Junta sat on opposite sides of the desk in the shelter's medical office. There was still almost no conversation between them, but at least they'd struck up a kind of routine.

In another notebook separate from Junta's diary, Koshimo drew the day's calendar symbols, tore the page out, and gave it to Junta. It was the Calli *trecena*, the Week of the House. On the day of Seven-Water he drew the symbols for House and Water and ⚬⚬. On the day of Eight-Dog, he drew the House and Dog and ⚬⚬⚬. On the day of Nine-Monkey, he drew the House and Monkey and ⚬⚬⚬⚬. Finally, on the day of Ten-Grass, he drew the House and Grass and ══.

Junta saved all of the sketches, and brought them all when he met with Koshimo. He hadn't shown any interest in the game consoles Yasuzu and Xia gave him, but he was clearly curious about the mysterious Aztec symbols Koshimo wrote. Sometimes, he tried to copy them and draw his own.

On the day of Thirteen-Eagle, the week of the House was over, and the week of the Vulture began. Koshimo drew the Vulture, Cozcacuauhtli, plus a •. In the Gregorian calendar, it was Thursday, August 12, 2021.

There was an undeniable change in Junta's eyes when he received the eccentric drawings. The boy had kept his heart closed off to everyone, yet now he was starting to accept El Patíbulo. This came as a complete surprise to Xia.

When the *sicario* met with the nine-year-old, he always asked a short question as they parted ways: What time did you take a bath last night, and what did you have for dinner? Junta always gave a brief answer, and the hitman departed the medical office to scribe the reply in the diary in his horrible handwriting.

As she watched their routine every morning, Xia began to feel that she was attending a kind of psychological test with a secret purpose. In reality, there was no goal other than to create a believable diary. Laba-Laba simply chose El Patíbulo because he was the best suited for the job. They needed diary pages to ship with the *choclo*, and they were getting them.

On the day of Two-Movement in the Week of the Vulture, Koshimo drew the picture like he always did, asked his brief questions, and turned to leave. However, he stopped at the door this time. Looking back at the boy, he said, "Junta, you wrote, *They're going to kill us all* in your old diary, right? Why?"

In the other room, Xia's ears pricked up, and she stared at the monitor intently. The mic under the desk had picked up Koshimo's voice. Junta had been asked that question before and had always refused to give a clear answer. No matter how many times he'd been pressed.

"Smells like blood," Junta admitted.

"'Smells like blood'?" Koshimo repeated. He was familiar with the odor of running blood. His nostrils flared, but the only scent in the office was of faint chemicals.

Junta stared at the tall man sniffing around the room.

Eventually, Koshimo asked, "Do you smell it from me, too?"

Junta nodded.

Koshimo lifted his arms to inhale their odor and did the same with the fabric of his T-shirt. They smelled like the oak he'd been carving early that morning in the workshop. The shavings had been blown off by the air cleanser at the entrance to the shelter, but the woody scent was still there.

"Are you smelling wood?" Koshimo asked Junta.

Junta shook his head. "It's blood."

Xia did as Koshimo had and pinched her high-neck blouse to sniff it. She'd never heard Junta talk about the scent of blood before. The blouse smelled like fabric softener. The shelter was cleaned and sterilized frequently, and the ventilation system was pristine. No odor of blood hung about the air. The surgery room was behind several doors, well out of the reach of the human olfactory system. And the children were always kept away from there.

This made Xia want to study more about the child's intuition, but then she remembered what Suenaga had said.

"This isn't a child-psychology research facility."

Saturday, August 14, 2021 was the day of Three-Knife in the Week of the Vulture.

That morning, Koshimo rubbed his sleepy eyes and got to the workshop earlier than usual. It was four o'clock. The sun hadn't risen yet.

From the light coming through the windows, he could tell that Pablo was already there. Koshimo opened the door and caught a whiff of freshly brewed coffee. That helped clear a bit of the fog over his head.

Pablo had specifically called him in at this early hour. The man had spent three days repairing the canoe the workshop's previous owner had left behind, cleaning off the mud and redoing the paint. He'd finished reinforcing the aging paddles as well. Pablo had always wanted to give Koshimo a chance to ride in it.

In the early morning hours, they wouldn't have to deal with the blazing August sun. More importantly, Koshimo left at eight o'clock these days, so they'd have to finish their trip to the river by then. Koshimo hadn't told Pablo anything about where he was going every morning, but it was easy for him to guess based on who picked the young man up. Although the reason was a mystery, Koshimo was clearly going to that shelter in Ota. To the depths of hell.

Koshimo showed up on time, so Pablo put a life jacket on him. The size didn't match at all, of course. They went outside the shop, carrying the four-hundred-and-seventy-two-centimeter, thirty-eight-kilogram tandem canoe and placing it upside down on the roof rack of the Citroën Berlingo. After tying it down with ropes, they tossed the two paddles into the back and closed the door.

The canoe sat in the predawn Tama, silently gliding downstream. Although Koshimo was the much bigger man, Pablo was more experienced, so he sat in the rear seat and did most of the rowing.

Koshimo's eyes sparkled in the dark at the wonder of his first canoe ride. It was like he was flying in his dreams. When they needed to fine-tune their course, Pablo would strike either side of the boat from the back, indicating the direction to paddle. The tiny, subtle sound of the paddles breaking the water was beautiful.

They caught a gentle current once they were out in the middle of the wide river. There was almost no need to row; the flow carried them along with it. The sky to the east was steadily brightening, the temperature was rising as the dawn approached, and mist began to form over the water's surface.

It was a completely different world from the Tama River as seen from land.

Koshimo envisioned the enormous Aztec capital built atop Lake Texcoco—Tenochtitlan. Canals running back and forth, people traveling them by canoe, just as they were doing now, carrying goods, moving from town to town, and sometimes going off to war.

The Maruko Bridge over the river drew closer, until the canoe went under it. The shadows of the bridge's girders and piers resembled looming *teocallis*.

Everything was quiet around them, broken only by the occasional splash of water. Eventually, they came across a small eddy, at the center of which a dead, twenty-centimeter perch rotated slowly. Its stomach had been chewed open, and little bones were visible through the softened flesh.

Pablo stared at the dead fish, which spun in place like some kind of signpost. He said to his rowing partner, "Hey, Koshimo. You're going to that shelter every morning, right? Over in Tokyo…"

Koshimo didn't answer. The sights of the shelter were the sights of the *teocalli*, secrets that belonged only to the *familia*. And for whatever reason, the men at the auto yard, who called Pablo "La Cerámica," claimed that he wasn't part of the *familia*.

Padre had said something similar.

"Listen to me, El Chavo. He's just an artisan. A very good artisan, but he cannot be our familia."

"Don't worry about it. You don't have to answer," Pablo said to Koshimo, when it was clear the young man wouldn't. "By the way, do you know what they do at that shelter?"

Koshimo didn't reply to that, either. He could have, of course. It was Toxcatl. The place where human sacrifices were offered to gods.

Pablo took out two tumblers full of coffee and gave one to Koshimo. "Just reach back, don't turn around. If you turn, it'll flip the canoe over."

They sipped on warm coffee as the current ferried them east through the cool mist.

The radiance gradually filling the sky seemed like the light of judgment, coming to expose their sins.

This enjoyable trip is nothing but an illusion, Pablo thought. *The boat we're on is taking us toward terrible sin, pushing us on a course down to hell.*

"I'm sure," Pablo muttered, speaking mostly to himself, "that you already know everything I keep secret."

He didn't believe he'd gone to the trouble of repairing the canoe and inviting Koshimo out here just to discuss this. However, the man also felt they'd gotten into the boat explicitly for this conversation. No, not *they*—*he*. Pablo didn't have the courage to broach this in the workshop.

How dearly he wished to run away, to avert his eyes. Koshimo had aided the men at the auto yard in murder, and witnessed the grisly execution of pitiful El Taladro. Perhaps there was nothing more Pablo could say at this point. He didn't have the right to say anything, either.

Still, Pablo felt compelled to try.

Now that Koshimo is going to that shelter, into the depths of hell, I need to tell him something very important. Otherwise, Koshimo, my first knifemaking apprentice, is going to spend the rest of his life as a monster. Bathed in blood and darkness.

"Hey, Koshimo," he began, closing the lid on the tumbler. The fish carcass traveled into the distance at the same speed as the river. "I should've told you what C-bone is. I know that. But I was scared. I was a coward and a hypocrite. I didn't want you to know that I was making money by selling products made from the bones of the children from the shelter. There was no point to me worrying about that. And while I kept that secret, you moved steadily in an ever-worsening direction. They found you and added you to their *familia*. Yet still, I couldn't tell you. I held my silence. Koshimo, C-bone is a femur taken from a dead kid. There are people in this world who believe that things fashioned from the bones of children have a magical power to them. Collectors want them because they're a rarity. A custom knife made with a C-bone handle goes for over ten times as much as one made with jigged bone or sambar stag. That's the business I'm in. It's inhumane. It's horrifying. But El Cocinero, your *padre*, he's..."

"He's involved in a far greater sin." Pablo decided to keep that part to himself. That wasn't what he wanted to tell Koshimo.

"Hear me out," Pablo stated. "Long ago, there was a man named Jesus."

"I hate Christianity," Koshimo replied, facing forward. "They destroyed the *indígena* country. They burned the temples down and killed everyone. They're bad guys."

"I agree," Pablo replied. "They were evil enough that they should've gone straight to hell. My dad was born in Peru, where there used to be a huge native country called the Incan Empire. The Spanish conquistadors destroyed them, too. Just like the Aztecs."

"Inca…"

"But Koshimo, the man named Jesus never told anyone to destroy Indigenous countries for their own gain. There isn't a single line in the New Testament telling people to steal gold, enslave others, and plant the flag of Spain in the ground. It says something else, and I want to tell you about it. If you wish to continue being my apprentice, please keep these words somewhere in your heart. You don't have to do anything else, just hold on to the words."

Staring at Koshimo's broad back, Pablo recited the words from the Bible page marked by his late father's two-hundred-nuevo-sol bill— Matthew 9:13.

But go and learn what this means: "I desire mercy, not sacrifice."

Eyes red and swollen, Pablo sobbed, mucus running from his nose, as he repeated the words again and again. He clung to the paddle like a walking stick, drawing it across the still-dark surface of the water.

With the sound of Pablo's sniffling in his ears, Koshimo slowly, carefully—so as not to overturn the canoe—turned around.

51

ömpöhualli-huan-mahtlactli-huan-cë

Where does betrayal come from? Enemies or allies? From allies, of course. You wouldn't call it betrayal otherwise.

Valmiro drank mezcal in the darkened room, *copalli* smoke filling his nostrils, as he considered his situation.

Who was the betrayer? Were they not part of the *familia*? Yes. They were *familia*. That was why they betrayed.

Valmiro first detected that something was amiss because of the skull smuggling, which was carried out in parallel with the *choclo* business.

After a child's heart was extracted, the skull was sent to Pablo's workshop, where he would give it an artistic finish and send it out into the world. They'd already sold Tham Hoa's, although it was not juvenile-size. Previously they'd peddled undecorated skulls to a religious group in South Asia, but now the margin on fashioned skulls for individual buyers was much higher.

The idea to cover the skulls in a mosaic of obsidian and turquoise came from an ornamental representation of Tezcatlipoca that had been taken from the Aztecs by the Europeans, and to this day, it still resided in the British Museum in London. It was a real skull, of course. The exterior was covered in lignite and turquoise, while the inside was lined with a fabric made of maguey fiber and deerskin, affixed with pine resin. Polished pyrite pieces were placed in the eye sockets, where they shone like eyes, and the nasal cavity was lined with red oyster shell, calling to mind the vivid red blood that coursed through the skull in life.

Although they weren't the same as the ornamental mask in the British Museum, the pieces of modern skull art produced at the workshop in Kawasaki were extremely popular, to the extent that a wealthy industrialist in Shanghai switched from collecting illegal ivory to skulls. He also enjoyed the custom knives with C-bone handles, believing them to be good luck. The man was the kind of person who proudly displayed his C-bone knives in his office, along with Siberian tiger fangs, which were just as illegal to sell as elephant tusks. He was the sort who desired the skulls at any cost. No price tag could stop that kind of person from getting what they wanted.

Valmiro was busy enough with other work that he left it up to Suenaga to sell the skulls on the dark web. All Valmiro checked was the quality of the finished decoration, and, on occasion, he oversaw the delivery records. He didn't focus on the documents as much as he did when clearing potential *choclo* customers, because he didn't need to. However, he couldn't help but notice that the same customer had bought skulls multiple times within the past three months. There was no outright problem with a satisfied customer returning to buy more. Some enthusiasts purchased C-bone knives practically every month.

Still, something was off. Valmiro had an inkling of wrongness that he couldn't shake. Had he not been a narco who dealt cocaine in Mexico for so many years, he might have missed it. Valmiro set aside the task of checking the specs on the Russian-made submarine sent by Guntur Islami and focused on the niggling feeling. The skulls were worth more than the C-bone. There was a waiting list for them. Over the course of three months, the skulls were essentially being monopolized. In other words, someone was being offered preferential access to the product.

The first thing Valmiro did was call Nomura to the office.

"Laba-Laba's been selling skulls to the same customer for a while. El Loco, do you know anything about this?"

"No," Nomura replied, perturbed. "I wasn't aware."

Valmiro stared icily at the former anesthesiologist. He thought back on what his brother Bernardo used to say all the time.

"Lies fly before bullets do. If you can't see them first, you'll wind up full of lead before long."

Nomura wasn't lying.

Valmiro finally let his piercing gaze drift away, much to Nomura's relief. The boss then commanded him to hire a hacker to find Laba-Laba's communications history.

Two brothers in Adelaide, Australia, were buying skulls from Suenaga in succession: Darren McBride and Brendan McBride. They had no criminal history, worked as film producers, owned their office jointly, and the younger of the two was married. They didn't pay an especially high price for the goods, so it was a mystery to Valmiro why Suenaga would prioritize selling the skulls to them over others.

The messages and files that Suenaga and the McBride brothers exchanged were encrypted with PGP, so Nomura's hacker couldn't pry into them. However, given the nature of the product, it made sense that all correspondence would be encrypted for secrecy anyway.

As the investigation continued, the hacker discovered that, in addition to the money for the product, the McBride brothers were also sending Suenaga separate e-payments. It totaled up to over ten million yen in individual transfers.

Neither Valmiro nor Nomura could tell what that money was for.

It was to the hacker's great credit that they discovered the child pornography site the McBride brothers were running.

Together, the brothers used the handle "bolz_ob" to run a members-only site called Blood Shot Eyes Wide—typically shortened to BSEW.

The community for trading child pornography on the dark web was worldwide, conducted in absolute anonymity, and constantly slipped through the fingers of any authorities attempting to stop it. It was similar to the online drug trade in that way, but it dealt with much smaller amounts of money. Unlike drugs, videos and images of child porn could be replicated with a single click. Some pieces of data were traded like accursed trading cards, but in the case of information so dangerous it couldn't afford to be exchanged, you had to track down the original.

A small but particular subset of this community, in search of a utopia that would grant its most perilous desires, eventually found its way to BSEW.

The draw of the site was that it periodically uploaded a notable number of new originals. The members of bolz_ob's site eagerly awaited each new drop, keeping their secret, grotesque hunger hidden from the rest of society.

Necropedophilia.

BSEW was a place the McBrides created to be a land of paradise for others like themselves, who combined the tastes of pedophilia and necrophilia into one.

To people who could only find sexual stimulation from the dead bodies of actual children, the site's operators might as well have been gods. On BSEW, you could see a naked child after an autopsy, alongside that same child's skull, which had been decorated and turned into an art trophy. And you could look at those pictures all you wanted, without committing the crime yourself.

Perusing the website, Valmiro recognized pictures of Pablo's skull work and the surgery room in the shelter under Saiganji. The faces and bodies of the children whose hearts had been extracted for transplants were clear as day.

The McBride brothers had bought the pictures from Suenaga.

Each image of a corpse taken from the security camera footage in the surgery room was paired with its decorated skull.

Suenaga's betrayal didn't stop at leaking images. He sent the money the McBride brothers paid him right to Ho Chi Minh City—to a man by the name of Minh Nguyen.

Valmiro remembered the name Minh Nguyen. When they kidnapped and tortured Nakaaki Morimoto, the second-in-command of the Zebubs, he'd dropped that name in an attempt to appease his tormentors. Minh Nguyen was a dealer from Ho Chi Minh City who supplied the Zebubs with their high-quality ice. He was gathering capital in the hope of building his own lab for production.

That was who Suenaga was sending his money to. He wasn't just buying *hielo*; he was investing in it. He used the money he got from the McBride brothers to become the sponsor of a new narco in Vietnam.

Valmiro didn't need to call the man in to hear his excuses. The flow of money told him everything already.

How unfortunate, Laba-Laba.

His investigation complete, Valmiro cut the end off a cigar with his knife and put a match to it. He gazed up at the dark ceiling, smoke trailing from his mouth, and placed a call to Jingliang Hao in Jakarta.

"Send me a surgeon who can do heart transplants," he told him. "I can't use this doctor anymore."

The *Dunia Biru* had already crossed the sea to Kawasaki again, and the ship date for a new *choclo* was approaching. Valmiro had to keep Suenaga alive until then, at least.

Laba-Laba. The Spider. The man could not be overlooked. *He's got the confidence of Mictlantecuhtli, lord of the underworld*, Valmiro thought. *He's cruel and merciless, and he could easily strike where we're weakest and then flee.*

If there was a moment Valmiro could guarantee the man's death, it was the night they shipped out the *choclo*. The four *sicarios* would do the job at the shelter. They were there to escort the transport vehicle to the container terminal at the port, so there was nothing unusual or suspicious with them being on standby at the origin of the shipment. Once Suenaga finished the extraction, he would be next to die, after which they'd deliver the *choclo* to the cruise ship on time. The lingering trouble would be finding another doctor for the shelter before the ship came to port again.

Valmiro exhaled smoke and placed a call to Chatarra.

When he received Koshimo's newest piece of art, Junta seemed disappointed. "Another rabbit. I got that one before."

There were pictures of a vulture and rabbit on the torn sheet, along with the symbol $\overset{\bullet\bullet\bullet}{=}$ to symbolize "thirteen." It was the week of Cozcacuauhtli, the Vulture, and the day was Thirteen-Rabbit—Tuesday, August 24.

The comment informed Koshimo that he'd drawn the entire rotation of twenty symbols since first visiting the shelter. That was just how the calendar worked, though. Thinking back on his time in juvy, he understood how Junta felt. Since he couldn't leave the shelter, getting a new sketch was something to look forward to each day. It seemed that the boy kept the papers with him at all times.

Seeing Junta looking so dejected, as though he'd pulled the unlucky short straw, caused Koshimo's expression to darken, too. He wanted to draw the boy something else instead, but he couldn't just invent a new symbol that didn't exist in the calendar.

Koshimo considered this quandary while Junta sulked. It was the start of another long period of silence; something Xia had become quite familiar with.

After twenty minutes, Koshimo folded his fingers behind his head, leaned back against the chair, pointed his face up to the ceiling, and closed his eyes. He went motionless.

Junta pulled every drawing he'd received from Koshimo out of his pocket, straightened out the wrinkles with his small fingers, and started lining them up on the table. He looked like a child fortune teller, silently arranging the twenty symbols in order.

While he did this, Koshimo was silent, eyes closed.

He isn't sleeping, is he? Xia wondered, clicking her tongue as she took off her glasses and leaned closer to the monitor. He was allowed to stay silent, but taking a nap in the meeting room was a wanton luxury he was not permitted. She was just about to call his phone when his eyes opened.

"Junta," Koshimo said slowly. "I won't draw anything. I won't light copal. I can't tell you my name. But just for you, I'll tell you a little about the god I know. The strongest god of all. The strongest god is the strongest mirror."

"…Mirror?"

"Yeah."

"…That's the strongest?"

"The god of war, the goddess with the snake head, the skeleton god of death, he's stronger than all of them. He's very mysterious."

"What kind of mirror is he?"

"Round, made of black stone. Have you ever had coffee, Junta? When you look into black coffee, you see your face, right? Your face shows up like that in the black mirror, too."

As Koshimo spoke, Junta picked up a pencil, chose one of the symbols at random, and began to draw in the empty space around it. He sketched a circular mirror that was made of black stone.

"The mirror isn't just an ordinary tool," Koshimo explained. "It makes smoke. That's why it's special."

"Not fire? Just smoke?"

"Smoke. It doesn't make sense, right? Mirrors don't smoke."

Koshimo watched Junta use the blank space on the paper, diligently sketching around the symbol. It wasn't good to reduce the magnificence of the gods into careless art, but he decided that since he wasn't the one drawing, it was okay. *Padre* would probably forgive him.

Junta put down the pencil. At the outer edge of the colored-in circle, he'd drawn fuzzy lines to represent smoke. That was the end of it. There was nothing else to depict based on Koshimo's story.

"I know this," said Junta. "I've seen it."

Koshimo's expression changed abruptly. He gave Junta a very keen, prying look. "Where did you see it?"

"In the sun." Junta went on to explain the celestial event that crossed North America on August 21, 2017. He had seen a video of the event on a TV program.

The sun? Koshimo thought. *Does he mean Tonatiuh?*

Tonatiuh, the Shining One, was the sun god placed at the center of the Aztec calendar. In the midst of the ring of time, he dangled his long tongue in search of sacrificial blood. But Tonatiuh was not Tezcatlipoca. He was not Yohualli Ehecatl, ruler of darkness, but the god who governed the bright daytime.

Koshimo thought Junta was mistaken, but the look of utter confidence in the boy's eyes caused him to falter. Junta didn't look like he was lying.

"Show me that drawing." Koshimo abruptly bolted forward. To Xia, watching through the monitor, it was as though a previously docile predator suddenly lunged at a helpless child. She panicked and reached for her tactical knife, but when nothing else happened, she exhaled. The only sounds that came through the mic were those of two people having a conversation.

"The sun turned black," said Junta. "The moon blocked it, so it was totally dark in the middle of the day. That's when the sun looked just like this. It was shining around it, like smoke…"

Koshimo could hardly breathe with Junta's drawing in his hands. His eyes bulged. He hadn't been this shocked since the night of El Taladro's execution.

What frightened him most was that Junta had chosen to sketch on the page depicting the jaguar. He'd drawn the symbol right above Koshimo's jaguar.

He was stunned and felt dizzy. The image leaped off the page, lurching right for Koshimo's chest. His breath was stifled, as though there were a knife stuck in him. He grabbed at his heart.

Why didn't I realize until Junta told me? Padre *didn't tell me. Maybe he hasn't realized. Does* Padre *know less? How does the Toxcatl sacrifice know something that he doesn't?*

The boy with all the day symbols was sitting before him. He was like a *tlamacazqui* priest from the Aztec days, a hallowed proxy of the gods, calling Koshimo to his *teocalli* to teach him the truth.

Koshimo recalled the news shows everyone watched in the juvenile detention center. During a school lesson period, the correctional instructor showed the inmates a photo. He remembered it clearly now. It looked just like a round mirror made of obsidian. That was the Smoking Mirror. It turned day into night, overpowered the sun god, and wreathed everything in darkness, even the *teocalli* of the war god.

Koshimo could no longer tell where he was or when. He couldn't hear Junta or Xia.

The pounding of drums. Flutes that sounded like screams. Terrified natives, praying for their lives. Titlacauan, Yohualli Ehecatl, Necoc Yaotl.

Tezcatlipoca. The black mirror was in the sky.

A total solar eclipse.

After leaving the shelter, Koshimo had trouble getting back to his usual work at the shop. He wasn't in any state of mind to cut out a blade with a grinder or perform precision sharpening. He returned to his apartment, closed the curtains, and lay on the bed. His feet stuck out past the end.

Koshimo fell into a deep, long sleep plagued by dreams. Within his unique sensibilities, time was asleep, and the dreams were watching him.

The gods came to him there, traveling to and fro.

An obsidian mirror hung in the darkened sky. A sacrifice was being offered on the ground underneath. *Padre* was there, Chatarra was there, El Mamut was there, and so was El Casco. El Taladro and Tham Hoa were desiccated mummies, tumbling in the arid wind.

No one was looking at the sky.

Padre, Koshimo thought. *That is our god. That's Tezcatlipoca.*

But despite all of his warnings, *Padre* would not turn around. He was staring only at the sacrifice. Somehow, Koshimo was there with them, holding down the body. The victim was Junta. He was looking at the sky.

"Stop," Koshimo said, his voice weak. "Padre *didn't know. He didn't know about the smoking mirror. And he's still going ahead with Toxcatl.* Padre, *who are you sacrificing him to?"*

Padre held up the obsidian knife.

"Stop!" Koshimo shouted. "You're a liar!"

The tip of the volcanic glass shard sank into Junta's chest, and his body jerked. Red blood spilled from his eyes, mouth, ears, and nose. His entire body spasmed. His ribs broke, and the knife severed his sternum. Blood erupted. Junta's screams filled the air, and from his throat came El Taladro's and Tham Hoa's shrieks. Someone was whispering in Koshimo's ear.

"I desire mercy, not sacrifice."

"I desire mercy, not sacrifice."

"Go and learn what this means."

Koshimo awoke with a shout. He sat upright and put a hand to his chest. There was a beautiful *teocalli* tattoo there. The tattoo artist had finally finished it recently. The carefully rendered stone steps of the pyramid, repeatedly inked with the shader, now flooded over with Koshimo's sweat. But he felt that it was blood. It *smelled* like blood. The room was dark, and he couldn't tell how long he'd been asleep.

His smartphone lit up in the darkness.

"Did you just wake up?" said Chatarra. "We're going to kill the doc soon, so get ready."

"Doc…" Koshimo repeated.

"Laba-Laba."

The plan to kill Suenaga, a member of the *familia*, had been concocted in secret and kept between Valmiro and Chatarra until the night of its execution.

"He was crazy. I kinda liked him for that," Chatarra remarked before ending the call.

52

ömpöhualli-huan-mahtlactli-huan-öme

Since the fall of Los Casasolas, Michitsugu Suenaga had spent more time with Valmiro Casasola than anyone else.

On the day they first met at the *kaki lima* on Mangga Besar Road in Jakarta, Valmiro was just the owner of a cobra satay cart, and Suenaga was merely a low-level organ smuggling coordinator.

Five years and two months had passed since then.

Narco and *médico*—the *choclo* business would not have come together without the both of them. They invented a new form of organ trade and became *corazón traficantes*, a new form of blood capitalism. But the two had never truly shared the same goal at any moment in their partnership.

Gonzalo García and Raúl Alzamora—Valmiro's real desire, hidden behind his many aliases, was to raise funds and muscle to return to Mexico, destroy the Dogo Cartel, and reclaim his *plaza*.

Suenaga planned to station himself on the *Dunia Biru* eventually. He didn't want to extract hearts in the basement of Saiganji, but to work in the state-of-the-art facility hidden on the mega cruise ship, leading an Indonesian staff in heart transplants. He didn't just want to be a black-market doctor. His goal was to be the primary surgeon controlling the entire *choclo* business.

But that would mean living on the ship, and once he left the land behind, he knew that El Cocinero would rewrite the system in Tokyo and Kawasaki to suit his own needs. That was a problem.

The *choclo* business was up and running, and El Cocinero's time as a crucial part had come to an end.

The self-styled Peruvian with a religious obsession with hearts had always been an alien presence. A business localized in Japan needed logic and rationality befitting the modern form of blood capitalism, not over-wrought weapons, a cultlike band of killers, and a Latin American crime family concept. Every time Suenaga heard the man's pet *sicarios* chant "*Somos familia,*" he felt a bit sick to his stomach.

However, the biggest reason that Suenaga gave up on El Cocinero was his treatment of the Zebubs. In order to demonstrate his strength to the Senga-gumi, El Cocinero loosed his *sicarios* on the Zebubs' leader, Tham Hoa. This was an obvious miscalculation. The Zebubs, in fact, was the smarter coalition when it came to the modern form of blood capitalism. An alliance with them was better than destroying them. The Zebubs was a much more rational group than the bloodthirsty hooligans at the auto yard and better suited for the *choclo* business.

El Cocinero didn't care as much about expanding the business as he did raising a paramilitary force. He spent huge sums of cash on weapons and ammunition and was looking into buying a Russian submarine and missiles. The man was clearly insane.

Leaving someone like that behind on land while Suenaga left to be a cardiovascular doctor on the *Dunia Biru* would end predictably. El Cocinero would take over the business.

Suenaga secretly hired a sixteen-year-old Japanese hacker and seventeen-year-old Vietnamese one, both subordinates of the late Tham Hoa. Suenaga convinced the two boys, who were terrified of being executed, to pry into El Cocinero's plans, and he now had a very accurate grasp of what was going to happen to him.

The two hackers came back with a grim report:

El Cocinero's going to send his hitmen to your shelter, and right after

you've finished the heart extraction, they're going to kill you in the sur-
gery room, where there's no escape.

It was just as he'd expected. The odd man out who needed to be removed
was going to remove him first. Suenaga knew that crying to Xin Nan Long
and Guntur Islami for aid would not earn him a prompt helping hand. If
anything, the two organizations considered El Cocinero more in line with
their thinking, and they'd prefer to make use of him over Suenaga.

The doctor would have to transcend both groups. He couldn't just sit
around with his thumb up his ass, waiting to get whacked. If El Cocinero
intended to send his *sicarios* to do the job, Suenaga would have to take
advantage of knowing that. In a sense, it was the perfect opportunity to
give the business a much-needed recalibration.

Once he'd eliminated all the unclean elements, he would remove the
next child's heart, then have one of the staffers take it to the Kawasaki port.
Nextli was sufficient for personal protection.

By the time Suenaga performed the extraction, his surgery partner,
Nomura, would already be dead. He'd have to complete the procedure
single-handed. Common sense stated that a one-man extraction was pro-
hibitively difficult. And perhaps that was true—for a common man.

Suenaga thought of the unprecedented challenge facing him and broke
into a smile.

This is what being a cardiovascular surgeon is all about.

After nine o'clock on the night of Thursday, August 26, footsteps filled
the hallway of the shelter while the children slumbered in their rooms.

All of the men carried golf caddy bags containing barracudas—
Remington M870 shotguns with Salvo 12 silencers. Chatarra's was the
only one with a twelve-gauge slug for deer hunting, rather than pellets.
That was to cut down on unnecessary damage to the surgery room, since
the pellets had a high spread. The other three had the usual double-aught
buck in their shells.

In addition to the barracudas, they'd brought sidearms. Chatarra had a Walther Q4 like Valmiro's, El Mamut had a Glock 17, and El Casco carried a Russian MP-443. Koshimo didn't have a pistol; he stuck his three-foot Aztec *macuahuitl* in the caddy bag with his barracuda.

Valmiro had instructed them to go fully armed. They were supposed to be protecting the *choclo* and had to be prepared for any trouble. Suenaga would be suspicious if they showed up empty-handed.

The gray wall split open as the automatic doors unsealed themselves, revealing a brightly lit surgery room spacious enough to fit right in at any university hospital. Suenaga stood there in a surgical mask, waiting for the four men with their caddy bags. He wore a blue cap and a surgical gown.

"I'm looking forward to this," Chatarra remarked. "I've always wanted to see a pro do a heart extraction."

"I went over this with El Cocinero already," Suenaga said cheerfully as the men walked into the surgery room for the first time. "I told him you just wanted to see blood."

The four observers wore surgical masks—tie-on, not ear loops. They covered their noses and mouths and knotted the strings behind their heads and necks.

Chatarra played along and acted excited, but threw a quick glance at El Loco, who was already in the room. The other doctor was aware of what was going to happen, but he ignored Chatarra and quietly laid out the extraction tools on the cart.

El Mamut and El Casco were trading words with Suenaga in a very natural manner, but Koshimo was silent.

The automatic door behind them was shut tight. It made almost no sound at all. Once it was closed, the personal sensor on the outside shut off, keeping it from reacting to any human presence in the sensor area. At a real hospital, a red sign over the door declaring OPERATION IN PROGRESS would illuminate at this point.

Toxcatl, Koshimo mouthed. *God's sacrifice.*

He felt adrift in a dream. The unpleasant sensation of that long vision still crawled through his body like tiny lizards.

The dream where he had shouted, *"Padre*, you're a liar!"

That dream is watching me carefully now.

Atop the surgical table was a boy wearing a Swedish rechargeable respirator. He was being given an anesthetic.

Koshimo studied the boy's profile under the surgical lights.

"Junta."

He whispered the boy's name. Junta was asleep already; a rest like death. Koshimo felt an itching at his temples that rapidly grew worse until he was assaulted by a headache stronger than anything he'd felt before. It was like having a hole drilled in his skull. He felt dizzy, his ears rang, bile rose to his throat, his heart hammered, his breath seized, and his vision went dark. Koshimo stumbled sidelong into the wall. That was when he saw the other members of the *familia* lying on the floor of the all-white surgery room, too. What was happening? Chatarra had fallen, El Mamut had, too, and El Casco was convulsing. El Loco collapsed by the wall, clawing at his throat, and kicked the tray. Stainless steel instruments and fluid-filled syringes clattered to the floor.

Only Suenaga stood on his feet.

He'd taken off his surgical mask to reveal that he was now wearing a thick, translucent mask. Through his stupor, Koshimo thought they'd been hit with poison gas. He didn't know what "anoxia" was. It would never have occurred to him that Suenaga had rapidly depressurized the sealed operating room and lowered their oxygen tension.

Suenaga was breathing through an oxygen mask connected to a small gas canister. He looked down calmly at Nomura, who'd progressed from breathing difficulty to the agony of cyanosis, and glanced at the number on the oxygen monitor. Based on the blood gas tension, Suenaga estimated that the other men's oxygen saturation (SpO2) had dipped below the 90 percent danger mark to as low as 60 percent. The only safe ones were

Suenaga and the unconscious Junta, who was wearing the rechargeable respirator while under general anesthesia.

If Laba-Laba was spreading poison gas in the room, then Koshimo needed to open the door. He wanted to blast it with the barracuda. With fumbling fingers, he tried to open the zipper on the caddy bag, grabbing feebly at the little metal handle.

Suenaga noticed that El Patíbulo was still moving, and frantically snatched a sharpened German scalpel. He would sever the carotid artery and ensure the giant was dead. But as soon as he took his first step, something grasped his left foot.

It was Chatarra, who'd crawled across the ground to grab his ankle. Suenaga glanced at the oxygen monitor again. The gas tension was even lower now. El Mamut, El Casco, and El Loco had all blacked out, and they were falling headfirst into the abyss of death.

Suenaga shook his head with annoyance. How could there be *two* men still moving in such a low-oxygen environment? They were hardier than the animals used for clinical trials.

He sliced Chatarra's right wrist tendon with the scalpel, but as soon as his left foot was free of the man's grasp, he felt a burning pain in his right. He'd been shot through the knee with a pistol.

Suenaga yelped in pain and fell onto the floor.

"Fucking monster!" he spat, rolling in agony as though he were the one running out of oxygen. It was a total nightmare. Who could manage something as logical and coordinated as hitting a target with a gun when his blood oxygen level was below 60 percent? It was a medical impossibility.

Chatarra's Walther Q4 fired again. The aim was off, so the bullet punctured the drainage bag, spraying heart preservation solution all around.

Suenaga, clinging to Nomura's motionless body, turned back to look, and could scarcely believe what he saw. Chatarra was standing. Suenaga let out a moaning shriek. Chatarra proceeded toward Suenaga, gun pointed, but abruptly toppled forward, like a boxer who'd been struck cleanly on the chin, and fell on top of the heart surgeon. The gun slipped out, but the man's open hand caught Suenaga's throat. Gasping, Suenaga picked up one of the syringes that had fallen off of Nomura's cart and jammed it into Chatarra's neck, sending the cardioplegic solution that was meant for Junta into the monstrous man's bloodstream.

While Suenaga and Chatarra were locked in mortal battle, Koshimo managed to open the caddy bag and pull the barracuda out. It felt heavier than a two-hundred-kilogram barbell. His oxygen level was even lower. Koshimo put all of his strength into the foregrip and pulled the trigger. Once was all he could manage.

The double-aught buck pellets destroyed the sealed door. The air pressure differential between the two sides caused an explosion, and the door was wrenched as though struck by a car, sending in gusts of fresh air.

Through dull eyes, Koshimo watched a shadow leap silently to the edge of the surgical cart, as nimble as a monkey. He looked like a child but also like an adult. He was staring closely at the sleeping Junta. There was a brilliant green feather headdress atop his brow, his face was painted yellow and black, a jaguar pelt was wrapped around his waist, he carried a shield covered in snakeskin, and his sandals were woven, red-painted deer hide.

He lifted his head and turned his eyes to Koshimo; they were not human. Two obsidian lights burned like dark flames.

The god stared at Koshimo. Like the quetzal bird, he nimbly inclined his head from one side to the other.

When Koshimo opened his eyes, he was lying on his back, staring up at the ceiling of the surgery room. He abruptly fell into a violent coughing fit, then breathed in as desperately as someone reaching the shore just before they drowned. His head and limbs felt as though someone were standing on them.

Very slowly, Koshimo managed to get to his feet and walk, but he stumbled and had to place his hands on the surgical cart. He reached out to rest a hand on Junta's chest. A faint heartbeat pulsed against his fingertips.

He wished someone in the *familia* would tell him if it was okay to remove Junta's respirator. Looking around the room, the only man still alive was the one who was no longer in the *familia*.

Chatarra's dead weight of over one hundred and fifty kilograms pinned Suenaga against the ground. He was reaching, desperately trying to grab the Walther Q4 that had slipped from the dead man's hand.

"If I take it out, will he stop breathing?" Koshimo asked, pointing at the oxygen mask over Junta's face.

Suenaga nodded. There was no autonomous breathing under general anesthesia. If the chargeable respirator was removed now, the boy would die, and his heart couldn't be shipped off to its recipient.

Koshimo checked the drip feed tube and found that the solution was empty. "Can I take this out?" he asked.

Suenaga didn't reply. Koshimo pointed the barracuda at him. He nodded without a word.

Koshimo removed the tape holding the IV syringe in Junta's arm and pulled out the needle.

He hoisted the caddy bag holding the barracuda onto his left shoulder, then picked up Junta and the respirator in his right hand. Koshimo started to leave the operation room, but stopped himself. He still feared the god. But this wasn't a *teocalli*, and Toxcatl was not being celebrated at this time. Of that much, he was certain.

But if this is *a real Toxcatl, that means I've stolen Tezcatlipoca's sacrifice.*

He should have at least prepared a gift to quell the rage of the highest god. Koshimo put Junta and the respirator down on the floor, opened his caddy bag, and took out the *macuahuitl*.

Suenaga noticed Koshimo approaching, opened his mouth, and screamed into the oxygen mask. He writhed and struggled under Chatarra's corpse, wiggling his head violently back and forth. Koshimo loomed over him.

"Wait," Suenaga stammered. His muffled due to the mask. "If I'm gone, who's going to take out the boy's heart? You won't be able to offer it to your god. If that happens, your beloved *padre* will suffer righteous wrath, as will you."

Koshimo considered this briefly. "Then tell me the name of the god."

Suenaga couldn't answer him.

Koshimo gazed at Chatarra's broad back, motionless atop Suenaga, then he glanced at El Loco, El Mamut, and El Casco. He could see their faces. All of them were dead and still, with their eyes open.

Koshimo lifted the *macuahuitl*. Suenaga spoke in Spanish, a desperate last attempt.

"No lo hagas. Somos familia."

"We're not family anymore," Koshimo replied in Japanese.

Suenaga's face distorted with hatred.

"Fucking kid."

Those were the last words he ever spoke.

Koshimo was exhausted from the ordeal, and it took four swings of the *macuahuitl* to finally cut off Suenaga's head.

Xia was transporting the icebox for the heart to the surgery room when she heard something rupture far down the hallway and stopped what she was doing. It was muffled by the usual layers of security doors, so she couldn't be certain, but it definitely sounded like an explosion. She set down the icebox on the floor and listened cautiously.

When nothing happened, she headed carefully down the hall and suddenly ran into Koshimo. He was carrying a child, respirator and all, and in one hand dangled the severed head of Laba-Laba, wearing a mask.

Without taking her eyes off Koshimo, Xia reached for the tactical knife on her belt. She also had her special carbon steel police baton.

Nextli stood in Koshimo's way. All around her, he saw a dark black aura of murder. "Move," he demanded. He wanted to get out of this underground place.

"Not until you explain yourself. That boy—" Xia said, pretending to start a conversation before abruptly charging at Koshimo. A step away from him, she tumbled head over heels to his right. Xia stabbed the young man's left foot with the knife and pulled it out as she fell. The CQC training she'd received during her tenure with the police force told her to attack the larger man's feet first. Then she drew her carbon steel baton in preparation for her next movement. However, something struck her in the face.

It was Suenaga's head, which Koshimo had swung with full force. A living face collided with a dead one; the impact was strong enough to fracture Suenaga's skull. Xia's glasses went flying, and her eye socket and cheekbone shattered. She rolled to the other side of the hallway as though thrown by a car. It gave her more than a concussion; her neck was broken.

Koshimo scooped up her tactical knife from the floor. He brought the knife up to his face before he'd even checked out his wound, just to see the blade and handle up close. It was Damascus tungsten, and the tan-colored handle had a thumb hole in it. The knife did not come from the workshop.

He was carrying Junta, the respirator, Suenaga's head, and the caddy bag with the weapons inside, and this was all while hobbling on an injured foot. Koshimo was looking for the stairs to the surface, but didn't know where to find them. He made his way down the hallway, then back, and had retraced his path several times when he heard a child scream.

Koshimo turned around and saw Yasuzu Uno.

"Malinal," Koshimo said, his eyes wide. "Yasuzu…?"

Yasuzu had escorted a six-year-old girl to the restroom and came out to a horrible, shocking sight.

An eerie, enormous man, holding a severed head that was still wearing an oxygen mask. She recognized the bloodied face on the grisly trophy. He wasn't wearing his glasses, but it was definitely the doctor. Farther down the hallway, Xia appeared to be collapsed on the ground.

Yasuzu stared up at the giant. She couldn't speak. It was the young man working at the workshop in Odasakae. In her mind, she screamed, *Why are you here? What did you do? And who is that over your…*

Junta?

* * *

Xia had assigned Yasuzu the night shift. When the little girl had woken up, Yasuzu escorted her to the bathroom, and was returning her to bed. The child's scream brought Yasuzu back to her senses. She grabbed the girl's hand and started to run, but Koshimo's long arm stretched out and snatched her by her hair, dragging her backward.

Yasuzu let go of the girl and pushed her tiny back.

"Run! Go back to your room and lock the door!"

If the young man was going to go after the little girl, then Yasuzu was prepared to die trying to stop him. She was alarmed at how quickly she came to that decision—but when she saw Koshimo's eyes glaring at her, she found herself overwhelmed by his presence. He looked even larger than the last time she'd seen him. Her heart was torn between the desire to save the child and the fear telling her to flee. Tears welled up in her eyes, and her body shivered.

It didn't make sense. Why was Koshimo here, with the doctor's head, and why was Junta with him? They'd just approved an elderly Australian couple to take the boy in as a foster son. Junta had been sent off last night. Why was he still here? He wasn't sick, but he was wearing what looked like an artificial respiration device and seemed to be unconscious. It wasn't adding up. None of it fit together. Still, Yasuzu had to protect herself one way or another. She had no weapons of any kind, though.

"I want to get out of here," Koshimo said, trying to keep things calm, pointing Xia's knife at Yasuzu. "Drive the car for me."

In his hand, the weapon looked as tiny as a butter knife.

That day, the rental car waiting at the Saiganji parking lot was a white Toyota Alphard, like the first time Yasuzu took Koshimo to the workshop. The license plate number was different, but the coincidence felt like a distillation of her poor fortune. Yasuzu gripped the wheel, sniffled back snot, swallowed, and turned on the engine. Her eyes were red.

"Where should I go?"

The severed human head—which belonged to someone she knew— simply rolled around on the floor at Koshimo's feet in the passenger seat. He didn't seem to care. He was holding a huge gun on his lap, the likes of which Yasuzu had never seen. This was insane to her. Junta was resting in the back, asleep, wearing the respirator.

Koshimo told her where to go.

Now that he no longer believed in Toxcatl, the only destination was the workshop. As the car pulled out of the Saiganji parking lot, Koshimo placed a call to Pablo; he'd gone home for the night. Koshimo told him, "I took one of the kids out of the shelter. I think *Padre* will be angry. I'm going to the workshop now."

Valmiro puffed on a cigar at his desk in the Sakuramoto office. He kept his eyes on the calendar tacked to the wall. It was Thursday, August 26, 2021 AD by the Gregorian reckoning. That was the year of Nine-House, the tenth month, in the *trecena* of Water, the day of Two-Dog.

They should have finished working on the kid with the type-O blood by now, but Chatarra had not checked in yet. There was no report from El Loco, either.

Valmiro blew out a large mouthful of smoke, then picked up his phone and checked Chatarra's location. Saiganji, Ota, Tokyo. His coordinates were right there on the map. Same for El Loco. El Mamut and El Casco were in the shelter, too. Even Suenaga was there. It was time for the heart to be shipped out, but no one had moved from the underground facility.

Except for one.

Koshimo's coordinates placed him in Kawasaki.

Valmiro became a statue in the darkness. He didn't even breathe. *What the hell are you doing, El Chavo?*

Pablo was already waiting for Koshimo at the workshop and wasted no time hearing him out. When he saw the bloodied head of Suenaga, he did not accuse Koshimo of anything, nor did he try to call the police.

That was shocking to Yasuzu. What was wrong with the men at this workshop? Were they both insane, homicidal maniacs?

"Did you know?" Pablo asked Yasuzu, his face stern.

"Know what?" She had no idea what he was asking. She was the one with all the questions here.

"We don't have time. Be honest with me," Pablo insisted. "How much do you know about this business arrangement?"

It was almost impossible for Yasuzu to believe the things that Pablo told her. It was a story of criminal acts on a shocking scale. Would he really tell lies like this to protect his apprentice-turned-killer? It seemed to her that Pablo's expression was nothing but pleading desperation.

Extracted hearts, a cruise ship carrying the recipient children of the ultrawealthy—all of it was beyond imagining. And if she were to accept the tale he was telling her, then all the children she'd brought to the shelter, played with, helped bathe, tucked into bed, and sent off to new families were...

It wasn't true. It couldn't be. Yasuzu closed her eyes. This knifemaker was a murderer, just like Koshimo, and he was enjoying filling her head with falsehoods. They looked at the severed head of a dead man and thought nothing of it. Of course they'd lie...

Taking custody only of undocumented children, oversized salary, a different rental car each day, Junta still at the shelter when he was supposedly sent abroad, wearing a hospital gown and put under—the doctors coming to the shelter, back-alley doctors—fresh hearts—

Junta still slept atop the blanket Koshimo had placed on the workbench.

"Get that thing away from him. Please," Yasuzu cried.

Koshimo promptly did as she said and took Suenaga's head off the table, placing it on the floor.

She screwed up her face and said to Pablo, "If this is all true, what happens if I tell the police?"

"You're going to call the cops here?" he replied.

Yasuzu just stared back at him with eyes reddened and puffy from crying.

"Koshimo," Pablo began. He was starting to panic, but did his best to remain calm. "If your *padre* got into a gunfight with the police here, how many people would die?"

Koshimo had just finished cleaning the stab wound on his left foot. He put his right hand on the worktable and began to count the fingers. In his mind he envisioned a barracuda spitting fire and police officers falling. He started with his thumb and counted up to his pinky. Then he paused for a while, and continued counting by extending the fingers again, starting from the pinky.

Pablo covered his face with his hands and froze. He didn't want any more deaths. Eventually, he dropped his hands, stared at the lights in the ceiling, and exhaled. He looked at the sleeping boy on the table. He thought of El Cocinero's eyes, all the C-bones, and all the skulls.

"Please. Save this boy," Pablo pleaded, walking toward Yasuzu. "Take him to the Kawasaki Police Station in your car, as fast as you can. It's only a mile and a half, so it should only take ten minutes. Pick him up, rush into the station, and plead for protection for the both of you. Got that? Kawasaki Station. Not one of those police boxes on the corner."

"I'll go, too," said Koshimo.

"Koshimo, if you go with her…"

Yasuzu could see the pain on Pablo's face. She knew what he meant to say. It was a bizarre sensation to her. Koshimo was clearly a murderer, but she didn't feel any sordid evil in his being. Perhaps that was what made him so terrifying.

Pablo opened the map over his worktable. He used a marking pencil to circle Kawasaki Station, explaining the directions to Yasuzu: under the bridge for the Nambu Line, then onto Kyomachi-dori Street until she crossed Dai-ichi Keihin. "Just gun it straight for the station's parking lot," Pablo told her. "As fast as you can. Got that?"

They heard a noise and turned around. It was coming from Junta, who was now writhing atop Koshimo's workstation. His eyes were closed, but the eyeballs were twitching under his lids. In his unconscious daze, he was reaching up to take the oxygen mask off.

Yasuzu rushed over to the boy, who was waking from the anesthesia, while Pablo walked to the corner of the workshop. He moved aside the bench holding the belt grinder that he and Koshimo used, examined the dusty floorboards, blew the sawdust away, then pulled up the boards and retrieved a smartphone and cash from the space underneath. The cash was split between yen and American dollars, each fastened with a money clip.

He beckoned Koshimo over.

"Once you've seen them off at the police station, you need to get out of here, Koshimo."

He pressed the phone and cash into Koshimo's hands, then wrote down a phone number on a scrap of paper.

It was the contact information for a deckhand on a container ship that regularly stopped at Kawasaki Port—an escape route he'd prepared in case he ever needed to flee the dirty business he'd found himself in. *Someday.* Pablo closed his eyes. *That day will never come for me. But that's all right.*

"Call him, then get on the container ship bound for Panama," Pablo instructed, pointing at the number on the paper. "You can speak Spanish, so you'll be able to get by."

"What about you?"

Pablo peered up into Koshimo's face and beamed. He would have hugged his only apprentice, but there wasn't time. "Get going."

Valmiro slowed down fourteen meters from the workshop, turned off his lights, and watched. No one was visible. There was light coming through the windows.

When the Jeep Wrangler was about seven meters from the shop, Valmiro killed the engine.

He grabbed his barracuda, got out of the Jeep, and knocked on the workshop door before stepping away and peering through the window. He didn't see anyone moving. Music was playing. When the song finished, a woman started speaking. It was the radio.

Valmiro went back to the door and put his hand on the knob. It was unlocked. He opened it and proceeded through, keeping the barracuda at a forty-five-degree angle.

Pablo was at his worktable, wearing a black-and-red plaid flannel shirt and sipping a fresh cup of coffee. The smell of beans was rich and bold.

Valmiro pointed the barracuda at Pablo. "Turn off the radio," he ordered in Spanish.

Instead, Pablo lowered the volume. He looked at the gun barrel. The silencer was large and blocky. Aside from the dot sight and flashlight accessories, it was identical to the shotgun Koshimo carried.

"It's over, El Cocinero," said Pablo. "The day of reckoning has come."

Koshimo's smartphone, which Valmiro had called repeatedly, was sitting on the worktable.

"Where is Koshimo?" he asked.

"I don't know," Pablo replied.

"What did he do?"

"That's a strange question, El Cocinero," answered Pablo wryly. "All I did was show him how to make knives. You were the one who taught him to kill."

The floorboards creaked beneath Valmiro's heavy boots. He spotted Suenaga's head on the floor, and walked over to pick it up and examine the cut. Flecks of black were stuck in the dried blood along the jagged flesh of his neck—obsidian shards.

"Where is Koshimo?" Valmiro repeated.

Pablo didn't answer. Valmiro placed his finger on the trigger of the barracuda, and Pablo closed his eyes.

* * *

Valmiro pumped the foregrip of the shotgun, expelling the empty shell. He picked it up off the floor and tucked it into his shirt pocket.

He left the workshop and was just reaching for his car door when he got a call from a Chinese man, Cao Xu—though he had three other aliases. He was one of Nextli's subordinates, and worked for Hao. His job was to circle ahead on the bridge along the *choclo* transport route and wait. If there was a car accident, construction traffic, or any other anomaly, he was supposed to contact El Cocinero and his *sicarios*. By all appearances, Cao Xu was simply going on a night walk over the bridge, wearing a tracksuit and an Apple Watch, carrying his smartphone, a fake ID, and no weapons of any kind.

"I was just walking over the bridge and saw a stopped minivan that came from the Kawasaki side," he said in English. "It struck the fence between the road and the pedestrian lane. A white Toyota Alphard, not significantly damaged. The plate number is…"

Cao Xu started the number with the sound *wa*. Valmiro knew that in this country, if the plate number was preceded by *wa*, then it was a rental car.

One of the rentals the people at the shelter use, he thought. *They might have just ditched it, but it's worth going to see.*

He turned on the Jeep Wrangler and examined the night sky through the windshield. The moon was out, and he swiftly found the Summer Triangle among the stars. He'd always been good at finding that one.

Valmiro headed for the bridge.

The Rokugo Bridge, a quarter-mile span, where the Dai-ichi Keihin crossed the Tama River, connecting Ota and Kawasaki.

During her short drive, Yasuzu found all kinds of memories flooding her mind.

The nursery school she quit, the screams and insults from the parents and guardians at the orientation meeting, the paper cup full of orange juice that hit her, the towns all over the country she visited in her leather jacket, the false smiles the violently abusive parents wore, and lastly, the children without papers—barely given a single decent meal in a day and wearing the same clothes for weeks at a time.

She passed a paid parking lot with a green LED sign indicating vacancy. Streetlights approached and vanished. There were no people walking along the road that ran parallel to the elevated Nambu Line.

We'll reach the station soon, Yasuzu thought. *Whatever the truth is, the boy will be safe once he's there. The police will ask me all sorts of questions. I have to tell them everything I know.*

An eerie calmness overtook her. A very different person from the one who tried to protect the little girl in the shelter hallway from Koshimo began to emerge.

If I was an accomplice in terrible crimes, then the detectives might decide to search my apartment. Of course they will. And in my room there's...

Cocaine.

The word hit Yasuzu like a bolt of lightning, and she yanked on the wheel. The tires screeched, and the Alphard shook.

If she got arrested, she wouldn't have a supply anymore. Anxiety bubbled up within her, until that was the only thought in her mind. She couldn't imagine a version of herself without that white snow.

Koshimo was alarmed that she wasn't going through the intersection. The Alphard suddenly revved its engine and raced north on Dai-ichi Keihin. The van passed under the Nambu Line bridge and accelerated.

Motoki Intersection, Kawasaki Fire Department, Kawasaki Ward Office—she kept her foot on the pedal, but she didn't even know where she was going at this point.

"Where are you going?" asked Koshimo.

She ran a red light, earning a horn as long as a steam whistle, but she kept her eyes dead ahead.

"Where are you going?!" shouted Koshimo. It was loud enough to rouse Junta, who was groaning and stirring in the back seat.

I can't get away from Padre. Koshimo was certain. *He'll catch us and take out my heart.*

The Alphard sped onto the Rokugo Bridge over the Tama going fifty miles an hour, which was over the speed limit. They were halfway across when Yasuzu suddenly slammed on the brakes. The tires slid and squealed as the Alphard fishtailed and knocked over a red-and-white-striped guard post. It crossed underneath the border sign listing the Ota Ward in Tokyo and Kawasaki in Kanagawa. The car slammed into the fence separating the road from the pedestrian lane and came to a stop. A headlight was cracked, and the front bumper was smashed.

Yasuzu pressed her forehead to the wheel between her hands and began to cry.

Junta was looking out the window, clinging to the back seat.

It was all Koshimo could do just to watch Yasuzu sob and mutter. What could he do? Not only did they go the opposite direction from Kawasaki Police Station; this location was dangerous. This was the route the hearts from the shelter traveled to the port.

Koshimo didn't know how to drive. A taxi was coming down the other way. He thought about stopping the cab so the two of them could get away, but *Padre* might find them on the way. He would shoot the barracuda through the taxi door and windshield, leaving a dead driver behind.

A sudden inkling struck the alarmed Koshimo—a premonition that *Padre* approaching.

He's catching up. We're doomed.

Not going to Kawasaki Station had spelled the end of their escape.

Koshimo was desperate now. His mind had been splitting apart from lack of oxygen in the surgery room underground, and it was being riven again now. He opened the car door and sucked in fresh air. Pieces of the headlight were scattered across the ground. The Tama was dark. The river where he rode on the canoe with Pablo. Night and wind.

Xochiyaoyotl. *Flower war.*

There was something within that word. It just popped into his head. Koshimo shut his eyes, diving to the riverbed of his memories.

The night he first used his *macuahuitl* against Tham Hoa, it didn't kill his target very quickly, so he thought he'd failed to make a proper warrior's weapon. Yet *Padre* had disagreed.

"No, this is good."

"In the xochiyaoyotl, *if you kill your opponent, you don't have a sacrifice for your god. How will the heart of a dead man beat? This is very important, El Chavo. The heart of your sacrifice must beat. Our god is the one who eats that heart, not us."*

Suddenly, Koshimo realized he had the answer. He knew how to save them.

That's it.

He bobbed his head up and down. Then he told Yasuzu his idea.

Leaving Junta behind in the car alone was even more unthinkable for Yasuzu than quitting coke. The ones staying in the car and leaving were backward. Leave Junta in the Alphard so the two adults could watch from a safe distance? Absolutely not. If there was a terrible man chasing after them, abandoning Junta was tantamount to killing him herself.

Koshimo opened the caddy bag and took out the cocobolo *macuahuitl.* It was stained with Laba-Laba's blood. He should have used the barracuda, but bullets were not the right tool for the coming *xochiyaoyotl.*

The sight of that ghastly weapon indicated to Yasuzu that Koshimo meant to fight, not to abandon Junta. The monster he called *Padre* and Pablo called El Cocinero. *But who's the real monster?* Yasuzu wondered, eyeing the weapon in Koshimo's hand. It looked like a rowing paddle with black razors lining the edges—and traces of blood.

She refused to listen to any of Koshimo's explanations, so he gave up and dragged Yasuzu out of the driver's seat. She struggled but did not scream for help. She'd chosen not to go to the police.

Xochiyaoyotl. Toxcatl. Koshimo could hear Valmiro's voice. He looked into the eyes of the boy alone in the back seat, nodded, and spoke a silent reassurance.

"*Padre* can't kill you. He won't shoot. He's only going to check inside the car to see."

Valmiro came to Rokugo Bridge in the Jeep Wrangler and illuminated the Toyota Alphard with his headlights. He pulled over to the left and stopped with a car's worth of space between them, lowered the side window, and listened.

After a minute, he quietly opened the door and got out. He kept the barracuda vertical, flush with his body. The gun's shape was invisible in the dark of night. He only pointed it forward as he came around the side of the Alphard. It was point-blank range, easily enough to shoot through the door. If a traitor inside the car shot at him now, he wouldn't react in time. The *sicarios* Valmiro had trained would never have allowed an enemy to get so close.

He peered carefully into the car. The driver's seat was empty. Koshimo wasn't inside. There was a child in a surgical gown in the back seat. A chargeable respirator sat nearby.

Valmiro couldn't see the kid's face, but it was clearly the *choclo* patient. Rather than opening the door, he peered across the bridge. Then he went up to the railing and looked for the river shore. He was staring into darkness. He could hear the Tama rushing underneath. Someone was standing on the Kawasaki shore. Based on the silhouette, it looked like a woman.

That was when he sensed something behind him.

Valmiro whirled.

Koshimo had been hanging from the railing on the other side of the bridge, and had pulled himself back up. He was holding a *macuahuitl* in his left hand, and slowly approached Valmiro. There was a center divider between them. Koshimo stripped off his T-shirt, exposing the stepped pyramid tattooed on his chest to the moonlight.

El Polvo had once stood at the peak of the narco world, and he was sharp enough to distinguish someone who was prepared to die in a fight from someone trying to act tough. Such finely honed power of observation wasn't necessary here. There were no bluffs in Koshimo's actions, which made his betrayal all the more obvious.

"El Chavo," Valmiro called out, as Koshimo approached the divider. "Don't you have a gun? No barracuda?"

"No," Koshimo replied.

"I'll give you a pistol," Valmiro offered. He took the Walther Q4 off his belt and tossed it at the young man. "Don't force me to kill you in cold blood. Pick it up and do the job yourself."

Koshimo glanced at the handgun at his feet, but ultimately ignored it. "It's a *xochiyaoyotl*, *Padre*," he said. "If you shoot me, my *yollotl* will stop beating. The sacrifice's *yollotl* must beat. It is the god who eats the *yollotl*, not us. You told me that."

Valmiro said nothing. He simply pointed the barracuda. In that instant, Koshimo raced toward the divider and up, launching himself into the air.

He pulled back the *macuahuitl*, soaring so far that he was above Valmiro without ever touching the ground.

It was a remarkable leap.

Valmiro looked up and stood stunned, as though struck by lightning. He didn't see a human being. It was Tezcatlipoca, among the moon and stars, his long hair flying. Why had he lost his brothers and family, been chased out of Mexico, and come all the way to this island in the far East? The epiphany was instantaneous. It was not for vengeance, but to meet the Aztec god. It was to offer up his flesh to him. He was entranced by feral beauty beyond measure. Terror engulfed Valmiro, and in his despair he tasted joy. He pulled the trigger, and the barracuda belched fire. He knew he could not win. All Valmiro wanted to do was prove that he was a warrior in the presence of his god.

He could hear his beloved *abuelita*'s ragged croak.

"Titlacauan. We Are His Slaves."

As the *macuahuitl* descended, Koshimo allowed fate to decide whether this single blow would kill *Padre*. That was the *xochiyaoyotl*. He would be kept alive until his sacrifice, or he would die.

The obsidian blades split Valmiro's hair and scalp, and the cocobolo wood dug into his skull. Valmiro looked into the shining eyes of the jaguar and felt its breath slip between glistening fangs like hot smoke.

They collided, toppled over the railing of the bridge, and plunged into the Tama River. There was a large splash, then silence. Yasuzu had been watching the bridge from the riverbank; she rushed back over and ran for the car. She started to get into the Alphard stuck in the fence, then eyed the Jeep Wrangler behind it. The key was still in the ignition.

She picked up Junta's little body—he was vomiting as a side effect of the anesthesia wearing off—got into the Jeep, and turned on the engine.

However, she didn't make for Kawasaki. Instead, Yasuzu drove straight on into Tokyo.

When the car reached the end of the bridge, Yasuzu felt as though she'd accomplished something of her own devising for the first time in her life. She would do anything to protect Junta. That was her only wish. And to see that done…

Yasuzu gripped the wheel and wiped tears away, only for more to come. How many people had died?

She looked forward, pressed the gas pedal, and gave herself a newfound piece of encouragement.

I can quit cocaine.

The dark river that divided two cities passed beneath them, as easy as that. Like the lost calendar, no one saw the two people who fell from the bridge.

A lost calendar.

According to the Julian calendar, the Aztec kingdom fell on August 13, 1521.

Today's date on the Gregorian calendar, August 26, 2021, if converted to Julian, would've been August 13, 2021—a coincidence that even Valmiro had been ignorant of.

The night they fell into the river was exactly five centuries after the fall of the Aztecs.

Days Beyond the Calendar

nemontemi

The prison built in the Mexican state of Sonora—located in the most brutal desert on the planet—housed 1,277 criminals serving sentences. Most of them were narcos, with a smattering of murderers for pleasure or personal gain.

The building was surrounded by armored vehicles twenty-four hours a day, and even if a prisoner were to miraculously escape, nothing but the forbidding Sonoran desert awaited him. It was impossible to survive without equipment.

Domingo Echevarría was just finishing a bland lunch in the prison cafeteria. Sitting next to Domingo was a man they called El Profesor. He was serving a life sentence for killing thirty-eight middle-school-aged boys. He was alive only because Mexico had outlawed the death penalty.

El Profesor was quite familiar with the thin Argentinian immigrant sitting beside him. There wasn't a prisoner in the place who didn't know that man.

A murderer whose body count was far beyond his own. The man who challenged the unparalleled ferocity of Los Casasolas, stole their *plaza*, and drove them into extinction.

Domingo Echevarría was the kingpin of the Sonoran prison.

By always starting his meal after Domingo, El Profesor demonstrated his silent respect for the king and his submission.

Two years had passed since a SEMAR special forces operation successfully arrested Domingo Echevarría, leader of the Dogo Cartel.

The major members of the cartel were spread out to prisons in various states. Without their leadership, the cartel's remaining forces split into three factions that proceeded to wage war on one another. Each gang pushed its legitimacy by claiming Domingo would return to lead it.

Sunlight flooded into the cafeteria through a special skylight that blocked the blazing heat of the desert. The prisoners ate their breakfast in silence. Their forks and spoons were covered with rounded yellow silicon rubber so that they looked like children's toys, preventing them from being used as lethal weapons.

A man walked next to Domingo as he left the room and clacked his teeth three times. That was a signal that he had information to give.

After-breakfast walks were performed in small groups. Domingo's group followed tape guidelines laid down on the gymnasium floor unerringly. You were not allowed to go outside the lines, because prison guards armed with assault rifles were watching from every direction. They called it a walk because you were walking, but that was as far as the description went. The only things to see were the ceiling, walls, floor, and gun muzzles.

A man named La Mandíbula casually approached Domingo. He got his name from the time he was hit by a shotgun blast and lost a third of his lower jaw.

"Domingo," La Mandíbula said as they walked through the gym, "El Polvo's been killed."

For once, Domingo's expression changed. He was startled to hear a name he hadn't in years. *He was still alive?*

"Where'd he die?" he asked.

"In Japan. The Japanese asked the Americans for help, and the DEA confirmed it. It's him."

"Who got him?"

"I don't know. But according to the Chinese, it was his own son."

Domingo said nothing. He stared at the tape on the floor. A guard warned him not to stop walking. He resumed pacing along the white line, and was coming to a boring, familiar curve when he questioned, "What happened to the son?"

"No information," replied La Mandíbula.

That was the end of their conversation. After one more lap of the gym along the white tape lines, the guards informed them that morning walk time was over.

A mother walked alongside her eight-year-old daughter, carrying a bundle of goods she'd bought at the home improvement store. The shopping mall parking lot was huge, and it was a long walk to the car. At three o'clock on a Sunday in Naha, Okinawa, the temperature was at its peak, causing heat haze over the asphalt and making the outlines of cars appear to melt into one amorphous blob.

"I should have parked closer to the entrance," the mother griped.

"Yeah," the girl agreed. "You always park too far away, Mom."

They both wore wide-brimmed hats, and the mother sported sunglasses. She opened the back trunk of the car, which was hot enough to cause burns, and placed the objects she bought into a tote bag. She started to push the door down, but stopped herself, letting it lift again so she could inspect her purchases. The mother had forgotten to buy dirt for the decorative plants. She sighed and looked up at the sky. It was too hot for the birds to bother flying. The only things shielding the Earth were a few measly clouds.

"Wait here for a few minutes," she told her daughter. "I need to go back and buy dirt for the everfresh."

She unlocked the door for her daughter, started the engine, and turned on the air-conditioning. They'd had to fix the AC twice already. To prevent the girl from getting heat sickness, the mother lowered the passenger side window just a little.

"The doors are locked, okay? Don't open them if anyone comes by," she warned, taking her hat off briefly to wipe away the sweat on her forehead. Then she hurried back toward the store.

Why didn't she just drive the car closer to the entrance? the child wondered. *And I'm not in kindergarten anymore. I can open the window on my own. If I'm afraid of getting heat sick, I can just open the door and get out.* But she knew that if she talked back, her mother would get upset, and they'd waste more time. She was always sloppy like that. The eight-year-old reached for the plastic bottle in the drink holder and swallowed the warm water inside. Through the windshield, she could see her mother's form wavering in the heat until it disappeared into the store.

A truck drove into the parking lot and took a spot about twenty yards behind the car. She watched it through the side mirror. Two men were in the truck—one got out of the passenger side.

The girl was astonished by his size. The colossal man wore a black T-shirt, and his arms were covered in tattoos. They made his limbs look purple from elbows to wrists. His hair went past his shoulders and was tied into a number of braids. He limped a bit on his left side as he walked, and his skin was a bit too dark for him to be Japanese.

He might be a Marine, the girl thought. Her teacher had been very clear during class, instructing the students not to approach the American soldiers when alone. She wasn't sure this man was a Marine, though. They didn't have men with hair that long.

The girl held her breath as he grew larger and larger in the side mirror. *Got to check the lock. Window. Must close window.* She was about to press the button to raise the passenger side window when she realized with great alarm that the giant man was looking right at her through the crack. She started to scream, but no sound came out of her open mouth.

"Are you Pablo's daughter?" Koshimo asked.

She didn't say anything. For a moment, she saw a glimpse of her father's face in this man's, despite the total lack of similarity. It had been three years since he died.

The girl clenched her hands, shut her mouth, and stared back at the man. She'd never seen someone with such clear, transparent eyes before. The black of his pupils ran far deeper than her father's, more pristine. However, it carried an indescribably strange light. They were somewhat like an animal's eyes, but not exactly.

When the terrified girl said nothing, Koshimo took out an envelope full of cash and tried sticking it through the gap in the doorframe and the top of the windowpane, like shoving a package through a mail slot. The heavy envelope landed on the girl's lap inside the car. He did this two more times.

After the envelopes, Koshimo slowly lowered a carved wooden pendant above the girl's head. It was shaped like a combination of spirals and lines, with a piece of obsidian embedded in the center and surrounded by bits of jade and emerald. The object hung on a yellow string, spinning to catch the light and reflect its colors, black and green. Koshimo released the cord, and the pendant dropped into the girl's hands.

"Do you...," the girl finally managed to say. "Do you know my dad?"

He nodded.

"Can I tell Mom about you?"

Koshimo gazed into her eyes again. After a moment of thought, he leaned closer to the window. "The night and wind cannot be seen," he said. "We were probably dreaming."

She considered this. There was something about the giant man that made her think she wasn't really looking at him. It felt like she was floating in a dream. The girl blinked, then gazed at the wooden pendant. There was writing on the back. ***Koshimo y Pablo***. At the sight of her father's name, she stopped breathing and closed her eyes. Thunder rolled in the distance.

A gust of wind blew through the parking lot, and the girl opened her eyes. The wind howled. She could see her mother coming back. The sudden wind buffeted her head-on, knocking her hat off. She turned to chase after the dancing thing. The girl checked the side mirror, but the huge man with the limp had vanished, as had the truck.

Look for an eagle atop a cactus,
eating a snake,
and that is where you shall flourish.

"What century is this in the white man's calendar?" Libertad asked the four.

"The twentieth," three of them replied. A moment later, Duilio copied his older brothers' answer.

"That's right," said Libertad. "The white man's time and Aztec time are very different, but just about eight hundred years ago, in the twelfth century, the Aztecs lived on a little island in the middle of a lake. There were herons there, *aztatl*, so they called it Aztlan. And the ones who lived on the island were the Azteca, the people of the heron's land.

"Then one day, a *tlamacazqui* heard the voice of Huitzilopochtli giving him a command, and from there, the Aztecs left their home in search of a new home. Huitzilopochtli is another form of Tezcatlipoca, and is his brother.

"The Aztecs wandered through the wilderness. They were poor and had few belongings, so everywhere they went, the people said, 'Here come strangers that no one knows.' If they tried to stop and raise a village, fights with the neighbors broke out, and they were driven back into the wilderness to wander.

"The Aztec warriors were headstrong and more powerful than any other tribe, but their equipment was old. They had only shabby clubs and shields to use. On top of that, they were hungry. They faced their foes regardless and were struck down and forced to flee. Their opponents had swords and long spears and carried shields made of animal skin stretched over firm wood frames.

"They traveled and traveled, but could not find a new home, and, exhausted at last, they went to the king of Culhuacán, who was descended from the Toltecs, and begged him for land.

"But now it's time for bed, boys. That's all for tonight. We'll continue the story tomorrow."

"Listen closely now.

"The king of Culhuacán gave the Aztecs a dry and desolate land, just like all the ones they'd traveled through. It was full of rocks and rattlesnakes. You see, he merely wanted to exile the Aztecs and get them out of his way. This was the closest thing to doing so.

"The Aztecs were trusting, however, and they were delighted that the king of Culhuacán had considered them worthy of being given a home. They ate the snakes and drank their blood, ate the scorpions and cactus fruit, and let their tired bones rest.

"Seeing the Aztecs living happily among the snakes and scorpions, the king of Culhuacán began to worry. He wondered if a proper exile would have been better.

"The oblivious Aztecs fought with other nations for the sake of the king and showed themselves to be alarmingly strong. Their warriors were utterly fearless as long as they had something to eat and a place to rest. They made use of weapons they stole from their foes. As thanks for being acknowledged, the Aztecs gave all of the gold and jewels they won in battle to the king.

"One day, the palace received a great load of human ears. The Aztecs had taken them from their prisoners. Instead of offering them to the gods, they gave them to the king of Culhuacán. Displeased, he ordered his men to take the ears and dispose of them in the mountains.

"Eventually, the Aztecs heard that the king was unhappy with their gift of prisoners' ears. They never offered him a pile of ears again.

"Well, boys, it's time to get into bed. That's all for tonight. We'll continue the story tomorrow."

"Listen to me closely, boys.

"The Aztecs behaved themselves well, and the king of Culhuacán was very relieved. He was so allayed that when an envoy came from the Aztecs and said politely, 'For the night before the festival, we would dearly like to invite the princess to attend,' he gave his blessing without a second thought.

"On the night of the festival, an Aztec woman playing the bride of Huitzilopochtli was dancing in the skin of the king's daughter. To ascend to the heavens and dance with a god was the greatest of honors to the Aztecs.

"But the king was angry, of course. All he saw was that his daughter had been slaughtered and skinned. The Aztecs were beset upon by the king's forces, and they were driven from their land by the man they trusted. They ran for their lives as family and friends were slaughtered, and they were chased to the shore of Lake Texcoco. There was nowhere else for them to go. Then, in a dream, the *tlamacazqui* had a vision and heard an oracle.

"'Look for an eagle atop a cactus, eating a snake, and that is where you shall flourish.'

"The *tlamacazqui* found that an island in the middle of the lake perfectly matched his vision. There was an eagle perched upon an exceptionally tall cactus, with a snake trapped in its sharp beak.

"The Aztecs gathered at the water's edge and surveyed vast Lake Texcoco.

"Everyone envisioned the world spoken of in myth. That world is flat land surrounded by water, with straight but invisible pillars penetrating the thirteen layers of the heavens all the way to Omeyocan, all the way down to Mictlan at the bottom of the nine layers of earth.

"This was the promised land. Two hundred years had passed since they left Aztlan. Their period of wandering had at last been rewarded. The story of the Aztec empire began on that island on Lake Texcoco.

"That is why, when you see the Mexican flag of green and white and red flying over the Zócalo, or the soccer stadium, or at a boxing match, there is an image of an eagle eating a snake on a cactus at its center. The white men stole the Aztecs' world, and left them nothing but the scenery in the prophecy.

"Now, go on, boys, into bed. That's all for tonight. We'll continue the story tomorrow."

"Who was the first king of the Aztecs?" Libertad asked the four.
"Acamapichtli," said Valmiro.
That's right. And what does that mean?
"It means Handful of Arrows."

"You're very clever," Valmiro. Libertad exhaled smoke from her pipe and rubbed his head. He promptly turned to his brothers and rubbed their heads too, sharing the strength he received from their *abuelita*. That was the rule for a warrior.

"Back when Tenochtitlan was just a small town," Libertad said, "in the days of Acamapichtli, your ancestors were proud warriors. They were excellent hunters, too. By the time of the fifth king, our line was the greatest of the jaguar warriors. The white men call the fifth king Moctezuma I, but his real name was Moteuczomatzin Ilhuicamina. It means Angry Ruler Strikes the Sky.

"There were bands of warriors within the Aztec army. The greatest among them were the jaguar warriors who served Tezcatlipoca. They had more experience and much more strength than the young eagle warriors who served Huitzilopochtli—even if you thought the brilliant eagle-feather helmets of those eagle warriors looked the bravest and boldest.

"The jaguar warriors painted their faces yellow and black, donned cotton-padded battle wear, and covered their powerful limbs with jaguar pelts. They were invisible to enemies in the forest, moved quickly, and, most importantly, the boiled leather deflected the enemy's arrows.

"Your ancestor led the jaguar warriors into battle, struck them down again and again, and brought great crowds of prisoners back to the city. Moteuczomatzin Ilhuicamina said, 'You are the true personification of Yohualli Ehecatl himself.' Boys, your ancestor was so honored that he fell to his knees, lowered his head, and exposed the back of his neck, right at the nape. It means he was so moved that he was willing to have his head cut off in that moment. For a human being to be compared to Tezcatlipoca is an honor that cannot be put into words.

"Moteuczomatzin Ilhuicamina told your ancestor, 'From now on, you will call yourself Tezcacoatl.' It means Mirror Snake. Why was he a snake instead of a jaguar? That's a good question, Bernardo. The Aztecs had a god named Quetzalcoatl, the feathered snake, and he fought against Tezcatlipoca in another land. So, to bear both the mirror and snake in your name, *tezcatl* and *coatl*, is to contain two opposing things at once—night and day, shadow and light, water and fire, moon and sun. It is a sign of true greatness.

"That is all for tonight, boys. We'll continue this again tomorrow."

"Have you finished your homework yet? Then let us talk more.

"It was decided that a new *teocalli* to Tezcatlipoca should be constructed south of Tenochtitlan, and the builders began constructing the foundation for the stepped pyramid. Tezcacoatl took hundreds of foreign soldiers as prisoners, and brought them to be sacrifices, buried in the foundation. With the *tlamacazque*, he helped remove the sacrificial hearts, learned their spells, and gained an understanding of the *tlamacazqui*'s job. He was allowed to do this because of his special name.

"Tezcacoatl's son also took the name Tezcacoatl, as did his son after that. They inherited the mantle of the greatest of jaguar warriors, from son to son, all of them taking part in the building of the *teocalli* of Tezcatlipoca. The construction took ages. Over months and years, they stacked the stones, added decorations, and finally finished a spectacular work of art.

"The eighth king of the Aztecs, Ahuitzotl, was one of the most powerful and aggressive of all the rulers. He was named after a water beast.

"The kingdom's domain expanded very far during Ahuitzotl's reign; no others could stand against the Aztecs. But at this very time, Tenochtitlan suffered a terrible flood. Many thousands of people died, the beautiful city was destroyed, and the new *teocalli* to Tezcatlipoca flooded. The *tlamacazque* drowned along with it. Even mighty King Ahuitzotl was struck on the head with a rock and died while escaping the floods.

"Tezcacoatl considered this. How could it be that such a mighty king perished and the holy city fell to ruin so easily?

"In mythology, it is said that Tezcatlipoca once destroyed the world by causing a great flood. This was known as Nahui-Atl, the Fourth Age of Water, and it lasted 312 years.

"Eventually, your ancestor realized that Tezcatlipoca was angry because they were short on sacrifices. To avoid another disaster like Nahui-Atl, he would have to take the part of the drowned priests and perform the rituals. He gathered craftsmen from all over the country and had them rush to build a new *teocalli*. It was a small building, but the jaguar warriors brought twice as many prisoners as before, and they were sacrificed every hour of the day.

"But that's all for tonight, boys. We'll continue this again tomorrow."

"Ah, there's a beautiful moon out tonight. You should look out the window later. But for now, let's continue where we left off yesterday.

"The ninth king, Ahuitzotl, had a nephew named Moctezuma Xocoyotzin. The conquistadors just called him Moctezuma, and historians call him Moctezuma II. His name means young, angry lord.

"Moctezuma Xocoyotzin put all of the *nahualli* sorcerers who failed to foresee the flood to death. They were responsible for allowing the old king to die. When the rainy season came the following year, the rains lasted, and the waters rose. When it seemed that the city would sink once again, Tezcacoatl's ceaseless rituals and prayers at last bore fruit, and Tezcatlipoca quelled the raging waters.

"For that, Moctezuma Xocoyotzin made Tezcacoatl an official *tlamacazqui*, allowing him to be both a warrior and a priest in charge of holy rituals.

"When he went into battle, your ancestor was allowed to wear royal garb, as befitting someone who was both warrior and priest. It was a great honor that even the greatest fighters were not allowed to mimic.

"On his face he wore a mask with a mosaic of turquoise and the teeth of nine jaguars, on his neck a jade necklace, in his ears two earrings fashioned from bat fangs, and in his hands an obsidian axe and a splendid shield. The shield was covered in shining green quetzal feathers and crocodile skin, green being the color of the finest warriors. It shone like a star, and in its center was a mirror that reflected his enemies' fear back at them.

"He looked no different from royalty, and he was close to a king. The only thing he lacked was an Aztec ruler's feather headdress. When your ancestor walked among the encampments, other bands of warriors quaked in fear and fell to the ground before him.

"Now, go and look at the moon before you go to bed. What you see up there is the very same moon that hung over Tenochtitlan in the days of your ancestors."

Reference Materials

TEXT

Arai, Takehiro. *Arai Takahiro no Peru Ryôri*. [Takahiro Arai's Peruvian Cooking] Shibata Shoten, 2014.

Asiain, Aurelio. *Shin Sekai Gendai Shibunko 5 Gendai Mekishiko Shishû*. [New Contemporary World Poetry 5: Poetry of Modern Mexico] Edited and translated by Hosono, Yutaka. Doyo Bijutsu Shuppan Hanbai, 2004.

Baquedano, Elizabeth. *Aztec, Inca & Maya*. Supervised by Kawanari, Hiroshi. Asunaro Shobo, 2007.

Basketball Summit (Ed.). *Basketball Summit: B-League Kawasaki Thunders*. Kanzen, 2018.

Batailles, Georges. *Guilty*. Translated by Ezawa, Kenichiro. Kawade Shobo, 2017.

Big Issue Japan, the. *The Big Issue Japan*, no. 311, May 2017.

Bolaño, Roberto. *Los Detectives Salvajes*. [The Savage Detectives] Translated by Yanagihara, Takaatsu & Matsumoto, Kenji. Hakusuisha, 2010.

Cardiovascular Institute, the. *Hajimete no Shinzôgekakango: Kara bijuaru de mitewakaru!* [My First Heart Surgery Care: Understand With Color Visuals!] Medica, 2014.

Carney, Scott. *The Red Market: On the Trail of the World's Organ Brokers, Bone Thieves, Blood Farmers, and Child Traffickers*. Translated by Ninomiya, Chizuko. Kodansha, 2012.

Chinen, Mikito. *Hitotsumugi no Te*. [Hands of the Soul Savior] Shinchosha, 2018.

Collis, Maurice. *Cortés and Montezuma*. Translated by Kanamori, Shigenari. Kodansha Gakujutsu Bunko, 2003.

Cretin, Thierry. *Mafia of the World—Transnational Criminal Organizations, News and Perspectives.* Translated by Kamise, Tomoko. Ryokufu Shuppan, 2006.

Díaz, Gisele and Alan Rodgers. *The Codex Borgia: A Full-Color Restoration of the Ancient Mexican Manuscript.* Dover Publications, 1993.

Díaz del Castillo, Bernal. *Historia verdadera de la conquista de la Nueva España.* [The True History of the Conquest of New Spain] Translated by Kobayashi, Kazuhiro. Iwanami Shoten, 1986.

Fisher, Mark. *Capitalist Realism.* Translated by Breu, Sebastian and Ruri Kawanami, Ruri. Horinouchi, 2018.

Girard, René. *Des choses chachées depuis la fondation du monde.* [Things Hidden since the Foundation of the World] Translated by Koike, Takeo. Hosei University Press, 2015.

Gonzales, Maruyama. *Gonzales in New York.* East Press, 2018.

Grillo, Ioan. *El Narco: Inside Mexico's Criminal Insurgency.* Translated by Yamamoto, Akiyo. Gendai Kikakushitsu, 2014.

Gruzinski, Serge. *The Aztecs: Rise and Fall of an Empire.* Translated by Saito, Akira. Sogensha, 1992.

Hogan, Andrew and Douglas Century. *Hunting El Chapo: The Inside Story of the American Lawmen Who Captured the World's Most Wanted Drug-Lord.* Translated by Tanahashi, Shiko. Harper Collins Japan, 2018.

Ido, Masae. *Mukoseki no Nihonjin.* [Undocumented Japanese] Shueisha, 2016.

Isobe, Ryo. *A Report From Kawasaki.* Cyzo, 2017.

Japan Bible Society. *New Interconfessional Translation Bible.* 1987.

Kanagawa Shimbun "Nature of the Times" Reporting Desk. *Heitodemo wo Tometa Machi: Kawasaki Sakuramoto no Hitobito.* [The City That Stopped Hate Demonstrations: The People of Sakuramoto, Kawasaki] Gendai Shicho Shinsha, 2016.

Kim, Tae-seong, et al. *Indonesia no koto ga Manga de 3-jikan de Wakaru Hon.* [Learn About Indonesia in 3 Hours Through Manga] Asuka, 2013.

Kizawa, Satoshi. *Dark Web Underground: The Net's Dark Dwellers Who Derail the Social Order.* East Press, 2019.

Kizawa, Satoshi. *Nick Land and Neo-Reactionaries: The Dark Thought in the Modern World.* Seikaisha Shinsho, 2019.

Kunimoto, Iyo, ed. *Gendai Mekishiko wo Shiru tame no 60-shô.* [60 Chapters to Explain Modern Mexico] Akashi Shoten, 2011.

Las Casas, Bartolomé de. *A Short Account of the Destruction of the Indies.* Translated by Someda, Hidefuji. Iwanami Bunko, 2013.

Le Clézio, J. M. G. *The Mexican Dream, Or, The Interrupted Thought of Amerindian Civilizations.* Translated by Mochizuki, Yoshiro. Shinchosha, 1991.

Matsuda, Hikaru, ed. *Shinzô Ishoku.* [Heart Transplants] Maruzen, 2012.

Miller, Mary & Taube, Karl. *The Gods and Symbols of Ancient Mexico and the Maya: An Illustrated Dictionary of Mesoamerican Religion.* Thames & Hudson, 1993.

Murata, Ramu. *Jukai Kô.* [Rumination on the Sea of Trees] Shobunsha, 2018.

Nicholson, Irene. *Mexican and Central American Mythology.* Translated by Matsuda, Yukio. Seidosha, 1992.

Nikkei National Geographic. *National Geographic, Japan Ed.* November 2010.

Ohtsuka, Kazuki. *Jûki Shiyô Manyuaru.* [Firearm Usage Manual] Data House, 2014.

Okudake, Bluelet. *Indonesia Yoasobi MAX 2015–2016.* [Indonesia Nightlife MAX 2015-2016] Oakla, 2015.

Onda, Riku. *Megalomania.* Kadokawa, 2012.

Sagawa, Fumiyoshi. *Yamanobori ABC Borudaringu Nyûmon.* [Mountain-climbing ABCs: A Bouldering Primer] Yama-Kei, 2015.

Sahagún, Bernardino de. *Kamigami to no Tatakai I.* [Battle Against the Gods I] Translated by Shinohara, Aito and Fujihide Someda. Iwan-ami Shoten, 1992.

Saviano, Roberto. *ZeroZeroZero.* Translated by Sekiguchi, Eiko and Tomoko Nakajima. Kawade Shobo, 2015.

Shibasaki, Miyuki. *Kodai Maya Asuteka Fushigi Taizen.* [The Complete Mysteries of the Ancient Mayans and Aztecs] Soshisha, 2010.

Suetsugu, Fuminaga and Takanori Ikeda (Supervision). *Circulation Up-to-Date Books 01: Shinzôgekai ga Kaita Tadashii Shinzôkaibôzu: Tôshizu -> Shinkate Danmenzu -> Shinekô Mitai Tokoro ga Mieru.* [A Heart Surgeon Draws Proper Heart Diagrams: Transparency -> Heart Catheter, Cross-Section -> Cardiac Echo, See What You Want to See] Medica Shuppan, 2014.

Suwa, Yasukazu. *Kachi ga Wakaru Hôseki Zukan.* [Gem Reference Book, Understanding Value] Natsume, 2015.

Tobe, Miyuki. *Nahua Dictionary.* Tairyusha, 1994.

World Photo Press. *Knife Magazine.* October 2011.

World Photo Press. *Naifu Meiking Tokuhon Saiko no Dôgu, Naifu wo Jibun no Te de Tsukuru.* [Knife-Making Primer: Making the World's Oldest Tool With Your Own Hands] 2004.

Yanagihara, Takaatsu. *Tekusuto to shite no Toshi Mekishiko DF.* [City as Text: México, D.F.] Tokyo University of Foreign Studies Press, 2019.

FILM

Eisenstein, Sergei, dir. *¡Que viva México!* Mosfilm, 1979.